Traders

of the

South Seas

JAMES FARRIS

ISBN: 978-1-7333199-4-2

Copyright © 2021 by James Farris
Printed by Charis Publishing
charispublishing.com
@charispublishing 🅵

Published July 2021

For my family,

for Kelsey,

for God

CHAPTER 1

Introduction

M Y NAME IS Christoph Swift, and my story began many years ago along the Tchefuncte River, nestled deep in southeast Louisiana, roughly an hour north of New Orleans. The time of year was right before the summer equinox when the purple flowers bloomed, and yellow pollen filled the air. The sun was bright with mild heat in the evening and cool, crisp air in the morning. Perfect weather, I tell you.

I lived with my Uncle Axelrod in a charming fishing house with a wooden dock surrounded by dense woods of tall oak and pine trees mixed with swampy marshland. He was a big ole man with massive hands embedded with calluses and covered in oil from working in his mechanic's shop. Aside from the messy black goop, he was a neat man—his hair combed and uniform tailored, a warm smile and a deep voice.

I can hear it now as I think back on those early mornings before school. "Get up boy, times wastin' away if ye want dreams to come true" was his usual saying to inspire me, if you want to call it that, to get ready for school.

I was eighteen years old with wide eyes of curiosity, a soft heart, and a ravaging eagerness to start my life. I was slow to figure things out and, more importantly, slow to see the bigger picture of life. I had an idea of what it was. I was just slow to act on it.

I was skinny with slight muscle tone and short dirty blond hair. I was decently tall at six feet. My skin was pale with some added color from fishing with my uncle and fixing up engines outside his shop next to our main house.

This was a fishing day. We woke up around 3:00 a.m. on the Friday before my last day of high school. My eyes struggled to open in the darkness. The cuckoo clock in the hallway jingled and cuckooed from that annoying bird. Axelrod loudly—*thump, thump, thump*— walked around the house with those damn boots on. I rolled out of bed and a book fell from my lap. I was reading *Caribbean Treasure: Tales of Lost Fortunes* before bed. It had a large schooner on the front cover.

I loved reading about myths and treasures. It pulled me from the dull existence I was trapped in. I blamed Axelrod for my curiosity. When I was child, I couldn't fall asleep—scared, I guess. Axelrod would tell me a tale of lost treasures, pirates, flying airships, cannibalistic tribes. The list goes on. It was my medicine to help me fall asleep and forget about the monsters hiding in my closet.

I hated waking up before the crack of dawn, but fishing with him early made the day a little bit more magical. It wasn't necessarily the fishing that I loved; it was my time with Axelrod. He brought me into a fantastic world where anything could come true and where life was tranquil. This was a place where swamp mud did not exist. What is swamp mud, you ask?

It's a terrible mud that traps a man or woman in a monotonous situation with no way to escape. Once trapped in the tangle, dreams begin to disappear. Then, a closed mind develops, furthering trapping its victim, sinking by the minute, in hopelessness.

Once the victim is waist deep in the mud and in distress, the opportunistic swamp monsters come out from hiding, creeping closer. One can see their yellow eyes glowing in the brush, watching.

When the mud reaches your shoulders and you're sapped by hunger and thirst, monsters of all shapes and sizes reveal themselves and take bites out of you. You try to stop them, but you are too exhausted to do anything of the sort. Only God can help you escape at this point.

Swamp mud can be seen and avoided easily with caution. One must always be on the lookout for it. Never let your guard down. Unfortunately, sometimes the mud is hidden by shrubs or, worse, by brackish water. I knew of a man that actually died by it. Everyone in our town of Fontainebleau knew the story of Mr. Guidry. Out fishing on the Tchefuncte, he decided to jump in the water to cool himself off on a hot day.

The river looked shallow enough. When he jumped into the brackish water, cloudy, light brown mud rose to the surface, but Mr. Guidry never came up. His companions on the boat looked for him but sadly could not find him in the flowing river. Mr. Guidry was swallowed whole by the swamp mud. May he rest in peace. Best thing to do is, if you come across it, avoid it with the most severe caution.

On this particular early morning, fog cascaded over the Tchefuncte River. I looked at it from my front porch while I sipped on dark chicory coffee that Axelrod had brewed earlier. The chicory coffee had an aroma of dark roast coffee mixed with a sweet chicory flower. I paid attention to the little things. Birds chirped, bees buzzed, and the river flowed down toward Lake Pontchartrain. Life was good along the river.

Axelrod prepared most of the fishing gear the night before, yet in the morning, he always took a long time meandering around doing who knows what. I usually had to force him out of the house by telling him that we had everything in the boat, but he always needed one more thing.

"I need one more thing. Hold strong," said Axelrod as he walked back into the house. *Thump, thump, thump.*

Only Axelrod and I lived together in that house off River Road. Our small Creole cottage was minimal with a silver tin roof, a light brown wooden frame, and a front porch. Next to the main house was Axelrod's workshop. It was large enough to fit two or three biplanes. It was composed of three hangar doors and a wide service area inside with tons of shelves and equipment, all protected by a sleek tin roof. He fixed things—all sorts of mechanical objects—for a living, everything from large planes to medium-sized engines and even small watches.

Near the workshop was an old white lighthouse that he renovated into his study. Sadly, I was never allowed in there. When I was younger, curiosity got the best of me. I picked the lock and made it inside the lighthouse. What I could faintly see through the darkness was a large map on a mahogany table and tons of connected red strings labeling places on the map to pictures of different people and objects.

There were different gizmos of all kinds, like mechanical arms, strange goggles, and all sorts of things scattered throughout the room—high-tech stuff. I had no idea what I was looking at, to be honest. Moments later, a siren came on. Axelrod found me and whipped me for my disobedience. I haven't been back since that day.

I returned from my reverie.

Axelrod opened the front door with two fishing poles in his hands.

"Quick, quick,.I got business later. Bait's on board!" Axelrod exclaimed as he hastily walked to the boat.

He wore his classic uniform: a light blue, long-sleeved button down shirt with a square pocket and navy blue pants held up by blue suspenders. He was partly bald, so he always wore a navy blue baseball cap. He was very self-conscious about the whole balding thing.

We hopped into the little fishing boat equipped with a small motor. The motor struggled to start. It puffed and roared but came up short of clicking on.

"Aye, this damn thing. Worked this mornin'. Even filled it up," stated Axelrod as he took off his hat to rub his forehead. Axelrod opened his toolbox, threw tools all over the boat, and tinkered with the machine. I looked it over and suggested he replace a specific part in the engine, but Axelrod claimed he'd done that already. I was a persistent young man. I pushed him out of the way and replaced the part in a matter of seconds.

To his chagrin, the motor started, and I couldn't help but smile. Axelrod was perplexed for a moment, then laughed. "I taught thee well."

Ever since I was a little kid, Axelrod taught me about the intricacies of machinery and life in general—how everything flows like connected cogwheels rotating clockwise. I could fix about anything mechanical—gears, engines, and the like.

Axelrod's favorite thing to work on was watches and clocks, especially cuckoo clocks—hence the annoying one in the hallway. Watches and clocks were quite difficult to master. It required a steady hand and patience, much different than an internal combustion engine. A clock had its own wonderful intricacies that dazzled me more than biplanes.

I didn't have so much time to dedicate to watches or planes. I did have time to fly planes though. That's where the fun was. Nonetheless, I appreciated all mechanical objects and had a good understanding of each.

Axelrod fixed planes more than anything because of his clients.

I learned the ins and outs of planes and how to fly them by helping Axelrod in the shop. He paid me to test drive the planes to see if they worked up high. I made some good money working under Axelrod as I grew up. I learned a lot.

I had a knack for operating machinery, more so than fixing it. I wanted to quit school and start working with Axelrod full time, but he would not let me. He demanded I join a club or sports team and save the work for later in my life, so I did thus so.

Axelrod was the closest thing I ever had to a father. I never knew my parents, other than that they died in a car crash, leaving me with ole Axelrod, my father's brother. I couldn't complain if it were a good or bad thing not having parents. I didn't know the difference. The only thing my parents left me was a purple-gemmed amulet necklace—circular and not too heavy or big. My uncle said it was a family heirloom. I wore it every day. It reminded me of them in some way. I didn't feel so alone.

I wished Axelrod got out the house more, but he kept to himself and his work. The only people that came to see him were clients, except one man from the United States government, or so I was told. His name was Mr. Charlie, a friendly man with military-cut gray hair, a clean-shaven face with a few wrinkles, and a powerful gaze. He wore a green decorated uniform.

I liked him when I was growing up because Mr. Charlie always brought me a different book to read when he came to see my uncle. He liked me a lot; I could tell. Usually, he brought me history books about great commanders and empires or, better yet, funny books, like plays by Oscar Wilde.

I loved each book he brought: it opened my eyes to certain things. Mr. Charlie caught a glimpse of me flying a biplane one day and wanted me to join some flying company he worked for and fly planes for them. He said I had some real talent. My uncle disapproved for whatever reason.

Mr. Charlie was quick with me and, like my uncle, never revealed too much about himself. One day, I asked Mr. Charlie, "Why do you come all the way out here? Is ole Axelrod fixing planes for the army?"

He told me Axelrod and he were good friends back in the day when Axelrod was in the army. I didn't know Axelrod was in the army, so I asked him about it. His response was the usual ambiguous, danced-around answer about how he was briefly in the Engineer Corps. or something like that.

Axelrod was a secretive man and never revealed much about my parents either, giving me the same answer every time I asked about them. It was that they were good people, that my mother was beautiful, and that I had her high cheekbones.

It made me bitter and sad growing up. I felt different from the other kids. It felt like there was an emptiness I could never fill. The only thing that came close to filling it was my time spent with Axelrod, flying high in the sky, or reading and retelling imaginative tales. Each pulled me from my normal life.

The moon in her celestial glory began to retreat below the horizon while the mighty sun took her place. Axelrod navigated the boat upriver to a nice spot where two streams intersected with one another next to a small outlet. The grass was high around the outlet, a perfect spot to catch fish swimming down the river hugging the bank. Lines were cast out, and we got some good bites that morning: sheepshead, redfish, and bass.

I caught catfish more than anything. It's a trash fish. My uncle told me cats counted as negative points in our little fishing game. We always threw them back. Most any other fish I caught were a plus.

After we caught a few, I sat down and took a sip of water.

"This be the life!" Axelrod proclaimed as he reeled his line.

I stared at the flowing river and dipped my fingers into warm brackish water. The sun slowly began to rise in the distance, breaking through the fog.

"Could you tell me the story about the treasure of Faustino again?" I asked.

"Why?" questioned Axelrod.

"No better time than now."

"Hungry for a tale, aye? Hungrier than Faustino seeking minosium."

"Even more than a sea serpent hunting a schooner!"

Axelrod put down his reel.

One thing to know about Axelrod is that he loved reading adventure tales and retelling them. It was therapeutic for him. I looked forward to his tales on our fishing trips more so than the actual fishing.

It was part of the whole experience: catch a few, then a tale.

When he would tell a story, he would get real into it. His warming smile would broaden, and he used his hands. My favorite story of all was "The Treasure of Faustino."

Axelrod positioned himself on the seat of the boat, gained that spark of glittery delight in his eyes, and began:

"Many moons ago, before Iberville and Bienville found our own Louisiana, came a time of great discovery: the Age of Exploration. Aye, a time where spices ruled the splendid world exchange and daring traders of all nations ventured across the seven seas to obtain these almost-mythical commodities of cloves, cinnamon, ginger, pepper, and other colorful hidden gems unknown to Western world to trade in the world markets.

"Worth their weight in gold, these spices and gems were created on islands far beyond the reach of Renaissance Europe, which at the time was cut off from the infamous Sinbad's Way—the famed sea route allowing the exchange of goods with India, China, and the Spice Islands from the Mediterranean Sea to the Arabian Sea.

"Europeans were forbidden to use this pivotal route by Islamic nations, who controlled Sinbad's Way and sought to maximize profits by silencing the Europeans from contact with the Eastern world—like a man with a noose around his neck gasping for his last breath of air, but a sound he cannot utter.

"For ages, Europe languished in decrepit darkness like a blind beggar with sores, unseen to Eastern civilization, until like a fiery phoenix reborn through black ashes, Europe with newfound wit and strength, demanded to find a new trade route to the Spice Islands, bypassing those cursed Islamic middlemen, to obtain these heavenly tasting spices directly.

"Aye, this is where ye friend, Salvador Faustino, enters the story. Faustino was a low-class sailor from the hills of Andalusia, Spain. He had deep aspirations to ascend from his hopeless, deep-mudded peasant class to that of richly feathered monarch class with an endless supply of wine, cheesecake, and a woman's delicate touch, free from that mudded caste estate system.

"With his wide ears, Faustino heard of an expedition under the royal Spanish crown, who was feeling the sweet breeze of fresh airy victory over the encumbered Islamic Moors during the Reconquista, to find a new route to the famed Spice Islands across the never-ventured Atlantic Sea route.

"Believing this was his chance to strike it rich, Faustino took a simple position aboard a doomed ship bound to circumnavigate the world with only one intention: find a western route to the Spice Islands and bring back spices to fill the king's hall. The ship set sail on the western trade winds of the Atlantic Sea.

"Many years went by, and not a soul knew the whereabouts of the fateful expedition across the Atlantic. If ye talked to anyone at the time in Spain, they would have said doom, common at the time, befell the traders.

"Then, through a mist-filled morning along the Rio Guadalquivir leading to Seville, like the one we have today on the Tchefuncte River, Faustino and a handful of others returned on a battered ship, sinking by the minute. When docked, the people of the port surrounded this decrepit ship, far past its expiration. Faustino and the surviving crew members came forth with a mountain of spices preserved well in the hold. Cheers rang through the city, celebrating the expedition's success.

"Unknown to the crew and the rest of Spain, Faustino secretly returned with a commodity far more valuable than any spice, hidden in his undergarments—minosium, a vibrant and glowing purple gem, more beautiful than a cut diamond, richer in color than a red blood ruby, and more powerful than chaotic plutonium.

"Where did he find this unknown gem? No one can discover the truth, for no one knows the real truth. Aye, legend says that Faustino encountered a mysterious Arabian figure somewhere in India, a magician or genii named Emir who made a deal with Faustino to trade the location of this secretive gem called minosium and the Spice Islands in exchange for Faustino's soul and the souls of his future employees. Eh, employees you ask? Wait and see.

"Faustino accepted Emir's offer and profited greatly from this trade. The moment Faustino stepped foot on dry Spanish topsoil, he used his newly acquired wealth to outfit an expedition to find this fabled minosium island, as instructed by Emir to do. Soon after Faustino departed his homeland of Spain, he found the minosium island Emir spoke of the day of the trade, and he begun to build his vast empire with this newly extracted mineral as its location was known only to Faustino.

"Shortly after, minosium became the rage in Europe for its beauty and elegance. Demand for it skyrocketed while plummeting the prices of spices. As for the power locked inside of this gem, like that of plutonium, it would be many, many generations later before someone would discover the power beyond the gem's sheer beauty.

"The world was falling into Faustino's hands, growing his wealth to never-before-seen riches by trading this mesmerizing gem across the world. Struggling to keep up with demand while needing to extract more,Faustino sold vast quantities of minosium faster than a breadline in a hungry countryside.

"Realizing this deficit in supply and demand, he bought slaves from Far Eastern countries and around the world to work the mines on minosium island, now called Faustino's Island. He developed the island into a magnificent trading port and constructed multiple forts on this island to protect his dearest greedy love.

"Faustino desired to diversify his holdings and continued to build extravagant ports around the world to exchange minosium for other commodities. He built vaulted chambers to keep and hold his endless supply of minosium and acquired treasures from his transactions. He became the master trader of the world, controlling world trade with his tongue and fingertips.

"During one of his usual monthly surveys of other minosium deposits on islands around the world, he met a beautiful, slender, arched back, sharp-featured face mulatto woman named Phara. Faustino fell in love at first sight with her fragrant beauty. She was known as a voodoo queen, a witch with hidden powers. Faustino made Phara his lovely wife, and her soothing velvet voice never left his ear thereafter. Life was perfect for Faustino . . . until the cunning buccaneers showed up."

"Tell me what a buccaneer is again," asked Christoph.

"Aye, lawless pirates sent by God to disrupt ole Faustino's devilish operations. An ulcer in his belly," replied Axelrod. He then continued, "As time went on, these crews of buccaneers began persistently attacking Faustino's trading vessels and ports, stealing his precious, dearly loved minosium. This allowed for black market trade of the mineral without Faustino's dominating hand taking a piece of the profit. The black market drove down Faustino's set price.

"In response, Faustino went to war with the sea dogs. The fighting was bloody, and at times, ships filled with minosium sank to the seafloor as far east as the South Pacific, India, Arabia, and even farther south than the Cape of Good Hope, and sometimes near Antarctica.

"The most well-known leader of the buccaneers, a terrible sore to Faustino, was the famous Captain Bird-Eye Edwards—a clever man who devised a system for trapping Faustino's ships filled with minosium and plundering them to the depths. Better yet, Bird-Eye got a hold of a few minosium-holding chamber locations scattered on islands among the sea like stars in the celestial night sky and raided a few with ease.

"Bird-Eye caused Faustino a great loss of wealth and an aching discomfort that kept his eyes wide open deep into the night at the thought of his dearest loved minosium falling into the hands of undeserving wretches! His heart filled with vengeful black hatred, causing dim purple bags to form under his brown eyes.

"Faustino wanted—rather, *needed*—a more-protected way to lower his risk of loss from the hands of these lawless rats. Phara, with her sensuous red lips, suggested he build an extravagant, fortified palace with gigantic walls around the island that none could destroy— walls higher than the walls of Troy or Babylon.

"Faustino was entranced with this idea but was paranoid about foreign enemies, say France and England, who could scale the walls with high ladders, which one day they surely would do.

"Phara, with her back and shoulders delicately exposed in a white dress, told him, with her charming eyes flushed with love's glow, to build an elaborate labyrinth cutting through the mountainous island and dense jungle and hiding the mine entrance deep within the labyrinth. Faustino smiled at her brilliant mind and flashing eyes, agreeing full-heartedly to the plan.

"Hastily acting upon it, Faustino brought world-renowned inventors, artists, and scientists, and even the most famous architect of the time, Casimir Wolfram—a God-fearing man—to construct the most sophisticated palace and labyrinth system ever planned since the labyrinth beneath the Palace of Knossos.

"It would not only protect his treasure. It would be a wonder of the New World—more beautiful than the Hanging Gardens of Babylon, more complex than the Acropolis, and grander in size than the Colossus of Rhodes—a labyrinth of natural barriers, weaving through the mountains, jungles, badlands, and rivers of the whole island.

"Faustino gathered the largest slave labor force ever assembled to create this wonder. In a matter of a few short years, his masterpiece was constructed. Only Casimir and Faustino knew how to navigate the maze without getting lost. Faustino could never allow another man to know the way through his maze.

"Casimir was smart. He knew of the evil inside Faustino, and so he sent clues to points across the world, places inaccessible to Faustino, outlining how to navigate the maze.

"Unfortunately, on the night Casimir and his workers planned to escape, a massive storm came, trapping him and all of workers on the island. Seizing the opportunity, Faustino and his small army forced all his workers into the labyrinth, fulfilling his promise to Emir.

"Before Casimir was thrown into the labyrinth, he sent a message hidden in the wings of a seabird to Bird-Eye Edwards, asking for assistance and carrying instructions on how to enter the labyrinth. Ye see, months before, Bird-Eye and Casimir had entered into an agreement to help one another. Casimir planned on freeing the slaves with the help of the buccaneers.

"Acting on the news, Bird-Eye Edwards and his crew attempted to free the people stuck inside the labyrinth without Faustino's knowing. He planned to scale the walls with intricate devices crafted by Casimir, find the architect, and escape the labyrinth with a few pieces of minosium, of course. Bird-Eye and the crew scaled the walls with tall ladders designed by Casimir, and the pirates entered the labyrinth. Sadly, no one knows what happened to Casimir, Bird-Eye and his crew, or the slaves after that.

"Besides, the end was near for Faustino, and he knew it. His hair turned grayer by the day as the sands of time fell around him, signaling his departure was near. Emir wanted the second half of the debt owed to him: Faustino's and his employees' souls.

"So it goes, Faustino eventually realized his wrongdoings versus the manipulations of Emir. He knew that no penance could save his soul blackened like a charred fish. Faustino decided to walk through the labyrinth into the volcanic mine, the epicenter of his wealth, the seat of the great minosium vein.

"Faustino cried out to God, asking the Lord to vanish the island from sight, only to be discovered again according to His will, hoping this last attempt might save his soul from the fiery lake of hell and the jaws of Emir. At that moment, Faustino jumped into the fiery magma, burning his soul evermore.

"Til this day, the island has yet to be found by scientists, enthusiasts, and adventurists alike. Some people say it was in the South Pacific, or off the coast of Arabia or India, or in the Caribbean, but no one really knows."

"Do you think the story is true, about Faustino, Bird-Eye, and minosium?" I asked.

"Why, ye ask?"

"My science teacher, Mr. Taft., he said—"

"That bald-headed buffoon! Aye, of course it's true. Don't listen to him, and frankly, never listen to non-believers. They never make it far in life," Axelrod counseled. "We need to get back. Last day of school. Cannot miss that."

I sighed. "You don't have to tell me twice."

"Cheer up. Soon enough, you'll be a college boy. You have no idea what good things lie ahead."

"I don't want to go to college. I want to work here with you."

"No, no, no! I worked too hard to put you through a private school. Ye will go to college and not waste away fixin' planes for a livin'. Soon enough, lad, ye shall be the one inventing new types of planes, for I have seen it. Ye are too smart not to."

"More school, waste of time," I sighed.

"College is different. Trust me, lad."

"Whatever you say, Axelrod."

"Good. Now don't forget, we must finish up Mr. Charlie's bi-plane this evening. The steering still feels stiff. Needs a tweak and spin."

"About that . . . The end of the year senior Mass is this afternoon, and most every senior's parent is going. I thought, well . . ." I hesitated.

"No, no, no," exclaimed Axelrod.

I exhaled in despair. "You never come."

"Christoph, that's not true."

"Of course, it is. Everyone else has someone there for them. Why can't I? It gets old after a while."

"I'm here for you, ever since you were a wee little boy, three feet tall. How about this? Give me call when I should leave, and I'll be there. Is anyone important going to be there?"

"Who's 'important'?"

"Like the archbishop."

"Him? No, this is a small Mass."

Axelrod constantly worried about if someone "important" would be at the school. It didn't make sense.

"Why does that matter anyway?" I inquired.

"Doesn't. Just wanted to know."

"So . . . you'll be there?"

"Indeed."

"You promise?"

"Promise."

I smiled, then gave ole Axelrod a hug. He didn't know what to do. We rarely hugged. He patted me on the back and steered the boat toward the house.

Looking back at those early days spent with my uncle, I can't help but relive those feelings of doubt and displeasure. Those days were difficult for me for the pure fact I did not know how to improve my situation of loneliness and despair. Axelrod rarely revealed anything about my parents—who they were, what their occupations were, and where this mysterious amulet that I wore each day came from.

The moment I tried to question him on these subjects, he would quickly defer to another topic or yield an answer insufficient to cure my curiosity, leading me to question where my sadness came from. It took much introspection and meditation to figure out that it came from a feeling that I didn't know who I was, creating an unanswerable void inside my soul.

This void caused me great confusion in my day-to-day life, bringing forth unwanted disturbances that reverberated through all facets of my life. This void pulled me deeper into the feared swamp mud.

The only vine I could reach to pull me out from this concrete mud was through continuous work in Axelrod's shop or reciting wonderful tales that pulled me from this hopeless situation. But that vine always snapped before I was free until I found the vine of prayer.

CHAPTER 2

In the Old World

I RODE MY motorcycle to school. It was a café racer with a 1930s look and a mix of beige and brown. Axelrod and I bought it for a good price and fixed it up together. She was a real beauty. I went to an all-boys private Catholic school called St. Francis, located seven minutes from my house. It was part boarding and part commuter.

My uncle sent me there because he was a hardcore Catholic, and God forbid I tried to switch schools. The school was in a wooded area outside Fontainebleau next to an abbey. One road went through the campus, which consisted of a couple of two-story red brick facilities with a few fountains and statues of saints scattered around the campus.

Being in an all-boys school, the only time I had an interaction with a girl was at theater practice, cracking jokes with them behind the curtain and a little bit more. The young ladies went to an all-girls school down the road from St. Francis. Having ladies in theater enticed me to do the theatrical plays in the first place.

I used to play basketball in high school before I got involved with theater. Axelrod told me to get involved, so I did. I was athletic and could really handle the ball. I just didn't like to practice. I was good at sports. I was quick and could pick up things fast. When I wasn't working in Axelrod's shop as a kid, I played sports at the local park near my house. I played almost every day. I loved the game, so I played in high school, which was far different than playing at the park.

The problem with me was that I struggled making it to basketball practice in high school for numerous reasons, the first one being that I was a rebel. It caused a real rift between the coaches, players, and me.

I couldn't quit because of Axelrod, so I felt boxed in, restrained. Confined, I gave a half-hearted effort in everything I did. Coaches seized upon this, seeing blood in the water, and made it hell for me during practice and in the classroom, encouraging me to give them my two cents about it all. It never turned out well when I gave my two cents.

Needless to say, I didn't last much longer on the team. The coaches and other players didn't like me, and I didn't like them. They didn't accept me in their pack. I didn't care; I was more focused on other things anyway.

It was ironic though. Axelrod never showed up at my games, but he was furious when I was thrown off the team. I had to find something else, or Axelrod would have thrown me out. Granted, it did hurt me at times, not being accepted. Maybe I should have gone about it a different way, but what the hell, I didn't let them see that side of me. Theater was more my speed—less crap and more women.

One of my only good friends was Arthur, a young, intelligent fellow. He wasn't too big. He was really skinny with lots of freckles and red hair. People called him a ginger, and it really pissed him off.

As small as he was, he threw a punch at anyone that brought up his hair color and pale complexion. I appreciated him for that. I liked a kid with guts. It was hard to come by in those days. He didn't play any sports—he was too small—but he was damn good at theater. He could sing better than Cole Porter, I promise you that.

Theater came into the picture from numerous places. It started with those books given to me by Mr. Charlie, reading those stories out loud, acting them out. I loved it. I had a great imagination and loved to put myself in the world of those characters. Their world was always better than my world.

After the fiasco with the sports teams, Arthur suggested I try out for theater. It worked out with my work schedule. I didn't have to show up until 6:00 p.m., practice was laid back, I made a few friends, and it brought out my artistic side.

The kids were good and nonjudgmental, less political; comparing it to machinery, I developed that same knack for theater and art, too. It made me appreciate a whole new world. I was a sponge, absorbing new skills and ideas. I finished out my senior year in theater.

I recognized I made a lot of mistakes during those days in high school, said a lot of regrettable things, fought way too much, and was all-around disappointed with my performance in life. Not many people respected me or liked me at school, but I didn't care.

I was a lone wolf the day I was born, and I'm a lone wolf now—no teams, few friends. Just me, my planes, and my tales. That's how I was, that's how I survived, and that's how it was always going to be.

I couldn't wait for the last day of school to end. Then, I would be off to the clouds, leaving this place and everyone in it for the birds. Before I could fly away, I had to make it through this last day and the end of the year Mass. Then, I'd be gone.

In the terms of Catholicism, Mass is a church service, in case you didn't know. The Archbishop of New Orleans at the time was Archbishop Narcisse. The archbishop would come from the city, say the Mass, and bless the graduating senior class.

Yes, I did tell Axelrod a lie, but why would it matter if Narcisse was there? Foolish, I said. The Mass was a huge deal for the school. Everyone's parents came to see their children accept a blessing by the great Narcisse. You would think Axelrod would be ecstatic for this opportunity, being a diehard Catholic, to see Narcisse.

Frankly, I thought it was all a big joke. I loved God more than anything, but this guy, Narcisse, in my opinion, was no different than these other yahoos at this school stinking up the place. Unfortunately, Axelrod never came to my school for any function, athletic game, or theatrical performance. I despised the ole bastard for it until I stopped caring.

Today was the day he promised to be there. Very monumental. I had to give Axelrod the feel-bad treatment for him to fold and come. Hey, it worked. It was all that mattered to me at the time. Little did I know, this day would change my life forever.

I parked my bike in my usual spot next to a tall oak tree in the Pit, a gravel parking lot secluded by trees, not too far from the school. Most of the seniors parked here. I met Arthur in the Pit every morning before class started. I hopped in his old brown sedan and talked about the usual stuff—dreams, women, and how we couldn't wait to get the hell out of there and start our lives.

Arthur was accepted into a private school up north. He wanted to become a doctor or something like that. Plans change as you get older though.

Next to us, sitting on his abnormally large, lifted truck tailgate was Tony Torino, leader of the Pack and son of Carlos Torino, a well-known public figure with immense power and wealth.

Tony was a well-built, tan boy with black hair and a strong attitude like mine. We were like each other, almost like brothers from another life. We liked the same women and played basketball together. We had the same height and build, even the same type of personality, though we differed in that I chose one road and he chose another.

His road was darker than mine. You could see it in his eyes, the dark, grungy look about him. I made the choice not to go dark. Every man makes this decision, regardless if he chooses to acknowledge it.

At my core, I'm not dark. Tony was a different story. Strange how in life the bad ones at times do better than the good ones, like the Bolsheviks in Russia and Tony Torino at St. Francis. Tony had everything in high school—a starting position on the basketball team, the pretty girlfriend, the many friends, and the large wealth. Quite honestly, I was never jealous of him, but I made observations. I connected the dots of the universe by comparing him to me, which I rarely did at the time.

I knew what having something looked like because I had nothing and, at this point, only something to gain. I evaluated my situation, saw what needed to be changed, and did what I had to do. I couldn't be negative.

I had to work hard, focus on the important things; it took me four years to figure these simple concepts out. The only person who could see and be the change was myself and myself alone. Too bad the only person that could see my gain was me and, well, Arthur, too.

Tony always hated me because we competed for the same things. We were always drinking from the same well. Strangely, I believed it was God manifested through destiny to intertwine Tony and me together. I saw what I could have been and what I could have had: success.

Sadly, I lost this round at St. Francis—hence the few friends and destroyed reputation. I accepted the loss honorably, but it would never happen again for the rest of my life, most assured. I would do whatever it took to win, to be better, to succeed; losing was not an option in my plan moving forward.

Granted, I still struggled with this uphill battle of having a good attitude, not fighting as much, and being respectful. Graduation was the sunrise on the horizon, the dawn of a new day, a chance to restart.

Until the day my liberty came, I was subjected to this world of St. Francis, Tony Torino, and the Pack—a group of the most popular and wealthy kids in our grade with extraordinarily superficial friendships. If you weren't in the Pack, you were labeled a nobody. If you didn't bow down and pay tribute to the Pack, you were left out of parties, gatherings, and an all-around stream of information.

Arthur and I weren't part of the Pack. Shocker, huh? It was all a load of crap, and I was over it. Now you see why I loved those imaginative stories and flying high. Each lifted me up from this dreaded world.

On this particular morning, the Pack had a group of some of the prettier girls around them from that all-girls school down the road. These women were pretty but mean and superficial, caring way too much about their self-image—luckily, a match made in heaven for the Pack. I'm so happy they found each other, and it all worked out.

I had a run-in with one of those girls. Her name was Caroline—bunny face, button nose, the classic cute blonde girl. She grew up down the street from me and did theater. She dated Tony Torino before me, and during one of their routine breakups, I had a fling with her behind the scenes.

The story went something like this: We were trying out for the fall play my senior year. She was the kind of girl that could sing, dance, act—the triple threat. Caroline sparkled on stage as she tried out for the lead role. Though I was more focused on myself, I also was trying out for a lead, and this just so happened to be my first time trying out for theater.

I told myself I would go for the lead and would accept nothing less. I had it in me, and I intended to capitalize on this idea. Arthur had laughed when I told him about going for a lead role.

"Lest you and rest of them laugh," I had said.

After coming off my losses with the basketball team, I intended to change, be the change, and obtain what I wanted and stick with something to the end. No excuses. It would make Axelrod happy and possibly even show up at a performance, more so if I got the lead. All were green lights in my book.

Thankfully, I had some hidden, magical natural talent conjured up from Mr. Charlie's books and Axelrod's tales. I had recited them a few times in the mirror and to the kids in class. I got the script for drama. It was about an occupied Okinawan village during WWII. Perfect. I loved WWII.

I played out each character to a T in my recitation, studied each one thoroughly, wrote out characteristics, and went from there. I told myself this was different, this was it, that success would come.

An actor is a storyteller at the core, and you couldn't find a better storyteller than me at the time, or that's what I told myself at least. I studied with diligence, went to that theater, and waited for my moment. My heart was beating fast; my hand was little jittery.

The theater instructor was Mrs. Anne Kay—a sweet old lady with curly, brown hair; a pale, white, narrow face; few wrinkles; and a lazy right eye. Her lazy eye was a small thing, but the only problem was that I never knew if she was looking at me or the guy next me when she talked to us. She was very confusing, but a lovely woman though.

Mrs. Anne Kay was super theatrical—in the way she talked, dressed, in her facial expressions, in her over-exaggerated hand motions. Even that crazy right eye moved theatrically. Each part of her moved harmoniously with theatrical magic, the sign of a true professional.

When the day came for tryouts, I went up on stage, laid it all on the line, and felt damn good afterward. I could tell I did well by Mrs. Anne Kay's smiling at my performance. I saw that glimmer in her eye. The following day, posted on the front doors of the theater was the list of parts, and God willing, I got the lead. God was looking out after me after all.

Everyone in theater was shocked, pissed, or amazed; some kid even cried.

Caroline, surrounded by her friends, stated, "Who's Christoph Swift?"

Arthur got the other lead. When he saw my name below his, he was shocked and amazed at first. Then, a smile grew on his face. He told me, "I don't know how you did it, Swift, but you did."

I replied, "That deep magic follows me, I'm telling ya. From here on out, God will blaze the trail."

Deep magic is that feeling one gets when he finds his destiny and life begins to work in his favor, manifesting into the physical form. I call it deep magic, but it's really the scent of God, a mysterious force working behind the curtain.

When I was at my lowest, trapped in my own swamp mud and had no one to turn to for advice, it was then I turned to God, my last hope. I asked Him to help me find my path, to save me from this dreadful mud of St. Francis. I made a promise to Him: If He would free me from that bottomless swamp mud, I would promise to live my life faithfully to Him, and with all things I do, I would never give excuses or have regrets. I would seek only honest progress.

I felt Him there that night; I knew He was listening. The next day, I kid you not, Arthur gave me the idea to try out for theater in the upcoming week, and the rest is history. It was deep magic working behind the curtain. I was starting to see life's big picture, and *starting* is the correct word.

I never missed a practice and studied those lines until my script fell apart. Luckily, reciting my favorite stories like Faustino's gave me a leg up. The lines came naturally. Who would've thought? My talents began to unfold and felt good, felt right, felt like a step in the right direction. When I told Axelrod, he was ecstatic for me. But once again, he was quick with me; then off he went to his study.

During those evening practices, I hit it off with Caroline. Since we were both leads, we were always around each other. We really clicked when we were on stage, and it continued behind the curtains.

I could tell when we were intimate with one another that a side of insecurity and superficiality would come out, holding us back from what we truly could have been. When I tried to move closer, she would back away. If I tried to inquire more about her personal side, she would fold up. I was frustrated, vexed.

She gauged her worth by how many friends and followers on social media she had, whom she hung out with, how much money they had—on all things superficial. At times, she would break through, but most of the time, she fell short. She thought I was her opposite—inferior, unpopular, poor, and destined to fail.

When her true colors came out, she had an ugly brown canvas. I knew our love wouldn't work out, but I didn't want to believe it, didn't want to end it. I could have been the same as her. Confused, I felt if she liked me, then everyone else would accept me. Hell, even fill that empty void.

For the performance, Arthur, Caroline, and I killed it on stage.

People were writing news articles about how good of a match the three of us were. It was a real high point in my career, standing on that stage as people cheered for us. The first time anyone cheered for me, I felt like I belonged and did something right for a change.

On that night, deep magic swirled on that stage—the same magic from flying high in the sky or listening to the stories of Axelrod. Sadly, he wasn't there to see me that night. I won't lie; it hurt a little. The Pack was there in full force, including Tony Torino, Caroline's ex-boyfriend at the time, with a look of anger in his eyes.

At the party celebrating the end of play, Caroline lightened up toward me. I guess she came to her senses. I made a move on her, and it went beautifully. I saw a piece of victory, and it tasted oh-so sweet. Love is mysterious—one day here and the next over there.

Tony Torino found out about us and what went on behind the curtains. He could not let that happen. I was an insignificant bug that he stomped on years ago. How could I make a return, especially with a girl he once had? That wasn't going to fly in his mind, so he spread malicious lies about me, stating that I was a clown who put on makeup and did drugs in the back instead of someone who stole kisses from Caroline. Dastardly, and that's just the half of what he said.

Surprisingly, the school believed him. I was kicked out of theater—no spring play—and that lie destroyed my reputation even further. I was "lucky," they said, that I wasn't expelled from school.

That little rumor made it all the way to Axelrod. He thought I was smoking pot in the woods. He raised hell, never let down, and put further restraints on me. Deeper I sank in the swamp mud, the damn monsters taking pieces from my soul. Soon after that fiasco, I caught Caroline and Tony together on a date walking along Lake Pontchartrain. I haven't talked to her since that day, told myself I didn't love her. It hurt; it did.

I was propelled back to square one—on the verge of expulsion, with a tattered reputation, once again stuck in the mud of St. Francis. I had had a brief taste of what victory looked like. I'll achieve it again one day—one day, I tell you—whenever I leave this school and bypass that filthy, no-good, heart-wrecking, soul-sucking mud.

I stared out across the Pit at the Pack, seeing Tony plant a kiss on Caroline. The Pack laughed with one another. I didn't care. Soon, there would be change; the deep magic would return once more. I knew in my heart that vine from heaven above would come down to pull me out of the mud.

Arthur had heard this story a thousand times while parked in the Pit. He demanded we get a move on to class. I agreed. One more day.

As Arthur and I crossed paths with the Pack in the Pit, they gave us deathly looks and, from what I could tell, muttered things about us to themselves. Caroline didn't look at me. She ignored me completely.

Tony laughed at one of the things muttered and called out to Arthur and me, "Too bad school's ending today. I'll miss my happy Ginger and Swift. Could y'all do that Japanese accent again from the fall play?"

The rest of the Pack laughed at the remarks, including the girls around them.

Arthur's face grew bright red. "Call me Ginger one more time, *dago*! I'll make you squeal *mamma mia* to Carlos when I'm done with ya."

The whole Pack booed at Arthur and me. Tony, with bitter anger, said, "Say it again, clown. I'll take you and Swift's manhood right here in front of everyone, makeup and all."

"No need. I gave it to Caroline already, far too many times to count," I exclaimed.

Caroline ran away in embarrassment. The Pack echoed my statements and laughed. Tony was furious.

Students in the Pit converged on the scene, waiting to see some action unfold, taking bets on the winner and loser.

"Twenty dollars on Torino giving Swift a new facelift. Twenty dollars! Come one, come all," yelled one opportunistic punk.

Another yelled, "Fifty dollars Torino slaps up Gingy and Swift."

"She told me you were no good anyway. Why do you think she came running back to me, clown face?" said Tony from on top his tailgate, gathering confidence from the crowd.

"Wasn't for the love. Probably was for that big truck and daddy's money 'cause she told me you weren't packing much in the pants. I guess the dollars and the truck made up for it."

A very tall, sturdy young man with short brown hair, beady brown eyes, tan skin, and a big bird nose stood up on the tailgate. His name was Marcus. His father was from Colombia, and his mother was from Fontainebleau. He was the star of the basketball team. He had those long arms to rebound and dunk. He was a "bad apple," and we absolutely did not get along when I played basketball. On the basketball team, Marcus was the favorite of the head coach, Mr. Taft.

"Funny, Swift. Talking about packing pants. Don't you and Gingy put on makeup every day for your little theater performance? My father would be ashamed of me if I put on makeup and acted like an idiot on stage. Oh, wait. You don't have a father or a woman to tell you that. Word around town, Caroline left you because she was embarrassed to be seen with you, a clown in makeup," Marcus exclaimed.

The Pack roared with laughter.

"That's what I've been telling y'all. Fruitiness happens when there's no father around. Your kid turns into a homo," exclaimed Tony. "Go smoke some pot, you quitter. You'll never be much more than that, you and Gingy."

"I'm gonna beat the hell out of him!" Arthur exclaimed.

"What did you say about my dad, *dago*? What did you say?" I yelled.

Acting upon the commotion, a couple of teachers hastily broke up the scene before anything could happen. They brought Arthur and me straight to the disciplinarian, Coach Billy Thomas. Tony was excused. No surprise there. I sat in the in the waiting room.

Billy Thomas's secretary was Betsy. She had curly black hair, put up in some 1980s fashion. She wore lots of makeup—bright blue around the eyes, pink on the cheeks, and bright red lipstick. I always caught her out back smoking a cigarette, talking on the phone with her lawyer. It was always about her ex-husband hoarding money from her or something like that. She always reeked of cigarettes and said, "How ya doing, darling?" Type, type, type on that keyboard was all she did. She wore headphones on the job, listening to music, I presumed.

"Betsy, send him in," yelled out Billy Thomas from his office.

She didn't hear him.

"Betsy, send him in . . . Betsy . . . Betsy!" yelled Billy Thomas.

She quickly took off her headphones. "I was sending the checks out like you asked."

"Oh, yes. Good. Well, send in Swift."

"Swift, he'll see you now, darling," Betsy said.

I was well-acquainted with Billy Thomas. I seemed to always be in his office. I blamed my mouth. I was routinely there every other week.

Billy Thomas had a bald spot on his head, wrinkles, and a bushy mustache; he was slightly overweight. He lived out in the country, so he had a Southern twang in his speech. He was not necessarily a bad man; tired was a better word. He was an older guy, and we had had a rough past of mixed ideologies and Saturday schools.

"Another fight, Swift? It's the third this month," Billy Thomas stated.

"This time was different, Coach. I promise," I replied.

He made a long, deep sigh. "You say that every time you are in here. How many detentions and Saturday schools will it take for you to realize to mind your own business and be a good kid. What's the problem, Swift?" He leaned back into his chair.

"Can I tell you a secret, Coach Billy Thomas?"

"A secret?"

"There's favoritism in this school, and I appreciate none of it. I demand a fair trial, a fair jury, and a fair place to state my case. I am preyed upon by the faculty and certain individuals, and I demand they are brought to trial. Demand, I say."

He sighed again. "Listen, Swift, if I hear anything else about you causing trouble, anything at all, you won't graduate from St. Francis. I promise you that."

"That's unfair!"

"Axelrod wouldn't like that, would he?"

"No, but—"

"But nothing. Keep your mouth shut, finish the damn day, and graduate for God's sake. Understood?"

"It's just—"

"Did I make myself clear, Swift?!"

"Yes."

"Good. Now get out of my office. I don't have time for this."

He leaned back into his chair behind his desk.

"Betsy . . . Betsy!" yelled Billy Thomas.

"Yes?"

"What were you doing?"

"Filing the paperwork with the state administrator, like you said to do," she said.

"Oh, yes. Well, send in the next one," he replied.

I left the office. I was pretty upset. I always felt shortchanged and disrespected. How could Tony get away with the things he said to Arthur and me? It was absurd! *Typical St. Francis*, I thought. I never got a fair shakedown.

Arthur waited for me outside of the office. "Don't listen to Tony, Christoph. He's just a punk."

"Yeah, just a punk. The things he said kind of hurt. I won't lie," I sighed.

"Lies, lies, lies. He's intimated by you, that's all."

"God forbid if he swings at me. It'll be his last. I'm tired of this stuff, Arthur. I've reached my limit."

"Pissed me off, too. Don't worry. If he ever swings, I'll be there, too."

"You're a good friend, Arthur."

He smiled. "Get to class. We'll talk after school before Mass."

I went to my nonsensical science class run by Mr. Taft. He was a bald-headed buffoon who used to be a male nurse turned basketball coach and teacher. Taft was tall and stocky, had a sleazy look about him, and acted absurdly tough. Too tough. He regarded his nursing knowledge highly and played favorites in the classroom. Students he disliked, usually the ones he could easily pick on, were subjected to his relentless jokes.

Some students loved him. Some hated him. Torino loved him. I didn't care at this point. I sat in my desk physically, but mentally and spiritually, I wasn't there. I looked out of the window, past the trees toward the blue sky, and imagined myself high above clouds soaring in a biplane.

Lucky for me, I was one of the few Taft picked on because I butted with his bald head when I played basketball. Our disagreement about showing up to early morning workouts led to my discharge from the team.

The story went like this: Before the basketball season started, long before my theater days, Taft hired this over-the-top workout instructor named Mr. Markel to condition the team to be in top shape for the season.

Mr. Markel was an ebony-skinned man, bald head, short, and

very stocky. He always wore a headband and red tank top. He used to play for some pro-football team back in his heyday, and he made sure everyone knew that. Mr. Markel was intense, always yelling at people and making us run suicides. It was terrible.

My big mouth got me and the team in trouble, causing us to run more. Torino and Marcus despised me for it. I couldn't help but question his tactics. They didn't make sense to me. We had to be there before the sun rose, but that was when I went fishing and did a little work around the shop, so I didn't always show up.

One time I showed up late, and Mr. Markel drilled me about it, spitting in my face, cursing up a storm, telling me I wasn't committed, or something bogus like that.

He told me to run until my knees gave out, and I told him no. That sent him into a frenzy. He almost passed out from my answer. Something broke in his head. He told me to get the hell out of his place, and I did, never to return. Looking back, I could've gone about it in a better way.

Basketball season started up with the first practice, but no one told me because I wasn't at those damn workouts. I showed up late to the gym and saw that they'd already started practice. I saw Taft and Markel talking with one another. I went up to them and told them I was ready to play. At that moment, Taft and Markel inquired why I didn't go to the preseason workouts. I was honest. I said it was counterintuitive to take the fun out of basketball, that I hated it, and that I did something else.

I questioned their methods. It probably wasn't the best thing to do at the time. Unfortunately, Taft and Markel yelled so loud at me to get the hell out of the gym, the girls school down the road heard them scream. I mean everyone in the school heard about it, talked about it, and tormented me with it. I brought it on myself. I'll accept that. I paid the price for it, and it was hard for a little while.

Needless to say, I was thrown off the team, and my relationship with Taft and the basketball team, especially Torino and Marcus, was rocky ever since.

Axelrod was angry with me when I told him about what happened. Disappointed was a better word. He told me to find something else, or I would be thrown out of the house. I said none of this was working out. I was frustrated and confused. I didn't know what the hell

I was doing. I felt alone in the whole situation.

If Axelrod cared so much about my playing basketball, why didn't he show up to any of my games? He never gave me a reason, only anger-filled yelling. Told me to learn how to stick with one thing and that working in the shop was postponed until I found another activity. Theater came into the picture shortly after that. I thought about my decisions as I stared out the window in Taft's class.

"Who can answer this question on the board? Tell me about the different types of lava," smiled Mr. Taft as he scanned the room, searching for a poor soul with a lost look on his face. "Jenkins, can you answer this question . . . hmm?" Taft would raise his eyebrows in anticipation of the question.

Jenkins had shaggy brown hair, unkempt hygiene, and terrible acne. He looked like he hadn't slept in days.

"Uh, lava?" replied Jenkins.

Jenkins stuttered once more, struggling to find any hint of an answer. The class laughed at his desperation. Tony and some of the Pack, such as Bubba—big ole guy, somewhat fat, with big buck teeth who looked like a real bully boy and played football—were in this class. Bubba hated me because Tony hated me. Mob mentality. He wasn't the brightest bulb in the shop. He always told me he disliked me because of my face. Well, I didn't like his face either, so we agreed on that.

"Last class, gentlemen. Final exam this Monday," remarked Taft. This might be confusing, but this was our last day of normal class. In the following week, we arrived at certain times only to take our finals exams in an auditorium.

Mr. Taft's eyes drifted toward me. A slight smirk popped up, and he said, "And no, the answer is not minosium."

The class laughed, as Taft referred to when I asked him about minosium a couple months ago, if it was a real mineral. Curiously before this, I had read an old book from the school library about minerals, and minosium was actually in the book, but little was said about it.

I asked Taft about it earlier in the year. He wanted me to elaborate on the story about Faustino and the mineral. I loved to retell stories, so I told the class the whole story. Taft thought I was crazy, laughed endlessly at me, and enticed the class to follow suit.

From that day on, he always referred to minosium and Bird-Eye when he called on me. I believed he did it as revenge because of our altercation during basketball.

"Wasn't it in that labyrinth?" Bubba joked.

"Along with dragons and elves," laughed Torino.

"He believed it to be true," Bubba remarked.

"I did and still do," I replied. "At least I believe in something."

"Class, now . . ." stuttered Taft, trying to hold back laughter. "I'm sorry. It is pretty funny." He controlled himself. "Can you answer the question, Bird-Eye. Wasn't that his name?"

The class erupted in laughter. Even Jenkins laughed with the crowd.

"Oh, he looks angry now. Come on. Do something about it, Birdy," snarked Bubba.

I clenched my fist. Billy Thomas told me one more fallout, and I wouldn't graduate. If I knocked out Bubba's or Tony T's two front teeth, Taft would surely stand against me. It wasn't worth it.

"Little Birdy upset? Do something about it," insisted Bubba.

"'Least I can fly, Bubba. I'll be sure to wave to you from above the clouds, bottom feeder," I replied.

I know I shouldn't have, but I couldn't take it anymore. Bubba was furious, stood up in his desk, red face and all. Tony pulled him back down.

"Everyone, stop. Let's get back to work! Bubba, since you are so eager to talk, answer the question on the board," Taft insisted.

Tony laughed. "Typical Swift, causing trouble."

When class ended, Bubba waited to tell me outside the class, "Last day don't mean a thing, Birdy. Can't go far once I clip them wings."

"Tick-tock, Swift," smiled Tony.

I told them to beat it. This was how I entangled myself in fights. Really, it wasn't this occasion alone that stirred the boat. This was pumped-up anger, four years' worth, from Tony Torino and the Pack, waiting to be released like a valve of air pressure.

The rest of the day went by relatively fast. I had my final theater class. We watched an old black-and-white film and said our good-byes. The seniors were let out early to attend our end of the year Mass. I thought about bailing on the whole procession and book it home. I was tired; the day weighed on me. I sat on my bike at the Pit, debating what to do. Axelrod didn't want to come anyway.

Trust me. I loved God more than anything, but screw that Mass, this school, all of this. At the time, I did not care if the Archbishop of New Orleans was coming to our school. In my opinion, he was the same as Mr. Taft, Tony, Caroline, Billy Thomas, and the rest of them superficial, vanilla characters at this school.

No one, not even Axelrod, cared if I stayed or went. I could jump off a bridge, and who would know? I grabbed hold of the amulet my parents gave me hanging around my neck and said, "Help me find who I am."

Arthur grabbed my shoulder.

"Stay. My mom is here. We can sit together," Arthur said.

"What's the point?" I inquired. "Nothing's left for me here."

"It's our last day. Love it or hate it. We had a good run. Don't let those punks take this day from you. Come on. My family is throwing a party for us after the Mass. All the theater guys will be there, even Mrs. Anne Kay. Bring Axelrod."

I gave it some good thought. I was flushed with a mixture of conflicted feelings. I turned off my bike and took off my helmet.

"You sure your mom is okay if Axelrod and I come to the party? It's okay if not. We were . . ."

Arthur smiled. "Please bring him. We have more than enough food. I'm begging the both of you to come."

"Okay, okay," I smiled. "We'll come."

"Aha, thatta boy. Let's get going then."

"Arthur."

"Yeah."

"Thanks."

"Don't go soft on me, pal," he smiled. "Come on."

We started to walk toward the assembly center at the center of campus. The big, square building looked like a large convention center made from tan brick and had a gray sloped roof. By no means was it an architectural feat, I'll say that. This is where all our Masses and assemblies took place, hence the name assembly center. Tons of parents and students stood in front of the center, talking and congregating.

Arthur's mother was standing to the side of the crowd in a pretty pink sundress. She was quite lovely, tall, and slender with poppy red hair, just like Arthur's. Her name was Mrs. Mary. She was a nurse at the hospital down the road. The doors to the center had not opened yet.

"How are we doing, love? Excited school's ending?" Mrs. Mary asked.

"Is the Pope Catholic?" I smiled.

"Indeed, he is. How's your uncle doing? I haven't seen him in a while."

"Fine, fine. He's always in his shop, working on who knows what. I guess there's always another plane or engine to be fixed."

"Whatever makes him happy. Arthur told me you can fly a plane. That's incredible."

"I'm a decent pilot. Still have lot more to learn."

"Shoot, if you're half the pilot compared to your acting skills, then I could only imagine. You acted so well in the fall play. I asked Arthur, where did you learn how to act so well?"

"Reading and rehearsing old books, if I had to pinpoint it."

"A man blessed with a thousand gifts. Keep it up. That's fantastic. I was wondering, did Arthur tell you about the party later?"

"I told him about it," interjected Arthur.

"Yes, thank you so much for the invite. I would love to come," I replied.

"You're more than welcome, and bring Axelrod. Tell him I insist he comes. It's a necessity. It starts right after Mass," she checked her watch, "which is soon."

"Right. I forgot to give him a call. Let me do that. One moment."

I checked my pockets for my phone, but it was empty. "Shoot, I left my phone on my bike. I'll be right back."

"Hurry! Mass is about to start," stated Arthur.

"We'll save you a seat, dear," yelled Mrs. Mary as I made my way through the crowd.

The crowd was so dense I could barely breathe. I nudged my way through. As I maneuvered through the crowd, a man in a fine black suit, slicked black hair covered up by a black trilby hat, and narrow face bumped into me rather violently. I fell, and my amulet popped out of my shirt.

"Excuse me, sir," I said with an annoyed tone.

He turned around, gave me a wide smile, and extended his hand to help me up.

"Nice amulet, Swift," said the man in a coarse, smoky tone.

"Not . . . a problem," I replied hesitantly.

I dusted off my clothes and put the amulet back under my shirt. But wait, how did he know my name?

"Wait, how'd . . . " I questioned then paused for a moment as I looked around for the man.

He was gone. I thought about the encounter. Strange. Then, coming upon the crowd with a large entourage was Archbishop Narcisse, glamorously talking and shaking hands with the parents, exhibiting a strong vibe around him, demanding attention.

He was an older man wearing his priestly black attire. He was roughly in his early fifties and slender, with circular glasses, brown hair parted to the side, and a pronounced forehead wrinkle and chin. He was quite tall, of good size, and seemed strong. He had a boisterous, strong attitude from what I could tell; he was outgoing, talked loudly, and had a thick New Orleans accent, sounding like that well-known Brooklyn accent: "I'm walkin' here!"

I didn't know too much about Narcisse, besides his being a big shot bishop back in the day. People worshiped the man, the biggest name in the state, more so than any professional athlete. Typical of Axelrod, he disliked Narcisse. I asked about the man one day; Axelrod told me, "He's no priest. He's a schemer! Deep pockets, deeper than the Gulf of Mexico, with greed more voracious than Faustino. Made a deal with the Devil, I say! Stay away from him, hear ye?"

It was a vague clarification, so I asked Arthur about the bishop. He was a diehard Catholic along with those other theater kids; more so, Arthur had a cousin who was a Dominican priest, Father Jean. Arthur said Jean strongly disliked the Jesuits, called them pompous. In turn, Arthur didn't favor the Jesuits either.

If you didn't know, in Catholicism, priests, monks, and nuns are part of a specific order. Even the pope himself is part of an order. The Jesuits were one of the most well-known orders. Jesuits were smart guys, credited for many scientific discoveries, like the Big Bang Theory. The order itself was powerful, prestigious, and old. Narcisse was one of them.

Jean, Arthur's cousin, said Narcisse was the most powerful bishop in America with connections all the way up to the pope. Story went that Narcisse came from a small town in the middle of nowhere Louisiana. He grew up on a sugarcane plantation. Family was poorer than dirt, so he joined the Jesuits to receive an admirable education. He was sharp, rose quickly in the ranks, and gained powerful friends intra- and inter-state.

I could say with certainty that Narcisse was the most well-known bishop in America. He even said Mass a few times in D.C. for the president of the United States. He remained in Louisiana for the time being, but I couldn't tell you why. Jean believed Narcisse had plans to become the first American pope—said he could do it, especially with the help of his wide variety of friends.

I looked through the crowd, and right in front of me was Narcisse giving a man in a seersucker suit an over-the-top hug. The man fortunate to have received such a hug was the infamous Carlos Torino. Narcisse announced his name with a loud cheer and open arms.

Carlos was a stern man with a bulldog face. He was a big guy but not fat, stocky with dark black hair, bushy eyebrows, and tan skin like his son, Tony. All the parents tried to move as close as possible to Torino and Narcisse, the center of the who's who in Louisiana, wishing, begging to receive acknowledgment.

Rumors spread around the school for years about Carlos Torino, a supposed mafia man with a hand in everything from casinos to politics in Louisiana and beyond. Carlos owned numerous restaurants and commercial real estate in Fontainebleau, New Orleans, and who knew where else.

Some of kids even said that it was Carlos Torino's uncle, Angelo Torino, who called the order to kill John F. Kennedy, a former president of the United States in the 1960s.

How the Torinos were involved with J.F.K. was quite fascinating. I believed it to be true. Lee Harvey Oswald, the man who supposedly shot J.F.K., grew up in a house down the road from my school, which was only forty minutes from downtown New Orleans.

The Torinos had been a prominent name in the city for quite some time, doing business in all types of licit and illicit things. Rumor went J.F.K. was cracking down on the mafia, especially targeting the Torinos' racketeering business in New Orleans. In response to J.F.K., Angelo hired Lee Harvey Oswald, who coincidently grew up in Fontainebleau for a short time, to take out J.F.K. Oswald's old house was right off the main street in downtown Fontainebleau. His house became a fantastic Thai buffet. Every time Arthur and I ate there, we talked of Oswald.

Carlos Torino was the direct heir to the mafia throne that had the power to kill J.F.K., a U.S. president. Needless to say, Axelrod did not want me fooling around with anyone named Torino.

One day, I told Axelrod about my trouble with Tony. His eyes lit up. He could not believe a Torino was in my school. Axelrod told me, "Remember this, boy: No politician runs Louisiana. They are puppets with strings, connected to the hands of good ole boys. Stay away from them, hear ye?!"

"Good ole boys" is a term used in the Deep South for people who contained power within their small circle, closed off to the rest of the public. They profited off embezzlement, racketeering, and layering. Louisiana is a game of good ole boys. Huey P. Long, an old governor of ours during Roosevelt's reign, tried to do something about these ole boys. He's dead—shot on the steps of the Capitol.

A group of well-dressed men in black suits surrounded Carlos, an entourage similar in size to Narcisse's. I finally made my way through the crowd. People turned, and the whole crowd funneled into the center.

No one, not a soul, was in the Pit when I arrived. I grabbed my phone from my bike bag and called Axelrod. He told me he finished up his work and was ready to come whenever I needed him. I told him to leave now and make the Mass, and we'd go to Arthur's party later. Axelrod was slightly reluctant, but I got him to budge. He asked again if the archbishop would be there. Once again, I lied to him.

I could tell when he was looking for a reason to bail on me. Not today though. I told him to park near the Pit, and we'd walk into Mass together. It didn't matter to me if we were late. All I cared about was that Axelrod said he'd be there in a few.

I was elated as I sat on my bike, taking in the moment. Maybe this day would turn around. Good things were on the horizon: Mass and a party later, no more Taft, no more of this school. It was over; it was all over. I was free, only clear blue skies ahead. I looked up into the sky. I closed my eyes and smiled. Damn. It felt good.

The sounds of unsettled gravel rustling about brought me back to reality. I opened my eyes only to find Tony Torino, Marcus, and Bubba ten yards away staring at me.

"Nice to see you here, Swift," exclaimed Tony. "Saw you run over here. Thought what better time to give you my goodbye while everyone else is preoccupied. Still need to get my service hours, so I can graduate."

"Fine public service about to be had," Marcus laughed.

Bubba whistled at me. "Nowhere to run now, little Birdy."

"Genius. No one around, no teachers, no friends, no one to save you, Swift," Marcus exclaimed.

"In fact, no one was ever around for you," added Tony.

"That's not true," I remarked.

They slowly approached me.

"Of course, it is, and you know it's true. No one cares what happens to you. No one ever did. You're an orphan. Your uncle doesn't care about you. If he did, why haven't I seen him?" remarked Tony. "Didn't see him at our games. Didn't see him at the plays. Where was he?"

"Go back to your parents. I'm not playing around. I'm done with this," I replied.

"'Cause he don't care about you, like Caroline and everyone else," laughed Bubba with his huge buck teeth.

"Except little Gingy," remarked Marcus. "He was so ugly, little racist ginger."

"What's your problem with me, huh? Why hate me so much all these years?" I asked.

"It's the way you carry yourself, the way you look, what you say. No respect," remarked Tony.

"No pops around to teach him respect," remarked Bubba as he moved around the Pit.

"I hate everything about you, everything down to what you stand for," Tony said.

"And what's that? What do I stand for that you hate so much?" I replied. "My clothes? My bike? My job? My pitiful family? What?!"

"You wouldn't subdue—submit to the coaches, to the team, to the teachers, to our school, to the Pack, to me," said Tony. "You are a disrespectful rat, causing us to run endlessly because of your bigotry, angering the coaches, sleeping with my girl." Tony spat on the ground.

"You're right. I would never submit to you or anyone at this corrupt school. Hear me, Tony. Go to hell, you and your fake friends, fake school, and fake life. I want none of it! Take it. It's yours. The only thing I'll give you three is a chance to kiss my ass."

"Let me at him first," yelled Marcus. "Just a quick pump. Get the blood going before the party tonight."

"Hold up! I'll give you one last chance, Christoph, to save your sorry ass from us splattering your head across this gravel. Bow down before all three of us, proclaim us your kings, kiss our feet, and say, 'I'm a dumb boy who disrespected Tony T.' Do this, and maybe I'll spare your face," stated Tony.

"That's a good one, Tony! Make him eat rocks, too," proclaimed Bubba.

"I'll make him lick my foot," laughed Marcus.

"Sounds like a wonderful deal, but I have knee issues," I remarked.

"Wrong answer, little Birdy," smiled Bubba, showing his buck teeth.

"Bad move, Swift," said Tony.

"Let's be done with this, right here and now," I stated.

I took off my shirt, cracked my neck, and took a deep breath. My purple amulet hung from my neck.

"Nice necklace. I think I'll take it," Marcus exclaimed.

"Marcus, before this day is done, your family will wipe the blood from your face, assessing how bad I broke your big, ugly nose," I replied.

Marcus took off his shirt and gave a deep growl. He moved forward while I stood still.

Marcus tried to jab me. I dodged it and uppercut his chin with great force. He fell to the ground. I hopped on top of him and beat his face to a pulp, striking at his nose purposely, breaking it severely. He could do nothing as his blood splattered in all directions. Anger filled my veins. I could see only red. Marcus cried out to Bubba for help.

Bubba quickly tackled me to the ground. He was a much bigger guy than Marcus, width- and density-wise. He began to punch me on my sides. Each blow he gave had strong force behind it, taking a piece of me with each strike. I protected my face, but I could only do so much.

I jabbed his face, but this bull wouldn't flinch. Bubba tackled me one more time to the ground and grabbed my leg, slowly trying to tear it apart. I screamed from the pain. He was breaking my leg, and I couldn't do anything.

Out of nowhere, Arthur jabbed his foot into Bubba's head, continuously stomping on his teeth. He moaned in pain. Blood spilled out all over my face. My eye was cut open. In a daze from lack of oxygen, I slowly rose.

Tony charged me, and we went at it. With all the strength I had left, I threw a couple of jabs at him. Tony was relentless and filled with hatred as he tried to strike my wounded face.

Upon hearing the commotion from the Pit, a large crowd of parents and teachers from the Mass hastily ran to the Pit and broke up the fight. Everyone from the Mass funneled toward the Pit; essentially, the Mass was ruined at this point. Trying to figure out what happened, people screamed at Arthur and me.

Marcus wouldn't get up. To be honest, I was in such a haze, I didn't know what was going on. The whole senior class was there, plus Tony's father, Carlos, and Narcisse. They were furious by what they saw.

Billy Thomas approached Arthur and me, grabbed us by the collar, and told us that we were expelled, possibly with criminal charges. A teacher pushed me to the ground, acting like it was an accident. I couldn't hear them so well because I was in a complete daze. Carlos bypassed his son, receiving attention from other parents.

"Dad, that punk, he . . ." uttered Tony.

Carlos ignored his son and kept walking toward me. Narcisse followed behind him closely. Carlos Torino picked me up forcefully and grabbed my amulet.

"Your name, boy!" demanded Carlos, staring directly in my eyes, then back at the amulet.

I was seeing everything in twos, bending, split vision.

"Carlos, he's wearing the amulet," stated Narcisse in a low tone. "I've seen it before. That's it!"

"Impossible," said Torino. "It went down with Kalendar years ago."

I grabbed onto my amulet and pushed him off. "Get off me! Axelrod! Where are you?"

"Where did you get that necklace?" yelled Torino. "Who gave it to you?"

"Tell me your name, son," asked Narcisse.

"Christoph Swift," I replied.

A burst of lightning struck from the sky, yet not a cloud was in sight. The crowd looked up in fear, questioning this strange occurrence.

The crowd uttered in loud cries, "Energy strikes without a cloud in sight!"

Another asked, "What does this sign mean? Is the Lord displeased with us?"

The crowd continued to chatter amongst themselves about the bizarre strike of lightning that followed the prior events.

"A sign!" Narcisse exclaimed. "The lightning was struck from no cloud. Surely an omen from above."

Narcisse and Carlos looked at one other with wide eyes.

"That can't be," said Torino as he backed away from me.

Axelrod broke through the dazzled crowd as they continued to stare toward the sky in amazement. He called, "Christoph! What in the name?"

Billy Thomas, disinterested in the strange lightning strike, tugged on Axelrod's shoulder. "Your kid has deliberately—"

"Quiet! Get away from us, you hear me? All of you!" Axelrod demanded.

"Take me home," I muttered as I tried to stand on my own.

Axelrod helped me through the crowd, ignoring the comments thrown at us. Directly in our path stood Narcisse and Torino.

"Axelrod," said Torino.

"You had the amulet! This whole time," Narcisse concluded.

"It's been a while, Torino, Narcisse," stated Axelrod.

His voice changed. I don't know how to explain it, but it was different, apprehensive.

"The boy bears the mark," said Narcisse.

"He bears nothing but good will," said Axelrod.

"As plain as day, I see the mark. Give it here!" exclaimed Narcisse.

"Back! Never touch him. Never come close to him!" Axelrod demanded.

"He'll find out sooner or later. You can't hide from him, Axelrod. You know that," Torino said.

"You got what you wanted at the expense of us. Is that not enough?" suggested Axelrod.

"This is different. You knew this day would come. No more hiding," Torino declared.

"*He* hears everything, like rats in the wall! Soon, *he* shall be upon us, on all of us. I can save the boy, only if you give me the amulet!" exclaimed Narcisse. He extended his hand outward. "Think of the boy."

Axelrod looked at Narcisse's hand with concern, contemplating what to do. He closed his eyes for a moment and said a prayer.

"You know them?" asked Tony as he nudged his way to the center of the action.

"Quiet," replied Carlos. "You're done here. Leave!"

The crowd of people were enamored by the scene. Axelrod opened his eyes—focused, stern.

"I am not scared of *him*, the Tughra, or the Terminal! A storm is coming, and it shall wash away thee and *him* from this miserable earth," echoed Axelrod. He turned to me, "We're leaving, Christoph, right now."

"No one can save you, Axelrod. No hole is too small to be found," Torino advised.

Axelrod guided me out of the crowd as they followed us with their eyes and silent lips.

"What about my bike?" I asked.

"We'll get it some other time," replied Axelrod.

"We must have it. Do something, Torino. Think of what *he'll* do to us!" exclaimed Narcisse.

Carlos Torino smiled.

"Why are you smiling?" Narcisse exclaimed angrily.

"The race is back on," Torino replied.

"Smile now, Torino. Soon enough our heads will end up on spikes!" remarked Narcisse as he walked away.

The crowd began to disperse in all directions. A deathly vibe filled the Pit.

Carlos Torino continued to stare in the direction of Axelrod.

"See you soon, Swift. See you soon," smiled Torino.

As I think back on that day, little did I know what earth-shattering event took place before me. Lightning struck when Carlos and Narcisse witnessed my amulet for reasons I knew not at the time.

This amulet, given to me by my father, harbored a hidden secret that tied Carlos Torino, Archbishop Narcisse, Axelrod, and me together in strange relationship. From this encounter, they acted as if they knew each other in a past life before my time.

They emphasized *he* shall know, but who was *he*? They further claimed Axelrod was in danger of being discovered by *him*. Narcisse offered a choice: give him the amulet to ensure my safety. This interaction caused my mind to run with curiosity, asking myself what made my amulet so valuable and who would harm me for it.

Axelrod had been withholding a secret from me worth a lightning strike from a sky without a single cloud. On that day, it seemed destiny felt the time had come to conduct its masterful design, beginning with a spark of light.

CHAPTER 3

Waltz of the New World

I WOKE UP ON a table with a single swaying lightbulb above me. My head pounded with pain, felt like I was hit by a bus. I rotated my body; pain radiated from my torso. I was in bad shape. I touched my side where most of the pain was coming from; it was horribly sensitive all around my ribs. I most likely broke a rib or badly bruised it. Either way, I was in terrible pain.

I lifted my shirt. My torso was covered with dark blue and purple spots. Better yet, my left eyebrow had stitches on it, and my left eye was swollen shut. I swung my legs off the table. Big mistake. My left leg felt torn, like a bad charley horse strain. I shrieked from the pain; sweat poured across my body

I looked around. I was in the lighthouse, Axelrod's study. It'd been so many years since I'd seen it. Quite impressive. At the center of the room was a mahogany table, and on it was a large map of the world, a gold magnifying glass resting on top of it. Scattered pieces of paper and books littered the table and floor.

Facing out the window next to a charting map and large bookshelf was an intricate telescope aimed at the stars. Situated on another table was some sort of mechanical device for an arm, almost like armor, with intricate, small valves and cogs of different sizes, all encompassed by light titanium plates.

I slowly got off the table, recovered my balance, and let the curiosity flow. I'd waited years to see what Axelrod was working on. Little did I know he was charting the world's seas and stars. I pushed the papers on the table to the side and examined the map. Red question marks and circles were drawn over certain locations across the sea and certain spots in the world. One circle was over a part in the Himalayan Mountains, another in South America, and one in the Mediterranean.

What in the world was this? Next to the table was a brown desk with a globe on top of it—littered with papers, sketches, and pencils. On the desk was a book called *The Mystical Treasure and Curse of Salvador Faustino*, Axelrod's favorite story. Below that was a thick volume with a green cover labeled in gold print, *Traders Terminal: Series Trials I & II.*

The door swung open. It was my uncle. Concern filled his face. I knew when he had that spark in his eye that something wasn't right. Axelrod hastily moved around the room, throwing different supplies into a blue duffel bag. Nervousness and worry grew within me by the minute; my heartbeat rose increasingly faster as I watched Axelrod act in such a strange way.

"Axelrod, what's going on? You're scaring me," I stated.

"Listen, Christoph. We don't have much time. I need ye to trust me and listen to everything I say. Do ye understand?"

"Yes. Yes, of course."

"First and foremost, I do not worry. Everything will be all right. Breathe."

"What's going on?"

"Breathe."

I took a deep breath.

"You will understand things in time. Everything is about to change drastically for ye, like you always wanted."

"Not like this."

"Ye are going to take our small fishing boat, the one from earlier, quietly down the Tchefuncte, across Lake Pontchartrain, toward Womack dock on the outer banks of New Orleans. The same one we went to see Mr. Charlie on. Remember that one?"

"I do. Long way away though."

"From the dock, ye will board a ship called the *S.S. Edwards.*"

"*S.S. Edwards* . . . but—"

"Listen! I outfitted the boat with a special muffler that will silence the motor, take . . . Do you hear that?"

"No?"

Axelrod peeked out of the window. Lights in the distance

shone through the woods. A few cars were coming toward us. Axelrod stepped back with a look of deep contemplation and stress.

"Is that someone you know?" I asked, concerned.

He pulled himself from his thoughts. "People are after us, Christoph. It is not safe for you here any longer."

"I didn't do anything. Who . . . Who are these people?"

"They've always been after us and always will be, as long as the springs run red."

"That doesn't make sense . . . Who are they?"

"Old friends of mine. No more questions. Ye must get going!"

A shot was fired outside the window. I turned my head. Axelrod grabbed my chin, keeping my focus on his eyes. Panic began to set in. *This can't be happening*, I thought.

"Ye must escape," he insisted.

"Aren't you coming with me?" I asked.

"Not yet. I still have some unfinished business here."

"I can't do this alone! Not without you. I . . . I—"

"Yes, ye can. Believe ye can, Christoph. Don't worry about me. This world ye are about to enter will challenge ye, scare ye, and hurt ye, but nay! It shall never defeat ye! For I have seen it. I've seen thee reach the top. I've tried to keep ye from this world, but Fate spoke otherwise. Ascend, Christoph. Ascend, and never look back."

"Axelrod, what world are you talking about?"

"Take this bag. It has food, water, instructions, and a GPS. No phones from here on out. It's everything you will need."

Axelrod moved the rug near the desk. Under it was a little hatch to an underground passageway. Sweat poured down his face. More cars rolled down the driveway and parked outside of the main house. A window broke with sounds of shattered glass. Then, the sound of another window shattered. I was frozen, unable to move.

"Take this coin to Villefranche, France." Axelrod closed my hand over the coin.

"But I've never been out of the country before, let alone the South," I replied.

"Take it to a small bar in an alleyway called Sinbad's Tavern. Give the coin to the bartender. He'll direct you from there. You must meet Captain Kalendar of the Victoria & Co. Tell him I sent you. This is critical."

"Captain Kalendar ... Okay," I repeated, trying to remember his instructions.

"Most importantly, never forget this: you can pass the Trials," he said with a dear smile. "It's in your blood. Listen to your mentor."

"Trials ... I'm good at some trials, I think."

"If ye choose a different path, sell the coin to the representative at the tavern, take the money, and stay hidden until this blows over."

"Different path?"

"The way to Kalendar is dangerous and rough. There is no turning back and no guarantees. But if do you succeed, which I know ye can, that life will offer ye great rewards and the answers ye seek. Reflect on it, and do not speak of this to anyone."

Men talked loudly outside of the lighthouse. They were getting closer. The chatter grew louder. I felt apprehension and fear. This was real. Real danger was at the foot of my doorstep. I was forced to deal with it.

"Bastards ... They'll never take ye alive!" Axelrod exclaimed.

"Axelrod! Come with me. Please. We can go together! Why must you stay?"

Axelrod pulled a sword out of the cabinet, but it was no ordinary sword. It looked like a cutlass, a curved sword with glowing buttons on the hilt. At the center of the hilt was a small, glowing, red circle.

"Never fear being lost or alone, for the Lord will be with ye. You'll find your way. I know ye will. Now, go!" Axelrod demanded.

The sword emitted a vibrant, electric red light, lining the crossguard—the sharpened edge of the blade about a centimeter wide. I couldn't believe my eyes. Seemed straight from a scene from a sci-fi movie, I thought. Has Axelrod worked tirelessly on glowing swords in his study all those years? Axelrod braced for the intruders. No time to gander at the fluorescent blade.

A window in the shop shattered, followed by a few gunshots outside the door. The men attempted to break in through the bolted door, but it was sealed shut with steel. After a few moments, a loud machine roared; then, electrical sparks created a small opening in the door. It was some type of welding tool with a pulsating purple light.

"What are you waiting for?" Axelrod exclaimed. "Before it's too late!" The sounds of the fiery tool piercing through the door violently roared over Axelrod's voice. It sounded quite frightening—a wakeup call that machines of this caliber existed.

I struggled to get into the small passageway. Once in, I closed the hatch. I hastily crawled through the dark passage, lit by my flashlight, and popped up at our dock, a good distance away from the house, covered by a tree line. I could see flashlights and car headlights in the distance.

With a slight gaze through the trees, I saw a man in a black suit with a familiar stature. It appeared, if I was not mistaken, to be Carlos Torino. I wasn't a hundred percent sure if it was him since the dark night masked the man's face. The next few moments, only bright flashes of lights and loud gunfire occurred in the lighthouse.

I needed to act quickly. I quietly got into the boat. The pain in my side was unbearable. I struggled to keep my mouth shut, withholding my shriek. The pain was so terrible, tears came from my eyes. I had to push through. I put on a black waterproof jacket, kept the hood over my head. I tried to start the motor. It didn't start but instead made a rather obnoxious puffing sound.

"Damn thing," I uttered quietly. "Why now?"

Flashlights shone in my direction. Men chattered in the distance. The voices grew louder; the men were getting closer. I started to panic. Sweat poured from my face. I could taste the salt of it.

I looked around the boat for a wrench and couldn't find one. I checked the red toolbox, but it wasn't there. In a frenzy, I tried to start it once again. It wouldn't click on! My heart was about to beat violently out of my chest.

I took a deep breath, closed my eyes, and thought for a moment. I tried to stay calm, think about what I should do. I visualized where I put the wrench earlier this morning. There—under the seat! I opened my eyes, and sure enough, it was there. I grabbed it. "Yes!"

The men were coming closer by the second. I tightened a few screws, which usually did the trick for a click. Tried once more to start it. Damn thing didn't catch!

The men started to yell to their other comrades. As a last ditch effort, I hit the motor with the wrench, and it clicked on. I grabbed the paddle to push myself off. Out of nowhere, a tan-skinned man grabbed the side of my boat. On his hand was a strange tattoo—black lines intersecting one another in an elaborate fashion. The symbol or word looked like it was from the Middle East or Turkey.

"He's over here!" yelled the man holding on to my boat as he reached for his handgun.

I quickly whacked him in the head with my paddle, and he fell into the water. I pushed myself off the dock and steered the ship downriver. What was that symbol? One of the men was carrying an assault rifle, the most unnerving image that still haunts me to this day, .

My poor uncle, I said to myself. *They'll kill him!* I cried and lamented for a whole hour. Tears dripped down from my eyes like raindrops falling from a midsummer's storm. I screamed, "Why? Oh why, God? If my life was not already terrible, why make it worse?" I cried for an hour or two until the tears dried up.

When the tears subsided and reason returned to my mind, I reflected on the past events that led me to this exaggerated point. I felt in that moment as if I were Odysseus floating down the River Styx to the underworld.

My world was changing before my eyes. This small fishing boat was my vessel to an unseen, dark world that lay before me. The moment my boat began its course below the crescent moonglow, I was moving into another realm, alien to my own. Danger was near, fear was close by, and everything was happening with great haste.

I had thought when the sun was high in the sky the day before that I had attended my last day of school. There I was enveloped in a fight with wretches that was grossly overdue. *Bizarre*, I thought as I remembered the bolt of lightning that struck the sky when Narcisse grabbed my amulet. *What was reason for that bolt of lightning, much less the significance of this amulet?*

Not long after the fight, when slumber fell to my eyes, light returned, and I found myself in the lighthouse, surrounded by questionable objects. No answer I received could satisfy my voracious intellectual appetite.

Axelrod arrived quickly without an answer to my predicament, only that I must escape and find Captain Kalendar of the Victoria & Co. With a coin I must beseech him, but for what purpose? Shelter, food, or protection?

Axelrod spoke of an opportunity to be associated with this captain and his company, perhaps a chance to join his company. If this company has anything to do with those strange and exciting objects in the lighthouse, this amulet, or the questions I sought, I concluded that Kalendar must be found, for he was a man worth more than gold to me.

I looked up at the moon as she sat on her purple throne, glowing in majesty. I said my goodbyes to Axelrod and the world I left behind with hope in my heart that I may return in the coming years. My focus would be tuned to the sweet sound of opportunity that would guide me through the dark unforeseen world that lay before me to find Kalendar, my own prophet Tiresias.

CHAPTER 4

Dance of the Victoria

The Womack dock wasn't too far from me, a few hours into the trip. It was along the Mississippi River on the outskirts of downtown New Orleans. The lake was quite calm.

I parked the boat, knowing I was never going to see it again, grabbed my bag, and searched for the ship on the dock. The dock was located a little way down the Mississippi River from downtown New Orleans. Even at 5:00 a.m., the dock bustled with energy. People of many different shapes, sizes, and colors moved in all directions—from workers on big cargo ships, sailors for private vessels, and merchants trading their wares.

I searched for the ship *S.S. Edwards*. I had no earthly idea what it looked like. Next to an old, salty sailor's bar next to the dock, I saw a few sailors smoking in a circle. They were tough guys and had the whole get-up—tattoo, big beards, smelled bad—perfect people to ask where the ship was. I broke into the circle.

"Pardon, any of you heard of the *S.S. Edwards?*" I asked.

They were rough, terribly standoffish to me.

"What?" replied one.

"*S.S. Edwards*. Heard of it?" I resumed.

He took a drag of a cigarette, squinted his eyes at me. The friend next to him chimed in. "What's wrong with ya, mate, eye lookin' all puffed up?"

The man had an English accent. It made sense: Womack dock was an entry point to the rest of the world.

"Eh, the *S.S. Edwards*, shipping vessel," said the man smoking a cigarette. "End of the dock. Big red ship. Can't miss it."

"End of the dock. Red. Got it. Thanks," I replied.

Before I pulled off, the man said "Take a sip; help the eye." He took out a flask from his coat pocket.

"I don't drink," I replied.

"Huh? Why not?" he replied in a deep tone.

"Don't know. Never had it offered."

"Down ye go then!"

I took the flask and gave it a sniff. Then down the hatch. The warm fire burned my throat and tasted dreadful. I almost threw up. The group of them laughed as the good man patted me on the back.

"Rum will do the trick," he remarked.

I continued down the dock, which smelled of brackish freshwater. The wind blew strong as it came off the Mississippi River. The rum helped ease the pain, but by no means was it gone.

I found the *S.S. Edwards*, a large cargo ship. I opened my bag and found the ticket. I was quite nervous. I had never done anything like this before. Where was Villefranche anyway?

A thought came briefly in my head: *Should I turn around? Go find Axelrod? Maybe all of this was a bad dream. What the hell was I doing here?*

The wind blew hard, and I was cold. I thought of my warm bed. It was harsh here. Goosebumps appeared on my arm. I could turn back now, return home.

I didn't think leaving meant this. Yes, I'd been wanting to leave, but faced with it, right here in front of me, was a whole different story. I told myself if I wanted change, I couldn't fear it. I told myself that I could do this, so I got in line to board the ship. Then, I walked up the gangway to a sea officer, who had a small black mustache and large circular glasses, wearing a tailored blue suit with gold buttons and a blue hat. He was accepting tickets for the vessel.

"Next please," said the man.

I pulled out my ticket from my bag. My hands were blue from the cold air coming off the river. The officer held up the ticket to examine it.

"Seeing someone in Nice?" he asked.

"What's Nice?" I replied.

"Not Nice. Pronounced like *niece*. Nice, France."

"I'm going to Villefranche."

"Ah, Villefranche-sur-Mer. Yes. Yes, you'll take a connection from Nice. Your cabin is on the lower decks. Look at your ticket for the cabin number. Next, please!"

This was a little overwhelming. I walked along the deck toward the stairs. I looked over the side rail at the city of New Orleans and Lake Pontchartrain in the distance. I said to myself that it could be a while before I saw this again. I would miss this place. When faced with my actual departure, it made me appreciate my home and what I had. You really never know what you have until you see it sail away.

As I stared off, I noticed running along the dock were the same group of men I saw earlier at my house. No way. No way! They were looking for me. It was quite frightening. Looked like there was no turning back now.

I made sure to get out of sight and headed for my room. The ship was big with many different sections to it. I went down to the lower decks and walked through the hallway. Smelled funny, like salty air and bad laundry. Different people were coming and going all around me, talking on the phone, texting, carrying bags.

I found my stateroom, 213. It wasn't much, just two steel bunk-beds on opposite sides of the room, a small closet, one dirty mirror, and a sink with a small circular window. I put my stuff down and sat for a moment, trying to come to terms with everything. My eyebrow was in excruciating pain as little bits of pus oozed out when I touched it.

I looked in the mirror at my side, horribly bruised. I was in bad shape—worried about my injuries, this ship, those men, Axelrod. A tear dripped from my eye. I had to be strong. I looked inside my bag and found Axelrod's book *The Mystical Treasure and Curse of Salvador Faustino*.

I opened the book and out came a small note.

Dear Christoph,

I know you must have a thousand questions and will have a thousand more after this letter. If you are receiving this, that means our departure has come. I write this letter on an autumn day; I didn't fish with you today on account of your theater tryouts. You're a bright lad. You'll get whatever ye put your mind to. Don't worry. I'll catch a glimpse of you on stage before it's all said and done.

For now, you must be on ye way to Villefranche along the French Riviera. See, lad? Ye dreams come true, finally out there. I suspected those damn bastards found us. I knew the day would come. Your only chance of survival is under the protection of Captain Kalendar, a friend from my past life.

Do not be afraid. Appeal to him, demonstrate your worth, and, most importantly, do not test him. If you fail in any of these things, kiss ye life goodbye. He is the only one who can protect ye at this point. Do not fail, Christoph. This is your future, for I have seen it in the waters of the oracle.

Give the coin to the bartender at the Sinbad Tavern to find Kalendar. Be cautious, Christoph. Keep your wits about you, and never reveal the secrets you discover. Do not return home. Never. I am giving you my favorite book as a pastime. Give it a good read. Might come in handy one day.

Keep focused, and trust in yourself and the Lord above. Remember, never stop searching, and you'll find the life you seek. Burn this letter.

Axelrod

I was terribly confused. Why would these people Axelrod spoke of be after me? On top of that, Axelrod wrote this letter in the fall. The ole man knew this was going to happen. I took out my lighter and burned the letter. I lay down in my bed, giving my weary body some rest. I shut my heavy eyes.

I woke up to ruckus in the cabin. I looked out the window near my bunk. *Up, down, up, down.* The sea rocked the large boat. Waves splashed against my small circular window.

We must've passed through the Mississippi River and hit the Gulf of Mexico. My right eye was swollen shut; I couldn't even open it. When I tried to, it faintly opened, then water would stream out of it. Terrible. My side was in even worse pain. Each time I moved, pain radiated from my ribs. When I lifted my shirt, purple and blue bruises covered my torso. This couldn't be good. I rubbed my head in confusion. How long was I asleep for?

"When did we . . ." I uttered.

"Beenz a sleep for awhilez, cozy boy."

It was an ebony-skinned man—tall, slender, in perhaps his early thirties—shaving in the small mirror. He was wearing a red coat.

I groaned. "For how long?"

"Eh, I woodz say at least for a whole dayz," the man laughed. "Judginz by yez look, yez must've needed it. What's yez name, cozy boy?"

"Christoph."

"Christoph. Likez it. Ma'z name iz DuBois. Pleazjah to meet yuz," he remarked.

"The pleasure is mine."

"De eyez. Somma juice?"

"Orange juice?"

DuBois laughed. "No, no. Greenz goop. Might help for a little whilez."

I was in so much discomfort, I would have taken anything to help.

"Yeah, sure."

DuBois put some dark green, mushy, rough dirt stuff around my eye. I took some more and put it on my cuts on my back.

"Up top better seez DuBois deedz," smiled DuBois.

"Thanks," I replied.

The green agent gave my cuts and bruises a cooling sensation and felt relieving, like a gust of wind on a hot day. He handed me some oats in a bowl. I was starving, ate them up. As we ate, DuBois told me he was on his way to France, searching for some sort of fellow that owed him a debt.

He talked all over the place. I could barely understand him with his thick accent, sounding like pidgin, a mix of a few languages. I talked about how I ended up on the ship and where I was going. DuBois said I would love France because . . . well, I couldn't understand his answer, but he said I would love it nonetheless.

I got up to wash my face. I took my shirt off. Upon seeing my amulet necklace, DuBois jumped up to analyze it. He bit it with his teeth.

"Ahh, haven't seen one of deez in long time," he said.

"It's a family heirloom," I replied, pulling it back.

DuBois gave a gregarious laugh.

"Beszt keep eyez peeled. Don't want a slip up," he stated.

"Thanks. I'll keep that in mind," I remarked. "So you know any-thing about Villefranche?"

"Villefranche?" repeated DuBois, stated with a better French pronunciation than mine on account of his pidgin tongue.

"Yeah."

"The Azure Coast. Beautiful. Follow ze coastline west. You'ze be zhair szoon."

We talked for little while longer about what to expect in France. It was making me quite excited. He told me about French women, croissants, and the sights. Still, I didn't understand all that he was say-ing from mixture of languages.

DuBois left shortly after to get some food. I asked if he would bring be back some. I couldn't move much. I fell asleep shortly after that—deep, deep sleep.

Call me crazy, but I woke up in the middle of the night, my body radiating pain. The sleep helped soothe it, but I still couldn't open my eye, which started to worry me. I woke up to a raging storm outside my window. I was starving. DuBois was in his bed, whistling as the waves crashed up against the ship. Lightning strikes illuminated the inside of the cabin. I was weak. DuBois's bunk was scattered with food, paper, pens, all sorts of things.

"Ze storm beckons us, calling out our namez," remarked DuBois, his face sparsely lit by his cigarette and the crashing lightning.

"DuBois . . . " I remarked faintly. My pain grew more, making it harder to speak. I had to eat something, but I knew the pain would make that difficult. "DuBois," I said a little louder.

"Shush!" remarked DuBois, putting his finger over his mouth. He leaned over quietly with wide eyes. "He'z here."

"I need food, DuBois. Please," I replied quietly.

Loud footsteps occurred in the hallway, moving back and forth, throwing doors open. My heart began to pound slightly faster. The sounds of doors squeaking open and closing caused my body to shiver. Our room was eerily still.

"Brings ze soulz to the labyrinth to feed hiz beast," insisted Du-Bois.

Thump . . . thump . . . thump were the sounds of the footsteps of this mysterious creature that lurked the halls. The lightning struck, followed by a loud sound of thunder. The ship tossed and turned, back and forth, back and forth.

"What's behind the door that makes such loud sounds?" I asked.

"A shadow whooz walkz to and fro in search of lost soulz," replied DuBois. "Make no sound to save ye soul! May the horned shadow pasz uz by."

A screeching sound filled the air, like that of a dying beast whose cry strikes the inner soul. I covered my ears in horror.

Thump . . . thump . . . .thump.

On the other side of the steel door in one of the cabins, a man screamed, echoing through the ship.

"We must help him!" I implored.

DuBois held me back, "Nay, cover ye earz to block out the horned beast who liez. DuBois protects ye, with hope Him above will see."

The heavy footsteps creeped closer to our door.

Thump . . . thump . . . thump.

This strange creature was at our door. Only a shadow crept through below the door. All was silent. I waited on the edge of my bed, covering my ears, waiting for this horror to end. Lightning flashed outside the window, illuminating the room. Then, I saw the shadow of a beast with large horns coming through the door. My eyes grew with fear, as the shadow came forward from the door.

"Back, ye demon!" screamed DuBois.

Thunder then struck! The ship tossed me hard from my bed due to raging stormy sea. I fell to the ground, and my eyes went fast asleep.

I woke up to the sounds of seagulls outside of the ship. I was out of my bed, must have slept on the floor. It was still raining terribly. Oddly enough, we were docked. How was that possible? Only been a day at most from my perspective. I must've slept for not one but a couple of days. I'd never done that before. I wasn't much of a sleeper.

My stomach raged with hunger, and my eye was worse than ever, severely infected. I turned over to see if DuBois was there, but the bed was completely empty. Not a speck of trash or any sign of anything. Where did he go?

I called out his name. No answer. I slowly got up, struggled with the pain in my side, and looked out the window.

Slight excitement filled my soul. The ship has docked. I was in France. My nerves started to creep into my mind. I reminded myself that everything would be okay. Axelrod wouldn't have sent me here if it were not in my best interest. I hoped whomever I was meeting might have something for my eye; it was getting worse by the hour. Hell, I thought I could the lose the thing if not acted upon.

I gathered my belongings, closed the door behind me, and made my way to the gangway. Crewmen and passengers were moving to and fro across the ship. The sweet smell of sea air filled my nostrils. The rain slightly subsided, giving some relief.

I looked around for DuBois. I thought it was a good idea for him to show me the exact direction to go. More so, he became like a security blanket for me. I clung to anything nearby that offered me certainty or familiarity. Soon to find out, nothing in the coming months would be certain or familiar. My security bubble had been popped.

The same man who checked the tickets when I first came onboard was on deck, giving directions to the passengers, pointing in different directions while asking to see their tickets. I needed to talk with him.

"Excuse me, sir," I insisted.

The man in uniform was talking to an older couple, directing them in French on where to go. One of the workers bumped into my shoulder, almost caused me to fall to the ground. He told me to watch where I was going in a raspy, mean tone. The ship's horn roared over the loud, chaotic mess on the gangway. I didn't work well in these types of situations.

"Excuse me," I insisted, slightly louder.

He finally turned to me. "Yes, yes. What do you need?" said the uniformed man, holding on to a clipboard. He checked his pocket watch.

"I'm looking for my roommate. His name was DuBois," I inquired.

"Speak up, son. I can't hear a single word from your mouth. Roommate . . . What's his name?"

"DuBois. Room 213. Port side."

The man checked his clipboard, pulled up his glasses to get a better view. "DuBois . . . DuBois . . . 213 . . . 213. Mr. Swift, I presume?"

"Yes."

He put the clipboard down and stared at me with an inquisitive face, then looked back at the paper. "213?"

"Yes, sir. 213. DuBois something or another," I replied.

"Not on record. It says 'no roommate,' Mr. Swift," he said. His face looked slightly agitated, as if I were pulling a trick on him.

"You sure about that?"

"The list never lies. Anything else I could help you with?"

Odd, DuBois was *definitely* in my room. The list must have been wrong. Never mind that. I needed to get where I was going fast. The thunder above me clashed. I asked him one more question.

"How do I get to Villefranche?" I inquired. "Know where that is?"

"Yes, yes. Take the train from the main station at the center of town. To get there, follow the main road up the hill. Hard to miss."

I told him thank you and got off the ship. I had to go through customs; that didn't take so long. The rain was drizzling at this point. Nice, France was pretty, had a French charm about it, though the beach was very rocky and cold. The pain in my eye and side was steadily growing the more I walked.

Here, everything was so different and bizarre to me. The only thing that was slightly like what I knew was the architecture, similar to that of the French Quarter. I didn't take the time to stop and smell the croissants on account of my pain. I was in dire straits, obsessed with getting to this other town.

Nice was surprisingly large. I walked over a black and white checkerboard plaza; I had never seen anything like it before. I finally approached the main train station. It had beautiful architecture of a classic French design, cream in color, and an elegant archway with a clock at the center.

The ticket counter wasn't too crowded. I couldn't read a thing on the time display showing the different train departure times. Some said 24:00; others 06:00. What did that mean? It was 8:00 a.m. All the directions were in French. I got up to the ticket counter. There was a woman smoking a cigarette behind the glass. She had short, curly, brown hair; she was young and very slender.

"*Bonjour. Coma ça va?*" she asked.

A train came roaring through the station.

"Uh . . . One for Villefranche, please," I replied, confused.

"*Villefranche, oui?*" she replied.

"Whatever is Villefranche. Soon, please."

"*Quand?*"

"I don't know '*quand.*' Whatever is soon."

She sighed, then mentioned a phrase in French to her friend. They both laughed. Her other friend was a taller woman with blonde hair, slightly older. She spoke English, and thankfully, she helped me out with the ticket. She explained to me my stop. She was much nicer than the original girl behind the counter. She told me the train was leaving in fifteen minutes.

I pulled out U.S. dollars to pay her. She laughed and said only euros. I was confused. I looked inside the bag and found some euros Axelrod had left for me.

I wasn't used to this currency exchange. I bought my ticket. That was a whole ordeal. I was in a completely different world here. The rain began to pour again. My hood was doing a terrible job of keeping me dry.

The train came, and I found a spot in it. This was the first time I'd ever been on a train. It traveled through the city of Nice and into the hilly countryside. I couldn't make out the coast from the rain. We bypassed a few towns hugging the coast. I was falling asleep, couldn't keep my eyes open as I rested my head on the window.

The train came to a stop, arriving at Villefranche. The sun was setting, and rain continued to pour. Villefranche was a small seaside town, constructed out of the wall of a cliff overlooking the ocean. It had small, winding roads and alleyways. The buildings were of all shapes and sizes, constructed in French design. Lightning crashed above me.

I couldn't find the damn place as I navigated this maze of small alleyways. I asked a Frenchman hanging outside of his shop where the Sinbad Tavern was, but he snubbed me, ignoring what I said. I went to a shop selling small confections. Upon seeing my terrible condition, the two women working there wouldn't let me inside their shop. I assumed they thought I was homeless.

I continued to walk down the street and saw an opportunity as another man walked toward me. I stopped to ask him a question. Sadly, he completely ignored me and kept walking.

The rain, my tiredness, and all my confusion started to break me. A tear of exhaustion dripped from my eye. I was scared, cold, and alone.

I sat down on bench in one of the small alleyways.

I'm going to lose my stupid eye! Why am I here?

I said to the sky above, "Please, good Lord. Help me."

Deep in my depressive state, I wished I were at home, fishing or with Arthur at our graduation party. Hell, Mr. Taft's class was better than this.

"Anything wrong?" said a man with a slight Middle Eastern accent.

"Everything," I uttered in a melancholy tone. "Wait! You speak English?"

I looked up with my one working eye. Standing before me was a man in a brown hood. I could faintly see his face. From what I could see, he had an olive complexion, a small black beard, and good posture.

"Who doesn't these days?" he remarked.

"Apparently a lot of people in France don't," I insisted with a faint touch of humor.

The man laughed. "Do you need help, my friend? You seem lost." The more he talked, I could hear a slight British-English touch to his accent on top of a Middle Eastern layer. It sounded very sophisticated.

"The Sinbad Tavern. Do you know where it is?"

He thought for a moment and said, "Yes, right around the corner. I'll bring you there, my friend."

I followed him along the cobblestone road around the windy corner of the alleyway. The sweet smell of that confectionary filled my nose. It felt warm and comforting, like home. I was starving. My energy was running out. The man led me to a side alleyway with a sign with a blue whirlpool and a woman's head adorned in jewels at the center of the whirlpool.

"Here it is," he said.

"Thank you. What is your name, sir?" I asked.

"Gabriel."

"Much praise, Gabriel; I'm Christoph."

"Christoph. A beautiful name for a fine gentleman. I'll be on my way, Christoph. May God be with you."

"And you, too," I said, perplexed. Interesting, he was a man of God, like a good Samaritan to me.

Gabriel moved out of sight, and then I faced the Sinbad Tavern. It was an old, dark, and grungy bar, had some music coming out of it, sounding like a guitar. I was quite nervous and had never been in a bar before. *What do I do? How should I act? Do I order a drink? I don't want to be awkward.* My pain throbbed.

I pulled the coin out of my bag. Etched on the silver coin was a picture of an Italian town, quite like Villefranche, which overlooked the ocean. In the sky was an old schooner vessel hovering above the clouds, as rays of light shined down on the town. I had no idea at the time what it meant.

The bar was dark with a few hanging light fixtures that dimly lit the place. The Sinbad seemed at least two hundred years old, with lots of smoke and a smell of alcohol and an old attic. People kept to themselves at each table. The bartender was wearing a vest with a white apron below his waist, cleaning a growler with a rag while three men—an ebony-skinned man with a lively smile in a duster coat, a stoic pale man, and an overconfident man with a well-kept beard—drank at the bar.

I waited for the bartender. I put my finger out; I told myself maybe that would get his attention. The bartender still wouldn't come.

The ebony-skinned man turned to me. "Ye speak the prairie tongue. Long way from the rolling corn fields."

"Swamp and sugarcane rather," I replied as I still held up my coin.

"Sugarcane yields me favorite cup. Smells of home and tastes of newly-gained hope," he replied.

"Cup of what, sir?" I asked.

"Rum. The taste of golden molasses. I get ye a drink!" The nice man turned to the bartender. "Aye, *boisson, boisson. Deux, deux,*" the man said with a heightened tone. "Me French is terrible."

His stoic friend next to him replied, "Your English is worse." He was smoking a cigarette and leaning on the bar.

"No one asked you, Marlow," insisted the ebony-skinned man.

The bartender came over and gave me a shot of rum. Before he left, I caught his attention and pulled out the coin. The ebony-skinned man watched the transaction with close attention, forgetting to take a sip of his drink. The bartender gestured for me to wait a moment. The ebony-skinned man gazed at me, perplexed under a newfound smile. I thanked him for the rum.

"What's ye name, lad?" he asked.

"Christoph," I replied. "And you?"

"Jeremiah," he said with a tone of question and eagerness.

The bartender came back and told me to follow him. I gave Jeremiah my goodbye, but he still kept his eyes fixed on me. *Strange*, I thought.

The bartender led me to the back of the bar to a tall, light-skinned man, rough around the edges, sitting in a circular booth. The man in the booth did not move, just took a sip from his growler. The bartender handed the man the coin. The man quickly snatched the coin without turning his head. The bartender walked away, and I sat down.

I saw the man in a better light. He had short brown hair and strong facial features composed of a pointed nose and chin, a prickly beard barely visible due to its shortness, and broad shoulders. He was wearing a black coat.

"*Parlez-vous Francais?*" asked the man.

"English?" I replied.

The nerves slowly crept up my spine. The man smiled when he looked up to see me. He looked to be around forty years old.

"American boy," said the man with a proper American accent. "Do you know what this is?"

"A ticket to safety?" I responded.

"This is a Traders Coin. Exceedingly rare to see these. It's an obligation. You're looking to become a Registered Extractor, yes?"

"Registered what?"

He exhaled in an annoyed tone. "This is how young lads like you die, ill-informed and ill-prepared. I'm not going through another one."

"Axelrod sent me to find a Mister Kalendar."

"I do not know an Axelrod. That's not a reason for me to bring you to Kalendar."

"Well," I questioned as I took a moment to ponder a response to convince this strict man of my worth. "I have tenacity on one shoulder and fate on the other. The coin bears my witness."

The man stared at me with a touch of curiosity and reserve, debating in his mind whether I was worth his effort.

"Not good enough. I accept only prior trainees from established Trader venues or on account of Captain Kalendar himself. Miscellaneous coins hold no obligation."

"This is no random coin. If so, how would I know of the man Kalendar?"

"True, you did speak thus." He thought for a moment, analyzing the coin. Then, he put it down, sliding it back to me on the table.

At that moment, I almost broke down, spattered by defeat.

"Please, sir." I pleaded with my emotional heart that spewed out from my lips. "I need to see Kalendar. I have no other choice."

Sadness seemed to overtake the man who rejected my plea. He got up from the table and spoke to me. "I can't take in another trainee for the Trials. Can't take on one more young soul."

He walked out of the bar, causing distress to fill my poor soul. I sat in the booth, languishing in self-doubt and the hopelessness of my situation. I thought, *This is it. I have nowhere else to go, especially in my crippling physical condition.*

The swamp mud further entrapped me below my nose, cutting off my air circulation. This was my end, and further deepening into my despair and depression, I thought of taking my own life. I picked up a knife on the table, holding it in my hand, thinking all my pain would whisk away in one small slice.

No, no, I told myself. *There must be a way. I must find Kalendar!*

To my astonishment, Jeremiah, the ebony-skinned man from the bar, jumped into my booth.

"Best not end here, lad. There's more on ye horizon," said Jeremiah with a smile.

"Not for me," I replied. "I'm stuck. Nowhere to go."

"Nonsense! There's always a way. I saw ye coin, a Traders Coin," he said, emphasizing its significance. "Ye want to see Kalendar?"

"You know Kalendar?"

"Indeed. I work under him."

My light returned to my face, for here was a chance to find this man of opportunity.

"Can you bring me to him?" I asked, excited.

Jeremiah laughed. "How do ye travel across the world with the intent to find an answer when ye has no map, friend, or knowledge of what dangers would befall a young lad such as ye, attempting to break into a closed-off world filled with snares and briar patches?"

"Much I do not know, but my soul steers me like a ship in the wind called to hoist the sail toward this degree," I replied.

His face widened with a smile. "Aye, the feeling of a trade wind on your back guiding you safely across the seas into unknown territories filled with beasts of prey. What would ye call that gut feeling that guides us through the unknown?"

"Belief," I replied.

"Aye, belief." He smiled. "I say this, our ship leaves very soon. I have a bet with two others that you board the ship before it departs. If you make it onto our ship where Captain Kalendar resides, I'll personally vouch for your safe passage and adhere to the obligation of the coin. The obligation means nothing to you now, but in time, it will. What do ye say? Time's ticking."

"How can I trust you?" I asked.

"No choice, lad. Yea or nay. I got four coins on you, so best get a move on."

"Well, where's the ship?"

"I can't tell you. Traders Rules. Rather, look to the coin and believe!"

"How do I know if I find the right ship?"

Jeremiah laughed. "Don't worry. Ye can't miss it."

I hastily got up from the booth; adrenaline filled my veins. I thought to myself, *Ship . . . ship . . . Dock . . . Yes, it must be at a dock. Wait, the coin.*

I took the coin out of my pocket, but it offered me nothing of a clue. I continued to think. *All I saw was this Italian town and a ship in the sky. What does it mean?*

Being on an incline, I stared out to the sea. I held up the coin, leveling it with my view of the sea. The etching on the coin had the same viewpoint as I was staring at now. Incredible. It was a mirror image.

Then, the ship based on its position on the coin was . . . in the sky? *Impossible. That can't be right.* My reason could not accept the ship in the sky, yet my soul ushered me to look up. I gazed upward then around the city, but the sky was cloudy.

As I scanned the mountainous terrain, I found what looked like a stone staircase clinging to the side of the cliff filled with people moving toward the top of a mountain overlooking the city. With my eyes, I followed the staircase, which led to an entrance a few yards away from me built into the mountain next to an alleyway.

I had time for only one choice: either go to the dock, which any reasonable person would do to find a ship, or ascend the staircase in hopes of catching a flying ship. I must have been crazy ... a flying ship!

I thought for a moment and looked inside of myself for the answer. I felt my soul pull me to the staircase, and to my great astonishment, I ran as fast as I could up that widening stone staircase to the top of the mountain.

At the top of the fortress, there were many of what appeared to be military personnel in green uniforms guarding the entranceway to the top of the fortress. All I had to show was my coin. I showed the personnel my coin, and to my amazement, they let me pass. I had no time to think since the ship could be leaving at any minute.

At the top of the open-air fortress, tons of different people from around the world were congregating, hauling cargo, and moving equipment. Why were all these people here? I hastily scanned the mountaintop for the ship.

At that moment, the sun shone through the foggy clouds, revealing the colorful city and light blue waters below while above me an incredible mechanical creation was hovering above the fortress. It was an airship.

The body of the ship appeared like an Arab dhow vessel from the Middle East though this ship was massive, at least one hundred yards or longer with a painted black metal hull. Keeping the ship in the sky was a black barrage balloon, resembling a blimp.

There was no time to gander. I had to find a way on board. There was a gangway connected to the ship through a series of ropes and levers. It appeared like a set of stairs to the heavens going up to the ship.

All around me people were screaming, "Disembark!" I noticed the gangway was being picked up. Now was my only chance to catch this miraculous ship before the opportunity slipped through my fingers forever.

I brushed danger aside and sprinted with all the energy I could muster.

The different individuals in uniforms were screaming and blowing their whistles for me to stop. It was all or nothing at this point. Either success or death.

I reached the edge as the gangway was being pulled up. I jumped over the edge and onto the gangway. I tripped onto the edge of it as my feet were hanging off the sides of it. The airship was ascending. I tried to pull myself up with all the adrenaline I had.

My right hand slipped due to the pain in my side from the days before. I hung on with all the power left inside of me. Glory! A hand grabbed mine and pulled me up! It was Jeremiah.

"Nice to see ye made it. Knew you could, lad," smiled Jeremiah.

Jeremiah ushered me on board this magnificent flying ship. The whole crew stared at me in great perplexity and astonishment, seeing that I risked my life to come aboard. Jeremiah vouched for me in front of the whole crew, attesting to my tenacity. I was starstruck and had no idea what to say.

The crew of around two hundred or so men and women of all ages and ethnicities muttered and spoke to one another about me, equally amazed at my feat of insanity.

The man at the bar who denied my coin stared sternly at me with a touch of compassion in his eyes and came forward to me to introduce himself. He nodded to Jeremiah, then made a slight bow to me. "I'm Fitzroy, a Registered Extractor of the Victoria & Co. I am honored to make your acquaintance."

"I'm Christoph Swift," I replied.

Jeremiah interjected, "I'll let you take it from here, Fitzroy." He then turned to the other man from the bar who had a well-kept beard and was part of this bet. "You owe me four coins, Spurwink."

Spurwink replied, "Aye, who knew the little twit had a brain?"

A tall woman with long blonde hair wearing a blue uniform came on deck. By her stature, she seemed to hold a great position of power within the ship. She seemed tough as an ox's hide. She yelled to the crew, "What's this commotion about?" Her accent sounded like she was from the American Midwest.

"Helga, I brought a new friend aboard," yelled Jeremiah to the blonde-haired commander.

"All of the hubbub for that?" replied Helga.

"Guess so," said Jeremiah.

"Bring him to Kalendar then," she said. "Rest of ye, get back to work!"

The crowd dispersed, and everyone went on with what they were doing.

Fitzroy gathered my attention. "Aye, forgive me, for my past has caused me much strife with trainees. Alas, it seemed I made a poor decision. Long journey, eh?"

"You could say that," I said as I was still catching my breath.

"Fitzroy is my good friend," said Jeremiah. "He'll look after ye for now."

"Come," insisted Fitzroy. "Let's go see the captain."

He guided me through this ship of wonders toward the captain's office.

"Welcome to the airship *Victoria*, the fastest airship in all of the seven seas," exclaimed Fitzroy.

Aboard the airship, I noticed that it resembled an updated schooner ship. The difference was that the sails were altered with a series of jets, and the large blimp helped it maintain a level position while hovering in the sky. From what I could tell, the deck was a mix of wood and carbon fiber.

Eerily, there were large, mounted machine guns on deck. I thought, *What was their use? Precaution? Probably not.*

The ship had many different levels. We passed through the deck to inside the hull, which was a large section of the ship full of supplies and tables. It seemed to be the meeting area. We came upon the commander from earlier. Her uniform shoulders were topped with the letters "R. E."

"One, two . . . Up, Up! Put your backs into it!" Helga yelled.

"Another load?" Fitzroy asked.

"Have to stock up for the off-season," replied Helga. "So who's the fresh meat?"

"Christoph Swift. He had a Traders Coin," Fitzroy responded.

We continued through the busy floor, maneuvering past people and cargo, utilizing an intricate staircase system.

"What does R. E. mean?" I asked.

"Registered Extractor. Now listen. When we meet with Captain Kalendar, do not speak unless spoken to. Understand?" Fitzroy warned.

We came upon two large, brown doors. Fitzroy knocked. A dark-skinned older crewman with a black beard and round belly, wearing a fez—a classic red Turkish hat with a black tassel—answered the door.

"Yes?" inquired the small man.

"We would like to see Captain Kalendar," Fitzroy replied.

"Who's we?" asked the crewman.

Fitzroy explained who I was, and the crewman closed the door for a moment then opened it back up.

"The coin," demanded the crewman.

I gave it to him, and he allowed us inside the room. Inside was an exquisite, two-level cabin with windows overlooking the sea, two-story bookshelves filled with books of many different colors and sizes, and another shelf filled with strange and exotic sea creatures.

The trim of the room was a blue coral, somehow wrapping around the room. At the center of the dimly lit room were large tables with holographic maps.

Next to the large circular windows overlooking the ocean was a magnificent brown desk with all types of strange devices situated on top of it. A large red chair faced outward to the sea. All I could see was the back of the chair and a man's hat. Captain Kalendar did not turn around; rather, he kept his back to us while seated in his chair.

"Captain, I bring you a hopeful recruit, courtesy of a Traders Coin. He seeks to become a Registered Extractor. His name is Christoph Swift," said Fitzroy.

"Christoph . . ." said Kalendar in a deep, sophisticated voice with an American accent.

"Yes. Do you accept him onboard? Do you accept the coin?" Fitzroy asked.

"Don't we have one recruit already?"

"Specksynder Spurwink's brother is a Doughboy."

"I see," Kalendar replied. "Is this young man worthy?"

Fitzroy gazed at me, contemplating my condition and value. Behind his eyes, I could see a reminiscent memory composed through a melancholic song that tuned his ears away from the sweet melodic tune of adventurous chance.

"Worthy?" repeated Fitzroy. "I believe so."

"Then he can stay for now. Begin his training, Fitzroy, and we will decide his ultimate fate at the Meeting of Fire, as stated under the Traders Rules," replied Kalendar. "I have a good feeling about this one."

My heart leaped with joy, but I kept it to myself, as Fitzroy suggested.

"One more question. Who gave him the coin?" asked Kalendar.

"His name was Axelrod," I replied.

"Axelrod," repeated Kalendar as if he were searching his head for a name once thought lost in time but had resurfaced like a buried grave rising from flood waters. "That'll be all."

Fitzroy accepted, and we left the room.

"Seems like a nice guy. Did I make the cut?" I asked.

"You're lucky," said Fitzroy. "It's usually a no. Then, we have to toss the poor would-be trainee off the side of the ship. Traders rules."

That gave me the chills—the thought of being thrown off the side of a ship hovering high in the sky.

"That's . . . reassuring," I said.

"Yeah, I would have been the one to do it. Not fun," Fitzroy stated grimly.

"I take it that has happened before?"

"What do you think? No more dumb questions, or I will still throw you off the side! You do what I say. Everything. Understand, Doughboy?"

"Yes."

"Good, let's take a visit to the infirmary. Looks like you're on your last leg and eye. The doctor will fix you up."

The moment I disembarked the *S. S. Edwards* onto French soil, I never in my most fantastical dreams thought the day would turn out like this. The twist and turns of rejection and triumph on the brink of death showed me how fast my life could end by one false step, one false word, or one missed chance.

I did not show my emotion or fear as I stepped aboard the ship. The moment I made that jump from the top of the fortress to the gangway was the scariest moment of my life up to that point. During that jump, I thought I was going to die, as any reasonable man would.

On the other hand, my soul convinced me that I could fly and that by the grace of the good Lord I would not miss my window of opportunity. I saw in that moment that when opportunity comes, the window was quite small, smaller than a needle eye.

I learned from my past days in high school to always look up and never down. By that stage in my life, I grew tired of people telling me that I was not good enough for anything I did—as in sports, academics, or social relations. In my mind, they were telling me to look down, and I was studied enough to listen to their condescending actions and words.

The moment I decided to look up and aim high, everything changed in my life. I wanted to be the lead in my high school play, even though Arthur told me that would never happen due to an infinite number of reasons. I didn't care for his logic. I wanted the lead and obtained it by looking up.

It's interesting that most reasonable people would tell you to look down at the dock for a ship. Defying all logic, a dreamer says look to the sky for a ship. Good thing I looked to the sky because here I was on a flying airship soaring through the sky.

When I had a moment of privacy before my visit to the doctor, I attempted to fully grasp the severity of my situation. I repeated the words "flying airship" at least thirty times to myself. My eyes were wider than the Mississippi River due to my complete astonishment.

Trying to play it cool in front of the crew, I tried to act like I'd seen something like this before, but inside, my mind and feelings were jumping around like a jackrabbit through the forest. I was scared, excited, amazed, and stupefied.

No emotion could capture what I felt as I continued to wait for the doctor in the infirmary. All I could do to rest my excitement was look out a small circular window to the open sky with a slight smile on my face.

CHAPTER 5

The Traders Terminal

T HE INFIRMARY ON the ship fixed me up; I needed it terribly. I thought it was odd. The surgical tools with sharp points like needles or knives had a glowing purple edge around their sharpest points. Also, the doctor injected my eye with some type of purple serum, healing it astonishingly quickly. I thought it was a medical miracle.

Once finished, Fitzroy brought me through the hull of the ship to a wall of cabinets. He told me I would be staying with him in his cabin until we docked at Port Victoria. It was a meager cabin—two wooden bunks, one closet with dividers, and a small window.

Fitzroy opened the curtain to my closet. He took out some clothes, a picture of a woman, and a few other trinkets. Above the cabinet read "Frederick Siltzer." Fitzroy replaced the name with "Christoph Swift" and placed all of the old objects in a bag.

"This will be your closet for now," said Fitzroy.

"What about Fredrick?" I replied.

"He's gone," replied Fitzroy without an air of sadness or emotion. He continued to clean out the cubby.

"Was he a trainee, like me?"

Fitzroy stopped for a solid five seconds, looked at me with an agitated look. "Yes. No more questions. Put your stuff in the closet, and let's get to the study room."

I thought, *What kind of man leaves pictures of his family and clothes behind?* Only a man that would never return.

Fitzroy led me through the series of hallways to a medium-sized room with two round tables and a couple of bookshelves lined with books of different shapes and sizes. There was a black electronic board attached to the wall. Fitzroy told me to sit, gathered a few books from the shelves, and threw them on my desk. Fitzroy began to explain our position:

"Ye have presented me a Traders Coin. When a Registered Extractor is presented with a coin, it is a duty, an obligation to train the presenter of the coin. This coin begins ye journey to obtain an Extractor's license with the Traders Terminal. For e to obtain this license, ye must complete and survive the Series Trials, which I will explain in the days to come.

"For now, I will teach ye the basics of our industry, starting from the ground up. Know this: Ye have presented me with this coin, ye have seen a Traders Passageway, and ye have stepped foot on the airship's bridge. For ye, there is no turning back. Either death or success.

"Ye have made your choice to enter the world of the Traders Terminal, and one cannot simply leave it after seeing it. The Traders Terminal will enforce all of these rules. It never ends well for those who attempt to break them. Consider thyself chosen by the Almighty, for precious few ever get this chance."

"I was never so good with rules," I replied.

"Stop being a snarky child, or off the ship ye go! I will not have another failed trainee on me hands. Ye must adhere to the rules of the Traders Terminal, which ye will know inside and out if ye wish to stand any chance of survival, let alone victory, in the Series Trials. If ye can't do this and take this seriously, then leave now. Make ye choice."

My heart began to pound at the seriousness of his tone.

"Look at ye with your scared eyes. Never show your fear. I can smell it on ye, and if I can, so will everyone else in this company," insisted Fitzroy.

"I'll commit," I replied faintly, mixed with fear.

"What did ye say?!" Yelled Fitzroy.

"I want to be an Extractor!" I yelled more loudly.

He laughed. "Ye don't even know what an Extractor is."

"Then teach me."

Fitzroy grabbed my collar with a fiery sensation burning in his brown eyes. "Will ye waste my time?"

"No!" I yelled. "I will listen."

He hit me across the face. I shrieked from the pain.

"This is no child's game, Doughboy! Understand?"

"Yes."

"Ye will listen?"

I nodded with sincerity as my heart pounded in my chest.

"Good. Now, let's get to work," said Fitzroy.

I let out a deep breath and sat down at the table. Fitzroy began to elaborate on this complex world that I had just entered.

He explained, "A Registered Extractor is a highly sought-after and dangerous profession, specializing in extracting the most powerful mineral in the world: minosium."

I interrupted. "Minosium! Like the story of Faustino and Bird-Eye."

"Faustino was credited as the first man to find the mineral, but the tale of the labyrinth and devil is no truer than Bigfoot or vampires. Remember this: Faustino discovered minosium in the late 1600s somewhere near India, we think," replied Fitzroy.

Fitzroy continued to explain that minosium was a highly prized mineral: "Beautiful in complexion, but more importantly, it harnessed incredible power like that of plutonium.

"Recently discovered in the past forty years, minosium contains a new type of power that has the potential to energize entire cities, new-age weapons, or once-impossible structures and vehicles—hence the *Victoria* airship.

"Minosium is extremely rare, found only on the most deserted islands or locations scattered across the seven seas. It is most likely found surrounding hot springs, places where magma reaches a small pool of water."

Thankfully, it wasn't my job to worry about the specifics of the geological information pertaining to the mineral. As an Extractor, all that mattered was that I could find it and trade it for a profit at the Traders Terminal. Only a minuscule amount of the mineral was enough to power any object. I recognized the power of the mineral and the devastation it could bring if used in the wrong way.

That was where the Traders Terminal came into the picture. The nations of the whole world came together to create the Traders Terminal, an exchange committee to regulate and enforce all information, extraction, trading, and their own bizarre traditional rules in order to protect this precious mineral from malicious activity—while profiting from it, of course.

The Traders Terminal oversaw all minosium trading on the exchange floor located at the Terminal on an island called Monte Carlo. A Registered Extractor may broker a deal for an approved Trader's client, usually a large institutional investor, like a corporation or a governmental entity.

The minosium can be traded in a variety of ways, such as in stocks, bonds, territory, gold—basically anything the Terminal can place a tax on. If an item cannot be taxed, such as a trade of minosium for land, the entities must still pay a tax in Trader Coins for that commodity, determined by the Terminal actuary. These trades must be pre-approved by the Terminal and are very costly to the Traders.

As for the companies that extract the minosium, each company member must be registered with the Terminal. Typically, each position affiliated with the Terminal was handed down either to a family member or someone close to the family.

It was a tradition among the Terminal Traders to keep the industry closed to the public though the Terminal was expanding at a rapid rate, allowing more outsiders a chance to enter the business through a variety of positions. Each position was highly lucrative and heavily regulated for reasons of safety, control, and power.

The most valued of all positions within an extraction company was a Registered Extractor (R.E.). This was how it worked: A Terminal-approved crew forms an independent company, like the Victoria & Co., to extract the minosium and trade it on the exchange floor. The company services individual outfits comprising five or six people within the company who do the heavy lifting of extracting and trading the mineral. The company provides each outfit with protection, information, and equipment. In return, the company takes a percentage of everything an individual outfit sells on the exchange floor. The Traders Terminal and minosium had totally escaped the body of public knowledge.

I still didn't quite understand all these intricate rules and structures. I felt like I was in some sort of business class more than a geology class.

Interestingly enough, the coins to an Extractor position were passed down through family members. Was Axelrod a Registered

Extractor? Impossible. From what I had seen, that would make him badass. I was not sure why he pushed me to go to college instead of teaching me about this wild endeavor. I did feel a little sadness at the thought of Axelrod.

Fitzroy stopped the lesson for the day and brought me to the deck of the ship. It was a busy day on deck as the crew handled their daily tasks.

"Look at thee. Brought a Doughboy from below?" asked a man in a raspy voice. He honestly sounded like Axelrod. Many people on this ship had been using the same vocabulary as Axelrod. They talked with words I rarely heard elsewhere.

The man with the raspy voice was a large man with a full black beard in a blue officer's coat and white turtleneck.

"Ahoy, Prince Rock. His name is Swift. He's training for the Trials," replied Fitzroy.

Prince Rock rubbed the back of his head in distress. "Oh my, another one . . . Welcome to our outfit. Best train hard, lad. We'll be in the cargo hold soon enough. Fitzroy, I've talked with a company specializing in robotics. Sounds golden, eh?"

"I'll look into it," said Fitzroy.

Prince Rock went on his way.

A more slender man approached us. "A new member of the gang. How nice," he said with an American Southern accent. He wore a navy blue sport coat and a white cowboy hat. He seemed young, not much older than I. Wildcat was fit and light skinned, and he had a slight twang nestled in his speech.

"How're we doing, shooter? I'm Wildcat," he stated to me, extending his hand.

"Christoph Swift," I replied.

"A Southern man!"

"How'd you know?"

"I hear that little twang. Guessing Louisiana?"

"Didn't think I had one. Texas, I presume?"

"Yes, sir," remarked Wildcat. "Big stuff shooting to be an Extractor. I'm part of Fitzroy's outfit, too."

Fitzroy broke into our conversation to explain the concept of an outfit inside of a company. It was a group of five or six people with specific roles to find and extract the minosium for Victoria & Co.

Usually, there were one or two R.E.s, a mechanic, a surveyor, a broker, and a roughneck. Prince Rock was the outfit's broker. Fitzroy was the only R.E. in our outfit. Each position had a different license with the Traders Terminal.

"Are you an Extractor?" I asked Wildcat.

"Hell nah. Never got a coin, and besides, too dangerous for me. I'm a surveyor, like my father before me. I find the minosium, so we can extract it."

"Makes sense," I replied.

"Now thinking about it," insisted Wildcat, "ole Spurwink won't like the sound of another R.E. trainee in the company."

"Why?" I asked.

Wildcat pulled my arm and told me to look across the deck to a group of other crewmen. One of them was a large, muscular man with a well-kept brown beard who seemed to be the leader of another outfit.

"See him there? That's Spurwink, a New England man, lead Specksynder, leader of the Nantucket outfit," said Wildcat.

"Specksynder?" I inquired.

"Means he's the top Extractor, MVP of the *Victoria*. Next to him is his younger brother Rabbit Run, your competition."

With broader shoulders and at least 6'5" in height, Rabbit Run was much larger than I and seemed to have been working out his arms a little bit. Similar to Spurwink in stature, he had a rough face, short blond hair, and a pointed nose. He was maybe a year or two older than I was. He looked intimidating.

"Why am I called doughboy?" I asked.

"It's tradition. You are the new kid on the block. Call 'em dough-boys," said Wildcat.

Fitzroy was called over by Helga to handle a few of the shipments. He told me it would only be a minute. Wildcat leaned closer to me. I could tell he was withholding a secret waiting to blurt out.

"Fitzroy had the last trainee. Loved the guy. Everyone thought he would make it through. We all did. Too bad he came up short. Really affected Fitzroy. I still think he hasn't gotten over the last doughboy," whispered Wildcat.

"What's the story on that?" I asked.

"Damn Trials," he said with anger.

I still had no idea what these trials were. All I knew was that I had to pass these trials to obtain my license.

Fitzroy came back to get me, and we maneuvered through the busy deck. We approached a man welding pieces on a large machine gun. I presumed it was machine gun. It overlooked the rail of the ship. Fitzroy called out to him. The man lifted up his goggles and put his tools down. He seemed to be a Japanese man with short black hair and small beard around his mouth. His hair was held in a ponytail.

"Zhen, meet our new trainee for the outfit, Christoph," said Fitzroy in a light-hearted way. I could tell they were good friends.

"I thought no more trainees, Fitzroy," said Zhen with a Japanese touch to his English.

"The winds spoke differently," replied Fitzroy.

Zhen walked around me with an air of contemplation, analyzing all aspects of me. "Looks good. Strong bones." He stared into my eyes without blinking. "Has something in him. See it in there."

"Think he'll make it?" asked Fitzroy.

"Too early to tell," replied Zhen.

"I feel confident," I interjected.

"Better you do, Doughboy," said Zhen.

Fitzroy explained that Zhen was the lead mechanic for our outfit. A typical company had around two to three outfits that answered to the captain of the company, then to the first mate, which was Helga.

Next in leadership was the second mate, known as the Specksynder, the overseer of all outfits. Below them were the registered Extractors. Only R.E.s and above could hold leadership positions within the company and enter the Traders Terminal to trade.

Next in line were the brokers, like Prince Rock. These guys worked closely with the extractors. They typically talked with companies from around the world to broker deals between the outfit and the company prior to reaching the exchange floor.

Followed by them were the lead mechanics and surveyors, and below them were the roughnecks. Roughnecks were typically the most skilled fighters in the outfit. The main job of a roughneck was to assist in the extraction process of minosium while providing protection to the whole outfit. They were typically the most skillful and cunning in combat and warfare tactics. The company relied on their prowess during violent confrontations.

At the bottom of the totem pole were the privateers. It was

still a distinguished position. These guys were the infantry of the ship, armed to protect the company as a whole first and foremost while they also cooked, cleaned, and performed clerical duties for the outfits.

Fitzroy explained that all these positions would make more sense during the upcoming months as I saw how they played into each other. This was the typical structure of a single company.

Back to the deck, I caught out of the corner of my eye a small aircraft flying toward the airship. It appeared to be a biplane. It had a narrow frame with two open-air seats, but instead of a singular propeller, it had four medium-sized propellers, like a large drone, with propellers on the four corners of the aircraft, like wheels on a car. I was amazed.

Electric blue lights lined the aerodynamic body of the aircraft. The pilot had a skull with a snake in its mouth painted on the body of this aircraft. Unfortunately, the pilot looked like he was in terrible distress as he flew in irregular patterns toward the ship. As the craft came closer, I noticed the engine was smoking. The body was filled with large bullet holes. I looked in awe, questioning everything I thought I once knew.

"Ever seen that before, Doughboy?" Zhen remarked.

"It's called a sloop. It's our means of transportation and firepower," said Fitzroy.

The pilot looked hurt. He attempted to land on the large open section on the deck.

"The cockpit is open-air. Why?" I inquired.

The sloop recklessly landed on the deck of the airship, and in an instant, the sloop burst into flames. The pilot scrambled and screamed for assistance. A group of privateers in blue uniforms rushed to the scene.

"Need a quick escape," Zhen suggested.

The privateers helped the screaming pilot onto the ground and hastily tried to put out the flames on the sloop and man.

"Zhen will take over repairs and flights for your training," said Fitzroy as he stared at the dismal scene.

"He'd better learn fast," replied Zhen.

I thought, *What in the hell did I get myself into?* This was on a whole other level than what I was used to. I was completely out of my comfort zone in a hostile environment where each person judged me with piercing eyes like sharks in the water.

"I bet it was Lennox, that bastard," said Fitzroy.

"Lennox?" I inquired.

"Best ace in the sky. You'll meet him soon enough," laughed Zhen.

"If he passes the Trials," interjected Fitzroy.

"By God, is that Christoph Swift?" asked a familiar voice.

We all turned around to see who it was. I jeered with excitement upon seeing—

"Mr. Charlie!" I yelled.

"Come here, you," he replied.

I gave him a firm handshake.

"I thought one day you would end up on an airship. I tried to recruit you, but you know how Axelrod was," said Mr. Charlie.

"He never told me about this world! Mr. Charlie, never in a thousand years could I have imagined this."

"Chairman, what brings you onboard? Perhaps, our new friend Christoph?" said Fitzroy.

"Nay, his presence was unknown to me," exclaimed Mr. Charlie. "Best take care of him, Fitzroy. He'll be your best pilot one day. As for me, just doing my inspection for the committee."

Fitzroy later told me that Mr. Charlie was an immensely powerful man, for he was a committee chairman at the Traders Terminal, one of nine people.

"Have you heard anything from Axelrod?" I asked.

"Not that I know of," replied Mr. Charlie concernedly. "Has something happened?"

"A dangerous man came to our house the other night. There was gunfire. I escaped . . . but Axelrod . . . "

"Axelrod told me something was brewing in the water. I can't say for sure say why." Mr. Charlie whispered closer to me. "Christoph, this is a different world you've entered into. A world where one must step lightly with his lips and feet. If you are a trainee, that means you shall face the Trials. From this point on, your only objective is to learn from your outfit and prepare for the Trials. This is critical."

"I've been told that, but I still know not what these Trials are."

"You will learn more soon. I promise that you can do it."

I nodded.

Mr. Charlie smiled. "I always thought you would end up in the business."

"Funny how life works. Please check on Axelrod. I have no idea of his whereabouts," I said.

"I'll look into it."

One of the privateers yelled in a loud voice that Mr. Charlie's sloop was ready to disembark from the moving *Victoria* airship.

"Leaving!" I questioned. "Where are you going?"

"Back to Monte Carlo," replied Mr. Charlie. "Do not worry. You're in good hands here, and I'll keep an eye on Axelrod for you."

Mr. Charlie gave me a firm hug and went on his way. Fitzroy was impressed that I knew Chairman Charlie and told me he was a big name in the Terminal, which might help me one day.

I was sad to see Mr. Charlie go, feeling the last piece of my home and past whisk away in the wind.

Axelrod told me many times that Mr. Charlie worked for the government, but never the Traders Terminal. Therefore, Axelrod must have lied to me about the true nature of his relationship with Mr. Charlie. I pondered the thought: What else had he lied to me about?

At this point, upon seeing Mr. Charlie and the coin given to me by Axelrod, my uncle must have been a part of this business. Astonishing. He must've gone through these same Trials and tribulations as I was about to endure. Still, the thought of Axelrod's whereabouts worried me.

In the heaviest point of night while tucked in my bunk aboard the ship, tears streamed from eyes from the gloomy thoughts and feelings of my past life. I had to move on, as much as the pain tore my heart in two.

For better or worse, for the next couple of months, the Victoria & Co. would keep my mind preoccupied. I told myself to detach from Axelrod and my past so that I may soar like bird in the sky without the chains of distraction and despair. This decision was a matter of my survival.

CHAPTER 6

Aboard the Victoria

I'D BEEN ON the airship for a couple of days at this point, learning all the ins and outs of the business. Victoria was the name of the airship and company. I was not considered an employee, only an "affiliate" until my training was complete. The ship was en route to a small island called Victoria Island, which was the headquarters of the company. It was located in Polynesia near the Solomon Islands.

I began to learn the intricacies of the business, which contained many complicated regulations and concepts difficult to understand. Fitzroy, my mentor, sat me down and explained the next couple months of my life.

"In order for ye to join this company and receive a Registered Extractor's license, ye must complete the Series Trials," explained Fitzroy. "The Series Trials are a set of different trials within twenty-four hours against eighty other cunning and ruthless trainees seeking their own license. Th Trials test ye knowledge, aptitude, and prowess. If ye fail at any of these during the Trials, ye will die.

"Tomorrow, ye will learn the intricacies of the Series Trials. My outfit and I will train ye to become a man able to pass the Trials and ultimately extract and trade minosium with ease.

"Ye will not like me for the next months, for I will push you to your limit. I demand excellence and will have it. When ye are crying in pain and suffering, that is when the true gains will be had.

"I am your master and ye are my pupil. Trust in my word, and ye will survive. We will adhere to a rigorous schedule on this ship and when we reach the island. We will wake up at 04:30, begin our training at 05:00 with exercise and study.

"Over the course of the day, you will rotate among the other members of the outfit, adhering to their will. Each person shall present different tasks and processes that must be completed for ye to compete in the Series Trials. This is a methodical process that will sculpt ye into a wise warrior, able to take on the world," Fitzroy explained.

Little did I know what the Series Trials and training would bring.

On the first morning, I struggled to get up, slowly moving to start my day. After that long journey, I felt like I needed sleep.

"One more hour. Please, Fitzroy. I am tired," I said, trying to cover my eyes with the sheet.

"Up, up!" he stated. "If ye sleep an extra hour every day for a month, that one hour would add up to thirty-one hours. That's thirty-one hours that could've been spent training. Now, get up! I won't ask you again."

I was scared to go against him and mustered what energy I had to get dressed and start the day. He brought me onto of the deck of the ship. It was a cool morning. The moon and stars were still out. My eyes were barely open. The wind brushed through the deck, creating a chill air. I rubbed my hands as goosebumps formed all over my body.

"It's freezing," I sighed. "Can I get a coat?"

"No," replied Fitzroy. "Let the cold fuel ye to warm your body. Now, follow in my way."

Fitzroy began to do burpees on the deck. He would jump up and then do a push up. These were dreadful. I had to do them for basketball. These were one reason I quit the team. I started to follow him. My arms were weak. I could barely do ten pushups, let alone jump into the air. I breathed heavily. I got on my knees to catch my breath.

"Get off your knees," Fitzroy yelled. "The moment ye rest gives your enemy a chance to strike!"

"I can't," I sighed.

Fitzroy grabbed me by the shoulder. He scared the daylights out of me. He pulled me to the rail of the ship and hung my head over the side. I panicked as I saw the clouds below.

"If ye can't do this," Fitzroy exclaimed in a serious tone, "then stop wasting my time, and get off the ship."

"Are you mad?" I exclaimed.

"Never say 'I can't.' Understand?"

"Yes. Yes, I do!"

Fitzroy pulled me back from the rail, and we continued doing the burpees. I pushed myself to the limit; my arms ached, and my legs were in pain. Of course, I wasn't cold after this workout.

It made me recall my attitude of the past during those days of the high school basketball team. During those practices and workouts, I tried to cut corners by avoiding the hardest weightlifting or running or any type of physical exertion. I did this because, well, I just didn't want to be at practice in general and thought working out to the extreme was useless. Hence, my loud mouth got me into deep trouble with the coaches and team members.

In high school, I thought I was smarter than the average guy by avoiding the workouts while the others slaved away by puking their guts out from a long run for Mr. Markel, the crazy coach with a red headband. Those workouts were hard and brutal, and honestly, I avoided them.

Now, as I worked out with Fitzroy, the past has come to haunt me due to my lack of conditioning. If only I had forced myself to partake in those strenuous workouts, I would've been in much better shape, and the team would've appreciated me more.

One could not cut corners with Fitzroy. Impossible! I was forced to push myself or else the grave would suit me. If only I knew in high school that my cutting corners would hurt only myself. I had to see my wrong ways and mentally strengthen myself, or I wouldn't last long in Fitzroy's presence. Was I strengthening my body or my mind?

Once we finished our morning workout, we moved to the mess hall for food. I was ready to gorge a mighty plate of different colored meats like a lion who hasn't feasted for days. I piled my plate high and sat next to Fitzroy.

Before I could dig into my colorful display, Fitzroy took three fourths of my food from my plate and placed it on his while feeding the rest to a dog nearby. I was left with only a scarce apple and two boiled eggs.

"Why do such a thing, to a dog at least?" I pleaded. "I'm starving. Please!"

"Doughboys are below dogs on this ship. Come down from your high abode and learn the value of food. Think not what ye believe you're owed, but be grateful for what ye are given. Besides, food is scarce during the Trials. One must always be hungry."

This concept he put before me caused me to ponder the idea of what I thought I should have rather than being thankful for anything given. I'll say this: by living off rationed food, it made me value each meal more and cherish what little I was given. Internally, my body morphed to live off less, counting each calorie ingested and expelled.

Fitzroy continued my training by bringing me into a study room. I sat at a table while Fitzroy handed me three massive textbooks.

"Ye will read these textbooks and outline everything ye need to know about the Traders Terminal, the companies, minosium, and the Series Trials," he stated.

These books were massive. I thought to myself, *How could I read through a whole textbook? I don't have the persistence or concentration for that!*

"It would take me forever to finish a single volume!" I exclaimed as I lifted one of the books. "I've never read anything of this size or this complicated. It must be a thousand pages long!"

"Good. Now is your chance to push yourself mentally. Ye will read these books through from the front to the back, multiple times, all day until I return."

"When will that be?"

"When I feel like it, and ye will be tested on this material at my discretion, so take notes."

Fitzroy left me a loaf of bread and went on his way. I analyzed these daunting textbooks. I could barely pass my classes in high school, let alone something of this magnitude. Once again, I had no other choice. Fitzroy was serious. I had to buckle down.

I picked up the first volume of the Series Trials and began my long endeavor of reading, learning, and memorizing. This would be my same routine for the next few months with only slight alterations in my days. From that day on, I saw why people ran for the hills at the mention of the Series Trials.

The Series Trials were the pinnacle of all my training and studying. The Series Game kicked off a week-long celebration for the Traders Terminal called the Festival of the Bazaar, or Festival of the Market. The Series Trials were a great spectacle like modern-day gladiators fighting in the Colosseum. For me to understand the Series

Trials, I had to learn how it began—with the Extractors.

An Extractor's job was to seek out and extract the minosium and trade it at the Traders Terminal. It sounded easy, but that was the furthest from the truth. In the case of fair-trade laws and extraction, the Terminal had set many rules concerning the extraction process and trading.

Only during the certain active months of the year may Extractors conduct extractions and trades inside specified extraction "zones," which were known or suspected hotbeds for minosium deposits. Within these zones, everything—yes, everything—was fair game—plundering, stealing, killing, all of the above.

Remember: the Terminal wanted fewer registered members, not more. This helped control how much minosium was extracted and traded for a fair market price, and the Terminal regulated this process in order to tax every piece of minosium traded on the exchange floor. Minosium can be traded only for commodities and products that can be taxed.

Once an R.E. and his outfit left a contested zone, they are in neutral territory; no fighting is allowed. According to Fitzroy, most of the time, the fighting is so fierce in those contested zones to control the deposits or transportation of the extracted mineral, the minosium ends up lost at sea due to "complications." Simply put, ships blow up.

There are a thousand or more rules concerning how minosium is mined, where it can be mined, what type of stone the minosium is mined from. The most important idea for me to understand was the risk I took every time I stepped foot into a contested zone.

If you were wondering about the general public, they had no idea about this, and the Terminal intended to keep it that way. Any position (privateers, surveyors, roughnecks, mechanics, and extractors) within a company that needed to be filled was usually passed down through family ties or sponsorship. For the lucky few, a position was filled by a connection, usually given to military officers or Ivy League college kids from California or New York.

Most of the time, each position was filled based on whom you knew, not what you knew. All nations were a part of the Terminal, but typically only a few companies from each nation were registered. It was a very closed industry.

In the old days, as in fifty years ago, competition was fierce among outfits and companies for minosium veins inside contested areas. Too many people were dying because these companies improvised by investing in technological advances through the harnessed power of minosium to have an edge over the next company—faster ships, deadlier weapons, protective suits of armor, innovative drills, etc.

Not only could the companies sell it, but why not harness its hidden power for warfare? This created a whole new world of weaponry.

The Terminal, upon seeing how deadly this warfare could be if allowed outside of contested zones, strictly enforced certain tactics, products, and use of these weapons within the contested zones. These tools were available for use only by the employees of registered companies who could enforce regulations and teach the nature of these weapons to their employees.

Above all else, fearful that large, unregulated quantities of minosium could fall into the wrong hands, the Terminal maintained that everything must remain hidden to the public. Thankfully, those very weapons, such as minosblades and sloops, were used extensively in the Series Trials, which brings us to why the Terminal created the Trials.

The Terminal needed a way to weed out hopeful R.E. prospects who were incapable in the Terminal's eyes of engaging in this highly lucrative and dangerous business. What young man wouldn't run to engage in a high-risk, high-reward business?

In response, the Terminal developed a system to test and train the R.E. hopefuls, who are called trainees, before they step into the contested zones and, eventually, the Traders Terminal.

The Terminal did not want any yahoos leaking the Terminal's secrets to unwanted persons with aspirations of romance and riches but with little substance within. The Terminal created a test to fulfill this need and learning curve by developing the Series Trials, the grand spectacle and achievement of the Terminal.

The Series Trials test the participants in various challenging scenarios: testing the trainees' knowledge of the rules and regulations of the Terminal, their ability to use reason under pressure, and whether they had the capability of outmaneuvering their fellow man.

The gist of the Trials went as follows: Eighty R.E. trainees descended upon an island maintained by the Terminal with the sole objective of acquiring a certain number of coins to reach the Victor's

Circle. These coins were obtained through an extremely dangerous series of different trials composed of puzzles, traps, beasts, and more—pitting trainee against trainee with the objective of acquiring a certain number of limited coins in order to move through the phase.

There were three phases of the Trials. In the first phase, the trainee was dropped on the island. He or she must seek out two trials, complete them, and retrieve two coins. Where it got interesting was that there was a limited number of coins and trials in the first phase.

The second phase was sloop aerial warfare. The two coins bought a trainee a sloop, and with that sloop, he or she must destroy two other sloops to retrieve two coins. Each kill counted as a single coin.

In the third phase, the remaining few entered the volcano at the center of the island for one last mysterious trial to achieve the final coin. Those that passed phase three received their extractor's license and a victory celebration. It is a rite of passage for all R.E. trainees and a way to deter half-hearted hopefuls from acquiring this job.

Was I scared? A little bit. Maybe a little more than a little bit.

I had to push myself to sit in that uncomfortable wooden chair with my neck bent over as I read endless black words on white paper for hours at a time, learning this information. I would get up, stretch, and then force myself again to keep reading. The more I read, the more I realized the severity of the Trials and how important it was that I studied and trained harder. That first day taught me what I was up against, and every other day continued in a similar fashion.

Typically, after my strenuous study session, I ate in the mess corridors. This was where I began to meet and see how the employees operated within the company. Captain Kalendar never left his office and very rarely showed his face to the crew. Below him was Helga, the first mate, and she had some grit.

A funny side story about her. One evening, I saw one of the privateers crack a demeaning joke about women in leadership positions. Helga found out and popped him right in the head, then threw him overboard with a parachute. I was amazed. She had some grit, and thankfully, from what brief conversations I had with her, she seemed to like me.

One of the most feared and respected of the crew, right below Kalendar and Helga, was Spurwink, the Specksynder. He was with Jeremiah at the Sinbad Tavern that day I boarded the *Victoria*.

Spurwink was a well-statured man with a well-kept brown beard, salty-keen eyes, and once-pale skin turned leathery brown from the long days in the sun. He was around forty years old, deep into his prime. He never said a word to me or looked my way.

Spurwink ate with his usual outfit and some of the other crewmen, including their group of privateers who bowed to their every whim. His outfit was composed of all New Englanders, mostly from Nantucket Island. Their names were Wyck, Spurwink's best friend and fellow R.E.; Locke, lead mechanic; Cudweed, surveyor; and Osprey and Pochick, who were the roughnecks.

The only one out of the group whom I was becoming acquainted with was Spurwink's younger brother, Rabbit Run. He gave me sinister looks at the mess hall. Rabbit Run looked like his brother: tall and well built with a stern, narrow face, trimly cut blond beard, a large nose, and slicked back blond hair.

In comparison to Rabbit Run, I had a defined jaw, high cheekbones, and a glowing face from being on deck all day. I had green eyes, no beard, and pale skin with some color, but by no means was I tan. With broad shoulders, I was slightly muscular and stood around 6'1", as opposed to the smallest Nantucket man in the group at roughly 6'4".

Rabbit Run was a 6'5", towering man with hunger in his eyes for me as he cut pieces of an apple with a knife while he stared directly at me. I wasn't scared of him. He viewed me as competition. We had not spoken to each other yet, but our heads occasionally locked. He was never in the study room. I assumed Spurwink was teaching him a different method of training. When we docked on Victoria Island, I had a feeling that during our physical training we would become acquainted with one another.

The next outfit seated at the mess hall eating lunch was the one I hoped to join—Fitzroy and his men. Fitzroy was as equally respected as Spurwink. Fitzroy had been with Kalendar and the Victoria & Co. the longest, longer than Helga or Spurwink. He'd managed to survive the Series Trials, and all these years, he had been extracting and fighting in the contested areas.

Fitzroy was well respected and kept to himself. I occasionally saw him wander into Kalendar's office. I heard privateer gossip that Fitzroy was one of the greatest fighters of the company, behind Jeremiah and Spurwink.

To give a better picture of Fitzroy's features, he was around 6'3", muscular, and rather on the slender side. He had a defined face with a striking gaze where his eyebrows knitted when he focused on something. His eyes contained harshness wrapped in sprinkles of sadness or longing for a feeling he does not have; I knew not what.

Fitzroy was a tough bastard. His skin was also once pale, turned brown from sun exposure. He was filled with scars and had a few strange tattoos that I couldn't quite make out hidden under his shirt. He was a man of few words; he spoke only when he had something to say.

The other members of this ragtag outfit were Zhen, the lead mechanic; Wildcat, the surveyor; Prince Rock, the broker; and Jeremiah, the roughneck.

Jeremiah was born in South Africa to a wealthy family. His father worked for the South African government, which moved him around a lot. From what he told me, he'd lived in America for most of his life and briefly in Jamaica and Egypt before joining the Victoria. I would say he was roughly thirty-five years old. He claimed he was descended directly from Shaka Zulu, a famous South African warrior.

His accent was quite unique, picking up subtleties from each country where he'd lived. His skin was dark with strong facial features, and a small nose; he was around my height, agile, and athletic. Best of all, he had a wonderful and hilarious personality.

We had four privateers who serviced the outfit's needs: Marlow and Cortez, two young lads from the states; Obasa, a tall ebony man from Tanzania; and a pretty woman named Aluma from Israel. She was twenty-six years old with olive skin, long black hair, high cheekbones, and a narrow face. In my mind, she looked like a princess from Arabia. She was short with a pleasantly curved figure accenting her hips. She mostly hung around the other women privateers.

I enjoyed her company and fragrance. I struggled to keep my eyes off her as she walked around the deck. Sadly, I didn't have time to converse with her or I told myself that, as I was too shy to give her anything but a simple hello.

The rest of the crew aboard were privateers whose main job was not to a single outfit but rather to the whole company. It was honor for an outfit to choose a specific privateer to assist them. This was one way a privateer could ascend to a higher position within the company.

On other days of my training, I worked closely with Zhen, the lead mechanic. His job was to teach me every component of a sloop and how to drive these flying beasts. We did this in the airship hangar where the sloops were maintained. Zhen walked me through all the specifics of this incredible vehicle. Our first day together training went as follows:

"Sloops. Powerful, fast, agile, and dangerous," Zhen began.

Zhen was covered in grease and wore large goggles on his head. We stopped to analyze a sloop.

"Most trainees never survive the dog fight phase," said Zhen.

"Dog fight?" I inquired.

"Aerial combat, sloops flying everywhere, bullets coming from all angles."

"Sounds intense."

"Yes, one must observe surroundings, maintain control, and avoid incoming missiles."

"How should I avoid missiles?"

"Outmaneuver your opponent and lead him into a trap—very important. Now, for the specifications."

Without going too much into the specifics, these bad boys were fast and could fly in all directions due to their versatile propellers. They were able to move side-to-side, up and down, and in a 360-degree motion.

Narrow and aerodynamic, a sloop sported an open-air cockpit comprising two seats, one behind the other with a bullet or torpedo-shaped body. It could fly up to 160 miles per hour, hitting its service ceiling around 16,000 feet, powered by a six-cylinder minosium engine, 250 horsepower. Rarely did it ever reach that high or fast. It mostly stuck toward the ground or above the tree line.

A sloop's main advantage was its mobility, quick movements, and protection. The back seat contained a mounted machine gun, and the pilot had a machine gun and a missile launcher in his control.

All in all, a sloop was a fighter prototype aircraft capable of incredible maneuvers. The controls and gauges were like that of modern biplanes, which were what I was used to. They were honestly simpler, carrying only the bare necessities to get a sloop in the air.

I sat in the cockpit and gripped the brown, leather steering wheel. I could feel the power and excitement in my hands. I was born to fly one of these things.

"This is incredible," I remarked.

"Ever flown before?" asked Zhen as he looked into the cockpit.

"A few times."

"Once we land on Victoria Island, we'll begin maintenance and flying lessons. Jeremiah will handle weaponry, Wildcat will teach you to survey, and Prince Rock . . ." Zhen scratched his head. "I'm not sure what he'll teach you."

I played with a few of the gauges, obtaining a feel for the components.

"So, dog fighting. How does that work in the Trials?" I inquired.

"Thirty trainees try to kill each other using missiles and bullets while flying at 160 mph, attempting all types of deadly maneuvers to attack and escape each other," Zhen explained.

"That's unsettling."

"You'll be fine if you listen to Zhen," he smiled.

After we worked a few hours on the sloops, Zhen would call it a day. On those days working with Zhen, I would also train with Wildcat in the evening. I could tell that he liked my company. He brought me into the same study room and taught me briefly about everything that concerned minosium with a more practical view of the matter. He explained the origins of minosium.

Without going into great detail and science behind this matter, minosium is formed deep within the earth. During violent volcanic eruptions, it is transported upward through tchouplite magma. The tchouplite magma is the only magma that does not dissolve the minosium, unlike basalt and andesite magma. The tchouplite magma protects minosium, like a traveler hitching a ride, on its passage to the surface.

The tchouplite travels though the magma pipe and is deposited into, typically, hot springs. The tchouplite, containing the minosium inside of its core, is then eroded over time by the hot springs, turning the igneous rock a yellowish color.

Wildcat brought out samples of the tchouplite.

"This is what we are after, kid," Wildcat stated in a Southern accent as he put the yellow rugged rock in my hand. "Ain't she a beaut?"

He took the tchouplite from my hand, then took a small handheld drill and drilled a small hole it. He took a hammer, hit it, and cracked it open; inside the rock was a glowing purple crystal, nestled deep in the tchouplite rock.

"There's the minosium," exclaimed Wildcat. "I'll be damned. It's glowing strong."

"Why does it glow?" I asked.

"It has radioactive elements. You see there," Wildcat pointed out, "the surface of the minosium burns when it meets oxygen, giving it that glowing ember color, and yet, this one is glowing stronger than normal."

"Must be a good batch."

Wildcat closely examined the vibrant ore. "It glows like that only when blood is around, exciting its fluorescent matter. Seen that only once."

"You cut yourself?"

"No, not human blood. Blood minosium, the most powerful and rarest of all minosium. Regular minosium is purple while the more powerful and rare stuff is blood red. So powerful, it lights up other minosium."

"Blood minosium sounds familiar. Wasn't that from Faustino's tale?"

"The kid's story?"

"Yeah, where the devil offered him blood minosium."

"In exchange for his soul."

"You know the story!"

"Of course, I do. Every member of the Terminal knows the story of Faustino. Regardless of how true the devil part is, he was the one to discover the mineral."

"Do you believe in the story?"

"Eh, I believe Faustino discovered minosium, not the part where he met the devil and built a labyrinth. That's like saying I believe in Atlantis."

"The story said Faustino had a large swath of blood minosium in that labyrinth. What say ye about that?"

Wildcat laughed. "Any fool that hunts for Faustino's treasures never finds it because it's a kid's tale, nothing more."

"Then where can we find more blood, if not in the labyrinth?"

"Shoot. If I knew the answer to that, I would be a rich man."

I stared at the glowing purple minosium.

"It's out there, so it can be found," I replied.

"True. How about this: you make it through the Trials, and we'll go search for some blood, you and I," he said.

"Sounds like a deal."

Wildcat loved to talk to me. I liked him, and he seemed to be a good man after his fortune. In time, I knew we would be good friends—if I survived the Trials. I enjoyed my time with Wildcat, and it was nice change of pace from Fitzroy's strenuous training.

The last thing I did on those specific days when I wasn't in the study room was training with Prince Rock after Wildcat. Prince Rock wanted me to meet him at the cargo hold at the back of the ship. The cargo hold was an open-air section of the ship, which allowed a nice sea breeze and sunshine to flow in.

Prince Rock was a big man with a loud voice similar to Axelrod's. He had a big jaw, a bald head, and large hands. He loved to shout orders. He typically wore a flat brown hat tilted to the left side, a white turtleneck, and a brown vest. He was a captain in the United States Merchant Marines prior to this, so he conducted his training and business in the cargo like that of the marines.

He was a jolly fellow who loved to pick on and jest with the small crew under him. His typical crew of privateers who helped him with the cargo was Obasa, the tall, ebony-skinned man from Tanzania; Cortez, a short, Latin-American man with a mustache; and Aluma, the pretty, olive-skinned woman from Israel.

Obasa and Cortez did all the maintenance, heavy lifting, and labeling of the cargo. Aluma serviced the company's balance sheets— tracking assets to debts, taxes due to the Terminal, and all import and exports of the ship from the cargo hold. Prince Rock managed all three of them and reported to Helga.

On this particular day, Prince Rock was carrying a large brown wooden cargo box on his shoulder and, upon seeing me, put it down.

"Doughboy, that time of day again?" asked Prince Rock with a smile.

"If I am so lucky," I remarked.

"Today ye are because we have a good one ahead of us."

"Let me guess," I said. "Could it be lifting heavy boxes?"

Prince Rock gave a rip-roaring laugh. "How did ye know?"

"I must be gettin' smarter, eh?"

"Indeed. Now remember: Pick up the box, and bring it to Aluma.

Understand the product and tax placed on it. The Terminal always throws out a tax question during the Trials," explained Prince Rock. "Chop, chop!"

Prince Rock's training was the absolute worst of them all. First, I had to pick up extremely heavy cargo boxes and bring them to Aluma. I would open the box with a wedge tool. She accounted for it and labeled the box. Then, I would carry it to the export section. I must stress how painstakingly heavy these cargo boxes were and how scorching the heat from the sun inside of the open-air cargo hold was.

I noticed Obasa carrying two large boxes on each shoulder. His shirt was off, revealing black tribal tattoos. I followed suit, took my shirt off, and wrapped it around my head like a turban to capture my sweat. My amulet hung from my neck.

I brought my first box to Aluma. She looked as pretty as ever, wearing her light blue button-down shirt with her rolled-up sleeves and khaki shorts. This was the typical attire for all privateers on deck. Her brown hair was put up in a bun, allowing her pretty facial features to stand out.

I'd gotten stronger since I had started my training. My biceps had grown, my thighs were more toned, and my abs had started to show. I tried to over-accentuate my muscle tone to Aluma. I placed my large cargo box next to her as I made an abnormally loud grunting sound.

"That was a heavy one," I said, drawing her attention to my efforts.

I tried to lean on the box, but enthralled in her beauty, I lost my balance. I tried to play it off, acting like I meant to do it. She laughed at me, keeping her attention focused on the clipboard.

"Open it up," she suggested.

I opened it, and inside were four elegant swords. I was amazed. I pulled one out to analyze it. The sword appeared to be like the one Axelrod used that night. I gripped it with my hand. The handle of the sword was silver with multicolored buttons. The tip of the blade was covered.

"What is this?" I asked.

"A minosblade," she replied.

"Can this be traded at the Terminal?"

"Anything that contains minosium can be traded on the exchange, as long as it is traded for a taxable security."

"Security?"

"Better get to studying," she remarked sarcastically. "It means a tradable asset. We'll trade these minosblades for trader coins, the Traders Terminal currency of the world."

"Wow, like the euro and U.S. dollar."

"Right, but trader coins can be taxed by the Terminal and traded around the world."

"Prince Rock told me to pay keen attention to that tax. Why?"

"That's how the Terminal makes its money. On every trade, they charge a fifteen percent tax."

"That's a lot!"

Aluma laughed. "Welcome to the real world. Now, get that to the export section. We're behind for the day."

I continued to pick up and drop off heavy boxes. My back was in serious pain. I was struggling. Seeing my sorry state, Obasa knew I needed help that day, so he placed his boxes down and came over to me.

"No, not like that," said Obasa as he referred to the way I was picking up the boxes. His accent contained a strong East African touch to it.

"Why do I have to do this, Obasa?" I sighed, on the verge of crying. "My back is aching. This is doing nothing for me, and I'm already stressed by everything else—and now this!" I kicked the box in anger.

"To learn good work," said Obasa. "Even if it seems meaningless, a man should take pride in good work, which will lead him to better work and a good night's sleep."

"How can the worst work lead to better work?"

"Opportunity comes to those who work hard."

"I can't work hard if one of these boxes breaks my back."

"Then change what you do. You pick up box wrong."

"How so?"

I would bend over and pick up the box. I didn't understand what he meant.

"You will break back if pick up like that," suggested Obasa. "Watch. Pick up again."

I bent over and picked up the box. Obasa came over and showed me how he would pick up the box.

"Bend legs and squat," suggested Obasa. "Keep back up, spread your legs, and . . . lift!" Obasa easily lifted the box between his arms. "Now you."

I followed his movement closely. He analyzed my movements and readjusted my feet and posture. I lifted the box. It was ten times easier than before.

"Don't work harder. Work smarter," he smiled. "Then get a better job."

I thanked him. His logic was breaking through my thick, stubborn head. Each day with Prince Rock was roughly the same task of moving things to and fro.

Two weeks into training and traveling aboard the airship, Fitzroy tested me on my knowledge of the rules and regulations of the Terminal. His test was a surprise that I wasn't expecting. Inside my head, I freaked out a little bit. What if I failed his test?

I took a deep breath and focused. He read off a series of questions, and thankfully, I was able to answer most of them correctly. He was pleased with me. I felt well accomplished. He told me that I was moving on to the second phase of my training, which would continue when we reached Victoria Island. I could tell he was slowly accepting me.

We celebrated with a few sips of rum. I could feel the tipsiness swirl around in my head. I felt the urge to learn more about Fitzroy.

"May I ask you a question, Fitzroy?" I asked.

He took another sip. "Sure."

"Where are you from?"

He smiled and swirled his rum around in the cup, contemplating his answer. He told me he was from Georgia. I persisted in knowing how he made his way into this business. He slightly opened up to me, saying that he grew up sailing in the Atlantic with his father. They owned a beautiful white sailboat, which they sailed all around the Caribbean.

Fitzroy said his dream was to be on a ship, sailing around the world like the old days of seafaring. His father was a well-connected merchant who traded his wares at the Terminal, most especially with Kalendar's company, the Victoria & Co. Fitzroy learned of the business and the dangers it entailed and wanted to join the Victoria & Co. as an eager young lad, but his father would not permit it.

Sadly, something happened to his father's business, but Fitzroy wouldn't offer details. Whatever happened finally prompted Fitzroy to join the Victoria & Co. Fitzroy wouldn't say any more and turned in for the night. I thought to myself as he walked away, *Strange how men and women fall into this deadly line of work. What pulls them to it? Was it the money, the power, or something more?*

CHAPTER 7

Round Dance of Fire

W E FINALLY APPROACHED the headquarters on Victoria Island, and it was . . . wow! I had never been to the South Pacific, let alone on this side of the earth. The whole crew went out on the top deck to see the island as we descended from the sky. On the observation deck right above the main deck, Helga steered the ship with the help of her privateers.

The water was crystal blue, clear enough to see the colorful coral reefs below the surface. The sun was shining bright. It was extremely hot and humid. I could smell the sea air and hear the crash of the waves along the shoreline.

The island, formed around a volcano at the center of the island, wasn't exceptionally large. The tip of the volcano reached into the sky. A cloud surrounded it. The island was mountainous, covered with green jungles, white sand beaches, and turquoise water.

The crew was ecstatic, hollering as we drew near the dock. Everyone on board was eager to disembark. The island had a small dock and colorful town, composed of a few contemporary buildings, docked boats, and smaller airships. I could see a few sloops buzzing above the treetops. Next to the small town was a lake and across the lake, accessed via white bridge, was a magnificent building. It was the Victoria & Co. headquarters at the center of the lake.

The building had a wavy, airy look about it with a white, elegantly shaped, wave-like roof. The roof was a continuous wave with its arch and curves. Under the roof were large glass windows, conforming to the airy white roof. There were no solid walls, only glass windows.

The whole building was three stories high, extending outward to the open terrain surrounded by jungle. I'd never seen anything of the sort, nor could have I possibly imagined a place as beautiful as this. This wasn't swampy Louisiana.

I would've enjoyed this view much more if I didn't have a constant nagging and concern inside my head at the time, reminding me of the impending Series Trials.

The *Victoria* airship docked on the water outside of the small town. Helga issued orders for the privateers to unload the cargo from the hold. Fitzroy nudged me on the shoulder.

"Where to now?" I asked.

"Gather your stuff from the cabin, and we'll leave it in my room. We have the fire circle," he stated. "That's where the company will vote to determine if you'll represent us at the Series Trials."

"I thought I was already cleared by Kalendar," I replied with slight concern in my tone.

"It's the company's choice, but don't worry, you'll make it through."

"Great, and if they vote against me, then what?"

"You return to Villefranche."

"Even better," I said gloomily.

"I wouldn't have trained ye if I thought ye weren't going to make it through the fire circle. Trust my words, as I've said before," Fitzroy commanded.

The threat of being sent back was added to my long list of worries. I was forced to learn how to deal with this level of stress, or it would have broken me. I had to let go of my fears. That was the only way to deal with this immense pressure that came from every angle.

I made my way off the dock and into this small South Pacific town appearing like an old Spanish port with cobblestone roads and a central cabildo. The town served as the living quarters, grocery, trading depot, and all other bare necessities for the company.

It was completely serviced by the privateers. I dropped my stuff off at Fitzroy's small teal house near the center of town. The whole outfit lived in the same house. From outside the house, I could see the whole company descending upon a large area outside the town.

Jeremiah—wearing big, flashy sunglasses, a Panama hat, and a colorful coat—stepped into the house.

"Good to be home!" said Jeremiah as he threw his stuff on the ground.

Marlow was right behind, carrying Jeremiah's luggage. Marlow was a privateer and Jeremiah's main companion in all his questionable endeavors and heavy drinking adventures.

Marlow was a stoic character, never offering much character at all, rather only when his character required much during death-defying situations, which exposed the true colorful character hidden under his stoic mask.

Marlow maintained a fixed, stern face—appearing as if he had killed a man, wanted to kill a man, or nothing. He often stared blankly at absolutely nothing. Marlow was Mr. Cool, and all the other privateers knew it. He was drunk mostly, smoked superfluously, and watched Jeremiah evidentially. Jeremiah would beg to differ.

Marlow was a pale man with a ruddy face and short, shaggy brown hair. I would say he was well built and roughly six feet in height. He always wore Acapulco shirts of many colors. His eyes ... his eyes ... well, his eyes were covered all the time by circular sunglasses, extremely hip and mysterious, or he was rather stupid, covering his masked drunkenness or insecurities. I couldn't quite make my mind up, but I liked him, and he liked me.

Jeremiah came into the room with a colorful button-down purple shirt and big sunglasses styled from 1980s, like he were partying in Miami. He wore a tan, wide-brimmed hat. Jeremiah looked ready for vacation.

"Christoph! My favorite trainee!" exclaimed Jeremiah. "I'm glad you're here. We start training tomorrow on my boat. Beautiful boat. Tell him, Marlow."

Marlow placed Jeremiah's heavy luggage on the ground.

"It's great. Can't beat it," Marlow insisted.

"And the fish!" Jeremiah said excitedly.

"If the day's right," remarked Marlow.

"Shush, you," said Jeremiah. "The day is always right when you are with Jeremiah. You'll love training with me. We spearfish each day and bring back our catch for a feast."

"Really?" I replied. "Why spearfishing?"

"Ah, you will have to find out, Doughboy," said Jeremiah. "It requires mental discipline. One must silence the nerves, control his breathing, and become one with his prey. Alas! Ye cannot wait till the morrow."

"I need a smoke break," insisted Marlow as he left the room.

"I wish I was excited as you, but the fire circle . . . " I sighed.

"The fire circle," laughed Jeremiah. "You'll be fine. Kalendar will have your back, I assure thee."

"Thanks."

Jeremiah looked at his watch. "We best be going. We'll go together."

I followed Jeremiah toward the sounds of loud drums echoing in the distance. As we drew further on, closer to the edge of town, I could hear loud chatter, drinking, and carousing. People were excited, surrounding a large circle in an open grassy field.

Jeremiah led me through the large crowd to the center of the circle since they would be voting for me. The center was lit by multiple torches surrounding a large pile of wood and hay. Overlooking the pile was a lifted stage with a series of chairs. At the center of the stage was an adorned wooden throne with exquisite carvings of sea creatures and minosium. Wildcat came up to me and gave me a few words of encouragement. I was scared.

The sun was setting, creating a majestic purple and pink sky. There was a slight sea breeze blowing through the island. A horn roared, and the crowd's chatter died down. Captain Kalendar, accompanied by Helga and few other privateers, appeared through the crowd. He appeared focused and reserved, with blazing eyes ready to pierce whoever spoke against him. He was chief of the tribe, ready to fight for his position.

Once Kalendar was seated on his throne, Helga gave an opening statement in which she congratulated the company on a successful and lucrative season. She vocally recognized a few notable people who served well and then spoke of the poor souls who perished in the contested zones. Last season, thirty-eight people died either from combat or instances relating to combat. Helga read off each name, followed by an eerie silence in the crowd. Helga continued:

"In honor of our passed brothers and sisters, we light this fire in remembrance of them and their sacrifice for this company. I remind myself that all things must come to pass, regardless of religion, who they were, or where they came from. We are all equal in the eye of death, and no matter how high we ascend the ladder or how low to the floor we go, death shall come for us.

"With that said, appreciate where you are, work for where you want to be, love passionately, and live fearlessly. Light the fire!" yelled Helga.

The drums began to play once more. A few of the privateers who surrounded Kalendar brought out lit torches and threw them into the large woodpile at the center of the circle. The fire grew as the wood crackled and hissed in the flames.

"Brothers and sisters of the deceased, bring out your memorabilia to place in the fire," Helga called forth.

Many people went forward to place pictures or objects related to the deceased members into the fire. Once the crowd died down around the fire, Spurwink went forward and dropped a small red ball and a blue hat into the fire.

"For Flintlock and Brockton," said Spurwink loudly. "Some of the finest Nantucket men I've ever met—extraordinary extractors, brave fighters, and good friends. I salute thee and make way for the new faces to come!"

Fitzroy asked Marlow for a cigarette, and he lit it. Fitzroy had a focused look about him as he dug into his coat pocket and pulled out a picture. From what I could see, it was man, no more than twenty-five years old, standing next to his mother in front of a cornfield. Fitzroy walked to the fire, placed it in there, and walked back to his spot. There was a moment of silence among all.

Staring deeply into the dancing flames, Kalendar maintained a fixed focus on the fire. Standing on the stage next to Kalendar, Helga gathered the attention of the crowd. Helga said a goodbye to the souls as they ascended with the smoke to the sky and continued:

"As with the seasons of the earth, when one season passes, a new season comes forward, blooming from the bleak death of a winter's night. To replace our lost friends, we first welcome two hopefuls in pursuit of the revered extractor's position, willing to face the deadly Series Trials," said Helga.

"We shall now vote as a company if we fully support our two new trainees as they pursue a dream few achieve. They will represent our company in front of the Traders' world; therefore, we must be diligent in choosing our trainees wisely.

"Our first trainee is Spurwink's younger brother, Rabbit Run. By vote of each class and outfit, yea or nay. Privateers collectively, one vote; each outfit has one vote. By tradition, if you step forward within the circle and you are refused sponsorship, accept your dismissal from the company with honor. Choose now, and bring forth your potential trainees!"

My heart began to beat rapidly in my chest. The thought of being dismissed did not sit well with me. Rabbit Run and I stepped into the circle. Two others stepped into the circle. They were two privateers, a young woman named Sheila and a man named Oscar.

"I thought it was only Rabbit Run and I?" I asked Jeramiah behind me.

"A privateer can attempt a vote. Don't worry," said Jeremiah.

I went forward and joined Rabbit Run and the two privateers. Helga began the vote with Rabbit Run. The first vote was the privateers, and they voted no, but Fitzroy's outfit voted yes. Kalendar had the last vote, and he did vote for Rabbit Run. The Nantucket men were delighted to see their trainee accepted. The next two were the privateers, who were voted on at the same time. Typically, the privateers would vote for their own but were outweighed by the outfit's vote and the captain's vote. Both privateers were dismissed in matter of seconds on account of a low vote.

I then stepped forward, and Helga called me to a vote. The stress was mounting. I tried to breathe and control it. Thankfully, the privateers gave me a sponsorship. I was popular among the privateers from working with them in the cargo hold under Prince Rock.

Spurwink's outfit denied me. It was 2-1. *Those bastards*, I thought to myself. Jeremiah screamed out a variety of colorful comments against the Nantuckets for voting against me after his outfit voted for Rabbit Run.

Kalendar had the last vote. My fate rested in his hands. The crowd grew anxious to see what would happen. Fitzroy gave me a steady look as he knitted his eyebrow at me. He could tell I was worried out the wazoo. I had to keep myself calm. The crowd's excitement grew as they called out my name.

"Silence!" screamed Helga. "The choice falls on our captain. What say thee, Captain Kalendar?"

Captain Kalendar with his fierce eyes arose from his throne, walked up to me, and looked into my eyes. I stared right back at him, never breaking eye contact. He grabbed my amulet and stared intently at it; then, he looked back at me without showing emotion.

This is it, I thought. I was going to end up back at Villefranche, trying to find my way back home. Then what? Whoever was trying to kill me would find me undoubtedly. No, no, no! This must work out for me. I had no other choice. There was no plan B. At that moment, I said a silent prayer to God in my heart: "O Lord, help me in my time of need, for I need you now more than ever."

"I sponsor Christoph Swift!" declared Kalendar in his booming voice.

I nearly dropped to my knees at those words. The crowd cheered in response. I thought to myself, *I can't believe it. It looks like I'm making it somewhere!*

Helga gave me a wink and declared, "Welcome, Christoph Swift and Rabbit Run to the Victoria & Co. May you achieve victory in the Trials and bring prosperity to our company. This concludes our fire ceremony and our past season."

Wildcat came running up to me with a wild smile. "I knew you'd get sponsored!" exclaimed Wildcat, with his twangy accent. "Get ready for my training. We got a lot to go over."

The rest of Fitzroy's outfit congratulated me with words of encouragement.

Fitzroy tossed out his cigarette as he approached the outfit and me. "The season may be over, but a wise prince prepares for war in time of peace. We continue with our preparation over the coming summer months. We will be the top outfit in the whole Terminal in the next season. I will not settle for less, and for that, I say this." He turned to me. "Christoph Swift, I promise ye that I will work day in and day out, preparing ye for the Trials and for the job afterward if ye give one hundred percent each day without excuses. Through this, ye will give back to our outfit tenfold after ye have conquered the Series Trials and wear the wreath of victory in the coliseum. I believe in thee. What say ye, Christoph Swift?"

"Wait a second!" yelled Jeremiah. "Before anyone says anything else, I wanted to say that I usually never help a trainee. Ye can ask anyone here. I always thought it was a waste of time because the chances of my own trainee surviving the Trials were slim to none. Not with you, Christoph. You're different. I believe ye have a chance, and with my help, ye have a real good chance. I stand with Swift through thick and thin."

"Me too, lad," said Marlow. "Can't let you and Jeremiah have all the fun."

"I stand by Doughboy!" Zhen exclaimed.

"He's got heart, and I like it," said Prince Rock.

Obasa was near Prince Rock. "I help you grow strong."

"I'm honored," I said, "and I promise to each of you, I will give everything I have inside of me, for I will survive the Trials and join this outfit."

"Good," said Fitzroy, "and as an outfit, we'll train and grow with Christoph and fine tune our own skills. When the new season comes, we'll have a new member and the strength to be the best outfit in the whole terminal. I smell blood minosium on the horizon. What say all of thee?"

With one loud roar, we all cheered, "Aye!"

Helga chimed in, "Looks like you're the prospect."

"Thanks to these guys," I replied.

"They say second phase of training is always the most brutal. Alas, I've known trainees in the past that have died while training on this island, long before they've entered the Trials," said Helga as she narrowed her brow. "Are you sure you can handle this challenge, Christoph, knowing the dangers that truly lie ahead of you?"

"Alone, definitely not," I replied, "but with the help of this outfit, undoubtedly yes!"

We all cheered, "Oohrah, oohrah, oohrah!" with gleeful zeal.

CHAPTER 8

Fitzroy and the Temple Dance

B Y THE LOOKS of it, I was doing well for myself. I had made it to
a beautiful paradise on the far side of the world. I was accepted
into a prestigious company (contingent on if I survived the
Trials) and seemed to have made a few friends along the way. I was in
the best shape of my life, mentally and physically.

Aye, at this point I thought things would slow down a bit—
catch a day at the beach, get some sun, see Aluma out there. But as
with all things, it was only pain, work, and determination ahead of
me—mostly pain. All of my dreamy thoughts vanished the moment
the sun approached the horizon, and my training for the day started.

It caught my attention during the fire circle when Kalendar
grabbed my amulet from my neck. From the twinkle in his eyes while
gazing at my heirloom, I could see a slight notion of familiarity. He
tried to keep this buried gaze withheld from me through his reserv-
edness, but I knew by his motion and sway, the way he grasped onto
the amulet, feeling the etchings on it, he appeared to have felt it before.

The thought of Axelrod's possible entanglement with Kalendar
never left my mind. Nonetheless, I kept that to myself; as I was learning in this deadly world, keeping secrets to the heart was crucial to my
success.

Regarding the logistics of the company, during the summer
months until October 31, business and extraction cannot be conducted. The Traders Terminal is closed, and contested areas are off limits.

The Terminal strictly enforced these rules. This allowed the participants in each company to return home and spend time with their

loved ones. It was a time to enjoy newfound wealth and forget about tomorrow. Most of the privateers stayed on the island in hopes of a better opportunity to rise in the ranks within the company.

Remember: Only the extractor position participated in the Series Trials. Privateers, surveyors, roughnecks, and mechanics had their own training and licensing with the Terminal and their own company.

Wildcat told me he started off as a privateer under Kalendar. He showed some wit and ability and eventually serviced an outfit, then had the ability to train to become a surveyor. Very rarely, if at all, either by tradition or fate, a privateer ascends the ladder high enough to become an extractor. It is true that only a select few can acquire the extractor's title.

As for Spurwink's outfit, they did not return home to Nantucket. Helga and Kalendar and their own privateers remained on the island to service the island and the needs of roughly fifty of them, which was a good number. Why would the privateers leave a paradise like this, especially when they can live here freely for the summer months?

I asked Fitzroy why Spurwink's outfit wouldn't take a vacation. He told me the outfits that take vacations are usually the ones that perish in the contested zones. He claimed that when we make our wealth, then and only then may we rest from this dangerous profession.

As for my continued training, it was mostly the same as it had been on the ship. The only difference was the more intensive studying and dynamic physical training.

During my early days on the island, my typical training regime went as follows:

I awoke at the crack of dawn before the sun ascended above the horizon in the outfit's teal blue house. Since the twenty-four hour clock is the time measurement used by both the Terminal and Victoria & Co., I had to learn it. Indeed, it took me more than a second to get used to a twenty-four hour clock, and it might take you a moment to understand if you've never seen it before. Trust me; you'll want to learn it.

Waking up around 04:30 was slowly becoming an easier feat. Fitzroy told me repetition was the answer to forming good habits. I knew I had to exceed Fitzroy's expectations if I wanted any chance to succeed at the Trials. I was learning a hard fact: the more I put into my training, the more I got out of it. The stakes were too high for me to frolic along the seashore. My life was at stake. I couldn't mess this up.

Mornings on Victoria Island were gorgeous with a calm sea breeze flowing through the trees. There was very little wildlife throughout this lush jungle due to wildlife migration patterns. The mornings were peaceful and calm, which was far different from the vibrant swamps of my homeland.

Fitzroy and I prepared for our morning run to start the day, and trust me, this was no ordinary run. The first part of the run was along the sandy coastline, then through the dense jungle along a dirt road. The arch of my foot ached from running barefoot on the sand. We carried a backpack with our shoes and supplies. I had a hard time keeping up with Fitzroy. He was relentless and demanded that I keep up with him.

Fitzroy's skin was quite tan from running in the sun. He was in phenomenal shape. Every part of him was well defined and sculpted, like an ancient Greek marble statue.

Past the beach and into the bush, we ran past sections of the jungle composed completely of bamboo. I'd never seen bamboo— this long, green, stalk-like plant, indigenous to this region—before. Through the bamboo forest, we swam through a small creek, all while ascending through this mountainous region.

It was one thing to run on a flat surface, but it was another thing to run on a mountainous terrain on a winding dirt path ascending around a volcano. This stuff was hard, and we rarely stopped for a break. For the first few runs, I had to stop and gasp for air. One of those in-stances went as follows:

"Wait," I gasped as I leaned on a tree. "I'll die if I go farther."

Fitzroy turned to me and said, "Life will not wait for you, even if you are tired."

"How great must a man push himself then? To the verge of death? A little rest hurts no one."

"Nay, I say to ye, Christoph. Rest is like debt: A little here is fine. A little there, why not? But each small debt incurred builds into great debts that weigh on a man's shoulder, crushing him like the titan Atlas. Be persistent in what you do. Give the enemy no rest!"

"Who is the enemy?"

"Your ego, your doubt, and your laziness. Ye, Christoph, are your greatest enemy. Now, get back on your feet and start running."

On that day, I continued on the hardest run of my life. We ascended to a large stone structure near a running river, covered by colorful white, pink, yellow, red, and blue hibiscus flowers, recently bloomed. It was a temple.

A stone staircase led up to more ruins. Fitzroy told me this was an old tiki temple from the ancient dwellers of this island. We ascended the stairs to an open room with wood and stone carvings of tiki gods. Each carving had a wide-open mouth, smiling or frowning, with small eyes and tall headpieces. Fitzroy told me they were similar to the carvings of the ancient Hawaiians.

There we stopped for a rest in the center of the ruins. Fitzroy told me to look at one of the stone carvings of the tiki gods.

"Look," Fitzroy pointed out.

I looked closely at the stone idol. There were scenes drawn into the stone of the structure's torso. Fitzroy called it petroglyph art, as in rock carvings. Fitzroy pointed out a scene of a group of people mining using stone tools around a hot spring. The next scene was of the indigenous people worshipping this mysterious crystal.

"What are they worshipping?" I asked.

"Minosium," he replied. "It means it's on the island and has been around for centuries."

I continued to analyze the drawings on the tiki god. The next scene was of a man adorned in jewels arriving on an old schooner ship. The next scene showed the man forcibly escorting the islanders, bound up in chains and carrying minosium onto his ship. The next scenes were destroyed by time and the elements.

"The people," I stated. "They were taken from here by this man."

"Indeed, they were," said Fitzroy. "I believe that man was Faustino."

"This could be evidence of his existence."

"Maybe, or evidence there's minosium or something more hidden on this island."

"We should look for it."

"No . . . Not yet at least. The Terminal would sentence us to death if we extracted minosium in the off-season, let alone laid eyes upon a hot spring."

"They wouldn't know if we found it."

"Stop!" insisted Fitzroy. "Learn the rules of the Terminal and follow them, or ye will end up at the bottom of the sea."

I nodded.

Fitzroy continued, "I cannot help ye if ye fall into trouble with the Terminal. Part of your training is to listen. If ye do not, ye will fail."

"I understand."

"Good. Finish the Trials, and we'll go hunt for this minosium together. Let's get back to town."

I remembered that particular day of training. It was insightful and played a key role in my future endeavors.

Occasionally, after my morning run, I would begin to study by 08:30 in an open-air classroom inside a small wooden cottage without air conditioning. It was in here that I continued my study of the Terminal. Fitzroy rarely lectured to me though sometimes he stopped by.

One day, I asked Fitzroy where Rabbit Run studied.

He replied, "Focus on yourself and no one else. He does not matter."

The studying was still strenuous. I had to practice my patience, mastering the art of focusing on one subject for hours at a time. At times, this meticulous studying was harder than the physical training. I was required to memorize all things the Terminal entailed: history, economics, business, regulations, and politics.

I began to understand the true meaning of a Registered Extractor. I was the person to trade the minosium for a variety of other taxable products inside the Terminal. It was my duty to negotiate and barter for a fair price and then invest my returns into financial holdings that would produce equity for the company. On everything I traded, I received a piece of the profit, further enticing an extractor to trade and turn a profit.

My job was less about the physical act of extracting the minosium but instead trading it on the exchange floor. An extractor's job required me to be a part of the extraction process, the shipment, and the trade of the ore on the exchange floor. Then, I would reinvest or trade from a pre-approved list created by my employing company outlining what the minosium or proceeds should be traded for on the exchange floor. Extractors had a hand in all operations of the minosium and, therefore, were paid the most.

Besides the specifics, I realized how much I could learn by reading a book consistently and improving my ability to teach myself. It was terrible, but I was absorbing the information by continually drilling it in my head through a structured learning regime.

Seeing my advancement, it made me think back on my high school days. What if I had applied myself like this, as if my life depended on my success? What if I applied this same work ethic to my studies and sports or, not just in school, but in jobs and even my relationships?

Maybe I wouldn't have been so low on the totem pole in that hierarchal societal structure of "status" prior to this. Success meant ascension, and ascension meant respect and loyalty. I was onto something, but I had to stay focused on my studies for the time being.

I descended deeper into the Series Trials, which were incredibly fascinating and scary. The Series Trials, as mentioned before, was the kick-off for the week-long celebration called the Festival of the Bazaar.

The Series Trials was a world-renowned spectacle for all participants involved with the Traders Terminal. One must be invited by the Terminal to watch the Trials at the massive coliseum near Eversa Island where the Trials take place.

The trainee and his trainer were introduced at the coliseum to a roaring crowd prior the start of the Trials. Trainees presented themselves and their company before the crowd. After that, they were transported to the island where the Trials took place.

The Trials began with the trainee starting from a singular origin at some point on the island. Each trainee began differently; some jumped from a sloop while others simply walked onto the island.

The main objective of the game was to collect Traders Coins. The more coins, the better. Each challenge offered two coins, though a trainee was allowed to take only one coin per challenge.

To move on to the second phase of the Trials, a trainee must have acquired one coin, either from a trial or from other players. Any coin was playable on the island, but a trainee could never have two of the same coins from the trial.

Typically, there were around sixty or so trainee hopefuls with only twenty-four coins available in the first phase. With pressure like that, things could get a little hectic and desperate in the first phase. Out of the sixty trainees, only twenty-four trainees made it to the second phase of the Trials. The first phase was composed of sixteen challenges or tasks with one, two, four, or even zero coins available per challenge, all depending on chance. The sixteen challenges varied by nature, changing by the year.

A note attached inside my used textbook referred me to an older textbook called *The Serpent's Den*. It was supposedly an unknown mythical trial on the island which harbored thousands of different coins from all years. That meant if a trainee completed this trial, he or she would have more than enough different coins to bypass phases two and three and complete the Trials. I was interested and searched the island for this book, eventually finding it tucked away in the town's library.

The Serpent's Den claimed there was one trial not made by the Terminal; instead, it was created before man ever walked the earth. It stated that a serpent from the Jurassic age lived deep within the island.

Our old friend Faustino, upon hearing of the serpent, wanted to use it to his advantage and built a chamber on the island to guard his treasure, especially silver coins similar to the Traders Coins. The Terminal modeled its coins from the same designs, weight, and specifications of the original Faustino coins. According to this textbook, one of Faustino's original coins matched a Traders Coin in every aspect.

They say only three trainees had found the chamber and used those coins to succeed in the Trials. The book stated the chamber was located on the northwest side of the island inside a cave. It sounded like an old children's tale, nothing I could rely on. Granted, I wanted to be armed with the knowledge of this mythical trial in case something went awry.

Moving back to my original textbook, it gave a few examples of past trials:

One trial was composed of a puzzle located in stone ruins created by the Terminal. The whole puzzle was a labyrinth containing a variety of scrolls with questions regarding Terminal regulations. If the trainee answered the questions correctly, the scroll would provide a route to the coin. If he or she answered wrong, the scroll provided a route to his or her death. In the book, it showed a picture of five trainees impaled on a set of spikes. I guess they chose the wrong scroll.

Another challenge required a trainee to fix a broken drill. If the trainee took too long, poisonous gas was released, causing the trainee to cough his lungs out. Luckily, if the trainee fixed the drill in the allotted timeframe, the trainee would take the fixed drill and drill it into yellow tchouplite.

Inside the tchouplite was a coin and a minosblade, a high-powered sword etched with minosium, able to cut through any matter like a hot knife through butter. It had become the ideal weapon of choice in post-minosium warfare, especially for trainees.

Some challenges offered weapons, supplies, or armor; other challenges would not offer a coin but rather supplies or, better yet, nothing at all.

The next page showed the devastation a minosblade can wreak on trainees—a gruesome sight!

Here was one last example of a past year's trial. This one stuck with me. In this trial, the trainees descended into a pitch-black cave, lit only by a light on their suits. Each trainee had to locate tchouplite hidden within the dark cave. Inside the tchouplite was a coin. The real kicker was that once the trainee entered the cave, the light on the trainee's suit was limited to twenty minutes before it shut off. The only way to refuel the light source in the suit was by correctly answering questions pertaining to the Terminal exchange floor written on the wall throughout the cavern. If a trainee's light ran out before he or she could recover the coin or find and answer another question, darkness and death awaited the trainee.

As you can see from these examples, the Terminal was not only testing a trainee's physical strength but, more importantly, his or her understanding and memory of concepts while under immense pressure.

The one point the textbook stressed was that a trainee must be prepared for anything and everything during these Trials. The Terminal was clever in its ways, always trying to trick the trainees, pit them against each other, or put them in deadly situations. The Terminal controlled the game and wielded it to their desire.

The Trials lasted a total of twenty-four hours. If the trainee did not complete the Trials due to lack of coins or becoming lost, the Terminal would release a terrible pack of a wolf-like beasts called Rougarou to tear apart the remaining trainees wandering the island. It was either success or death.

The second phase was aerial combat, plain and simple. The trainee bought a sloop with the coin from the first trial. During this phase, the only objective was to kill or be killed. The whole island was open for combat. Each kill equaled one coin.

A trainee must shoot down four other trainees to gain four coins and access to the gateway on top of the island's volcano that led to the third and final phase before the Victor's Circle. The price of admission through the gateway was the five coins earned through the first two trials.

The third and final phase was mysterious and changed each year.

All these concepts and comprehensive material took me a few weeks to master. By the end of the textbook, I knew I was prepared.

In my heart of hearts, I felt during those months the Traders Terminal was evil for subjecting me to this terrible test. Who did this to people? Sure, I could've escaped at any moment, run away to a distant land using one of those sloops. But I told myself, *No! I chose this.* I genuinely felt I could pass the Trials.

Those sloops played an integral part of the Trials. I had experience with flying, so I should have a leg up. For the other trials, I analyzed how past trainees had failed. They usually ended up impaled or cut in half by a minosblade. Worse, a trainee could cough up his or her lungs from exposure to mustard gas.

I had to think outside the box, a game plan that would save my ass. I remembered that Fitzroy had stressed repetition. I needed to continue to train and study each day without missing a beat. Through hard work, I should, God-willing, achieve victory.

CHAPTER 9

Zhen and the Sloop Dance

I TYPICALLY STARTED my training with Zhen in late afternoon
every Monday and Friday at the hangar next to the town. The
hangar was where all things mechanical were serviced. A few
buildings along an airstrip formed the hangar. In one of those buildings, Zhen taught me the ins and outs of the mechanical aspects of
the business.

As Zhen observed, I tinkered with sloops and a special type of
armor worn in contested zones and during the Series Trials. It was
called the minos-assault body armor system, or just minos-armor. The
armor implements the energy within minosium, changing the state of
warfare in the contested zones and in the Series Trials.

Minosium powered a suit of slim ceramic plates with a wide
range of motion. The minosium offered an invisible barrier, almost like
a vibrant force field around the armor. These companies were clever
and conjured up some pretty amazing technological advancements
utilizing minosium.

The invisible barrier powered by the minosium could deflect
incoming bullets to a degree. Flying shrapnel and bullets would be
deflected, but the invisible shield would be able to stop continuous
penetration, as from a machine gun. The only type of weapon that
could easily pierce through the armor was a minosblade or, well, large
missiles.

The headpiece of the suit had a transparent glass for the face.
Each suit was painted a different color; some were pure black, others
were a mix of different colors and designs, like painted floral. *How in-*

teresting, I thought. *Warfare has gone back to the time of knights in shining armor fighting with long swords.*

Zhen taught me the inner workings of the suit. I won't go into the schematics of the armor and blade. Zhen kept the information light with me. He mostly taught me how to wear it, fix the suit or blade if damaged, and how to use its embedded features.

The suit was a tight fit, high tech, and not too hot because of an internal cooling agent powered by the minosium. Other than the suit, Zhen wanted me to focus on the sloop, the main component of phase two of the Series Trials: aerial combat.

After four long weeks of continuously maintaining, cleaning, and tweaking these high-flying dodgers, I was ready to get my hands on one. I couldn't wait to hit the sky.

Zhen finally allowed me to fly one after persistent agitation on my part. He relented, and I finally got my chance. I was sitting in a sloop for my first time on the open runway next to the turquoise ocean with the shining sun above.

"Don't be scared in the sky. Trust the vehicle," Zhen said through the radio.

"Got ya, Zhen," I replied as I clicked the buttons to start the sloop.

"Remember: Not too high. Right above the tree line. Nothing more. Keep the sloop in cruising mode."

"Yep."

"Oh, and one more thing, you crash, and it's your head on the pole! Not mine."

"I'll do my best."

The four propellers on the sloop roared, and the back jet rumbled. This aircraft was quite loud. The electric blue lights that lined the body of the sloop lit up.

Damn, I thought. *I've been waiting for a chance to swirl this baby around. It's been too long since I've been in the sky.*

I floored it upward. The sloop jolted upward with great ferocity, almost stopping my heart from excitement. I grabbed the steering wheel, gripping it tightly with my hands.

This was going to be a good one. I smiled. Adrenaline poured through my veins. I turned the wheel to the side. The sloop jolted unnaturally to the right, turning upside down. Thankfully, I was strapped in. I could see Zhen with his glasses reflecting the sunlight, screaming words in Japanese mixed with English at me. I grabbed the wheel, turned the sloop upright.

"My bad. I got it now!" I screamed below to Zhen with a smile and thumbs up.

Zhen was going stark raving mad below, worried I would crash the sloop. He was telling me over the radio to bring it down. I acted like I couldn't hear him. I gripped the wheel and stared forward. I had been waiting for this.

For one brief moment, I thought of Axelrod. Over the past month, I'd completely forgotten about my past life at home because I'd been so focused on my training and studying. Axelrod would be happy for me right now, seeing me live out my dream flying high on some exotic island.

A wave of excitement and power came over me; I pushed the throttle. The jet roared, and the sloop went zero to sixty miles per hour within a second. I gripped the wheel, pushing her into the sky, flying over the jungle and around the volcano, and hovering no more than six feet over ocean. I could see my reflection in the clear, crystal blue water. The more I looked, I saw magnificent orange coral reefs. A tear trickled down from my eyes as I whirled that bad boy over the water.

This deep, magical feeling brought me back to my days at home. Nothing felt more right than being in the sky. It was a high point for me and showed what progress I'd made. When I landed back at the hangar, I excitedly jumped out. Waiting for me was Zhen with a long bamboo stick. He whacked me with it, hitting my right arm!

"What did I do?" I yelled as I tried to cover my face.

"You did not listen to me!" he yelled. "I said bring her down, and you no listen! You must listen, Doughboy, or you die like the rest of them!"

"You're right. I should have listened. Fitzroy told me the same thing. I'm sorry, Zhen. I guess I still have a long way to go."

A smile slowly crept on his face.

"Good. Now get going. We have flight lessons next week. Don't be late," smiled Zhen.

"I won't be," I replied.

That was a good day. Throughout those couple of months, most of what Zhen and I worked on was flying sloops. In exchange for helping me, I helped him maintain and clean the sloops, suits, swords, and airships. It was a job I enjoyed. Zhen was impressed that I was able to quickly pick up the gist of flying and fixing the sloops the more I showed him my ability to learn quickly and fix things on the spot.

CHAPTER 10

Wildcat and the Game Dance

O N OTHER DAYS, I trained with Wildcat out in the jungle. His training was unique. I was more like his partner in crime in whatever he was doing. He gave me a few books to read about extraction and the process of mining minosium though he told me I wouldn't have to learn the complicated figuring to extract it. Instead, he advised me to learn how to seek out minosium and drill it from the tchouplite.

His training went as follows: He took me hunting using a classic rifle. I carried my own rifle and backpack containing a special drill that required two hands to use.

I'd never used a firearm, let alone a rifle, in my life. Wildcat loved hunting and everything about the whole process. He loved to talk the whole time, too.

To begin, we would go to the shooting range outside of town. I occasionally caught Rabbit Run working on his shot at the range with a few of the Nantucket privateers assisting him. For at least an hour, Wildcat and I fired at different targets from a variety of yards.

At the shooting range, he taught me everything there was to know about a rifle: how to shoot it, reload it, clean it, etc. At first, I had a hard time firing the rifle. I was a little nervous, especially of its kick. Eventually, I got the hang of it and began to nail a few bullseyes.

Wildcat always cheered when I hit the bullseye. One time, Jeremiah and Marlow showed up with their guns. Jeremiah had a large assault rifle.

"Hey, hey, hey," smiled Jeremiah. "Check out my new toy!"

Wildcat laughed at Jeremiah. "What do you need an assault rifle for?"

"I told him he didn't need it," interjected Marlow.

"Give it a hold, Christoph," stated Jeremiah as he placed it in my hand.

I aimed it at the target.

"It's not for show," exclaimed Jeremiah. "Hit that target."

I fired at a target two hundred yards away. I hit it right in the bullseye.

"Weehoo!" Wildcat remarked. "Nice shootin', partner."

"Good shot, Swift," said Marlow as he smoked a cigarette.

"I like it. It has some kick to it," I smiled.

"She'll be good for this season," said Jeremiah as he took the gun from my hand.

Walking up to the gun range, I could see Spurwink, Pochick, Cudweed, and Rabbit Run. By his gaze and mannerisms, I could tell Rabbit Run wasn't too fond of me. If I had to give a reason why, it would be none other than I was his competition in the company.

As these thoughts passed through my mind, I started to see Rabbit Run resembling a figure from my past that I thought was removed by the continued setting sun. He brought to the surface my old feelings of Tony Torino and the Pack from Louisiana. Tony had drifted far from my mind, and yet seeing Rabbit Run and the Nantucket outfit brought out forgotten emotions. They were eerily the same to me as Tony Torino and the Pack, who had come back to haunt me.

I believed what I had experienced during my days at St. Francis was a phenomenon, uniquely limited to that terrible environment that I was subjected to. As I laid my eyes upon the combatant Rabbit Run, a realization sparked in my mind: What if there's always an enemy, a Tony Torino, a Pack in my life, and no matter where I went in this world, these people and situations would exist? If it were true, then I must tackle this problem head-on before it becomes the same situation as in my ghostly past.

"Tucks want a piece of this action!" exclaimed Jeremiah. "Well, I'll show them. Hey! What brings the Tucks around here?"

Spurwink with his intense gaze smiled at Jeremiah.

"We want no trouble, Spurwink," said Wildcat.

"Is that so?" replied Spurwink in a deep tone. "We're here to shoot. Nothing more."

"Did us dirty at the fire circle," said Jeremiah. "We voted for Rabbit Run."

"I thank thee for that," replied Spurwink. "Your trainee just wasn't the best fit. Did what we thought was best."

"Best . . . Best, eh?" questioned Jeremiah. "Hear this, everyone. Spurwink and I had a bet at the Sinbad Tavern. I wagered Christoph would make it on the ship without help; Spurwink said not. Needless to say, his coins enlarged my pocket." Jeremiah hit his pocket with his hand, pointing it outward in a provocative fashion. He then pulled his fingers back. "While Spurwink's pocket became shallower than an inch." Jeremiah smiled at his own raunchy joke.

"Funny man," said Spurwink. "How about another bet if ye are so confident in your lad. Double or nothing, or is your pocket not as big as you once thought?"

The Nantucket outfit laughed at Spurwink's sly remark.

"Jeremiah, come now," sighed Wildcat. "What's the point?"

Jeremiah's face grew stern. "Shooting contest, one shot per person—three hundred yards, five hundred yards, seven hundred yards, one thousand yards. "Our outfit against yours, four on four. What say ye?"

"Deal, Mister Big Pocket," smiled Spurwink. "Oh, and one condition."

"Yes?" replied Jeremiah with a raised eyebrow.

"Trainees shoot for the one thousand yards," said Spurwink.

Jeremiah laughed. "Sounds fine with me, Specksynder."

Wildcat sighed, but Jeremiah felt confident in our abilities.

"One thousand yards?!" I exclaimed to Wildcat. "I'm not sure about that."

"Look down the sights, control your breathing, and you'll hit it," replied Wildcat.

Marlow and Cudweed went first, firing at three hundred yards. They both hit their targets. The pressure began to mount inside my stomach. I felt like this was a test of my worth. Wildcat and Pochick went next, five hundred yards away. Wildcat went up first, aimed his rifle, fired, and missed! Pochick hit the target spot on. The Tucks laughed.

"Not looking good," smiled Pochick.

"Shut your face," replied Wildcat.

Spurwink and Jeremiah went next, seven hundred yards away. Spurwink, with great confidence, aimed his rifle, fired, and missed! We had a chance now. Jeremiah aimed his rifle, fired, and nailed it. We all cheered.

"That's right!" exclaimed Jeremiah. "You got this, Swift."

My palms were sweating from the tension, making it harder to hold on to the rifle. Rabbit Run and I were next to each other, aiming our rifles one thousand yards away. I could barely see the target in the distance. I looked into my scope and saw the circular bullseyes dead ahead.

"You weren't cut out for this," whispered Rabbit Run as he looked down his sights.

I was shocked that he said such a thing to me. Indeed, my suspicions were true. His voice resembled the devil of my past, Tony Torino. At once, I thought this was a dream, a nightmare more so. No, it was not.

Rabbit Run was real, in the flesh, speaking to my past self, causing doubt to resurface in my mind. He echoed the feelings that drove me to my deepest despair. In the bleak darkness of a moment that felt an eternity, I broke through the deep abyss of doubt.

I told myself never again would I let this dark entity fill my head with lies. My mind had grown since then, stronger than ever before. Confidence filled that once-dark void. I must attack this situation.

I turned to him and said, "Back, ye demon, for I rarely miss when I aim right!"

"Demon?" echoed Rabbit Run. "Pull your tongue back, boy. You made an enemy out of me today."

"Keep the air in your lungs before you say one more stupid thing," I replied.

I looked through my scope, keeping my hand steady, and pulled the trigger . . . Hit! I nailed the one thousand-yard shot. The whole outfit erupted with cheers. I smiled at my success. Rabbit Run, upon seeing my victory, hastily aimed his rifle, fired it, and missed.

On that day, Jeremiah won the bet, and I solidified my worth to the Nantucket outfit, better known by Jeremiah as the Tucks. I learned on the shooting range to stay focused on the target at hand, even when scorpions tried to sting me.

On that same day after the shooting range, Wildcat and I went out on a hunt for wild animals. Wildcat was meticulous in the way he taught me to hunt. He told me to always pay close attention to movement in the shrubs. For hours, we searched for a hog but came up short, as usual. We rested upon a rock to drink and eat a small snack. It was there when Wildcat told me how he got into the minosium business.

"So where did you get the name Wildcat from?" I asked.

"I think I told you this before," said Wildcat, "about my dad in the oil industry back in Texas?"

"You've mentioned it to me before," I replied as I took a sip out of my canteen.

"Right. Well, my great-granddaddy Floyd was an oil man back in the day. He made his fortune during the wildcat days in the early 1930s. Wildcat oil basically stood for searching for oil in unexplored places. Floyd struck oil in the middle of nowhere. Soon after, he bought the surrounding land, and my family grew wealthy.

"I am an explorer, just like Great-granddaddy Floyd. This time I'm seeking minosium, not oil. That's how I got the name Wildcat. Sadly, my family's oil reserves dried up by the time I came around, and crude oil prices dropped far below a reasonable market price.

"My father knew a few well-connected people and got me into the minosium business. I started out as a privateer under Kalendar. He liked me because I knew so much about oil and because of his relationship with my father. Kalendar thought my knowledge of exploratory oil programs just might come in handy for finding untapped minosium."

"So you inspect the land," I interjected.

"Yessir."

"Have any clue where to find more minosium for the new season?"

"I've been doing some research and my own figuring. Hot springs are near impossible to find on their own. I would have to use seismic waves and all other sorts of fancy devices to maybe—yes, *maybe*—stumble upon a hot spring containing tchouplite."

"I take it you found a way to find it."

"Indeed, I've found that certain creatures are drawn to tchouplite—better yet, tchouplite in a hot spring."

"Do tell."

Wildcat leaned in, as if he'd found the secret to life. "I believe these creatures called kilbits, small glowing worms, are attracted to the tchouplite containing the minosium."

"I see, then if the worms are nearby, then tchouplite is nearby. Therefore, minosium is nearby."

"Bullseye!" exclaimed Wildcat.

"Do we know why these glowing worms like the tchouplite?"

"I believe they feed off the minosium's radiation, giving them their glowing, fluorescent color. You see, the tchouplite has been eroded over time, allowing it to be soft enough for a little kilbit worm to feed off the energy source and the nutrients in the hot spring."

"Genius!" I proclaimed. "But where can we find these worms?"

"Inside dark caverns, hanging from the roof of the cave. If you see them, that means minosium is nearby."

"There are mountains on this island, so why not start here?"

"You're right. I believe they are on this island," exclaimed Wildcat as he pulled a geographic map out of his backpack. "I found an entrance to a vast cavern system below us. That's where I'll start. Do you want to come? It might be dangerous. I've heard sea serpents live down there." He smiled jokingly.

"Sure," I replied. "I'll be ready."

I enjoyed my time spent with Wildcat and the hunts we went on. I was eager to see the caverns below. It sounded like fun, and the possibility of seeing glowing worms and minosium amped me up.

CHAPTER 11

Prince Rock and the Offer Dance

M Y NEXT TRAINER was Prince Rock. His job was to teach me everything I needed to know about how the Victoria & Co. conducted business since I would be the one to trade the minosium on the exchange floor. Prince Rock's duty during the extraction process was to assist in the drilling, weigh the minosium by scale, and document the logistics of the project.

Prince Rock knew down to the cubic meter how much minosium would bring on the market, making him an asset when meeting with potential clients prior to the beginning of the season. Typically, the outfit and person came to an agreement before the start of the season. They signed a deal obligating each other to their agreement.

So it goes that when the season started, the outfit extracted the minosium and traded it with that said person at the Terminal. Prince Rock served as our specialist for trading minosium.

I went to him every other day. His office was essentially a massive treehouse, supported by large beams and trees. It was an architectural masterpiece. It was on the outskirts of town, overlooking the ocean on a cliff. This provided easy access for clients to come to and fro from the island. This structure comprised three separate buildings connected by wooden bridges.

A clear glass elevator brought me from the ground to the house. Weaving through the treetops, the treehouse was made mostly of glass windows and wood. I stepped onto a wooden platform from the elevators.

The roof was white and conformed to the pattern of the trees.

The main section of the structure was an old wooden schooner renovated with glass windows, two floors, and a balcony and placed in between the trees. It was covered with beautiful greenery and colorful hibiscus flowers that gently twirled themselves around the boat.

Next to the treehouse was a landing pad for incoming sloops. This was our outfit's base of operations elevated in the sky. Prince Rock and his privateers handled all the trading intricacies for our outfit.

Aluma handled the bookkeeping for the company, and she reported the outfit's balance sheets and activity to Helga, so nothing could happen under the table. Obasa and Cortez serviced the treehouse and the needs of visiting clients.

My job was to keep record of our outfit's personal inventory and learn how business was conducted during the off-season. I would report our outfit's activities to Aluma and Fitzroy. All information flowed to Fitzroy since he was our Registered Extractor and would conduct our prearranged trades at preset prices. The reason this was crucial for the Series Trials was to understand the process of the trade during the off-season.

One day in particular stood out to me. We were meeting with a representative of Capeltronics, a company that specialized in computer chips. Usually Prince Rock, Aluma, and I went to the meetings, but Fitzroy thought this was important enough for him to attend.

The representative of the company landed on the helipad. He was a pale man with brown, slicked-back hair. He wore sunglasses and a suit and carried a briefcase. The helicopter pulled away, and he came up to us. His name was Gibson. We brought the meeting to our open-air office at the top floor, granting a beautiful view of the sea.

Aluma brought out cucumber waters for everyone. Business was a nice change-up from the usual physical training. We sat in elegant wooden chairs around a table at the center of the room. Fitzroy opened the meeting, welcomed Gibson to the island, and gave brief small talk. Then, business began.

"Mr. Gibson," said Fitzroy. "As I represent my outfit, tell me, what brings you here today?"

Gibson placed his cup on the table.

"What any man wants," smiled Gibson. "Minosium."

"Are you cleared with the Terminal?" asked Prince Rock.

Gibson pulled out a piece of paper and handed it to Aluma. "Of course, we are," said Gibson, "and I'm cleared to trade on the floor."

"He's approved," Aluma stated.

"Good," Fitzroy said. "So why would a computer chip corporation seek out minosium?"

"Imagine this," said Gibson. "The power of minosium inside a computer chip. Think of what it could do to our computers or cloud services. Our computers would be lightning fast, able to process incredible amounts of data in an instant. What if minosium could be the secret to artificial intelligence?"

"Like robots?" I interjected.

Gibson smiled. "Yes, like robots, or better yet, digital weapons, like a digital virus. Let your mind go free on the potential of what can be done with minosium and the profit that could be had for your outfit and the Victoria & Co. as a whole."

"What are you offering in exchange, Mr. Gibson?" Fitzroy asked speculatively.

"We want you to trade half a season's worth of minosium to us in return for stock in our company," Gibson replied.

"Half?" Prince Rock shouted. "Twenty-five percent!"

"Half," remarked Gibson.

"Thirty-two percent," said Prince Rock. "That's a fair value for stock in a business development company."

"No, half," Gibson said.

"Calm down," Fitzroy interjected.

"This could be a lot of money for us, Fitzroy," Prince Rock insisted.

"I understand," said Fitzroy.

"I respect your company," stated Gibson, "especially the great outfit led by Fitzroy. Know this: I give this offer only once. I have other buyers dying for a chance."

"Who?" exclaimed Prince Rock.

"Belle-Claire," stated Gibson.

"Ugh," shrugged Prince Rock. "Belle-Claire . . ."

Fitzroy stood up. "Your offer is very generous, but I do not accept it."

"Why?" asked Gibson.

"I do not have a good feeling about your company," said Fitzroy. "I do not believe the Terminal would accept your proposal. More importantly, trading minosium for potentially harmful purposes goes against my ethics and those of Victoria & Co. I respect you and your company, Mr. Gibson. Perhaps in the future we may come to a more fruitful deal. Obasa, would you please show him out?"

Gibson was furious with anger. "The world is changing. Best not stand in the way of progress."

Obasa led Gibson out of the room, and he boarded his helicopter.

"Who's Belle-Claire?" I asked.

"Our leading competitors," replied Aluma.

Fitzroy stared out the window, watching Gibson's helicopter disappear into the distance.

"That could have been a lot of money," said Prince Rock.

"Or a lot of suffering," replied Fitzroy as he knitted his eyebrow.

CHAPTER 12

Jeremiah and the Bar Dance

THE LAST MEMBER of the outfit I had the honor of training with was Jeremiah. Good ole Jeremiah, such a delightful character. He was the best fighter of the outfit—an expert swordsman, a martial artist, and a top-notch spear fisherman. Jeremiah was a man who has been everywhere in the world during his years aboard the *Victoria* airship.

At each port, he made a new friend with his positive attitude, and he acquired a new skill. He fenced in France; dueled with short, curved blades in Turkey; wrestled in the streets of Rio de Janeiro; cut through air with a katana in Japan; and practiced yoga by way of India. He had a story to tell for days—with a drink or two to accompany it.

Jeremiah lived in his small boat connected to the dock outside the town. Jeremiah had a classic boat, all wood with a white deck and a small cabin. His ship was outfitted with steel plates to protect it from misfortune on the high seas. He loved his boat more than he loved any woman, until he had a drink or two.

His boat was spotless. Its wood glistened in the sun. Marlow was the bossier of the vessel and helped Jeremiah with everything he did, most especially spearfishing. On the ship, Jeremiah dressed in a white skipper hat, a tattered burgundy vest, and brown pants and wore abnormally large and showy 1980s-style, Miami-esque sunglasses.

He had a rugged look about him, ebony skin with great stature, strong and broad shoulders. He always smelled of fish, the sea, and rum.

Marlow was from Savannah, Georgia and no more than twenty-nine years old. I had to think about what he looked like that day: a skinny lad with a bird-like face, a pointed nose, and pale skin, but he was a little sun-kissed from the water. Marlow always rocked those multicolor Acapulco shirts while wearing large shades that added to his stoic attitude.

During those first months, I met with Jeremiah down on the dock every other day early in the morning. There was one day that I remembered:

I stood on the dock before our disembarkation. I caught glimpses of the Tucks preparing their medium-sized fishing vessel. The body of their vessel was red with a white deck. It had a large observation deck with at least five windows in a row. It had an assortment of nets, lines, and storage.

Rabbit Run gave me a look of distaste when we locked eyes. Funny how competition drives such division among other men. Jeremiah came next to me.

"Aye," suggested Jeremiah. "It's not about the size of their boat that matters, but the crew that works it."

"That is a big boat though," I replied.

"Eh, I like mine more, and besides, Tucks fish as well as they shoot. Not well. Let's go."

Jeremiah and Spurwink exchanged words any time their ships crossed paths. I never saw Rabbit Run training. Rabbit Run appeared to be growing larger in size and stronger by the day, and so was I.

We disembarked the dock and set out for our fishing spot. Jeremiah brought the ship around the island to a small outlet. It was beautifully clear. We pulled out a few spearguns, and my training began.

Jeremiah set the boat near a cliff to observe the shallow turquoise water. He took off his vest, grabbed his spearfishing gun, and hopped into the water without any diving equipment besides a pair of goggles.

I had no idea how to use a speargun before those days of training. I'd had some familiarity using a rifle with Wildcat, so my aim was precise. As for the speargun, it took me a couple tries to get the hang of it. The gun was simple: it fired a spear underwater. Jeremiah demanded that I should not use any type of equipment, only my natural lungs and the gun.

In order to keep up with Jeremiah, I had to learn to breathe underwater for extended periods of time. A few of those times, I almost passed out underwater trying to keep pace with him. Jeremiah was a master swimmer, able to hold his breath underwater for long durations. Marlow stayed on the ship to assist Jeremiah and me in case anything went wrong in the water.

"Yes, yes. We go under, catch a few, and be back before the Tucks," said Jeremiah.

"Peachy," I replied.

"I'm seeing lots of big fish on the radar, more than usual. Why you think, Jeremiah?" asked Marlow, staring at the sonar next to the steering wheel.

"The Most High is giving us this day. Receive thy manna," exclaimed Jeremiah, diving into the crystal clear turquoise water.

"Keep an eye out, Swift," remarked Marlow.

I gave him a thumbs up and dived into the water. Jeremiah loved swimming near a magnificent coral reef filled with fish of all different sizes and colors. Those reefs were the large cities of the sea, harboring life to the greatest extent.

Swimming out of the tentacle path of a large purple jellyfish, I bypassed an entanglement. In my haste to avoid the poisonous fish, I accidentally bumped up against the orange coral reef. It was incredibly rocky and sharp. A piece of the coral cut my arm, letting out the scent of red blood. The pain wasn't too severe.

I could see two yellow eyes hiding in the reef and staring at me. It looked like an eel waiting for me to draw near. I had to swim up for another breath of air. Gasping for a few bits of oxygen on the surface, I dived down once more.

I saw Jeremiah a few yards away, aiming his speargun at a large tuna. After a few seconds, the spear shot from his gun, hitting the tuna in the fin. It was a massive blue fish refusing to go down without a fight. Blood filled the water as the tuna attempted to free itself from the spear. Jeremiah was pulling with all his might, causing more blood to spill into the water. I debated whether to assist Jeremiah as I swam in the water.

Strike!

A large predator grazed me from behind, sneaking up on me. It was a reef shark, trying to bite my arm. The reef shark swam back into the dark blue water, disguising his whereabouts.

My heart was pounding as adrenaline poured through my veins.

I narrowly escaped a damaging bite that could have taken my arm clean from the bone.

Then out of the corner of my eye, I saw at least ten different types of sharks, including one tiger shark, all heading right for Jeremiah as he struggled to catch his prey. Jeremiah was completely oblivious to the incoming predators. He was too fixated on reeling in the massive tuna.

I was running out of breath, but I couldn't go to the surface. I had to alert Jeremiah before he became fish bait. I swam further down to meet him. The sharks were moving closer to us, now coming from all angles of the reef. The small fish hid in corridors of the reef to avoid slaughter. More and more sharks swam toward the blood red water.

I'd never seen so many sharks in one place. I was petrified as I realized my chance of survival was dwindling by the second. I swam as fast as I could to reach Jeremiah, grab his attention, and point to the incoming sharks.

Jeremiah was startled, trying to figure out a way to safety. A school of sharks began to swim all around us. I pulled out the amulet around my neck, gripping it with fear. My breath was fading by the minute. The large tiger shark drew near to us.

Amazingly, my amulet began to glow red! I'd never seen my amulet do this. Incredible! The red was majestic, projecting outward. The sharks dispersed the moment the magnetic red light emitted from my amulet.

Jeremiah and I, upon realizing there was an opportunity for safety, swam to the surface. Marlow pulled the boat up to us, and we climbed aboard.

We gasped desperately to give our lungs air. I was still in shock, trying to come to terms with the dangers barely escaped. Marlow stared at my glowing amulet with fixed eyes, wide in astonishment.

"What in the world?" exclaimed Marlow.

The light on the amulet dimmed back to its original state.

"It's . . . never done that before," I replied as I struggled to catch my breath.

Jeremiah grabbed my amulet and stared at it intently. "I've never seen magic like this or the markings it bears."

"Looks Egyptian," interjected Marlow.

"No," Jeremiah replied. "This be different. Dark magic."

"I've had it my whole life," I said. "It's never glowed red."

"Where did ye get this?" asked Jeremiah with great perplexity.

"A family heirloom," I replied.

"I wonder . . . " Jeremiah raised his eyebrow. "Impossible," he remarked quietly to himself.

"What is it?" I asked, concerned.

"Keep it to thyself," said Jeremiah. "Tell no one of its properties."

This incident dwelled with me for a while. Returning to the dock, I was speechless. My mind could not rest on account of nearly avoiding death and the questionable glowing agent that hung around my neck. I pondered the thought for days on end: *Why do I have this amulet, and what is its significance?*

The sharks swam away from us when the amulet glowed red. My mind grew angry from the questions regarding Axelrod, who my parents were, and how they are tied to the Traders Terminal, which all filled my head. I wanted to tell Jeremiah all these issues, but he refused to listen, saying to keep those things to myself for now and that time would reveal what needs to be known. Jeremiah and Marlow never told a soul of the events that day.

I believed Jeremiah saw that amulet as something far greater than he was and debated as to whether it was worth involving himself in my affairs. The amulet seemed to hold a power tied to an unknown origin, linking my past life to this new one.

It was becoming more difficult to distinguish what could be real in this world the more I pondered the events unfolding before me. At times, it drove me mad, questioning my own existence and purpose within this astonishing new world, different than my questioning of my days in Louisiana. It was best, I concluded, to let my eventual flower bloom in secrecy in its own time, as Jeremiah stated. I would know the right time to reveal the connection of the story of my past to this present, like a constellation of stars in the outer spheres of time and space.

In my training with Jeremiah, we also practiced swordsmanship on the boat. The first day of sword training at sea went as follows:

Jeremiah tossed a fencing sword to me. The boat swayed back and forth. The waters were so rough that day, I barely had enough balance to stand up, let alone with a fencing sword.

"Best way to learn sword is on rough waters," Jeremiah told me.

"Are you mad?" I exclaimed. "We always practiced on calm water or, well, calmer water."

"Do you want to survive the Trials?"

"Yes, but—"

"You will always fight in less-than-favorable conditions, so best be prepared. Now, *en garde!*"

Jeremiah drew his sword, and we clashed our swords back and forth. It was there on those rough waters where I learned how to use a blade adequately. The only downside of it all was that I could never keep a shirt on out on that boat. I received some of the worst sunburns of my entire life during those months; those yellow bumps of pus all over my back made me shudder just thinking about them.

One of the most enjoyable aspects of training with Jeremiah was the fun we had after our daily training. Once docked, we went to the only bar on the island on the edge of town. It was completely serviced by privateers.

It was a tiki bar composed of a long wooden bar with roped railings and carvings of the different gods, all lit by a variety of exotic lanterns from across the world. It was quite impressive. Helga ran the bar with her privateers and made a killing from that place. Helga owned the whole market and was always there, overseeing the cash register and her privateers.

It got wild up in that joint. Since most of the privateers were young, it didn't shock me that few privateers left the island for the off-season. The summer months were like spring break for them. The only difference was that these privateers were from all over the world and made enough money to throw at drinks. I didn't blame them. Why would they leave? It was a tropical paradise here, and some of those women privateers got my blood hot.

Jeremiah loved the tiki bar. He went there every single night. He drank a lot, sang along to the songs, and hit on the women, especially Helga.

One night, Jeremiah was talking to an older male privateer at one of the tables in a secretive manner. I noticed them exchange objects with one another under the table. Jeremiah took a shot with him and walked back to our table.

"Ye, ye, ye," smiled Jeremiah.

"What was that about?" asked Marlow.

"Gold, boys," replied Jeremiah.

"Gold?" I remarked.

"Shh . . . A map to the gold. Keep it on the down low. How about another drink for you two before I start?"

"If you must," shrugged Marlow in a stark tone, "but I never like deals with privateers."

"Nonsense," exclaimed Jeremiah. "You are a privateer. What's the difference?"

"I don't make deals," said Marlow.

Jeremiah shook his head and went to the bar to get us a drink.

"Why the sketchiness?" I inquired.

"No one on this island can keep a secret," stated Marlow as he took a drag of his cigarette.

I looked around the bar curiously, seeing if anyone was eaves-dropping. I then noticed Rabbit Run and the Tucks were there. The Tucks were always engaged at the tiki bar; drinking, socializing, and gambling were the quintessential pastimes of the group.

My eyes drifted toward the bar, and there seated in an elegant fashion with her back upright, brown hair curled around her shoulders, was Aluma. She was the hot issue of the bar as all men converged upon her. I even caught Jeremiah take a glance and smile at her.

"Stay away from her," warned Marlow.

"What? Who?" I asked, surprised.

"Aluma. I see how you look at her. Stay away."

"It's not like that," I insisted. "Besides, why should I stay away from her?"

Marlow took another puff of his cigarette. "Privateers talk. She's gone to the dark side. That's all I'll say."

"Dark side?"

Jeremiah returned with a round of dark amber rum shots. I was a distressed by what Marlow had said, so I took a sip of this dark sailor's drink of cane sugar. Down the hatch it went without a chaser nearby. It was terrible. I almost threw up from the intensity of the alcohol, burning my throat as it went down.

"So, so, so, tell me young lad . . . Like the rum?" Jeremiah smiled.

"I want," I said as I coughed, "more."

"Aye, his eyes are blood red," laughed Jeremiah. He then hit me on the back as he took a swig himself.

"A drink of the seas and seafaring men," laughed Jeremiah. "You'll get used to this amber, Swift. I started drinking the devil's gold when I was only fourteen years old. The more ye drink, the better thee feel." Jeremiah took another swig of rum. "Eh, bartender! Another round on the tab!" He banged the empty glass on the wooden table.

Marlow pulled out another cigarette. "Better slow down, partner."

"Me? Slow down?" laughed Jeremiah, "Not with a midsummer's night like this! Fine work today for each of ye. I say fish today, gold tomorrow."

"You can't trust them privateers, Jeremiah," Marlow sighed.

"Blasphemous," cried Jeremiah. "The gold is in the mountain, buried within an old temple of some sort. We're going to find out."

"Gold? Here? No way," interjected Marlow.

"We didn't have trouble finding jewels in the Valley of Kings," insisted Jeremiah, "or the magical vases of Arabia blessed by King Solomon himself. This be no different. Easier, in fact."

"I agree," replied Marlow, "but we found them far from Terminal zones."

"I thought you two were joking," I laughed. "Gold? Vases? Jewels? The drink must be in the veins."

They both looked at me as if I said a tune of madness or was a child never seen beyond his or her gate.

"What ye mean, lad?" Jeremiah asked.

"You two sound like treasure hunters," I replied. "The map you referred to must be a jest."

"*You're* a jest," stated Marlow without emotion.

"Ah, let me assist," said Jeremiah. "We hunt for jewels in the off times using our sound equipment. Don't forget: minosium is a jewel nonetheless."

My face slowly turned at the realization they were telling the truth.

"Amazing . . . as if in my dreams," I said.

"Pinch yourself, for it's true," smiled Jeremiah.

"Count me in!" I cheered.

Jeremiah gestured for me to quiet down. "I knew ye be on board. Now, let's take a look at the map."

Jeremiah pulled out an old map of the island, dated in the Year of Our Lord 1636. He looked inconspicuously over his shoulder. "As I said, it's a chamber of gold, hidden deep in the island."

"What kind of chamber?" I asked.

"The privateer said it was built by a wealthy Spanish merchant who did business in the Philippines. He stopped on Victoria Island on the way back to Veracruz. He needed a place to store his wealth and built this chamber. This map will lead us to it," Jeremiah suggested. "We go soon, gentlemen."

"And the Terminal?" said Marlow as if referring to a hole in Jeremiah's plan.

"Worry not," said Jeremiah. "They'll never know. Besides, we seek gold. Nothing more. We'll speak more on this later where ears cannot hear and eyes cannot gaze." Jeremiah quickly folded up the map.

From the corner of my eye, I noticed Prince Rock and Obasa. Upon seeing us, the two men with great excitement walked up to our table.

"I saw each of ye talking sternly. About what?" asked Prince Rock.

"About you overworking my poor trainee Christoph here," suggested Jeremiah.

"I know that look," smiled Prince Rock. "You're hiding something from me."

"From you?" Jeremiah replied. "Never!"

"I wager you have something worthy to address," Prince Rock challenged.

"Nay. Lay out the bet, and ye will come up short," Jeremiah said. "I have nothing but a few more shots to pour."

Prince Rock chuckled to himself. "A wager it is. Ten Trader Coins." He lifted the bag and placed it on the table.

Jeremiah's eyes became like those of a hungry lion about to strike a zebra. The temptation weighed heavily on Jeremiah, unable to resist the clinging of the coins or the thrill of the bet.

"Ten coins for what?" asked Jeremiah.

"Obasa carries the magical bones of his homeland," said Prince Rock. "He throws them, and the spirits tell him the secrets of the well."

"That's cheating!" remarked Jeremiah. "Dark magic, I say."

"The spirits reveal what they think is dear," interjected Obasa.

He pulled out of his backpack a small brown bag containing

the small bones of different animals. Jeremiah looked on with terror, worried his secret would be revealed.

"We're good friends, Jeremiah," smiled Prince Rock. "All I ask for is a piece of whatever ye find for the bones brought me here tonight."

Jeremiah thought hard for a moment, debating his trust with Prince Rock and the assurance of the bones.

"Aye, throw the bones!" said Jeremiah.

"Ten coins wagered if the bones prove me right," smiled Prince Rock.

"Aye," said Jeremiah.

Obasa took the small bag, shook the bones in his hands, said something indistinguishable, then flipped them onto the table. It was five small bones which seemed to be that of birds. He moved his hands over the bones. The table watched Obasa analyze the bones with great anxiety. Obasa stared with perplexity, unable to come to a prophecy.

"What does it say, Obasa?" Jeremiah asked eagerly.

"I can't read it," said Obasa.

"What?" remarked Prince Rock. "Shake it again."

Obasa continued to attempt to read the bones but came up with nothing. Obasa explained that a stronger power was at work, rendering the bones useless. Distressed, he couldn't fathom what this object could be. I wondered what object rendered the bones void, as did the rest of the table.

Needless to say, Jeremiah was happy to collect his earnings from the vexed Prince Rock and keep the secret of the map to himself. Prince Rock and Jeremiah bickered back and forth for a few minutes until the two men came to an impasse.

Moving past the wager of the bones, I in my drunken state became fixated on the object of my desire: Aluma. She moved across the bar in a light fashion like a butterfly landing on a flower. She was wearing a white dress that accented her olive skin beautifully.

"You're a fool, Swift!" exclaimed Marlow. "No experience."

"I assure ye I've had more girlfriends than you," I replied.

"If you're so sure of yourself, go take your shot, shooter," said Marlow as he took a swig of his rum.

I thought to myself that if I saw what I desired, I couldn't stop until I had it. My desires turned into an obsession. I was tired of being told no. This life was different from life back home. Anything was possible. I couldn't stand the word "no." Why should I not have the prettiest girl at the bar?

At that moment, Rabbit Run, who was seated at the bar, made a move on Aluma. Jeremiah analyzed me. As my hopes were let down, that strength inside of me deflated like a balloon letting out air. My shoulders changed from a straight posture to a slouched position.

Seeing me stare at Aluma with Rabbit Run, Jeremiah with his sly grin said, "Go! Get up there. Take a swing at it!"

Prince Rock laughed. "Anyone with eyes can see you're after Aluma."

"Not so!" I replied stubbornly as I took another shot of rum. By that point, I was really feeling the effects of the alcohol.

"Go up there, and give it an ole Trader's try," Jeremiah said.

"Trader's try?" I questioned.

"Aye. Like a Trader, go ask for the business. Barter your price, and if she refuses, at least ye did it," Jeremiah replied.

"Well, good luck with her. By the looks of it, she's a python. Best stay away from her, Doughboy," Prince Rock warned.

"The young and eager always hunt for the pythons until they're bitten and feel the venom run through their hearts," exclaimed Marlow. "Find a nicer one."

"I like that one," I replied. "What should I do? Rabbit has the higher ground on me."

Jeremiah chimed in. "Buy her a drink at the bar. Keep an eye out if she looks your way. If she doesn't, still bring her the drink. Be a man of few words. Then, come back and sit down."

I took a deep breath, took another shot, felt the wobble in my legs, and walked up to the bar. There were a few spots near Aluma and Rabbit Run. I awkwardly stared at them, waiting for my chance. I began to psych myself out, telling myself Rabbit Run already had her which, well, he did. Aluma never looked my way. Damn.

I ordered her some a shot of rum and made my way in between her and Rabbit Run.

"Thought a drink might do us well after dealing with Prince Rock," I said.

Rabbit Run had a look of distaste.

"Christoph! Yes, indeed. What kind of drink?" she asked.

"Rum."

"Just rum?"

"And ice ... What were you drinking?"

"A pineapple cocktail, but I'll give this rum a try."

She took a swig of it and had a horrible face of displeasure. "Good," she said faintly.

Rabbit Run chimed in. "We haven't had a formal introduction besides our little quarrel on the gun range. Forgive me for that day. Competition drives my blood hot. I'm Rabbit Run."

"Christoph Swift," I replied. "No hard feelings from the range?"

"Of course not. Lost fair and square."

"How's your training been? Feel ready for it?"

"It's been splendid. Been pumping iron and crushing the textbooks. I'm not worried. How's training been under Jeremiah?"

"Great. Why?"

"I couldn't stand him or anyone in your outfit for more than five minutes. All of us can't stand them."

"Your opinion, but they've trained me well."

"If you call running around a mountain, hunting in the bush, and dancing on a boat training, then I disagree," chuckled Rabbit Run.

"And what have you been doing?"

"I work out at the facility in town doing drills—sprints, weight training, stability and core, boxing, wrestling, and swordplay—all measured by state-of-the-art scientific instruments, which constantly analyze my heart rate, breathing, and movements. The old school way of running up hills is over."

"Now I know where you've been. I guess I'll take my chances with those hills."

"You have no idea what you're up against," said Rabbit Run. "Drop out. Save your life while you still can. Don't worry. Your outfit won't be around much longer anyway."

"Calm down, Rabbit Run," Aluma interjected.

"Why do you and the Tucks despise my outfit, eh?" I asked.

"It's full of unorganized clowns clinging to the old ways of doing things. Your unwillingness to change impedes the progress of the company and our profits. There's a reason my outfit is number one each year. There's a reason my brother is the Specksynder of this company. We want our larger cut that's due to us."

"You have no respect," I remarked.

"Watch what you say, Christoph," Aluma cut in.

"I thought more of you, Aluma," I replied.

"Who do you think you are, telling me that?" Aluma asked. "I was trying to be nice to you before this. You're a kid with no name set to die in the Trials. Get out of here."

Rabbit Run laughed. "Once again, your outfit brought in a trainee who is unqualified for this position, tossing him into death, just like with the last trainee. Do yourself a favor. Run, or they'll get you killed."

My blood was boiling with anger. I recalled the past, the feeling of exclusion and rejection. No, that would not enter my life once more.

"Ye know, I've dealt with people like you and Aluma my whole my life," I said. "It seems life is the same everywhere I go—the same people, the same arrogance, and the same fights to be fought. Know this both of ye: I will ascend like a phoenix from the ashes in due time, and my wings of flames shall burn thee to smithereens. Good day."

"Why wait for the Trials when I can end you right here?" demanded Rabbit Run.

He pushed Aluma away and attempted to grab the collar of my shirt. I quickly grabbed his arm. He tried to break free, but he couldn't break my grip. I stared at him with my fiery eyes.

Jeremiah and Prince Rock stepped into the scene to break it up. Spurwink and the Tucks quickly followed suit. Hostilities were high in the air.

"Let's all stay calm. No need for violence," Jeremiah exclaimed.

Spurwink stepped forward. The bar was silent.

"Keep your trainee away from my brother, or we'll have some serious issues," demanded Spurwink.

"We'll do our best," smiled Jeremiah.

"Best you do," replied Spurwink.

"Or what?" Jeremiah responded.

Spurwink fixed his eyes on Jeremiah. "What did you say?" he asked.

"I said, 'Or what?'" repeated Jeremiah.

Spurwink laughed then looked to the Tucks behind him. Then, he turned around and tried to punch Jeremiah. Jeremiah dodged, then jabbed him in the stomach. The whole bar was drawn into a fight.

Everyone was throwing jabs at each other. Privateer against privateer, Jeremiah and Prince Rock threw punches at the Tucks.

Rabbit Run made his way to me. He attempted to throw a stool at me. I dodged it, and we went at it. He and I were throwing punches left and right at each other. I was holding my own quite well. He had a hard time catching me. I was quite agile, able to dodge his moves. Rabbit Run eventually caught my neck and started to choke me up against a pillar. Rabbit Run's face was savagely beaten and bruised. I couldn't breathe as I struggled to free myself.

"I said unqualified!" Rabbit Run yelled.

At that moment, a glass bottle broke over Rabbit Run's head. He fell to the ground on impact. It was Marlow, still smoking his cigarette.

"Thought you needed help," said Marlow.

"Thanks," I replied.

Helga then fired a gun at the center of the bar. Everyone froze in the place. She yelled at everyone to clear out of the bar. Jeremiah had Cudweed in a choke hold and then let him loose.

"All of you, get out!" screamed Helga, "before I throw each and every one of you in the dungeon. Don't test me."

We all cleared out of the bar, each tending to our own wounds, avoiding any more contact with one another. A clear division was set between the Tucks and our own outfit. Other than that, I would say it was a good night at the end of it all.

Looking back in comparison to my old life in Louisiana, I was gaining a wide variety of friends from all different places of the world. Before, I'd never been part of anything special or felt the powerful feeling of inclusion. When I had my disagreements with the coaches and players on the basketball team, I was alone in fending off their attacks.

The only person who came to my aid was Arthur, but still, the weight of resentment from that high school world around me broke my legs and shoulders due to its heaviness. It contrasted with my time on Victoria Island where I was included in a company of incredible people of all different colors, shapes, and sizes. They accepted me as one of their own and defended me in my time of need.

That feeling of being accepted was unknown to my heart, but when my companions came to my defense at the bar, I could've cried in joy. It meant that I was accepted into their pack, and each one of these amazing people would fight with me no matter what.

It dawned on me that perhaps the world wasn't as gloomy or deadly as I previously thought. Instead, this new world around me must be changing or, rather, this old world inside of me was changing.

CHATPER 13

Waltz of the Bridge

I HAD BEEN training every day in my continuous cycle for the past three months. I felt much more mature than when I stepped foot on this island. I had improved my relationships with each person in the outfit. My muscles had grown, my skills had increased, my focus was centered. All I needed for the Trials was on the horizon.

By this point, I'd rarely encountered the Tucks since the brawl that night. My old life felt a world away, a distant memory. I was so focused on my goal of finally becoming an outfit member for the upcoming season that nothing else mattered in my mind. Little did I know what cunning fate had in store for me during my last weeks of training and the impact it would have across the celestial spheres.

Dawn rose upon her throne wearing a beautiful robe of fire to start the day. Fitzroy woke me up for our daily run around the island. I cracked a few raw eggs over orange juice, and we hit the trail up the volcano. Over the last month, I had made progress. I was now able to follow behind Fitzroy without stopping. Not only that, I could hold my own around the winding, deadly trail.

We moved incredibly fast through the narrow wilderness trails that cut in and out of the bush. Before this day, I would stumble on roots, scrape my knee on the rocks and stumps, hit my nose from a hanging limb; but now, things had changed. As I ran behind Fitzroy, I used my weight to tightly hug the rocks, scale large boulders covered in green vegetation, swing on the luscious vines from one plane to another. We came upon a part of the trail where five stumps stuck out of a small river in diagonal fashion, providing a platform to venture across the flowing river.

Fitzroy hastily jumped in elegance from one stone to the next, then waited for me on the other side of the river. I took a confident deep breath and dashed from one stone to the next. I almost lost my balance on the last smooth, slippery stone. Fitzroy grabbed my shirt in the nick of time with a smile, pulling me up, and we continued up the fiery volcano.

We approached another dangerous pass high up in the mountainous terrain. It was a wooden, roped bridge over a valley of water far below. The bridge was much too old to run over, and yet, that never stopped us. Fitzroy ran ahead of me and grabbed a sword from a lockbox situated next to the bridge, obviously placed there prior to this excursion.

Fitzroy then ran to the middle of the bridge, waiting for me to cross. He stared back at me with a twinkle in his eyes, preparing himself for a duel to the death. Fear was non-existent in his stature.

I grabbed an old steel sword from the lockbox and twirled it in my hand, feeling the edge of the blade cut through the air. I was the master of this blade and all who crossed swords with me would face the sharp edge of defeat.

I stepped on to the swaying bridge moving side to side as the wind cut across the valley. The sounds of leather stretching echoed across the hilltop with each step I took on the rickety bridge. I slowly moved toward Fitzroy, omitting any fear or flight in my mind. As I walked on each wooden board that made up the bridge, I stepped through one of the rotted pieces of wood, brittle as a dead leaf. I grabbed hold of the rope railing to keep myself from falling to my death.

Fitzroy was in a position ready to fight, so I approached him. Fitzroy drew his sword and screamed, "*En garde!*"

I knew there was no way I could outmaneuver him one on one. I knew I had to do something out of the ordinary and use my greatest weapon: my mind.

Feeling the wind sway the bridge, I decided to sway the bridge in a stronger fashion. The bridge started to rumble as the ancient ropes broke from the strain. Fitzroy flinched for a moment, attempting to assess the condition of the bridge.

Seizing that moment, I jumped forward with a scream, attempting to strike him with the bridge still vibrating from its decrepit state. I knew the only way I would have any sort of chance fighting Fitzroy would be by eliminating any fear I held deep inside.

We clashed swords, and the fight began. I was on the defensive, parrying his attacks. I struck him in the arm, and then he cut my left hand. We clashed together, meeting each other face to face. I screamed vigorously as my adrenaline skyrocketed.

The wooden planks broke with each step, leaving us only the roped sides. I clung to the side—utilizing hands, feet, and even my mouth—all while balancing myself and continuing to strike. At times, I was hanging under the bridge striking upward at Fitzroy's feet as he jabbed his blade below.

My strength was extraordinary, seeing that I could hold on the rope with one hand and still strike. Our swords met once more, locking each in place. Fitzroy had a fire in his eyes. He pushed me off and struck at my shirt, cutting through it while accidentally slicing a section of the roped bridge. I ripped off my shirt, revealing my amulet dangling upon my neck. Fitzroy's eyes were fixed on my amulet.

"The Amulet of Faustino!" he remarked.

The final ropes on the bridge began to pop and twist off from the blow delivered by Fitzroy. The bridge began to rumble like an earthquake as it was dismantling itself. I looked behind me. The whole bridge was unwinding.

"Run!" yelled Fitzroy.

We ran to the other side of the bridge, like monkeys jumping from treetop to treetop. All of the boards of the bridge were falling off behind us. The bridge then broke, causing Fitzroy and me to free fall. We hung onto the bridge for dear life. We hit the side of the rock; my heart was beating out of my chest. Fitzroy and I dangled from the bridge. He laughed.

"Why are you laughing?" I screamed as I clung to the boards of the bridge.

"What a day to be alive!" he replied.

A loud snap occurred at the top of the cliff. The bridge fell about a foot. The ropes were snapping off. My eyes went wide with fear.

"Climb!" screamed Fitzroy.

We climbed for our dear lives, using the remaining ropes; by the good Lord's grace, we made it to the top before the whole bridge fell to the rushing waters far below. I lay there to catch my breath.

Fitzroy hastily got up. "We're not done yet, Swift." He offered his hand, pulling me up, and we continued on the trail around the volcano until we arrived at the tiki temple. I finally was able to catch my breath. That was the hardest run I'd ever done in my life. The tiki temple was majestic as ever, filled with its carvings of their strange gods.

"You're almost ready for the Trials," smiled Fitzroy.

I was still trying to catch my breath. "I hope so. How much longer before the Trials?"

"Next month."

"Thank you, Fitzroy, for training me."

He nodded at me. "Now tell me, where did ye get that amulet?"

I looked at the amulet around my neck. "It was a family heirloom. My father's."

"Who's your father?"

"William Swift."

Deep contemplation filled Fitzroy's face. He uttered to himself, "Of course. How did I miss that?"

"What is it? You've heard of him? Was he a part of the Terminal?"

"No, I haven't heard of William Swift."

"Oh, but you've seen my amulet before?"

"Only once in my life." Fitzroy held the amulet from my neck, closely observing its details. His eyes grew wide with excitement.

"What is it?" I asked.

"Listen to me, Christoph. Tell no one that you have this amulet. It's not my place to say any more."

"Why does everyone tell me that?"

"Everyone?" questioned Fitzroy with a raised eyebrow. "Who else knows of this amulet? Speak truth, or I'll cut ye where ye stand!"

"Jeremiah and Marlow. Only they have seen the amulet!" I pleaded as I held my hands up.

"Any more?"

"No!"

"Leave it that way. Tell not a soul, yes?"

I nodded.

"Kalendar will want to know of this. Let us go back."

"Why should Kalendar know of my amulet?"

"No more questions," replied Fitzroy sternly. "Take this shirt.

Cover up the amulet."

Fitzroy pulled a white shirt out of his bag, and I put it on. My head swirled with angst. Our conversation only fueled my desires for more answers.

We ran back to the town. Fitzroy led me to the main head-quarters of the company, the airy white building at the center of the lake. To get to the building, we went across a glass bridge toward the entrance of the building.

Inside was an open-air factory filled with all sorts of unique mechanisms for refining, shipping, and crafting the minosium. Priva-teers were creating sloops, large airships, and drills. It was one room filled with wide windows and hangar doors. Fitzroy led me up a spiral staircase to a section of the building that overlooked the ground floor. This was where Kalendar resided.

We stepped into his office, like that of a ship's corridor with wooden walls and an observation point overlooking the waters of the lake and the ground floor. His privateer let us in and led us to Kalen-dar, who was conversing with Helga over a large map of the sea. Part of the map was holographic, demonstrating landmasses and weather conditions. Kalendar was immersed in the map as he scouted out dif-ferent points.

I was able to capture a better view of this esteemed captain. He was tall and broad-shouldered, likely English or French descent by his skin tone and features. He had a long scar down the side of his right face, coming from his eye intersecting with his well-kept black beard. His gaze was fixed, and he kept perfect posture. I was nervous to inter-rupt the man, let alone utter a word. The privateer introduced us and left. Kalendar lifted his eyes upon me.

"I presume this pertains to Mr. Swift, correct?" asked Kalendar.

"Indeed, Captain," replied Fitzroy.

"Speak plainly," said Kalendar with a serious undertone.

"This young man carries the Amulet of Faustino. Did you know this?" asked Fitzroy.

"Helga, take young Swift outside for a moment. Bring him in when I call you," asked Kalendar.

"Yes, Captain," replied Helga.

She escorted me out of the room. Inside, the meeting between Kalendar and Fitzroy went as follows:

"I did know of that, Fitzroy," remarked Kalendar.

"And you didn't tell me? You've cursed me to a fate worse than death, for I've touched the amulet," stated Fitzroy.

"For good reason. No one must know of the amulet until the time is right."

"The curse—"

"He alone bears the burden of the amulet, as I still do. The amulet chooses its bearer and those in company of it. The fate directed by God has chosen us to beat the amulet once more."

"I thought you threw it into the ocean many years ago."

"That is true, but destiny said otherwise."

"The last bearer must have been his father, passed by blood."

"Nay, the old expedition maintained the amulet. You were a privateer then."

"I remember them."

"The work is unfinished, and the amulet must be restored before anyone else finds it."

"The only man that knew of it was Reszo Zoltan . . . and the others."

"Do not say that name!" Kalendar yelled, striking his desk with his fist. "He's dead."

Fitzroy took a step back in retreat and said with slight response, "If we do not toss that amulet into the sea once more, the same fate as the old expedition will happen once again to young Christoph Swift and to the company as a whole.

"Don't you see? Destiny chose this young man and us to bear this responsibility. We will restore the amulet to its place. We will set out after the Festival of the Bazaar. The labyrinth shall fall into the sea and never into the hands of Zoltan."

"Swift came to us in distress. I presume someone knew he had the amulet, or he wouldn't have been here."

"I have thought such."

"What if it is the Tughra after him?"

"It could be," said Kalendar. "But nothing can be done until after the Bazaar. Continue on your way. Send the young lad in."

Fitzroy bowed and signaled me to come inside the room. I was hesitant.

"Come in, lad," remarked Kalendar.

"You wanted to see me?" I asked hesitantly.

"Yes, Fitzroy said you've made great progress. What say ye?"

His accent was almost identical to Axelrod's, using the same types of words and phrases.

"That is true. I've been training hard. I want to become an R.E. and serve honorably under the Victorian flag, whatever the cost," I replied.

"Aye, a very high price indeed. I wanted you to know that I was dear friends with Axelrod. We served together in an expedition many years ago."

"I thought so. He's the one that gave me the coin, told me I belonged here."

"He was right, and you were wise to listen to him."

"Thank you. Has he contacted you at all? It's been a few months since I've heard from him. He told me he was coming to meet us, yet he never showed up."

"No, I heard nothing."

I nodded my head.

"I'll try to get in contact with him, try to find his whereabouts," Kalendar proposed.

"May I ask you a question, Captain?"

"Yes?"

"What was it like working with Axelrod?"

"Smart man who loved the sea."

"Did he ever mention anything of my father, William Swift, or my mother, Charlotte Swift?"

"Nothing that comes to mind."

"Indeed. Well, thank you for this chance to be a part of this company."

"You can thank Axelrod for the coin. That was his."

"I felt like this was my destiny to come here, a deep desire within me. If you do not mind, do you know anything about my heirloom? Fitzroy said it was tied to Faustino."

"It's a relic that Axelrod must've found on the job. It supposedly opens Faustino's labyrinth and reveals the way to the island and through the maze."

"Do you believe that to be true, Captain?"

"We'll see," he smiled. "That's a story for another time. For now, you need to focus on the Series Trials."

"Right," I remarked.

"I have a book for you. This is part of my training for you," said Kalendar.

He walked over to a modest wooden bookshelf filled with many books. He withdrew a red one and handed it to me. It was called *The Ways of a Prince*.

"Who wrote it?" I asked.

"I did."

"Wow! That's an achievement."

"Read it front to back. Then, we'll talk about it in a few weeks," said Kalendar.

"Yes, and thank you, Captain Kalendar."

"Better get back to training."

I flipped to the first page and read the inscription: "May the wise man learn to be a lion who eats the wolves, Kalendar."

I pondered my encounter with Captain Kalendar. What first came to my mind was how far my communication skills had come, which had profoundly increased since my days in Louisiana. I was speaking more like a man, paying keen attention to the topics discussed and the reaction they caused to a third party.

My training had sharpened my skills not only physically and mentally but also socially. I was constantly put in situations where I was dealing with different people with various linguistic and ethnic backgrounds embedded in the hierarchal society of the company, strangely similar to the society I encountered in the days of my youth.

This melting pot of Victoria & Co. provided me a hands-on experience where the test was to communicate in pressure-based scenarios and political situations. I realized I was building a reputation in the company, starting from the bottom and working my way up.

Comparing this to my high school days, the reputation of my youth was tarnished due to my continually bad attitude and subpar performance in school and athletics.

In contrast, on Victoria Island, I was giving one hundred percent of my effort every day of the week, pushing myself to accelerate to my highest potential. The people in the company—such as Jeremiah, Rabbit Run, and Helga—were a high-caliber breed rubbing their excellence off on me.

At first, I had no idea this change was occurring until I witnessed the craftiness of my newfound skills. I never had exposure to such excellent people during my time in high school, nor was I ever pushed to become excellent in this newfound way. I felt blessed to be surrounded by the best of the best.

Regarding my meeting with Kalendar, I learned over the past months to pay attention to the words I spoke. I watched each word I uttered to the umpteenth degree. I discovered that words can be more dangerous than swords.

During my meeting with Kalendar, I spoke to him of my amulet, parents, and Axelrod, even though Fitzroy begged me not to. I did this to gauge his reaction to these subjects. I knew Kalendar would never reveal the answers I truly sought; rather, I began to discover that a man's eyes were just as revealing as the words he spoke.

At the mention of these sensitive subjects—Axelrod, my parents, and the amulet—I noticed Kalendar's eyes flicker like a firefly in the night. I knew in that pivotal second that Kalendar was well-acquainted with my family and this amulet, but his words spoke otherwise. Listening to Jeremiah's advice, I decided to keep my reserved wall fortified, protecting my innermost secrets from this world.

CHAPTER 14

Interlude

T HE TRIALS WERE at the end of next month; the pressure was
on. I could feel the tension and excitement pulse through my
veins. Over the course of my training, I learned the many vari-
ables and layers of this job. It was more than a job. It was a way of life,
a type of warrior class, like the samurai during the Edo Period. An
extractor was the most well versed and trained of all employees within
the company. They were not only the most physically adept, but they
were also more mentally savvy.

The Traders Terminal had created a culture and tradition surrounding its practices and the companies intertwined with it. All who
were a part of the Terminal adhered to its rules, taking on the risks
involved with this tumultuous job.

Being in a constant state of warfare changes a man. I could see it
in the eyes of Fitzroy and Kalendar, that their values and views of life
had changed. The others in the outfit maintained the same view since
they had firsthand experience with death, riches, and glory. They acted according to their surroundings. They lived in the moment—ready
to have fun, drink the most, laugh the most, and fight to the death.
Tomorrow was never guaranteed.

I learned how to appreciate life by observing how they lived, remembering death was always just around the corner. In return, I must
seize the day, perform, and obtain my riches.

Why did these men continue this way of life, this dangerous
job? Because the rewards were bountiful, beyond measure. Glory came
to a trainer who trained a successful trainee; riches came to an outfit

that struck minosium. The thrill of finding and recovering minosium was an obsessive hunt that was like striking an oil well, spewing black gold. The ore changed the way a man thought.

The lifestyle of striking it big then blowing it all on lavish parties, gambling, and vacations made up for the danger of each strike.

Jeremiah loved to splurge on exotic materials from each port he went to and on the incredible parties after a strike. The women flocked to Jeremiah as he wore his fine silks from Arabia.

Prince Rock loved the lifestyle, the hunt, and the power he gained with each strike. He desired the wealth and status working for the company had gotten him. He saved each coin he earned for when he would retire to a bed with fine linen sheets and a beautiful mistress awaiting him.

Zhen, from what I could see from his situation, needed this job as a mechanic. Working for the company paid higher dividends than anything he could find from his homeland. He told me the pay from the outfit was beyond amazing and nothing could compare. He sent all his money to his family on a small island off the coast of mainland Japan. He accepted that one day this job would kill him, so he earned as much as he could until that day came. He was not scared of death; rather, he embraced death as eternal peace.

Wildcat kept his eyes fixed on the prize. I had surmised that Wildcat felt that he needed to bring honor to his family, once prestigious but now fallen from grace. From what he told me, his father incurred massive debt and had to file for bankrupcy on his family's oil company. Wildcat took it upon himself to join this dangerous line of work in hopes of bringing great fortune to his family. He fought for his family, to reclaim his lands taken by debtors and bring honor back to his name. He constantly searched for the perfect vein out in the world. He rarely drank and socialized. Instead, he constantly surveyed the islands for the greatest minosium deposit in the world. He wouldn't return home until he struck that great vein. Then, and only then, would he return home as a conqueror.

Fitzroy was the most mysterious of the outfit. He never revealed much about his past. From what I could gauge, he was the most well respected and experienced of all in the outfit. He was one of four R.E.s in the entire company. He was no more than forty-five years old with wisdom behind his gaze. I believed that he was the most valued employee of the Victoria & Co.

I never knew how Spurwink became the Specksynder. From the little interaction between our outfit and the Tucks, they feared Fitzroy; even Spurwink did. It amazed me how long Fitzroy survived this in the company and dangerous profession.

Out of the whole outfit, and honestly the company, Fitzroy and Helga were the only ones who spoke to Kalendar. Spurwink occasionally did but not as much as Fitzroy and Helga.

Fitzroy became fond of me over the past months though he still kept me at an arm's length, keeping our conversations short and focused on the topics of importance. I felt he was not ready to connect with me, scared that I may be whisked away in an instant, as his last trainee. was

Fitzroy, hidden in his conscious mind, knew something about me that I did not know. I could tell by the way he looked at me. He held a secret but would not reveal it to me, nor did I press him about it. I believed only time would bring forth the truth.

CHAPTER 15

Dance of the Firebirds

T HIS WAS THE last day of training with Zhen. By this point, I was whipping that sloop in all sorts of directions. I had fully mastered the art of flying this machine. Zhen was amazed by my evasive and free style of piloting, like a bird in the sky.

I was up above the tree line in a sloop that day. Zhen stood at the base of the airfield, talking to me through the radio. Wildcat came out to the airstrip to witness me in action. He had his own communication device linked to my helmet. He stood right next to Zhen. I had the sloop leveled in the air.

"How do the controls feel?" asked Zhen in his Japanese-English accent as he looked through his binoculars.

"You look like a young lad ready to break in a wild steed," stated Wildcat.

I did a horizontal barrel roll in the sky.

"Yeehoo!" I screamed.

"Don't fly off now!" laughed Wildcat.

"Good," stated Zhen. "Vertical. Up and down."

I pushed the sloop vertically up then down, working the controls perfectly. Wildcat and Zhen both cheered at my mastery of the sloop.

"Watch out, trainees. The best pilot in the sky is here," I remarked.

Down on the airstrip, one of the hangar doors opened slowly behind Wildcat and Zhen. Behind them flew out two sloops, whizzing toward me. It was Rabbit Run and his companion, Osprey.

"Looks like company," said Zhen.

"The worst kind," said Wildcat.

"What? What is it?" I asked.

Rabbit Run and Osprey tuned into our frequency.

"Rabbit Run here. Do you copy?" asked Rabbit Run over the radio.

"Yes, speak. What do you want?" asked Zhen.

"I want to make a wager with Swift, reclaim my lost coins from the gun range. Ten coins to the winner of dog drills. The rules are simple: If the missile-locking system successfully targets your sloop, you lose immediately, just like in the Trials, but we use no missiles, only jest. Winner takes the coins. What say ye, Swift? I'm still a little salty from the gun range. We both need the training, and nothing is better than dog drills unless you feel inadequate against Osprey and me."

Zhen and Wildcat eyed each other with concern.

"I don't know about this one, Doughboy," said Wildcat.

"What's the worst that can happen?" Rabbit Run asked as he leveled his sloop to me.

"It's your decision, Doughboy," replied Zhen.

I thought for a moment. I knew they were trying to pull something on me. Maybe they tried to bring out apprehension within me.

"What's wrong? Can't play with the big boys?" asked Rabbit Run. "We can see whose training paid off in the end, eh? Ten coins to play."

"Let's move on. He's too scared to play. Swift knows his lovable Jeremiah can't protect him up here," Osprey said.

"I don't need protection. I'll play," I replied with a strict tone. "But it's uneven, two vs. one."

"I'm here, buddy," stated Wildcat over the radio. Wildcat was flying a sloop toward me. "Can't leave you hanging!"

I was overjoyed Wildcat came to help me. He leveled his sloop next to mine and gave me a thumbs up.

"Good. The rules, as I've stated, are if you're locked on, then you forfeit. We begin at exactly 10:30. Set your watches, and pick a spot," declared Osprey. "We will tune back into your frequency at the end of the game. Zhen, are you there?"

"Yes," Zhen remarked.

"You will referee the game from below," Osprey stated.

"Roger that," agreed Zhen.

"Any questions?" Osprey asked.

"I'm clarifying. If my missile lock turns green, signaling a confirmed lock, then you lose, correct?" I asked.

"If you can get a green lock," laughed Rabbit Run.

"Yes, now to your positions," Osprey announced. "Tuning out."

"Don't try anything too fancy, Doughboy. Keep on their tail. Don't fall for their tricks, and we'll clock them out. Sound good?" Wildcat said.

"Roger that," I replied.

"And if I say pull out, you pull out. Don't need to lose a leg in this, okay?"

I nodded, and we got into our positions. I could see them a few hundred yards away. The clock was counting down.

Thirty seconds.

I gripped the wheel with excitement. My heart pounded as I watched the time tick down. I said a quick, solemn prayer to the Lord for guidance in the game.

The clock struck zero, and I pushed the throttle. We approached them in the sky, and they whizzed past us.

"Here we go!" echoed Wildcat.

We flew in all sorts of patterns in the sky as we attempted to tail each other. I caught a glimpse of Osprey's sloop. I began to tail him. The computer system within my sloop would alert me if someone were attempting to lock onto me. There was a small screen next to my wheel that showed my digital tracking system, which constantly tracked and traced the target, like a camera using autofocus.

I pushed my sloop to its ultimate potential. Osprey was a damn good pilot. He threw all types of maneuvers at me. I stayed on him, swaying left to right, trying to get a lock on. Osprey wouldn't allow me. I didn't think he expected my skill set to be on this level. He couldn't shake me in the sky.

My target system said someone was trying to target me. Rabbit Run was on my tail, trying to trace me.

"Wildcat, Rabbit's on me!" I stated.

"I see him. He's a squirmy bull. Trying to lock now!" replied Wildcat.

Rabbit Run was getting too many close locks on me as I pursued Osprey. I had to pull off Osprey in order to lose Rabbit Run. Osprey pulled a maneuver and now followed behind Wildcat.

"Damn bastard. He's getting a hold on me. I'll try to shake him," stated Wildcat.

Wildcat pulled off, and Rabbit Run was still on my tail. I was pulling all types of aerial maneuvers, trying to cut him off, but he wouldn't budge. He was a magnificent pilot; I couldn't break him. He knew all my tricks. Wildcat was struggling with Osprey, and in one brief moment, Wildcat was locked on. He lost.

"He got me! Damn it! He got me!" Wildcat screamed.

That wasn't good for me. Now Osprey was turning toward me. I was already struggling with Rabbit Run chasing my tail.

"You can do it, Doughboy," Wildcat stated. "Trust your instincts."

I wasn't going to lose this match. I knew what I had to do. Osprey and Rabbit Run were now both on me. I descended to right above the treetops, hugging the mountainside. It was a dangerous move. Rabbit Run and Osprey did not back off; they followed me along the treetops.

"What are you doing, Doughboy?" Zhen demanded. "Trying to kill yourself? Pull up!"

"I got this!" I remarked.

"I order you to disengage!" Zhen screamed.

"Zhen!" I countered.

"You are not listening again," stated Zhen. "Your life is worth more than a game."

"I need you to trust me."

Zhen paused, then replied, "All right, I will. Descend into the valley. It's your only chance to lose them. Trust your instincts, and feel the sloop."

I descended into the valley of this mountainous terrain, brushing just above the flowing river, gliding through the winding valley. They followed me ever closer. I knew if I followed this winding canyon above the river, as dangerous as it was, I would hit the side of the steep mountain where the bridge fell when I ran with Fitzroy.

If I pulled off the right maneuver, I could scale the side of the mountain vertically, giving me the upper hand on both them. I couldn't move out of the canyon because they could both use the open air to maneuver around me and lock onto me, so this was necessary. It was either death or victory at this point.

I gripped the wheel, focused my attention, and calmed my

thoughts. Each turn required masterful precision to guide my sloop past the rocky edges of the narrow valley.

Osprey struggled to maintain control. He was hitting the sides of the cliff, but he wouldn't pull up. Rabbit Run almost had a lock on me. He was seconds away from victory. I knew he was going in for the kill, which was what I wanted him to do.

I'd reached the fallen wooden bridge and the vertical mountainside. I took a deep breath, approached the rock face, pulled up delicately hugging the rock face at a ninety-degree angle. An explosion occurred behind me. Osprey ran into the mountain. I could feel the vibrations of the explosion rumble my sloop.

Ignoring his dead comrade, Rabbit Run pulled up, hugging the rock, persistent in locking on me. I then pulled up on wheel, punched the throttle, and caused the sloop to backflip off the rockface.

Rabbit Run bypassed me as I turned upside down, flipping through the air. Within a brief moment during the flip as Rabbit Run ascended the rock face, I locked onto Rabbit Run.

Green. Click. I won.

I landed the sloop at the airfield. I looked up and saw Fitzroy, Jeremiah, Prince Rock, and Wildcat standing with a mass of privateers and Tucks that all came out to watch. There was a heavy sadness in the air.

Wildcat ran to give me a hug.

"Hell of a flyer. Knew you could do it, slick," stated Wildcat. "Ole Osprey, though . . . " He trailed off.

"I bet you to win," smiled Jeremiah. "Those Tucks are going to have to pay up big!"

Zhen came before me with a look sincerit. "You are more than ready for the Trials. Never have I seen a trainee fly like that." He then handed me a Master's Coin, which signaled my training with him was complete.

A Master's Coin was a purple coin, etched with minosium, labeled "Master," which circled the bottom of the coin, while the words "Traders Terminal" circled the top portion of the coin. At the center was the letters MEC (Minosium Exchange Commission); the M was large, and the E and C were small, intersecting with the M. The Terminal gave these coins to the outfit trainers. They were highly regarded and exhibited a sign of brilliance when a trainee earned one.

I was elated to see it.

Zhen continued, "I have nothing left to teach you at this point. Perform for us."

I put the coin into my pouch.

"There is always something to learn from you, Zhen," I remarked.

I looked around at the large crowd watching this event. Helga was conducting numerous privateers to help in medical attention. Behind me, two sloops landed. One was Rabbit Run, and the other was a sloop carrying Osprey, burnt to a crisp. He was dead.

The Nantucket outfit and their privateers were there to assist at the scene, carrying Osprey's body off the ship. Rabbit Run looked terribly disgruntled. Spurwink pushed through the crowd.

Upon seeing his dead companion, he began to scream in anger. He then grabbed his brother, Rabbit Run, by the neck and threw him to the ground. Everyone was silent. Spurwink's eyes, full of fire, gazed at me, cursing me in that moment.

We held a funeral pyre for Osprey that night. Everyone was in attendance. It was held at the fire circle. Osprey's body was laid upon a bale of hay and a woodpile, surrounded by his friends and the rest of the company. Kalendar was present and spoke of his regard of Osprey.

It was custom to place a hibiscus flower on the pyre before it was lit. Each privateer placed a different colored hibiscus on the pyre. Spurwink stood close by Osprey. I placed my own white hibiscus flower that I found near the bush. Spurwink and the rest of the Tucks gave me a sinister gaze as I placed my flower.

The privateers played in a drum circle to the sounds of a passing soul. Spurwink grabbed a flaming torch and lit the pyre on fire. We all watched Osprey's soul ascend to the heavens.

After that night, the rest of the outfit offered me their Master's Coins as the summer season came to an end, signaling the end of my training.

On one of the last hunts with Wildcat, we searched across the island for wild boars running through the shrub. During the hunt, we conversed about all things pertaining to minosium and what I might need to know for the Series Trials.

Then, out of the blue, Wildcat actually saw a hog, shot at it, and missed. It came screeching at us. Wildcat, scared out of his wits, climbed up a tree faster than a tiny squirrel. The hog then turned on me and charged me with lightning speed based on the sounds it was making.

I did not have a clear view of the beast; rather, I saw only the leaves rustling in the bush as the hog came upon me. I trusted my instinct, aimed my rifle, and waited for the right moment. I shot right through its heart, killing it instantly.

Wildcat was a little embarrassed by the whole thing. We gave it a hearty laugh. Wildcat patted me on the back and told me I was a good hunter. He believed we would have a prosperous future working together. After that incident, he granted me a Master's Coin.

As for Prince Rock, my last few days of training were composed of meeting with different companies offering trades to our outfit. Aluma and I stayed clear each other ever since that night at the tiki bar. Besides the occasional meetings and shipments, Prince Rock was gearing up for the upcoming season. I could tell his mindset was changing, becoming more serious. He didn't have time to talk to us much. He was mostly at the main headquarters.

On my last day, Obasa would not let me give him a farewell. He did not believe good-byes. Instead, he honored me with the word *salaam*. I asked what that meant. He said it was an Arabic word, his mother tongue, for "peace be upon you."

Prince Rock returned from headquarters to finish up some paperwork. I told him goodbye and thanked him for all the training he provided me. He was shocked to see the last day of training complete.

"We must celebrate with a drink!" Prince Rock exclaimed.

Prince Rock convinced Obasa to stay for a small drink to reminisce on a summer well spent. Prince Rock grabbed a fine bottle of Spanish red wine from his cabinet, and we toasted to good fortune. The wine tasted dry with a sweet scent that caressed my nose.

We sat in the main office overlooking the ocean as the sun set in her purple and orange majesty. With the wine in hand, we reminisced about the homes we left behind. Prince Rock told us he was from New York City and had worked as stockbroker on Wall Street until he landed the job as the outfit's broker by handling Captain Kalendar's financial positions. No wonder Prince Rock was savvy on the deal.

Prince Rock loved to down a bottle of wine, stating that the ever-encroaching edge subsided the moment the sweet grape touched his tongue, offering his soul relief.

As for Obasa, he spoke of his time in Tanzania, living on the seaside of the country. All of his family were wealthy merchants, traders of exotic wares that seafaring men could not resist, not even Captain Kalendar.

Through his family's intercontinental exchange connections, Obasa landed a job with the Victoria & Co. as a broker's assistant. Obasa claimed Kalendar was more inclined to hire him because of his gift of seeing the unknown, hoping Obasa's throwing of the bones could predict if a trade would be profitable.

Laughing and celebrating life itself, we continued to tell stories of our past until the crescent moon was high in the dark sky. At the end of our gleeful chat, Prince Rock dug in his pocked, turned to me, and said, "If I didn't think you would make it, I wouldn't give you this, lad."

He pulled out a Master's Coin and handed it to me.

I gave him a large smile.

"Your training with me is complete. You are ready! May the seafaring spirits guide ye to victory!" Prince Rock yelled.

CHAPTER 16

Appearance of the Fable

T HE NIGHT BEFORE my last day of training with Jeremiah, I
received a note slipped under my door, addressed to me. I
opened it up.

Tomorrow is the day. Be on deck at sunrise, lad.

Jeremiah

Oh boy, I thought to myself. *This must be the day he planned to
search for that gold chamber.* I was skeptical of the whole situation. Did
Jeremiah honestly believe there was a chamber filled with gold on the
island? I was doubtful, but I knew it would be fun nonetheless.

I made it to dock at the set time. The sea breeze was blowing
through the dock, bringing cool air to the island. The sun began to rise
upon her fiery throne on the horizon. I could hear the boat brush up
against the wooden dock as the waves crashed against it. The water
looked beautifully clear today.

I noticed the Tucks were out early on their ship, preparing it for
what I presumed to be an early morning fishing voyage. I saw Rabbit
Run following close behind Spurwink as he conducted the privateers
stocking the ship. It looked like a bit much for a fishing trip. What
were they doing? I turned my attention to Jeremiah and Marlow, who
were hastily outfitting our ship, pulling lines, and checking the lights.

Jeremiah, upon seeing me walk up to the boat, yelled with a
great smile, "The best pilot and trainee in all of the seven seas, Christoph Swift!"

I couldn't help but smile from his compliment.

Jeremiah swung from his ship to the deck to greet me. Marlow followed closely behind him.

Jeremiah jokingly bowed before me as I walked before him. "We're in a hurry, Swift."

"Why?" I replied. "Let me guess. It has something to do with the Tucks."

"I wish it weren't true," cried Jeremiah. "It was that no-good privateer that sold me the map. Curse ye!"

"Told him not to trust any privateer," said Marlow as his smoked a cigarette.

"What happened?" I asked.

"I was at the tiki bar last night, rather drunker than normal," started Jeremiah.

"Oh no," I sighed.

"Indeed," remarked Marlow.

"I was playing a game of dice with the Tucks, Pochick and Spurwink. All was fine. I was winning each roll. Then, Spurwink wagered a bet for my map for four Trader Coins. I thought he was mad. That damn privateer that sold me the map told Spurwink about it."

"And did you accept it?" I asked.

"Of course, I did!" sighed Jeremiah. "I felt coerced, as if this were planned out. Spurwink demanded I show him the map to claim its legitimacy. I pulled it out of my vest pocket where I always kept it and laid it on the table. Then, we rolled for it."

"Bad roll, eh?" I remarked.

"No, I rolled winning dice and won the coins," said Jeremiah.

"Then why the long face?" I inquired.

"The map was stolen," interjected Marlow.

"Stolen it be, right out from under me, as I was celebrating. I know not who took it," cried Jeremiah, "other than those damn Tucks."

"So, what do we do?" I asked. "We can't call the Tucks out."

"I made a copy of the map in my notes, wrote out and memorized how to get there," exclaimed Jeremiah.

"That explains why the Tucks are out and about," I said, contemplating the whole situation.

"That's right, lad," said Jeremiah. "Best we hurry!"

"Here they come," pointed out Marlow.

On the other side of the dock, the Nantucket outfit, led by Spurwink, was boarding the ship.

"Fancy seeing you all here. Eager to fish, eh?" yelled Pochick from the other side of the dock.

Jeremiah changed his demeanor, acting as if everything was normal, but he was doing a horrible job of it.

"Just fine, fine. Setting out now. Nothing to see here," assured Jeremiah poorly. He whispered to Marlow, "Unhook the lines. We're setting off now. Go!"

Marlow began to untie the lines from the dock. We launched the boat and made our way out.

Pochick yelled with great delight, "See you there soon, you sea dogs!"

"No, you won't!" yelled Jeremiah out of the window of his boat.

The Tucks raced aboard their ship, attempting to gain some ground on Jeremiah.

"The Tucks are gaining on us," said Marlow.

"Aye," said Jeremiah. "Luckily, I know a shortcut to the cavern."

"You sure it will lead us there?" I questioned.

"Indeed. It's through the jagged cliffs," Jeremiah replied. "Their boat is too big to follow me through there, and we'll use that passage."

"That passage is dangerous, Jeremiah," exclaimed Marlow. "One brush with those rocks, and this boat goes under."

"Need not worry, mate. This boat will ease past all obstacles ahead. We will return to the dock without a scratch on this boat and a mountain of gold in our hands!" Jeremiah reassured with a smile.

Marlow whispered to me, "Last time he said that we ended up in a Turkish prison with no gold."

"Let's hope this is different," I said, hesitant.

We sailed around the island, past the orange coral reef and the shallow waters of our old fishing spot. I could see our outfit's large treehouse near the cliff.

We circled the island, bypassing the airstrip. I could faintly see the sloops outside the hangar with an assortment of privateers working on them. I turned around and could see the Tucks were catching up to us. We passed into rough seas on the edge of the island with large, jagged cliffs and rocks scattered in the water. The sky turned gray as a storm was on the horizon. We came upon a small opening in the rugged cliffs.

"There she is—the passage," said Jeremiah. "Did my research

about the island. It's called the Merchant's Passage."

Jeremiah maneuvered through the rock cliffs and jagged edges piercing the water. He had a hard time avoiding each rock, pulling the wheel left and right. The waters were rough. Above my head, I saw an albatross with a tan head with white and black feathers. For some odd reason, it gave me a bad feeling in my stomach.

"I hope you're right, Jeremiah," I said. "Might be hard to turn around in such a tight gap."

"The passage will shoot us out on the other side of the island. This is part of the river that flows through it," said Jeremiah.

We passed through the rocky gates into this widening canyon. The current pushed our ship deeper into the tight canyon. It was so narrow that our only option was to follow the current.

Jeremiah looked at his notes to see where we were going. Marlow helped to direct him. We came to a wedge in the rocks, moving the water in two different directions. On the right pass, painted on the rock was a black emblem that was vaguely familiar to me.

Concern filled Jeremiah's face. I asked him what was wrong. He struggled to make words.

"It can't be. Not here!" exclaimed Jeremiah.

"What's wrong, Jeremiah?" I asked.

"We can't turn around. The current is too strong and narrow. We must go forward," stated Marlow. "Pick right or left."

Jeremiah unveiled a variety of medallions and symbols around his neck, chanting all types of hymns to himself.

I stared deeper into the symbol as the boat drew nearer to it. The black-painted symbol on the rock face was similar to Egyptian art—a man with a jackal head adorned in Egyptian jewels, holding a scepter pointed to the right side of the canyon.

I had seen this symbol before. I pulled out my amulet and held it up to the symbol painted on the rocky surface. It was the same. The hairs stood on the back of my neck, realizing this was . . .

"The symbol of Faustino," said Jeremiah. "I knew the symbol on your amulet was familiar. Now I know why the sharks swam away."

"I didn't think I would see the symbol here," I said as a mountain of questions filled my head.

"So what if he carries this old amulet?" questioned Marlow. "What makes it so special, eh? Other than that it glows."

"That amulet, forged with magic, is said to be the key to the labyrinth of Faustino," remarked Jeremiah, "the key to the greatest minosium deposit to have ever existed yet lost to time."

"Sounds like it's right up our alley," said Marlow.

"Not this piece," remarked Jeremiah.

"What if Axelrod . . . that map in the lighthouse . . ." I said to myself.

I pondered the memory of the great map in the lighthouse back in Louisiana, which had different circles of locations. Could that map Axelrod tirelessly slaved upon be linked to Faustino? Was my uncle trying to uncover this mythical labyrinth? For what purpose?

Yes, yes, he told me in that note to read the book on Faustino when I was traveling from Louisiana to Villefranche. He said the book might come in handy, and my questions would soon be answered. Could this amulet be the key to my past?

"No map reveals the labyrinth," Jeremiah remarked. "The legend said the architect of the labyrinth left only scarce hidden clues."

"Well, we got a map," interjected Marlow.

"And this be a clue," I said, referring to the black symbol on the rockface.

"Aye, 'tis true," said Jeremiah. He held up the map. "Something tells me this is only a map to forbidden jewels, not to the hidden labyrinth, but we shall see what dark magic lies ahead of us as Fate begs us forward. Ah, Fate, ye evil mistress that ties us to our untimely doom."

Marlow stared intently at the symbol, judging its authenticity. He said, "I'm doubtful of this symbol. It could be a trick done by privateers in their spare time. We all know that Faustino was a child's tale and nothing more as opposed to a pharaoh's tomb, like the one we discovered in Egypt. Was it Ramses or Seti? I can't remember."

"Seti I," replied Jeremiah. "Buried in the Valley of Kings."

"Hold on. When was that?" I asked.

"Oh, a couple years back," said Marlow.

"That's incredible. What was in the tomb?" I inquired.

"Minosium," smiled Marlow.

"You jest," I remarked.

"I do not," replied Marlow.

"Minosium?" I questioned in astonishment. "In an old tomb? Impossible!"

"Only the King of Kings knew of minosium in ages past, a fact still unknown to the modern age," explained Jeremiah. "Marlow and I searched around the world for those hidden vaults containing minosium in silence."

"Never could I have imagined that," I replied. "Does Kalendar know of this?"

Jeremiah shook his head. "Best keep your treasures to yourself, lad. As I've told ye, tell no one of your conduct."

"Why then was I told minosium was only recently discovered?" I inquired. "And here you say it was buried with an ancient pharaoh. Makes no sense."

Marlow laughed. "That's what the Terminal wants ye to think. Can't tax the past. But we be more clever than that."

"All treasure starts out as myths," Jeremiah remarked, "until we reveal its true nature."

"Then the tale of Faustino could be true," I said. "We must go on to see!"

"I feel dark magic swirl up my back and arms, raising my tiny hairs as it caresses my soul," said Jeremiah.

"We can't turn back now," said Marlow. "We must go through the passage regardless."

"Aye, Fate worked her hands upon us," said Jeremiah. "We go forward."

We all agreed to follow the map and the symbol down the passage to the right around rocky edges. We came upon a cave, which the river flowed through. Marlow turned on the ship's lights as we were engulfed in complete darkness. All I could hear was the rumble of the ship's engine and the current below us. I pulled out a flashlight and looked at the redrawn map Jeremiah was holding.

"Where does it say to go?" Marlow asked.

Jeremiah read his notes out loud.

Follow the stream, hugging the right side.
Do not venture left, for death awaits those who venture too far.
Fear the teeth and tail, all too long for those that cannot see.
Stay the right course, guided by the kilbits of light.t

Find the chamber full of riches.
Life is above.
Do not tarry,
Best to look and not touch.
Only touch the key,
and life will be given to thee.

"Sounds like a bunch of hoopla," remarked Marlow.

"Kilbits," I uttered. "Wildcat told me of them."

"What did he say?" asked Jeremiah.

"Kilbits signify minosium is nearby," I replied.

"Minosium, eh?" said Jeremiah.

"What is it, Jeremiah?" asked Marlow.

"I'm starting to think this chamber is not of gold but of minosium," said Jeremiah.

I continued to use my flashlight to see inside of the cave. There were small ledges of sand on both sides of the ship. In an instant, the shores along cavern were littered with carcasses of fish, hogs, and what appeared to be humans.

"Ma . . . Marlow," I said.

Marlow turned and gasped at the sight of all the bones.

"Must be shark-infested waters," stated Marlow.

We continued to follow the stream through the dark, eerie cave. Out of the darkness, a blue glowing light appeared along the ceiling of the cave. As we drew closer, I noticed it was colony of majestic, bioluminescent creatures, illuminating the cave with a sparkling blue light. I remembered Wildcat said kilbits glowed like this.

"Kilbits!" I said. "Just as Wildcat described them."

"If he was right, that means minosium is nearby," said Jeremiah.

At the end of the tunnel, I could see light. Our ship crossed into an enclosed area inside of a mountain with light shining from the outside world through openings in the rock, illuminating massive golden and stone structures resembling those of ancient Egypt.

"Oh my," I remarked in complete shock.

"This must be it," said Jeremiah. "This is no ordinary merchant chamber. This is something much greater."

Green vegetation surrounded this dome structure built into the mountain. Stone walls painted with symbols resembling ancient

Egyptian hieroglyphics encircled us. Roughly thirty feet in height, two large black statues of Anubis, the Egyptian god with a human body and the head a jackal, stood on opposites sides of this circular chamber; the statues held large purple crystals in their hands. At the center of the dome was a surface to walk on, leading into the mouth of a massive sphinx.

"It must be a Faustino chamber," explained Jeremiah. "A place to hide his minosium from—"

"Pirates," I replied, finishing his statement.

"Maybe you guys are onto something," said Marlow.

We parked our ship at the small stone dock and approached the open-mouthed sphinx.

"Be careful," suggested Jeremiah. "If there is minosium in here, do not touch it. The Terminal forbids any time of extraction during the off-season."

Jeremiah and Marlow descended with flashlights into the mouth of the sphinx. I began to question why my father would give me this amulet and why he had it in the first place. Were these fantastical stories true? What was Axelrod hiding from me?

I wanted to know the truth. That mouth would reveal the secrets I desired, for my soul told me so.

CHAPTER 17

Waltz of the Chamber

E DESCENDED A dark, narrow corridor. Only our flashlights lit the way before us. Sweat poured down my face.

"Where do you think it leads?" asked Marlow.

"I've seen this before or, I mean, something like this," replied Jeremiah.

"Really?" I asked. "Was it filled with booby traps?"

"If I can recall, it was. The worst trap of all was bad air," said Jeremiah.

After about one hundred yards of walking, we entered a room. It was pitch black, but I could tell from our echoing voices that it was spacious. Jeremiah stopped us from walking forward. He took out a brown rod from his backpack, wrapped some linen cloth around the tip of it, and lit it with his lighter, creating a torch. He then lit a tray of black powder in a small plate next to the door.

In an instant, the whole room illuminated as the powder was turned into fire. The flame moved through the black powder that lined the walls of the room, lighting it.

This room was supported by four magnificently painted pillars marked with Egyptian art and colorful hieroglyphics. The ceiling was painted a rich blue.

"Yes, yes, yes. Now I know where I've seen this—Egypt, in the Valley of Kings. Faustino adored the ancient Egyptians and Greeks." Jeremiah examined the pillars, trying to read the hieroglyphics. "He brought artists and architects from around the world to make his wonderful imaginations come true. A place to store his minosium, a labyrinth to protect it from thieves."

"This! Could this be the labyrinth?" I asked excitedly.

"No. This . . . This is something else," Jeremiah replied.

Jeremiah examined two figures on each of the pillars, which were on all four pillars and identical to each other. One figure on the pillar was a red man with horns, offering the other man what seemed to be blood minosium. The other figure was receiving the minosium. He was a man appearing to be in a sickly state and dressed in rags.

"Strange. Very strange," remarked Jeremiah as he examined the pillar.

"Why?" I asked.

"This horned beast . . . Usually, it is of Anubis or Osiris, the Egyptian gods. This figure I've never seen before."

There were footsteps behind us, slowly climbing down the staircase.

"Someone is here!" I whispered.

"What if it's the Tucks?" asked Marlow.

Jeremiah unhooked a whip on his belt.

"Get ready," said Jeremiah as he gripped his whip.

Before we could strike, stepping out into the light was none other than Wildcat. We were relieved to see him. He was shocked but happy to see us. He couldn't believe it. He explained he'd been following these kilbits for the past few days, which led him here.

"I never thought something like this was on Victoria Island," exclaimed Wildcat.

"Keep your wits about you," said Jeremiah. "If minosium is here and any bit of it is extracted, let alone touched, the Terminal will come for us all."

"Got that, partner," Wildcat said. "I was just surveying. Strangely, I saw the Tucks' boat docked not too far from here. Think they know about this, too?"

"They're coming for the chamber," I said.

"And they're not too far behind us. Let's keep moving," said Jeremiah.

The room led to another narrow corridor, descending further into the belly of the beast. We encountered a hallway adorned with hieroglyphics and artwork painted in Egyptian fashion. It showed the same once-sickly man, growing stronger as he mined the minosium from a hot spring. It sparkled with blue paint.

Jeremiah intently studied the paintings. "It's the story of Faustino. He gained wealth and riches from the minosium, growing more powerful by the day."

The next set of paintings on the wall was of Faustino dressed in Egyptian fashion, whipping other men and women in rags as they mined the minosium under a scorching sun along the Nile River.

The next painting was of these same slaves walking into the Nile River where they encountered a horrible, massive serpent with the head of a viper, a dark blue body, and a golden underbelly. The beast feasted on the slaves. It was a terrifying painting.

"The Leviathan," uttered Jeremiah.

"These are a little perplexing," stated Wildcat.

"You know what? I need a cigarette. I'll be back at the boat," Marlow stated as he turned around and ran for the exit. "Too much bad air for me."

"Wait! Come back, Marlow!" I yelled.

Jeremiah and Wildcat shrugged, and we continued forward. I was more scared in that moment than at any other moment in my life. I had to go forward. Something inside me, my soul perhaps, pushed me to go forward.

We entered the next room. Jeremiah lit it using his torch and the black powder.

"The main chamber," Jeremiah remarked.

This room contained six pillars richly painted with scenes of souls passing into the afterlife. The pillars surrounded a natural hot spring filled with red, hot water.

"I'll be damned," said Wildcat. "There's the hot spring! Thanks be to the kilbits."

Above the hot spring was a beautiful blue ceiling of the seven seas. The continents were adorned in gold. Jeremiah and I stared at the ceiling.

"Can this be? Look!" Jeremiah pointed.

My amulet began to emit a reddish glow unlike I had ever seen before, glowing ever more brightly.

"That looks old," Wildcat stated as he stared at my amulet.

"Take it off. Trust me with it. Take it off," said Jeremiah.

"This is way over my head," said Wildcat. "I'm going to survey the hot spring."

I took it off and debated if I could trust Jeremiah.

"Give it here," said Jeremiah.

Jeremiah took the amulet and followed the ceiling to a circular hole in the wall. It looked like a perfect fit for my amulet. Jeremiah placed it in the hole. The whole room illuminated with a mesmerizing red light, outlining all the hieroglyphics.

"Look there!" Jeremiah indicated.

The ceiling began to move like a mechanical machine, reshaping itself in different positions. It eventually stopped, and reflected in the water was a map of the seven seas and the continents.

"That's pretty cool," said Wildcat.

Numerous bright red sparkles, brighter than anything in the room, shone on different key points around the world like sparkling diamonds in the night sky.

"What are those sparkles scattered across the map?" I asked. "Look how many there are!"

We gazed at the ceiling, trying to guess the meaning of the numerous points on the map.

"I'll be damned," said Wildcat. "There's a sparkle over Victoria Island."

"These points must show the locations around the world of the other chambers like this one," said Jeremiah.

Then, the mechanical ceiling rotated once more, causing glowing red lines to extend from each sparkle converging on the brightest point of all, located somewhere in the Indian Ocean. When all the lines reached the brightest star, its red glow turned into a bright blue light.

"Another chamber?" I inquired

"No," said Jeremiah softly. "It's the entrance to the labyrinth."

"Looks like it's near the Spice Islands," said Wildcat.

"Legend said the greatest deposit was found around there," Jeremiah exclaimed excitedly.

The blue light shone brighter than a lightning bolt. Then, a burst of white light, like that of camera flash, emitted from the blue point. In an instant, the light faded away, and the red lines returned to their original points, slowly fading away. The powerful red lights dissipated, and the reflection in the water disappeared. I grabbed the amulet and placed it in my bag. Wildcat was feeling the stone in the crystal blue hot spring water.

"It's tchouplite," said Wildcat. "Right here below us is a great fortune. We'll come back then, Jeremiah. The season starts soon. We'll get the others and extract this well, analyze this chamber, study it, and formulate a plan."

"A plan?" said a mysterious voice from behind us. It was the Tucks walking into the room, armed to the teeth. Spurwink held a minosblade in his hands. "Rest assured, none of you will be planning any time soon."

"What are you doing here, Spurwink?" Wildcat asked.

"I could ask you the same thing," replied Spurwink.

"Ye stole my map!" Jeremiah screamed.

"Stole is a harsh word. Rather, *borrowed*," smiled Spurwink.

The whole Nantucket crew walked into to the room and began to surround us.

"Now, don't do anything you'll regret, Spurwink," Wildcat warned.

I slowly backed up toward the hot spring.

Spurwink walked around, analyzing the paintings on the wall. "I've been searching for this chamber for years. Stunning, isn't it? Tie them up."

"What are you doing, Spurwink?" cried Wildcat. "The Terminal will kill you for this."

"The Terminal's power is fading by the day," Spurwink said, "eclipsed by the future."

"The only future ye shall see is the bottom of the sea," Jeremiah echoed.

The Tucks—Rabbit Run, Pochick, Cudweed, and their three privateers—aimed their guns at us. Rabbit Run and Pochick tied all three of us to a pillar. Rabbit Run made sure to make my restraint extra tight around my wrist. He tied our hands with a rope around a pillar. Rabbit Run smiled at me then punched me in the stomach. Grunting in pain, I fell to my knees as he laughed.

Pochick felt one of the pillars with his hands. "Our friends will enjoy knowing we're one step closer to the labyrinth."

"Who are your friends, eh?" asked Jeremiah. "And what of Marlow? If you goons did anything to him, I'll . . ."

"He's in safe hands," said Spurwink.

"Once Kalendar hears of this," said Jeremiah, "he'll—"

"Do nothing! Kalendar has no power over *him*," Spurwink countered.

"Over whom?" asked Wildcat.

"The man whom Kalendar fears most," Pochick interjected.

"No, no, no. He's dead," Jeremiah said.

"Is he?" smiled Rabbit Run.

"You dirty, lying, no-good traitor! Turned on ye own company for a man resting six feet below!" Jeremiah said.

"Who are they talking about, Jeremiah?" I asked.

"Reszo Zoltan," said Wildcat in a distinct tone, pronouncing his first name as *Re-saw*.

"Let me avenge Osprey, right now!" Rabbit Run demanded as he unveiled a minosblade in front of me.

"Back, brother," demanded Spurwink.

"All of you are working for the Tughra, Zoltan's hidden army," stated Wildcat.

"You always were smart, Wildcat," smiled Spurwink.

"Whatever they have told you, it's lies. Turn away from the Tughra," Wildcat insisted, "before it's too late."

"Lies?" questioned Spurwink. "The only lies we've been subjected to were by the corrupt Terminal. They fatten themselves as we kill one another for a piece of rock. Zoltan offers us a solution: our revenge. Look at my brother and your beloved trainee, fighting like gladiators to the death. For what? For the enjoyment. I've faced the Series Trials before, and they have left their mark on me. Nay, enough is enough!"

"What's in it for you?" asked Jeremiah.

"A place in Zoltan's new world. You could join us, Wildcat. We need men with spirit. Help us exact our revenge on the Terminal. No more shall they tax us, control us, and subject us to their cruelty."

"The Terminal brings order to our world," Wildcat stated. "Without it, anarchy would ensue."

"Indeed, anarchy. First the Terminal shall fall. Then the world governments shall bend at the knee. We will take power from the hands of those mongering officials thriving off the labor and killing of the common man and give it back to the people."

"Bourgeoisie, eh?" Jeremiah interjected.

Spurwink chuckled. "What say ye?"

"The catch?" asked Wildcat.

"Give us the Doughboy," remarked Spurwink.

"I've done nothing to this Tughra!" I remarked.

"What does the Tughra want with him?" Wildcat asked.

"I am not sure, but we have strict orders to bring him with us. That's all I know," smiled Spurwink. "Now, hand him over, walk away, and never speak of this to anyone."

"Ye won't kill me," Jeremiah proclaimed.

"Aye, over my dead body," I shouted.

"With pleasure," Rabbit Run responded.

"If we refuse?" asked Wildcat.

"We take the Doughboy with us and leave you to rot here with Jeremiah. We cannot let Kalendar know of any of this," Spurwink said.

"Ye don't know Zoltan or what he's capable of," replied Jeremiah.

"I'll take my chances elsewhere, shooter," Wildcat said. "I stand by my outfit."

"So be it," Spurwink remarked.

"Let's be done with this!" Pochick yelled.

"Let me kill them both, brother. It will be easy!" Rabbit Run insisted.

"No, they will stay here and die attached to that pillar," Spurwink replied, "in darkness."

I whispered to Wildcat, "What do we do?"

"I'm thinking" was his response.

"Rabbit Run, take pictures of the chamber and the ceiling. Document the hieroglyphics," Spurwink commanded. "As for the others, bring in the extraction drill. We're taking this minosium with us."

"What if the Terminal finds out we've drilled? It's the off-season," said Cudweed, a pale man of strong stature with red hair and green eyes.

"They won't find out, and if they did, the Tughra will protect us," said Spurwink.

"Brother, I couldn't compete in the Trials though," said Rabbit Run.

"Stories have been told of the bounty of a Faustino spring. It carries blood minosium. We cannot pass up this rare opportunity, brother,"

Spurwink said. "The Terminal will not find out. Now, let's get drilling."

Steam from the hot springs filled my nostrils, filling them with an eggy scent. I turned to my left. Before me was the next dark corridor of stairs, descending into darkness. I tried to wedge my hands out of the restraints. This was going to take some time.

Pochick and Cudweed returned with two handheld spear-like drills. I'd studied these in my textbooks. They were used to extract the minosium from the tchouplite. The drill was powered by minosium and maintained a type of central computer system that would pick up the radiation from the minosium deep inside the tchouplite.

Cudweed and Pochick slowly got into the hot springs, roughly four feet in depth, eight feet in width. They wore a special type of goggles to protect their eyes from the bright drill. On top of the extraction drill was a small radar. Pochick and Cudweed scanned the rocky sides of the red-hot spring.

"Tchouplite, yellow rock . . . It's here," Cudweed stated.

Cudweed and Pochick continued to drill into the rock.

"Zoltan's back from the dead. Kalendar will love to hear about that. So what's the deal?" asked Jeremiah. "You join his little army, the Tughra, and find the labyrinth. Then what?"

"You'll just have to wait to find out," smiled Spurwink. "My mistake. You won't live to see that day. What a pity."

"Aye, I've been told that a few times before," Jeremiah replied.

"Quiet!" demanded Rabbit Run. "Or I'll do the dirty work now." He pointed his gun at Jeremiah.

I was able to free my hands from the restraints and pull a small knife from my pocket, all the while keeping it hidden.

"There! Move more lightly with the drill!" yelled Spurwink, directing them toward a specific section of the rock. "Do not crush it. Be gentle with it."

Cudweed lifted his goggles and said he struck the minosium. Spurwink excitedly hopped into the water. Spurwink told Rabbit Run to bring a titanium container forward. Rabbit Run noticed my bag near the hot spring.

"We'll use this bag for now to store it. Then I'll grab the container," stated Rabbit Run.

I was growing nervous. They picked up my bag with the amulet. At that moment, Cudweed stopped drilling; a glowing purple aura shone through the opening in the tchouplite. The Tucks were mesmerized by its beauty, engrossed in its glowing, fluorescent color.

"I've never seen this much minosium," said Cudweed.

"We're going to be rich!" Pochick cheered.

Cudweed pulled out small fragments of the glowing crystal, holding them up in pure ecstasy.

"Here! Here!" called Rabbit Run as he held my bag next to him. "Put it in here!"

Cudweed hastily chipped away pieces of the glowing minosium and placed it in the bag.

Back on the pillar, I whispered, "I've freed my hands."

"Good. I've almost freed mine," said Wildcat.

"This is what we'll do: we'll sneak up on the privateers, take their guns, and shoot our way out of here," Jeremiah directed.

"That's a terrible idea!" I whispered.

"And ye have a better one?" said Jeremiah.

"I'll move from pillar to pillar without them knowing, slowly take out each privateer, and then bring back their weapons," Wildcat said.

"Sounds good. Get to it while they're distracted," Jeremiah insisted.

Wildcat slowly began to move from pillar to pillar while the Tucks were fixated on the hot spring. He slowly moved behind the first privateer, threw hand restraints around the privateer's neck, and pulled the privateer back into the shadows.

"One down," I counted.

Wildcat then did the same technique to the next one. One more privateer left.

I looked back at the spring. Cudweed unveiled from the rock a jagged, glowing, burgundy crystal about six inches in diameter. The Tucks were salivating at their treasure. Spurwink grabbed hold of the minosium with a great smile, feeling its power in his hands.

"We'll need something bigger than that bag," exclaimed Cudweed.

Rabbit Run then tossed my bag toward the pillar. Sadly, that was the bag that I put my amulet in after the whole moving ceiling ordeal. It was of great importance that I retrieved my bag before leaving this chamber. Thankfully, the Tucks did not know my amulet was stowed away inside of it.

"Never in me life have I witnessed minosium of this color," stated Spurwink. "Zoltan will make us kings!"

The whole Nantucket crew cheered with excitement. Rabbit Run turned to look at the prisoners on the pillars and noticed immediately one was missing.

"Look, brother. Wildcat is gone!" Rabbit Run cried.

I began to panic.

"Hey!" Pochick yelled. "Where's Wildcat?"

"He's gone!" screamed Rabbit Run.

At that moment, gunfire echoed up the stairs near the pillars. It was Wildcat firing an automatic rifle into the privateer. From the force of the bullets, the privateer fell off the ledge and into the hot spring.

"He's got a gun!" Pochick shrieked.

"Shoot him," Spurwink declared, "and protect the minosium."

Wildcat walked to the ledge, aimed the assault rifle at the pool, and unloaded his clip on the Tucks. Bullets flew in all directions. Pochick was instantly shot in the arm.

"Move! Hurry!" Jeremiah commanded.

I quickly grabbed my bag. Rabbit Run grabbed onto it also. We locked eyes.

"Give it here!" demanded Rabbit Run as he pulled on it.

A bullet ricocheted right near us, causing Rabbit Run to let go of the bag. I quickly made way for the stairs, bullets ricocheting around us. Wildcat gave me some fire support.

Jeremiah and I moved behind the pillars. The Tucks continued to volley bullets at us, hitting the pillars. Wildcat tossed us two guns. A firefight ensued.

"We can't hold them off forever," Jeremiah yelled over the roar of bullets.

The Tucks were moving closer to us, utilizing the protection of the pillars in the room. I took my amulet out of the bag and put it around my neck. I caught Spurwink gazing at the amulet around my neck. He carried his minosblade.

I tried to fire at Spurwink, but he hastily ran toward me. In an instant, he was on me. He sliced my gun in half, crumbling it to pieces. I fell to the ground and attempted to back up slowly.

"You bear the amulet," Spurwink said. "The one Zoltan seeks.

Give it to me!" His eyes grew wide with desire.

"No!" I replied.

Spurwink raised his minosblade at me. Then at that moment, his blade was caught midair. It was Jeremiah! He caught Spurwink's sword with his whip. The tip of his whip contained glowing purple shards of minosium.

"Aye," said Jeremiah. "Over here, Specksynder."

Spurwink laughed and turned toward Jeremiah.

"I've been waiting for this," smiled Spurwink as he and Jeremiah circled each other.

Jeremiah cracked his whip. "As have I."

"*En garde!*" echoed Spurwink as he jumped toward Jeremiah.

Spurwink struck with lightning speed at Jeremiah. He dodged it, then attempted to whip Spurwink at a distance. Spurwink was blocking every strike until Jeremiah, in an instant, struck Spurwink's right leg, cutting it clean off. Spurwink cried from the pain, falling backward off the ledge and into the hot spring.

Jeremiah and I stared at the ledge. Then, there was a loud scream, and the gunfire ceased. Coming from the dark corridor that led to the next chamber was a large blue serpent with a yellow belly and red diagonal lines on its body. It had yellow eyes and was larger than any beast I had ever seen before. Cudweed tried to shoot at it, but the serpent picked him up in his mouth.

"What in God's name?" I wondered.

"Time to go!" yelled Wildcat. "He's red on yellow. Bad fellow! Bad fellow! Get out of here!"

The serpent propped itself up on the ledge, staring at us with yellow deadly eyes as Cudweed, screaming and hollering, struggled to free himself from its mouth.

The serpent was a viper with fangs sharper than the tip of a knife. Cudweed continued to scream in pain; then, the serpent lifted its head up and swallowed Cudweed whole. I couldn't believe my eyes. My jaw dropped at this unbelievable sight. I was frozen in shock as I gazed at this ancient beast.

Jeremiah grabbed my shoulder, breaking me from my daze, and we ran out of the chamber and up the corridor. Behind us, I could hear bullets firing and people screaming. We ascended though the dark corridor and out of the sphinx's mouth. We saw our ship and two Tuck privateers watching over Marlow, who was bound to a rock on the small surface.

"Halt, or I'll shoot," said one of the privateers.

"Your comrades need you. Can't you hear them?" Wildcat said.

"They need you down there. A beast! A beast, I tell you!" I yelled.

"A beast?" asked one of the privateers as they both lowered their guns in confusion.

I jabbed one of them in the mouth, catching him completely off guard. The other privateer turned his gun toward me. Jeremiah punched him in the side, took the gun, and hit him over the head with it.

"I'm sure happy to see you guys. Sounded like hell down there," Marlow said.

A loud crash resonated from the corridor. The crash had such force behind it that large rocks began to fall all around us.

"Boat! Chop, chop!" remarked Jeremiah.

We freed Marlow and hastily got into our small ship. Marlow pushed us off. Rabbit Run, carrying Spurwink on his shoulder, was coming out of the sphinx's mouth, yelling for assistance. Unfortunately for them, we kept going and refused to turn back.

I was in amazement and fear, looking back at the abandoned and helpless Rabbit Run and Spurwink. I never could've dreamed a beast of that size could exist. On top of that, I was trying to recall what Spurwink said about this mysterious Zoltan figure and the Tughra. I replayed the whole event in my head, starting from the beginning. My attention turned to Wildcat.

"How did you get here without a boat, Wildcat?" I asked.

"I found the kilbits in a different cavern and was taking samples of them when I saw a light down the tunnel. I broke through the rock and walked into the chamber," Wildcat explained. "There I met you two, coincidently."

"And Marlow, what the hell happened?" asked Jeremiah. "A little warning would've helped us out."

"I was watching the ship, smoking my cigarette. Then, the Tucks came up and took me by surprise," Marlow remarked. "I can ask you the same question. What happened down there? I heard drilling, screaming, bullets, and hissing sounds. I thought I was going crazy."

There was a moment of silence on board.

Jeremiah shrugged his shoulders. "I'll tell ye later. Let's just get out of here."

"The Terminal will want to know what happened. Minosium was drilled, and we were there," stated Wildcat.

"We were tied up," I said. "There was nothing we could do."

"Doesn't matter. We'll have to explain ourselves to the Terminal on Evisa," said Wildcat.

"Oh great," sighed Jeremiah. "The Tughra *and* the Terminal will be after us."

"I heard them say the Tughra," I questioned. "Zoltan's army?"

"Yes," replied Wildcat. "An old secretive order started by Zoltan with the sole intention of destroying the Terminal and taking over the world through minosium, or so they say."

"They saw your amulet," stated Jeremiah, "the key to the labyrinth—the world's richest minosium deposit."

"Oh, that's right, Jeremiah," said Wildcat. "If the Tughra does exist, I bet they're after Faustino's long-lost treasure."

I pulled out my amulet and stared at it intently. *Why and how did Axelrod have this amulet?* It didn't make sense; it was just a family heirloom.

Obviously not. I was missing something.

Why was I really here? A thought occurred to me: Spurwink said *he* would know. Was he referring to this Zoltan character?

I began to connect the puzzle pieces in my head. What if this was the same *he* whom Narcisse and Carlos Torino referred to when they grabbed hold of my amulet that day the lightning struck without a cloud in the sky?

Perhaps Axelrod was hiding from Zoltan and this Tughra army. Yes, which could mean Narcisse and Carlos Torino were affiliated with the Tughra. I needed time to think on this, and now was not the time.

"Did anyone catch a glimpse of that sea serpent?" Wildcat asked.

"He looked at me with bright yellow eyes," I replied.

"I saw it come from the dark corridor," Jeremiah said. "Alas, a beast from the deep."

"A prehistoric one if I had to say," said Wildcat.

"Now we know where these bones from earlier are from," I pointed out.

"Couldn't this sea serpent be under us now?" Marlow asked with concern.

We all looked at one another. Then, Jeremiah pushed the throttle down to speed up the boat.

"Ye best hope not," said Jeremiah.

We continued through the cave system using Jeremiah's notes. As we approached our point of origin, sadly, it was shut solid by fallen rocks.

"The devil! The way out is shut!" exclaimed Jeremiah. "We must take the way to the left."

"I don't know about that, Captain," said Marlow as he examined the sketched map. "The map says not to go left."

"What about the way Wildcat came from?" I suggested.

"No," said Wildcat. "The rocks most likely closed it off. I say we stay on the water."

"Give me that map!" Jeremiah demanded.

Jeremiah examined the map, thinking decisively what the next step should be. The way to the left showed a large X to the left. Past the X showed a simple passageway to a lagoon that led to the ocean.

"Aye, as captain of this ship, we take the passage through the lagoon," said Jeremiah. "I must've made a mistake by putting an X there when I sketched the map."

I looked to Marlow with an apprehensive look.

Marlow shrugged his shoulders, accepting the order. Jeremiah took the left route at the wedge in the cave. The waters turned into rough rapids with sounds of rushing water around us, rocking the boat back and forth.

"Little rapids. Nothing more," exclaimed Jeremiah. "If we get stuck, push us off with the poles on deck!"

The rapids grew increasingly rough, faster and faster.

"This seems more than little," I echoed.

Boom! We hit the side of a rock, almost propelling all of us from the ship. *Clash!* We hit another rock. Marlow violently fell forward. Wildcat tied himself to the railing. The medium-sized boat jumped up and down on the rapids, as the great force of the rapids tossed us effortlessly.

"Hold strong!" screamed Jeremiah as he gripped the wheel tightly.

"To what?!" I yelled.

"Anything!" screamed Marlow.

The boat crashed into a larger rock in the middle of these tumultuous rapids. It caused a crack in the body of the ship. Water started to pour in.

"Push us off! Hurry!" exclaimed Jeremiah.

Marlow, Wildcat, and I picked up the wooden rods and pushed as hard as we could from the rock. My arms were shaking from the weight of the task. After a few strong pushes, the boat was set free. Unfortunately, we were turned in the opposite direction of the flowing water and were helpless.

"We're dead. Dead, I tell you," cried Marlow as he hung on for dear life.

"She's a wild steed, all right! An Arabian thoroughbred," said Wildcat. "Don't let her kick ye off."

Water continued to pour into our boat. The rapids grew stronger, making the ship spin in all directions. The sound of falling water grew louder the farther we continued down the rapids.

"I hear something disturbing," I insisted.

"Ole bitter creek," said Wildcat. "She stands between ye and the Almighty!"

"When we hit the drop, take a deep breath and hold it!" yelled Jeremiah, gripping the steering wheel.

"Why?" I yelled.

"Waterfall," echoed Marlow.

The sounds of crashing water was distinguishable by its terrifying roar. The ship hit another rock. Marlow flew overboard.

"Marlow!" I screamed.

"Say your prayers to your God for mercy!" exclaimed Jeremiah.

The ship turned in all directions, and a small amount of light cutting through the rock revealed the waterfall ahead. I made the sign of the cross.

"Deep breath!" screamed Jeremiah. "Till the depths shall we part!"

The ship went over the side of the waterfall. I flew off the ship. I don't remember how long we fell for, but the falls were extremely steep. Free falling for a second or two, I descended into the water with great speed. The ship sank, whizzing right past me. Those long trips spearfishing under water were coming in handy. I was underwater for a while. I learned how to control my heart rate and breath.

I gazed up toward the surface, illuminated by sunshine. I swam up with great haste. I saw a small plot of land roughly twenty yards away from me. I swam to it and lay there for a moment. Once I caught my breath, I turned to the water. I saw Jeremiah swimming with Marlow on his back toward us. Wildcat was next to them, swimming toward me with a backpack on.

"That was one hell of ride," stated Wildcat. "I got your backpack. Helped me stay afloat."

"Wow," I replied as I put on my backpack. "I didn't think I would get this back."

Jeremiah placed Marlow on the sandy beach. Poor Marlow was barely breathing.

"Come on, Marlow," exclaimed Jeremiah as he tried to smack Marlow's face. "Don't die on me!"

"Give him some air," Wildcat instructed.

Jeremiah checked Marlow's breath, then gave him mouth-to-mouth and pumped life back into his lungs. Marlow coughed up water and opened his eyes.

Wildcat grabbed my shoulde. "Almighty chose not today, gang."

"What happened?" Marlow asked. "Did we make it?"

Jeremiah gave Marlow a big hug.

"Me boat didn't," remarked Jeremiah sadly.

I looked around to assess our situation. We were in a turquoise lagoon, in between the sea and the cave system behind us. The lagoon was a circle, fortified with large rock formations covered with tropical trees, green vines, and colorful flowers. The lagoon's ceiling was partially covered by the rocky terrain above our heads. On the other side of the lagoon was a small exit seemingly leading to the sea.

"This must be the lagoon on the map," I pointed out.

"And the exit must be through there," Wildcat pointed.

About four hundred yards from us was a small exit wedged between the rocks, leading upward. A small strip of land circled the lagoon, allowing us to walk to the exit. I helped Marlow up and offered my shoulder to him as a crutch.

Marlow cried out with eyes wide with fright. "Something is in the water. I saw it!"

"What did it look like?" I asked.

"Yellow eyes, like you said," replied Marlow.

"Blast!" Wildcat remarked. "If there's one, there's probably more."

"Hurry! Best not take a chance. To the exit!" Jeremiah commanded.

I stared into the lagoon intently. The serpent appeared briefly above the water, showing bright blue scales covering its slithering body, moving through the water. My eyes caught a floating object, relinquishing red plasma, adding a red dye to the turquoise water.

"It looks like a . . . body," I said.

"Pochick," Jeremiah stated. "Must've floated down the rapids."

I made the sign of the cross.

"Another Tuck down," remarked Wildcat.

"The horror! The horror!" Marlow cried.

A large mouth, like that of a large viper, came from below the surface, rising above the water and grasping Pochick's body between its teeth. There it stood, this monstrous sea serpent. I could see its light blue scales glistening in the water, protruding from the surface with its pointed, dark navy fins lining its back. The eyes were a magnetic gold.

"That ain't no rattlesnake," remarked Wildcat. "That's one of them sea dinosaurs."

Another large serpent lifted its head from the water and attempted to take a bite. The first serpent ripped it apart, flinging pieces of Pochick's body in all directions. The other serpent ate a piece of it.

Pieces floating above the water revealed two or three other serpents biting for it. The first serpent, once finished, caught a glimpse of us, hissed, then went back below the surface.

"Oh my," exclaimed Marlow.

"Help Marlow, Wildcat," said Jeremiah. "I'll stall them."

Jeremiah quickly unhinged his whip with vibrant purple minosium tips. Jeremiah clicked a button on the hilt, lighting up the tips of the whip with electricity. Jeremiah cracked the whip.

"Don't tarry," warned Wildcat.

"Aye," said Jeremiah.

Wildcat and I helped Marlow to our shoulders. His leg was severely broken.

The large serpent rose from the water in front of us, hissing as he watched our movements. Jeremiah moved in front of us and whipped at it. The serpent shrieked from the pain and bared its teeth to us.

"Go!" Jeremiah demanded.

Wildcat and I took off with Marlow, helping him run with his limp. We darted through the sandy surface toward the exit. Jeremiah cracked his whip in the air at the serpent. The serpent waited for an opportune moment to strike.

"Ahoy!" declared Jeremiah. "I will cast thy head into the sea from the tips of my whip."

The serpent lunged forward, attempting to strike. Jeremiah moved out of the way like a matador to a bull, then whipped the serpent in the neck, gashing it. The snake shrieked in pain. It attempted to strike again. Jeremiah elegantly danced out of the way. He attempted to whip the beast, but the serpent dodged.

We continued to run toward the exit. Marlow was struggling, trying his best to run with his damaged leg. Looking at the water, I noticed two serpent fins slithering toward us. We picked up our speed. One of the serpents sprang from the water and attempted to strike us. Wildcat pushed Marlow and me away to dodge the lunge and bite.

Another serpent propelled itself from the water, attempting to bite us. I pulled Marlow's head down as the snake struck above our heads. It missed us, crashing into the rocky edges of the lagoon, then thrust its back into the other serpent. The two serpents began to fight with one another. Wildcat was at the exit.

"Come on! Hurry!" insisted Wildcat. "While they's fightin' amongst themselves."

I helped Marlow climb up the rocks to the small opening in the cave. I could see the cave ascend toward the surface. Wildcat grabbed Marlow's elbow, and we brought him into the small crack in the cave and laid him on a rock.

"Jeremiah!" echoed Wildcat.

I went out of the cave to see if Jeremiah was behind us. Jeremiah was running toward us, wounded on his left arm.

"We need to help him," I proclaimed.

The body of the first large snake rested dead on the surface. I saw more serpents, roughly five or six, on the other side of the lagoon, slithering toward Jeremiah. The two snakes that had bickered with one another smelled Jeremiah and turned toward him.

Luckily, Jeremiah was near the exit. The two snakes blocked the exit with their mouths wide open. One serpent tried to strike him. He dodged it and whipped it in the mouth. I needed to do something; I needed a distraction

"Get the rocks. We'll throw them at the serpents," I said.

"Better than nothing," Wildcat remarked.

Wildcat and I picked up a few rocks and began to throw them at the serpents' heads. We got a serpent's attention. It turned to me and tried to strike me. I maneuvered out of the way. The other snakes were almost upon all of us.

I looked back at the lagoon, and at least twenty or more large serpents were coming toward us . . . no, thirty . . . no, fifty. They kept coming, more and more of them, swimming toward us.

Jeremiah came upon the rock, cracking his whip at each bite. Wildcat and I continued to throw rocks at the serpents.

Jeremiah quickly made it into the small exit between the rocks. The serpents did not give up. They all ascended toward us, fifty or more serpent heads attempting to bite us. I could see nothing but the glowing golden eyes in front of me. We ran into the passage. The serpents attempted to break through the opening, causing the rocks around us to fall.

We hastily ascended through the passage and toward the surface. Through a small crack in the ceiling, we could see the surface and sunlight.

"Quickly!" said Jeremiah. "They are breaking through."

We ascended large stone staircase of rocks. Wildcat reached the top first and helped pull up Marlow. Below us, two of the serpents made it through the small opening. Jeremiah and I hastily reached the surface.

Crash! Rumble! A violent collision occurred below us, like that of an earthquake. Rocks fell in all directions, closing off the lagoon entrance completely.

I lay down in a grassy cliff overlooking the ocean below, attempting to catch my breath.

"So much for the gold," remarked Marlow.

I never thought venturing out from the dock that day would end this way. My eyes took in the sights, buried in secret delight. My heart felt thrills on tumultuous white waters and sprinted from numerous slithering serpents' venomous bites. The day was tragic yet revealing.

Inside the Faustino chamber, I could not help but contemplate the hieroglyphics painted on the walls of the chamber, depicting the same story Axelrod told me that morning on our fishing boat. Funny how Taft and the class, most especially Tony Torino, mocked me with the story of Faustino, framing it as lunacy.

Alas, the joke was on them, for Faustino was real—the chamber and minosium, too. As for my amulet, I questioned how Axelrod got a hold of it. He must have ventured into one of these many chambers scattered across the world to obtain this ancient key.

If this amulet was the key to the labyrinth, then it would make sense that Narcisse and Carlos Torino demanded to have it that day the lightning struck without a cloud in the sky.

My mind still rattled in madness, trying to discern whether this Zoltan figure was a character in the play of Axelrod, Narcisse, and Carlos Torino. If, in fact, Zoltan was the *him* Torino spoke of that day, then I'd been surrounded by this Trader's life since the day I came from the womb. The amulet on my neck bore witness to his statement.

One question still lingered in the air: How did Kalendar and the Victoria & Co. play into this whole debacle? I assumed the answer would come, for the cards had been dealt and my hand was hidden from the rest of the table.

CHAPTER 18

My Variation

C OMMOTION RAGED ACROSS the island. Everyone knew what
had happened. Shock, anger, fear, and unrest filled the island,
causing great panic and mistrust among the privateers. No
one knew who was working for the one they called Zoltan and the
Tughra.

Kalendar ordered the privateers to search for the Tucks in order
to hold them accountable and assess the damage. The Tucks were nowhere to be found, not even some of the deceased bodies. The entrance
to the lagoon and cave were walled off by the massive rocks. To drill
through these massive rocks would take a great deal of time. The only
bright thing out of it all was that Marlow's leg wasn't broken. He was
patched up and put in a boot.

As for all of us, shortly after our ill-fated expedition, we met
with Kalendar inside of his office. We relayed to him the spectacular
events of the cave. Jeremiah wished to keep it a secret, but we had
no choice. At the end of our explanation, Kalendar remained calm,
considering our story. Kalendar knitted his eyebrow, contemplating,
thinking of his next move.

Helga came into the room bearing my bag. She pulled out pieces
of the minosium, which were illegally extracted during the off-season.

Kalendar shook his head. "Do you know what this means?" He
held up the minosium shards. "The Terminal will undoubtedly hear of
this, if they have not already, regardless of the truth of your story. The
Terminal will investigate this, and you four will be put on trial. Right
now, I say, you four are criminals in the eyes of the Terminal."

I attempted to plead with Kalendar, telling him how I had no idea that was in my bag and the circumstances that led to it. Jeremiah chimed in to explain himself, blaming everything on himself and condemning the Nantucket men for their misdeeds.

"As for the Nantucket outfit," explained Kalendar, "their claims of the Tughra and betrayal are quite dangerous and concerning. I will investigate this matter myself. This incident will sweep through the Terminal in a matter of days, damaging the Victoria & Co. reputation. Nothing is worse for a company than an outfit extracting in the off-season." His head shook with the great anger boiling inside of him.

Wildcat attempted to explain to Kalendar his thoughts and concerns, but it was of no use.

"You four will be lucky to survive this," Kalendar stated. "The Terminal could make an example out of you. I will have to defend myself and the honor of this company. Worst of all, if Zoltan is alive and the Tughra still thrive, we are all in danger. Luckily, we know what they are after." Kalendar lifted my amulet. "The key."

"They'll be back for it," remarked Jeremiah.

"Yes," said Kalendar. "I will do what I can to save your four when the time comes. As for now, you are prisoners of the Terminal. I will keep this amulet safely with me, and we will return to the topic of Zoltan after the Bazaar . . . if you four survive."

"We're innocent, Captain," Wildcat asserted.

"I believe so, but we cannot take any chances," Kalendar replied.

"I guess we'll be on our way then," Jeremiah said as he stood up from the chair.

"Helga," said Kalendar. "Lock these four men into the dungeon for now. We wait on the Terminal. If I speak any more to you four, I put the company and myself at risk. Leave."

"Yes, sir," said Helga.

"The dungeon!" shrieked Jeremiah. "Is that necessary, Captain?"

"The Terminal must know we are on their side," said Kalendar.

Our downfall came at the hands of the minosium drilled in the chamber and placed in my bag. We could have potentially avoided the dungeon if this minosium was discarded prior to our interaction with Kalendar and Helga.

I reflected on how the minosium ended up in my bag. I had no idea illegally extracted minosium was put there. The Terminal took this offense, punishable by death, extremely seriously.

I had been chained to the pillar in the chamber when the Tucks extracted the mineral. They needed a container, anything to hold the minosium for the brief time being. Rabbit Run was close by the hot spring and grabbed my bag to put the mineral inside of it. I was too busy paying attention to Wildcat to notice the minosium being placed in my bag. No wonder Rabbit Run wanted my bag so terribly.

I should've noticed the excess weight in my bag or seen it when I pulled out my amulet to put it around my neck, but when I was pulling out my amulet in great haste, my attention was drawn to these man-killing sea snakes, not on the sparkling jewels resting inside in my bag. Aye, the thought never crossed my mind that minosium would be there.

Regardless of the minosium extracted, the Terminal would have heard of the deaths of the Tucks, causing all of us to stand trial to bear witness.

Besides those unfortunate mishaps, my gut told me a far worse enemy, the one they called "*him*" and *his* mysterious Tughra army, would soon find out, too. Above all of that, the thought of not competing in the Trials crept into my head, causing my psyche great distress.

What if all that work and training were for nothing? No, no! I started to slightly panic inside Kalendar's office at this thought. My world was turning on me. Fate chose to throw me into the most abhorrent of swamp mud, my oldest, dearest enemy.

It was astonishing to see how well my life was going, and in once instant, my opportunity vanished faster than a hummingbird strokes it wings. Fear, frustration, and confusion swamped my soul at that moment.

Four privateers, accompanied by Helga, began to shackle each of us.

"Alas, the dungeon," sighed Jeremiah.

"Jail . . . No, no, no," I said as I was being shackled by a privateer. "This can't be."

"At least a cigarette for the road?" Marlow asked, but he was denied one.

"No need for shackles, love," said Jeremiah to Helga.

"The Trials, Kalendar. The Trials!" I pleaded to Kalendar, but it fell on deaf ears.

"That's the least of ye worries, my friend," Jeremiah said.

Helga smiled and placed shackles on Jeremiah's wrists. Helga and the privateers led Jeremiah, Marlow, Wildcat, and me to a tower made of stone on a hill overlooking the town. It served as the island's jail. The tower used to be an old fort in the 1600s. Victoria & Co.'s orange flag with a navy blue V and C next to each other waved above the tower.

Helga led us down a spiral staircase into a desolate cell at the bottom of the tower. The floor was covered in hay. It had three large cells with one window per cell. Helga threw us all into one large cell that reeked of urine and excrement. The guard was a large, pale brute privateer with a pointed chin and long, brown hair. Helga called him Raphune and told him to shoot us if we tried to escape, a rather harsh order.

"Yes, madam," he replied coldly.

Raphune went away, leaving us to our own devices within the cell. There were two other privateers in the adjacent cells, a woman and a man, both of whom had passed out.

I kicked the bars angrily upon entering the cell, letting out a succession of grunts. I was furious, angered by this mistake. I didn't plan on this! Locked away for a crime. What crime? Kalendar had my amulet, my dear amulet! How would I ever find my past now? I continued to shake the bars of the cell.

"It is no use, Christoph," sighed Wildcat as he sat in the corner of the cell.

"Now what? We're innocent! What if I can't compete in the Trials. Then what?" I cried out. "Oh, and my amulet, the only piece to my past, is now gone."

"Eh, quit ye whining!" said Jeremiah.

"Christoph, we'll get it back. I assure you of this," said Wildcat.

"If it weren't for Jeremiah, pulling me into a wild goose chase, I wouldn't be in this predicament right now," I said.

"Hold ye tongue. Remember who you're talking about," Jeremiah said. "You, not I, chose to come aboard my ship. Better yet, we realized where the labyrinth lies. We hold the key, a key more important than that amulet."

"Won't do me any good if I can't participate in the Trials," I replied. "It's your fault we're here."

"That's not true, Swift," Wildcat countered.

Jeremiah arose. "You fool, putting the blame on someone else, eh? I see you're ready to throw me under the bus . . . What gratitude, wretch!"

"For fishing?" I exclaimed. "What did spearfishing ever teach me?"

"How to control yourself in unfavorable conditions," Jeremiah replied, "but it seems ye never learned."

"You're a roughneck and nothing more," I remarked.

"Aye, true words of immaturity and ignorance," said Jeremiah. "Think ye better, smarter, stronger than the seasoned ones, eh? And yet, having nothing to prove of it. Ye are a child with an ego bigger than Faustino's greed and pride greater than that of the devil himself. You're a fool and will always be one with an attitude like that."

Anger pulsated through my body. I tried to jab Jeremiah, but it was of no use. He grabbed my fist, threw me to the ground, then beat me without interruption. Wildcat jumped in to break us up and pulled Jeremiah from me.

As I lay on the ground, I was confused by the punches and the words I endured, equally piercing my soul. A wave of exhaustion consumed me as I lay upon the cold floor, contemplating what Jeremiah said to me.

Was it true? Did I blame other people for my decisions? I always took responsibility! It was his fault that I was here.

I did agree to board his ship though, and it was Jeremiah who helped me aboard the airship that fateful day in Villefranche. Jeremiah saved my life, trained me out of the goodness of his heart, and here I was blaming him for our misfortune. I sighed at how ungrateful a wretch I still was. Tears cascaded from my eyes at my own stupidity, but I kept them hidden. Perhaps there were things I still needed to learn.

I awoke from a deep sleep. Raphune brought small pieces of hard bread and water. My right eye was swollen shut. I took the bread silently, grunting from the pain in my face, and quietly sat in my corner. No one in the cell conversed with one another upon the realization that were here to stay for a while. We all kept to our thoughts. We were all upset, disgruntled with our situation.

A few days of silence went by, then a whole week. I started to become aware that life inside of a prison cell was terrible. It was boring, first and foremost. I was offered very little food, my back ached from sleeping on the hard floor, and we had only one window to let in the sunlight.

Life in a cell did lend me time to my thoughts, time to reflect on what had happened—how I got here and what my next plan of action was. Every single day, I prayed to the Lord to save me from this swamp mud. At first, I was angered with Him, asking why this had happened. Over time, the pain turned into sadness as I reflected on the past, seeing where I went wrong in my past life.

Looking back to my life in Louisiana, I blamed Axelrod, Tony Torino, Mr. Taft, the basketball team, St. Francis, and even God for my misfortunes; yet here I was still blaming my misfortunes on Jeremiah, Rabbit Run, Kalendar, the Victoria & Co, the Traders Terminal, and once again God himself.

It seemed the universe was playing a trick on me, mirroring two existences together that on the surface appeared to be black and white but were strangely the same. Perhaps the problem wasn't my external environment but my internal one. I asked myself such questions.

Occasionally, Raphune stopped by our cell and would offer fresh water and fruit to us.

"Here, Christoph. Don't ye look hungry," he'd say with a smile.

I went to grab the food and water, but Raphune poured the water out and threw the cup at me.

"Why do this to me?" I sighed.

"For my brother Tucks," replied Raphune and then walked away.

"Stay away from him. The kid is from Nantucket," said Wildcat. This was his first utterance of words in at least two weeks. His beard grew out in a mangled fashion. All of us looked rough. I thought this was the right moment to speak.

"Jeremiah," I said.

"Yes?" he replied.

"I wanted to say that I am sorry for what I told you two weeks ago. I've had time to think about it and realized where I went wrong. Would you accept my apology?"

Jeremiah smiled. "Apology accepted." He let out a sigh of relief. "Forgive me for leading you and Marlow to what I thought was a chamber filled with Spanish doubloons. Indeed, I should have turned us around at the sight of Faustino, which cursed us all to this fate."

"Curiosity lassoed all of us," said Wildcat. "We all chose to venture forward knowing the risks."

"Jeremiah," said Marlow, coming from his deep silence. "I would follow you to the ends of the earth if you asked me to. My only regret was losing your beautiful ship."

At that moment, I could the feel the tension in the cell fade away. The pumped-up anger and pent-up ill feelings were vanquished by a moment of humility.

"I've been thinking to myself the past few days about what was said in the chamber," I stated.

"Yeah?" replied everyone in the cell, tuned into what I was about to ask.

"Jeremiah, how did you know about this Zoltan person and the Tughra?" I inquired.

Jeremiah was a smart man. He could see the spark of desire in my eye. Jeremiah told me that when he started his training with Fitzroy years ago, he became well-acquainted with another trainee on the island. His name was Lennox, a smart Englishman, recruited by another outfit in the Victoria & Co.

Jeremiah and Lennox became friends as they worked together to pass the Series Trials. They trained together, ate together, and drank together—all while becoming the best of friends.

One day, Jeremiah caught Lennox conversing in the tiki tavern with a mysterious figure in a black cloak, bearing a symbol on his right hand in turquoise and gold—three straight lines, intersected by three more lines flowing like a musical note, which spiraled around those straight lines and one more line that looped around the three straight lines.

Jeremiah said it was a strange symbol, so he asked Fitzroy if he knew of this symbol. Fitzroy's face grew pale, and he told Jeremiah the symbol was called the Tughra, an old Turkish symbol of the sultan, but specifically used to represent an order under a dangerous man called Reszo Zoltan. Jeremiah told Fitzroy of Lennox and where he saw the man bearing the mark of Tughra.

After countless days of searching, Lennox disappeared with no sign of the cloaked man. It was only then that Fitzroy scarcely revealed to Jeremiah who Zoltan was. Reszo Zoltan was a part of the original

Victoria & Co. outfit when Kalendar first started the company. Zoltan was from Eastern Europe with an ambitious and warlordlike mentality. He passed the Series Trials easily and obtained his license.

Kalendar believed he was a brilliant extractor but knew deep down something about Zoltan was off. The company operated during a lucrative time, capitalizing on minosium and the trading of it.

Zoltan despised the Terminal's taxes, rules, and regulations imposed on his extracted ore. He always sought more minosium, more power, more equity, but it would be impossible with the Terminal in the picture, or so he thought.

In response, Zoltan convinced Kalendar and the crew to seek out the greatest deposit of minosium to have existed: Faustino's minosium deposit lost in time. Zoltan believed he who found Faustino's collection of minosium could destroy the Terminal and rule the world. Zoltan never revealed this true intention to the company. Zoltan persuaded Kalendar to search for the mythical Faustino labyrinth.

Jeremiah was unsure what exactly happened on the expedition. All he knew was that something went terribly wrong, scarring Kalendar for life. Supposedly, Kalendar told Helga this story, Helga told Fitzroy, and Fitzroy told Jeremiah.

After the expedition, Zoltan left the Victoria & Co. and created his own order, calling them the Tughra—an order of rebellious, pirate-like ex-outfit members who had left their company behind in pursuit of riches without the interference of the Terminal. In response, the Terminal sent a fleet of man-o-war airships to hunt down and kill Zoltan.

Not long after, it was said that Zoltan perished during a fight with these airships high in the sky, bringing an end to the Tughra and his legacy—until the Tucks brought up the name Zoltan and Tughra.

I thought deeply of the story Jeremiah related to me, especially of Zoltan's intentions and my own anger toward the Terminal for subjecting me to the Series Trials. Strangely, I could see Zoltan's point, though all of this wouldn't matter if I perished at the hands of the Terminal.

"Jeremiah," I said. "What should we do? Will the terminal execute us?"

"Possibly, depending on their verdict," replied Jeremiah. "They are some ruthless bastards."

"Not all people on the committee are bad," Wildcat interjected. "Some will be fair to us."

"Aye, we'll provide a solid case. I've talked my way out of several court trials, municipal trials, and scandalous trials. This one is no different, and we have a good case," Jeremiah said.

"Not from what I've seen," Marlow remarked.

"Then have your eyes checked," Jeremiah replied.

"Even if I survive this trial before the committee, I have the Series Trials right after," I stated, "and I haven't been training."

"That's right, kid," said Wildcat.

I was worried, and my face showed it.

"I have an idea," said Wildcat. "I'll do my best to train you for it, and I know Jeremiah will help, too. We'll continue your training in here."

"Indeed," remarked Jeremiah. "We all need some training, even I."

"Beats sitting down all day," sighed Marlow.

"Yeehoo! I would owe a debt to each of you," I exclaimed. "But when do you think the trial with the Committee would be?"

"In a few weeks," said Wildcat.

"Don't worry," said Jeremiah. "You'll make the Trials and be well trained for it. Rest assured. You have the best trainer in all of the seven seas."

Raphune approached the three cells, delivering food and water. When he came to our cell, he had a sinister look on his face. "A lot of chatter for men set to die." He laughed. "We have friends on the Committee."

"As do we," replied Wildcat.

Raphune grabbed a bucket of water near his foot, chuckled, placed it near the cell, and walked away. Coming down the stairs was a man wearing a large coat, keeping his face concealed by the shadows. It was Fitzroy; I could tell by the way he walked, upright and pronounced. He handed Raphune some coins, then walked toward us. He unveiled his hood at our cell.

"Fitzroy!" I cheered.

"Nice to see a friendly face," said Wildcat.

"Shush," insisted Fitzroy.

"Where have you been?" asked Jeremiah.

"Helping you four up top," replied Fitzroy. "I can't talk long. We have a tough trial ahead of us, so be prepared to defend yourselves. Seemed the Tucks have friends in high places."

"We'll be fine," reassured Jeremiah. "Any news from Kalendar?"

"He's concerned, from what I can tell, but he hasn't given up hope on you four or the company's reputation," said Fitzroy.

"That's a relief," said Marlow.

"Here," said Fitzroy, handing me a large brown sack. "Supplies, from Kalendar and me."

"How much longer until the trial?" asked Wildcat.

"Four weeks," remarked Fitzroy.

Fitzroy gave his adieu and left. I opened the bag. It was filled with bread, water, fruit, and my textbooks on the terminal. I was delighted to see the books. It meant I still had a chance. I dug deeper and found the book Kalendar gave me earlier in the year: *The Rules of a Prince.*

CHAPTER 19

Pas de Quatre

I CONTINUED MY training with the help of Jeremiah, Wildcat, and Marlow in our cell. In the morning, Wildcat would test me on all my knowledge that pertained to the Terminal's rules and regulations. He knew them quite well, more than I thought prior to this. We used the book as a reference point.

"When was the Terminal established?" asked Wildcat.

I took a moment to think. "1986."

"What law was enacted by world leaders to protect and regulate the minosium exchange?" asked Marlow, using the book.

"Minosium Act of 1995," I said.

"Ye know it well," stated Jeremiah.

"Now for the Trials," said Wildcat.

Wildcat went into further detail about the Series Trials, which types of obstacles I should look for and how to survive. We would do this every day for a few hours.

"If something looks too good to be true, it is. Move on, or find a key to the trap," suggested Wildcat.

"Like what?" I inquired.

"If the trial looks strangely simple, do not fall for it. There's always a hidden trap waiting to kill you. The Terminal is smart, too smart. Do not try to outsmart them. Play your game. Control is key," Wildcat coached.

"What about the time limit, or what if I can't find a coin to move on?" I asked.

"That's a myth. There's always a coin available. You just must find it. Don't be too hasty; only fight on favorable ground. Remember: Control your game. Do not let the game control you. If something seems off, move on," Wildcat directed.

"How do I know if I'm choosing the right trial to engage in?" I asked.

"You won't know for sure, but you can choose by your gut instinct. Trust it. Do not second-guess yourself," Wildcat advised.

After occasional reading and lecturing, the whole cell engaged in combat training and rigorous cardio workouts. Jeremiah pushed all of us to the limit during those cardio workouts.

First, we did burpees for an hour straight. That was where we jump up, then immediately do a pushup, and repeat. It was exhausting. Sweat poured from my face; my shoulders, chest, and abs ached. Jeremiah would call out each one. 1 . . . 2 . . . 3 . . .

Next, we would mix in pull-ups using the bars in the cell while the others would lightly box with one another in between each set. Jeremiah said lightly boxing, but it was definitely not lightly. It was outright bare-knuckle boxing.

Marlow and I typically went at each other, jabbing at each other's sides and faces. It was painful. My face was swollen every day with an occasional black eye or a hurt rib. When I was fighting, Jeremiah would jump in and correct our form, and then all four of us would fight simultaneously.

Jeremiah was well trained, having an eye for all types of martial arts. After boxing, we would wrestle. Jeremiah showed us intricate moves utilizing jiu-jitsu, emphasizing body contact, judo for pinning my opponent, kung fu for kicking, and tai chi for fluid motions. Most importantly, we practiced our breathing and keeping peace of mind. Jeremiah was sculpting me as a great warrior—mastering all arts of combat, motion, and thought.

Jeremiah demonstrated the art of controlling the mind, the lungs, and the spirit—all flowing in unison with one another. When following Jeremiah's tai chi movements, I fell into a meditative trance, unlocking portions of my mind I'd never believed or knew existed.

It was there in those meditative states that I would pray to the Lord above. All the clutter and noise of my head was subdued, and in those moments of silence, I heard the Lord whisper to me with words only tangible through the spirit. The whisper told me to believe in myself and Him, to remain strong, that He would be with me.

Jeremiah sensed that I entered a place few had ever seen or felt during those meditative trances. He would not disturb me but gazed at me with joy, seeing his methods unfolding before his eyes. I was touching a place where the great men of history had been before, a place of greatness and heavenly genius. I could see over the mountain to a place of my greatest potential.

It was there in my deep meditative state that I decided to put my childish ways behind me—arrogance, overconfidence, excuses, and useless distractions. I would focus on my goal and my mission, and I would not rest until I achieved them. I would uncover my hidden past along my path of becoming an extractor. The next step was the Series Trials. It was crucial that I obtained victory, for my life and future depended on it.

I did not know where Axelrod was, but I knew he sent me here, knowing I would face the Series Trials while also unfolding this mystery of the Amulet of Faustino. For now, I narrowed focus completely on the Trials—victory or death.

At the end of those six weeks in the cell, I was a sculpted man, ready to take on whatever life threw at me. There was a great air of peace within our cell. We worked hard during those days. We each found our own piece of enlightenment during those isolated times. It was a retreat from the noisy world above us, a blessing in disguise.

Before my time in the cell ended, I finished the red book Kalendar had given me. It spoke of how a prince should act in all his affairs and how one may rise to power, outlining concepts such as how a prince should act with justice and mercy but act severely if contested. A prince should keep his mind focused on his kingdom, preparing for war in times of peace. It listed many ways to justly ascend to power and how to maintain that power with love and discipline versus fear and hatred.

The one concept I took to heart from this manuscript was that Fate was like a volcano. No matter what we did as humans, we could not stop the volcano from erupting. The eruption would happen, and if the prince's city were built near a volcano, then the eruption would devastate the city.

The book told the story of two kingdoms living side by side on the slopes of a volcano in Italy. One day, the volcano roared out of the blue, causing great speculation among the two kingdoms. The first king relied on sorcerers for his information. They told him the gods would never destroy his beautiful city by a volcano, nor could a volcano have such power to destroy a city as large as his.

The king believed his high walls would suffice as protection. The king took the sorcerers' word and built up a great army and high walls. The king thought with his high walls and great army that he could conquer the kingdom next to his while they trembled from the weak volcano's roar.

The other kingdom was much smaller and full of good, hard-working men. The prince of this small kingdom heard the roar of the volcano and brought the wisest men from around this kingdom for advice. From their research, they said the volcano was set to erupt and destroy everything in its path.

The prince took heed of his advisors and built great ships to sail away and return after the eruption. The prince did so and sailed away.

The king of the neighboring kingdom delighted in this, believing he was right. The king deployed his army and took over the vacant city without a drawn sword. He laughed at the other prince's stupidity of leaving his city vacant. Not long after, the volcano erupted, sending its eruption high into the celestial sphere. The king and his people could not escape the menacing, fiery ashes exploding from the volcano's crater.

His subjects had not built enough means of escape; rather, they used their funds to supply a great army and high walls. Sadly, all the king's people perished under the volcanic ashes.

On the other hand, the prince returned with his people to their destroyed kingdom after the dust had settled. He reclaimed not only his old lands but the neighboring king's lands, too.

The moral of the story was that Fate is an unstoppable volcanic eruption that no human can control. What we can do is listen to Fate's signs and when it strikes, which it will, be prepared for it; fortune would come to the prince who does.

I felt from this story, Fate was like Tony Torino coming for me that night when I left home. No matter what I could do, he was going to come. Axelrod was prepared for when he came, allowing for me to escape. I need to be the prince, prepared for when Fate struck again.

That story gave me solace in the fact that Axelrod could have possibly survived, given how prepared he was. Regardless of my thoughts, I had to keep my focus on the Trials first and foremost.

On our last day in the dungeon, all four of us awoke to Helga and three privateers accompanying her. She told us the Terminal would see us for our trial with the Committee. We had been in that cell for six weeks total.

She bound each of our hands and walked us up the spiral staircase and into the open sun. It was a beautiful sight to see. I hadn't seen this beautiful island in so long; it felt like an eternity. Jeremiah cheered once he felt the sea breeze on his face. Marlow kissed the ground. Wildcat gave a smile of contempt.

"No tarrying," Helga commanded. "You four are not free until the Terminal decides such."

"Where are we going?" I asked as my eyes squinted upon seeing the sunlight.

"To clean up and then to the Traders Terminal," Helga replied.

"A shower! Oh, thanks be!" Marlow exclaimed.

"Where is the Terminal?" I asked.

"Evisa," she replied as she hurried us along.

"Where is Evisa exactly?" I repeated.

"Off the coast of Italy near Corsica," Wildcat answered.

Helga and the privateers brought us to the dock where an airship floated in the sea, waiting for our departure. This airship was smaller than the great *Victoria* airship. It looked like a medium-sized sailboat, larger than a sloop. It was composed of a wooden deck and white frame. Instead of sails, the lines were connected to a dartlike blimp above the ship.

We were directed to the hold below deck to our seats, chained to the wall and accompanied by our privateers. Helga was the captain of the vessel, operated by her army of privateers. She gave the call to disembark.

I looked out the window and saw the ship slowly rise from the water and direct itself eastward. The ship retracted the blimp into the hold, allowing the four hovering jets to keep us level in the air. After a few moments, we jolted off at great speed.

It did not take us long to arrive at Evisa. We descended from the clouds, allowing the island to be seen from the sky. The island was surrounded by beautiful blue water. It was a small, semi-arid, mountainous island with large cliffs covered in slight green vegetation, like Capri and other Italian islands.

At one corner of the island was a small city called Monte Carlo. This was where the main Traders Terminal headquarters was located. Monte Carlo was a classic Italian town surrounded by a fortified wall in classic fashion like that of a medieval city. All the buildings had red tile roofs with walls painted red, tan, orange, or blue. On the highest cliff on the edge of the town was a massive fort with an elegant Italian palace at the center of it.

The ship slowly descended, extended the narrow blimp above the ship once more, and docked, coming to a soft touchdown. The lights came on, signaling that we had docked.

After a couple of minutes, a group of Trader cadets in olive green military regalia came into the hold, led by a pale, sturdy woman with brown hair and a deep voice. She must have been an officer. Two large T's were on the armpatch of each cadet. The woman read our names aloud, then took us into custody. Finally, she led us off the ship.

As we stepped off the ship, I realized how ahead of the times this island was. While walking through the docking area toward the walled city, I noticed airships of different sizes and designs. Some airships appeared more like futuristic spaceships in design with two small blimps holding them up instead of one large one.

Another ship looked exotic to me, appearing to be like an updated look of an ancient Chinese ship called a junk. The wings of the ship were red, curved like a crescent moon with bamboo-like battens situated between different parts of the wings. On top of the narrow blimp holding up the ship was another red crescent-curved tail and rudder, like shark's fins. The body of this Chinese airship was of classical design, like the schooner style of the *Victoria* airship.

I couldn't believe my eyes. There were airships and sloops of all different origins, demonstrating the culture and sophistication of each region around the world from which it came. We walked up through the stone archway with glass doors leading into Monte Carlo.

The city was awe inspiring, like something from my dreams. Each building was kept in classical Italian fashion, though outfitted with the most up-to-date technology, lights, doors, and furniture. The city was clean and properly maintained.

Artwork pertaining to minosium, the Traders Terminal, and

the unique world cultures intertwined with each part were painted throughout the city—on the narrow cobblestone roads, on the buildings, on the baroque-style fountains, and on marble statues. This place exhibited beauty reminiscent of the Florentine Renaissance but in the contemporary world.

Each apartment window was decorated with dazzling flowers. In the piazza were magnificent marble statues of sculpted men and women in classical ancient Greek style, either naked or adorned in minos-armor.

As the cadets led us through the bustling, narrow cobblestone streets, there were no cars, only flying sloops above. I could smell the most beautiful fragrances: a mix of cedarwood, rose, vanilla, jasmine, and ginger, all coming from the markets.

We walked through a smaller alley into a marketplace full of the finest wares: gorgeous Turkish rugs of all colors, gems of the finest cuts, fruit of every flavor, minosblades dazzled with intricate golden designs. This was a finer display of goods than that of Fifth Avenue in New York City. This was the center of trade in the entire world.

Finally, we reached the Terminal.

The Traders Terminal was a magnificent, five-story structure, appearing in classical Italian fashion with seven Roman arches with intricate floral designs, marble pillars, and red doors—all adorned with gold. It had a dome at the top of the structure, like St. Peter's Basilica in Rome. It was an architectural masterpiece, combining the contemporary with the classic.

We hastily pushed through the doors and climbed the large marble stairs that led to the trading floor. For only a brief moment, through the white marble arches, I saw the exchange floor filled with electronic screens and holograms of trading tables. Then, I was whisked away up a series of stairs to a large courtroom, which resembled an ancient theater where sound resonated from the center.

The roof was open air, providing sunlight and fresh air into the courtroom. Regular individuals sat on one side, and the Minosium Exchange Committee (MEC) sat on the other. The MEC was composed of eight main members, seated at the center of the circle. The courtroom was packed to the brim. I could see Fitzroy, Helga, and Kalendar within the crowd. Upon seeing us, Kalendar and Fitzroy moved toward center stage.

"Pray to ye God for help. We'll need it," Jeremiah whispered.

"Should I do anything?" I asked.

"Speak only if you are called on," Wildcat said.

The cadets brought us to the center of the stage and seated us behind three desks. Kalendar and Fitzroy entered the circle and stood next to us, representing us as our lawyers. I looked at the Committee members composed of men and women of all different nationalities. I counted seven. Where was the eighth member? I counted again; as I counted, I realized I knew one of the Committee members. Seated on the far end of the Committee table was a face far too familiar to me . . .

It was Carlos Torino of my Louisiana past—the father of Tony Torino, the leader of a mafia family suspected of killing John F. Kennedy, the man who destroyed my home and, if my word was true, a companion to the Tughra. He was my enemy, the hatred of my soul, the destroyer of my past world.

I clenched my fist as my blood boiled to steaming. *Shush*, I said to myself. *Reveal not your emotions, for you are a mere mortal dependent on his sway.* Arthur, my red-headed theatrical friend of St. Francis, was right to say Carlos Torino was well connected and powerful. I stared at him with piercing eyes, trying to subdue my resurfaced emotions and my past thoughts.

The force of my fury felt stronger than that of Caesar Augustus exacting revenge on poor Brutus. My mind pondered the day the lightning bolt struck the empty sky. If he was Carlos Torino and a Committee member, then how was he connected to Archbishop Narcisse, and what did Torino want with Axelrod? Wildcat caught my gaze as we were ushered to the table.

"What's wrong, partner?" Wildcat asked. "Did someone tell you something?"

"That's Carlos Torino on the Committee, an enemy of my past life," I replied.

Wildcat gestured me to kept quiet. "Let's hope today he's not."

The strings of Fate played their harmonious tune once more with the return of such a pivotal character in my life story. Coming from behind the Committee desk in an elegant navy robe was Mr. Charlie, a dear friend from days past, bringing forth jovial feelings of times with Axelrod and the hangar.

It had completely slipped my mind that Mr. Charlie had told

me on my first days aboard the *Victoria* airship that he was a part of the Committee. He caught my gaze, and he gave me a wink that felt more assuring than tomorrow's rising sun. My heart leaped with joy as my mind was trying to cope with the two forces working against one another to determine my ultimate fate.

The Committee chairman was an old, pale, Dutch fellow named Torsten. He had a brown mustache curling upward with small circle glasses resting on the tip of his pointed nose. Torsten began the trial. The room fell silent.

He called all four of us before the Committee.

Carlos Torino briefly stared at me with his malicious eyes, trying to place me. He knew I looked familiar as he searched the far recess of his mind. Then, in an instant, his eyes grew wide, realizing I was Axelrod's nephew, the one who bore the amulet. His eyes told me everything I needed to know, but he did not utter a sound. Torino kept his reserved composure, acting as if I was none other than a faceless criminal.

The proceedings began. Torsten introduced us to the Terminal and listed out our crimes as follows:

"These four gentlemen engaged in extraction during an off-season. More importantly, none of them are R.E.s," stated Torsten. "During this little expedition of theirs, another outfit of the Victoria & Co., also under Captain Kalendar, engaged in illegal extraction and combat out of season and not within the contested zones. There were casualties during this encounter."

Torsten listed the confirmed casualties and continued, "I hold the Victoria & Co. responsible for these mishaps and plan to show them the consequences of not adhering to the Terminal's rules and regulations. We all know that the penalty for illegal extraction and combat is banishment or the penalty of death. The defendants may step forward and state their case."

Jeremiah stepped forward and delivered an eloquent speech, entailing the entire story from beginning to end, detailing every specific point of where he was misjudged by Torsten. Jeremiah proclaimed that we did not engage in any sort of extraction or enter into an organized project.

Torsten asked for Jeremiah to elaborate. Jeremiah then spoke the name Faustino, and the crowd grew excitedly louder. Torsten demanded silence. Jeremiah had the crowd wrapped around his finger. Jeremiah then delivered the entire story of the Faustino chamber, providing a powerful argument for our case.

He demonstrated that we had no idea minosium was in this chamber, emphasizing that we had not engaged in this illegal activity; rather, it was the Nantucket outfit. At that moment, Jeremiah went silent. The crowd was on the edge of their seats. Jeremiah turned to the crowd behind us.

"The head of the Nantucket outfit, Spurwink, bore a Tughra, the symbol of Reszo Zoltan!" yelled Jeremiah.

The crowd cried out at this revelation. Torsten was shocked, trying to deduce the authenticity of this claim. Carlos Torino stood up and said these were false claims, attempting to undermine their crimes based on a mythical symbol and a claim on witnesses who could not be present. Torsten was conflicted, pulled on both sides.

Jeremiah continued, "Spurwink declared he worked for Zoltan. Spurwink had been searching for years on Victoria Island for the Faustino Chamber to extract and acquire secret information and minosium. Spurwink tied us up, threatened us with death, screamed 'Down with the Traders Terminal!' and began to drill from the hot spring inside the chamber. We were not extractors. We were prisoners and have been such ever since that day!"

The crowd cried out. Some said Zoltan has returned while others dismissed Jeremiah's claim. Torsten called for order in the court. Carlos Torino stood up to give his reasoning, attempting to appeal to the crowd.

"These are outrageous claims!" exclaimed Torino. "They have no way to prove these statements. How could someone believe Zoltan has returned, let alone influence a prominent outfit in the Victoria & Co? I believe this is a conspiracy conjured up by Captain Kalendar to illegally mine the minosium deposit during the off-season! Believe what you want, but I say the Victoria & Co. created a fake story to cover their illegal extraction from multiple places, not from this make-believe Faustino Chamber, but from who knows where else. Lies, I tell you. Lies!"

The crowd began to sway with Torino's reasoning. Torsten demanded evidence to back up our claims. Jeremiah knitted his brow, seeming to come up short of physical evidence.

This was it. They had us. Kalendar and Helga stepped forward. They handed a cadet a leather-bound book, which he handed to Torsten.

Kalendar explained in beautiful fashion that there was the evidence of our claims. "Inside that leather-bound book were years of surveillance and study of the men who claimed to be a part of Zoltan's hidden Tughra army. I have been following them closely, and there is our evidence of their dealings. I have sent my privateers to each of the places outlined in Jeremiah's story. Inside are pictures and statements from the Faustino Chamber and witnesses who can testify that the Victoria & Co. and these men seated before the Committee have played no part in the illegal extraction of minosium in the cavern. Therefore, based upon solid evidence, I say these men are innocent and should be relinquished of these charges and the Victoria & Co. dismissed of these unjust claims."

The crowd applauded Kalendar's stunning compilation and defense.

Torino screamed, "Lies! Lies, I tell you!"

Mr. Charlie stood up and gave a gripping speech about how he believed our story and said he'd been in contact with others who had said that Zoltan has returned. "This incident of betrayal and injustice is not solely related to the Victoria & Co. My agents, whom I trust with my life, have given me evidence that Zoltan and his Tughra pirate crew have been recruiting from many, many companies. This will continue to happen and instead of convicting four innocent men, we should be after the Tughra and stop them before they grow any stronger, for the power of the Traders Terminal and safety of the world are at stake!"

The crowd cheered at Mr. Charlie's oration, agreeing with his proposal. Torino fought against him on the other end. Torsten called for order in the court over the loud, argumentative screams coming from all over the courtroom.

Torsten called for a vote. He went to each Committee member. We needed at least five to have the majority. Torino and the two others next to him voted guilty—three against us. The vote moved to the other side of Torsten. Mr. Charlie and the three committee members next to him voted innocent. My heart was beating incessantly at the suspense of obtaining my freedom. Everything in the past months—

honestly, years—came down to one vote. My future, my life all came down to Torsten's vote.

Torsten stared at us with an intense gaze. He then looked to Kalendar and shrugged with a sigh. "Innocent. All four of ye are relinquished of the charges."

My heart fell out of my chest with those words. The crowd behind us cheered at the ruling of the court. Tears fell from my eyes. I cried out a thank you to the gracious Lord for saving me once again.

Jeremiah picked me up with great excitement.

I saw Mr. Charlie smiling at me from the Committee table. Torsten approached me, followed by the crowd.

"I'll keep an eye on you for the upcoming Series Trials," smiled Torsten.

"Please do. I intend to do well," I exclaimed.

He laughed. "Good sport."

Torsten went on his way, accompanied by a large group of cadets and the other Committee members. It was a joyous day in my life, one of the finest. I felt that deep magic swirl within my soul during that moment.

A feeling of uneasiness still crept in my spine at the thought of Carlos Torino knowing of my existence and whereabouts. If my gut was true and my logic sound, I believed Carlos attempted to kill Axelrod and me for my amulet for either himself or this him character Torino spoke of. The fact that Carlos Torino was a Committee member and potentially part of the Tughra demonstrated the interconnectedness of this unseen force bound by no chain.

This force sought out Axelrod and me. Nowhere but with my most-trusted friends was safe. I knew Mr. Charlie would work behind the scenes for my safety, and my friends would protect me with their lives. The unknown weighed upon me like the world on the shoulders of Atlas and kept me wondering what songs Fate's stringed instrument had left to play for me.

CHAPTER 20

Monte Carlo Serenade

J EREMIAH, WILDCAT, MARLOW, and I met with Fitzroy in a small café after the courtroom session to plan out our next moves. The day was beautiful. The sun was out, the sky was blue, and I could hear the birds chirping. It was around 15:00.

We sat outside at the wooden tables. I was noticing that most restaurants in Monte Carlo had outside seating, which was different than in America where people rarely sat outside to eat, drink, and chat at restaurants.

The waitress came to the table. Jeremiah ordered me an espresso, and he ordered some limoncello. Jeremiah wanted to know if Wildcat wanted any.

"Eh, some limoncello to celebrate?" smiled Jeremiah. "Served best on sunny days."

"I'll stick with the Italian beer," Wildcat countered.

"Have any rum?" Marlow asked.

"Sì," replied the waitress. Her English was spotty. "And you?"

"House white, my lady," said Fitzroy.

She brought out the drinks. Jeremiah and Marlow inhaled theirs and immediately ordered another round.

It'd been a long time since I'd had coffee, and I'd never had espresso. I asked why the cup was so little. It didn't look like much coffee. Jeremiah insisted that I taste it. I took one swig of it; it tasted bitter and rich and gave me a jolt.

The group laughed when I puckered my lips from that powerful shot of espresso.

"It's nice to see you, Fitzroy," said Jeremiah. "A dark cell can do things to a man, especially his back."

"I did what I could to help," said Fitzroy. "And it all worked out in the end."

Fitzroy talked about the Nantucket crew and where he believed they were hiding out. I thought they had died in the cave, but Fitzroy begged to differ. He said he was about to embark on a mission, given to him by Kalendar, to personally seek out the Tughra and the remaining Tucks and find out if Zoltan was still alive.

"I want to point this out," I remarked. "Carlos Torino, the Committee member—I believe I saw him the night I left home."

The group turned their eyes toward me, focused on what I said.

"Speak," Fitzroy replied. "What are you saying?"

I elaborated on my story, starting from the fight I had with Carlos Torino's son, Tony. I continued with the part about strange men approaching my house, attempting to abduct or kill me.

Out of those men, I thought I saw Carlos Torino as a part of that coalition. I told them I never spoke of this because Axelrod told me never to tell a soul of my past or where I came from other than to Kalendar. Fitzroy pondered on this.

"Axelrod was right. Do not repeat that story to anyone, especially about a Committee member. I'll look into it as a part of my investigation. Focus on the Trials for now," Fitzroy commanded. "Luckily, the Series Trials are next week on a nearby island, so it would be pointless for you three to leave."

"There's four of us," I pointed out.

"Yes, but Wildcat will be leaving tomorrow," Fitzroy said.

"Why?" Wildcat asked. "Swift needs me here."

"Kalendar needs you back on the island," Fitzroy explained. "He wants you to research more about these glowing worms before the upcoming season. A transport will pick you up tomorrow morning at the dock."

"Can't it wait a week?" I remarked.

"It's all right, Swift," Wildcat comforted me. "I'm needed elsewhere."

"As for the rest of you, Kalendar gave instructions that Jeremiah, Marlow, and I help Swift prepare for the Trials here on Evisa. Jeremiah will represent the company with Swift in the coliseum. Furthermore, trainees from around world will be arriving today for the Trials next week.

"Marlow, keep your eyes and ears open for anything you hear about the Tughra. Muster yourself amongst the trainees and privateers. See what you can find out," Fitzroy directed.

All agreed on the plan set forth by Kalendar.

"I say we celebrate tonight," cheered Jeremiah. "I need a night out and a sweetheart on my knee."

"I second that," said Marlow. "Fitzroy, have any cigarettes?"

Fitzroy pulled a pack from his pocket and gave one to Marlow. He smelled it with incomparable happiness. It was one of the few times he broke from his stoic attitude.

"Ah, it smells sweeter than a cookie store," smiled Marlow.

"Where will Kalendar—and you—be?" I asked Fitzroy.

"Kalendar had immediate business to attend to here on the island. He gives you his regards and good fortune for the Trials. As for me, I will be setting out on my search for the Tughra the day we finish your training," Fitzroy explained.

"I see," I said gloomily.

"Don't worry. We'll see each again other soon enough," reassured Fitzroy.

"And me too, gunslinger," said Wildcat.

"Aye, more the need to celebrate," echoed Jeremiah.

We all agreed excitedly. Fitzroy told us he had rooms for us in a small apartment on the edge of town. He gave us each a key and said we were free to go. Fitzroy wanted to join us that night and told us to tell him where we would be going.

Before Fitzroy left, he gave me a few coins and told me to spend them however I pleased. Jeremiah and Marlow were going to start the celebration early by checking out the beach. Wildcat said he wanted to check out the rifles and knickknacks at the marketplace to send back to his family.

"I want to mail my family one of them fancy postcards," said Wildcat.

"Beach, rum, and ladies, my friend," said Jeremiah.

"Cigars, too," winked Marlow.

"I'm feeling some alone time. Been needing it," I replied.

I gave them the go-ahead and decided to see the town for

myself—catch the sights, smells, and vibe of the world swirling around me. I wanted to enjoy this moment of free air without the thought of danger, which always seemed to be lurking around, creeping into my mind. I had to assure myself that I had this, and I would succeed at the Trials. I needed a peaceful walk to clear my head.

Walking around the town was wonderful. Feeling the heat of the sun warm my skin was like a warm fire on a cold, white, wintery day. I could smell the different sausages, pizzas, exotic spices, and all types of other international dishes flowing from the restaurants along the promenade. I had to try everything. I'd been starved of real food for weeks.

My eyes were pleased to see the dazzling and colorful culture around me—fruits and vegetables of all colors, mosaics, painted walls— and just the Italian architecture itself was rustic and enchanting.

I noticed a barber shop at the corner of the street. I moved my coarse hands through my helmet of hair and unkempt shaggy beard. I walked in and spent a few coins on a haircut and shave. It felt splendid. The barber spoke to me in Italian, so all I could do was nod in response. The barber knew what to do, so he fixed me up nice.

Next door was a bathhouse, and boy, did I need a bath! I looked and smelled homeless. I took my time in the delicacies of the bath-house. I first received a relaxing massage to work on my stiff knots all across my torso and back; then, I sweated out my worries in a steam room, followed up by an elegant bath. I felt like I stepped through the golden gates of heaven.

I ventured further down the promenade and saw through a window of a shop an assortment of fine Italian clothes. I walked in and chose anything that caught my eye. I bought myself a wide array of new clothes since I had none at the time. I bought beautiful linen shirts and pants and other pieces of clothing I needed, such as new shoes, socks, and underwear. I didn't care if it was from a high-end Italian designer. I wanted it and got it; it was such a liberating feeling being able to buy whatever I pleased.

I went to a fine Italian leather store. A man dressed in fine Italian apparel waited on me. He said all the merchandise in the store was handmade in Florence. The shopper's high came upon me, and I bought a leather backpack, belt, and jacket.

I felt like a changed man. When I saw myself in the window

along the promenade, I looked like a real man—mature, well-dressed, and refined. I hadn't seen my reflection in two months, at least. I could tell I was much more built with strong, broader shoulders and thicker arms than when I left home. My face looked more defined, concentrated, and stern, void of a baby face. My eyes had a different look about them. I felt that my innocence had washed away from my eyes.

My posture had improved. It was straighter and more upright. I could visibly see my progress over the last year. I was no longer a kid, mentally or physically.

The promenade led me to a beautiful, stone Catholic church, built around the Middle Ages. The inside was adorned with vibrant stained glass and golden mosaics. I knelt down in a pew and prayed to the Lord. I thanked him for keeping me alive and asked him to be with me when I fought in the Series Trials—to grant me victory, so that I may find where I fit into to His grand picture that intertwined with this ever-changing world around me.

As I was praying, a man sat next to me in the pew. He caught my attention on account of his familiarity. I'd seen him before, I knew, but from where? He had an olive complexion, a black beard, and short black hair. He was in his mid-forties.

Yes, I remembered. It was the man who helped me find my way to the Sinbad Tavern in Villefranche. What was his name? He was deep in prayer, but I wanted to give him something for helping me out that day.

I tapped him lightly on the shoulder. He opened his eyes and gave me a warm, attentive smile.

"Hello, I know this might be strange, but do you recall being in Villefranche, France, a couple of months ago?" I asked.

"Yes, I believe so," he said in perfect English mixed with a slight Middle Eastern accent.

"I thought so. My name is Christoph Swift, and what was yours again?"

"Gabriel," he said warmly.

"That's what it was. Gabriel! Sorry for interrupting your prayer."

"Not a problem. I'm always in commune with the Lord, and we were just finishing up. And you are?"

"Christoph Swift. We met in Villefranche a few months back. I was that poor fellow on the bench, moping in the rain. You showed me to the Sinbad Tavern. Do you remember?"

Gabriel thought for a moment. "Indeed, I do remember you now. Did you find what you were searching for?"

"I did find what I was searching for. Been a little bumpy along the way, but here I am."

"And here you are on Evisa Island, a secretive place few ever get to see. You must be an apple of God's eye to have this privilege."

"I could only dream such. I'll need Him now more than ever. I have the Series Trials in a week."

"Those Trials are tough. Most who enter into them fall."

"I know. I've been told that many times already. There are moments I feel inadequate to win the Trials. I tell myself I can, but I still feel that fear inside of me, telling me I won't survive. It's a battle inside of myself."

"Anything is possible, Christoph. If you believe in yourself, no challenge is too big or difficult for you to conquer."

"The chances of me surviving though . . . I don't know if I can do it. Who am I to survive? These trainees are from royalty, the Ivy League, and the military while I'm just a small-town guy from nowhere."

"I think not. I see you as a young, brilliant, worldly lad with great potential to go far. You are what you believe you are, Christoph. Believe in your worth and abilities and reach beyond the clouds, and you shall gain what you desire."

I felt his words enter not through my ears but into my soul.

"Alas, how does one know if he's going in the right direction?"

"Faith, my friend."

I pondered what he said.

"Thank you. I'll keep that in mind," I said. I stared at him for a moment, looking to his eyes, which told me a warm story that I could not put into words. I snapped out my small trance. "Here, I wanted to give you something for helping me that day in Villefranche."

I attempted to hand him a coin, but he refused it.

"Keep it. I have more than enough," he responded with a smile.

"If you say so," I replied. "I am leaving now. I'll let you get back to your prayer. Hopefully, we'll see each other in the future."

"As do I. Goodbye, Christoph Swift."

I left the church with a good feeling in my heart. It was the confidence that I dearly needed. I felt the worry—worry that had stressed my being ever since I left New Orleans—slowly fade away. Gabriel's words gave me a small sanctuary of peace.

I continued my solitary walk through the winding cobblestone streets of this small city. I could feel my lips were parched. I was growing hot from walking on this sunny day. I noticed a gelato shop, and I decided to take a gander at its collection. The gelato shop had a cozy feeling, resembling a rustic café. It was cold on the inside. I looked at the selection and choose a lemon sorbet. I smiled as I took a bite. It was a scoop of heaven.

While I was tasting the gelato, a hand tapped me on my shoulder. I turned around, and it was woman wearing big circular sunglasses, a tight white dress, and a red wide-brimmed hat. She appeared to be no more than twenty-five years old. She was fit with tanned skin, a sharp chin, and high cheekbones. In that moment, her beauty paralyzed me. I had gelato all over my face.

"Hello, I heard your accent. American boy?" she asked in an American accent.

"Uhh," I replied awkwardly as I tried to wipe my mouth. "Louisiana. You?"

"California," she replied quickly as if she were trying to figure me out. "What's an American boy your age doing on Evisa?"

"What do you mean 'your age'? I'm old enough," I said with bravado.

"Right," she responded quickly. "Why are you here?"

"Business."

"You're here for the Trials. I can tell you are a trainee."

"Does that shock you?"

"Yes, it does."

"Why so?"

"I thought I knew every American trainee, yet here you are, an unknown trainee."

"Here I am." I smiled. I was starting to like this. I could tell it was ruffling her feathers.

"I don't believe it."

I shrugged as I took a bite of my gelato. At that instant, she tried to snatch my gelato from my hand. Her hand moved quickly, quicker than lightning. I hastily moved it out of the way.

"Hey! Why did you—" I remarked.

She tried to kick me fast. I dodged her strike once more. Then, she tried to jab my side, and I elegantly moved out of the way. This was fun; she must be a trainee.

"Oh, too slow," I said.

She was growing frustrated. She then tried to jab me once more with great force. I grabbed her hand, and my gelato hit the ground. That was the last straw. She chuckled at the sight of my gelato on the ground. I ran out of the shop.

The woman continued to throw all different types of moves at me. I dodged and countered every single throw, jab, punch, and kick. She was good—great, in fact—though not better than I was. After a couple of minutes of fighting in the street, she backed off.

"You're damn good. You're not from an American company," she stated. "I would know, for I've beaten the best. What's your name?"

"Christoph Swift. And you?" I asked.

"Sophia," she replied as she relaxed her shoulders. She smiled at me. I could see her features now. Sophia had beautiful blue eyes with shoulder-length blonde hair. She meant business, a serious type girl.

"Where did you train?" she inquired.

I could tell she was growing more interested in me by the minute. She was like a mongoose. I had mixed feelings about her. She had the look I could fall for faster than Jeremiah's boat plummeting down a waterfall. If I had to guess, her looks were a part of her game. I took a deep breath as I gazed at her tentatively.

"Walk with me, and I'll tell you," I replied.

Sophia fixed her brow upon me and gave a small chuckle. She then walked toward me with a powerful womanly strut.

We walked along the promenade talking about our experiences with our companies. She was quite fascinated about my story and how I ended up there. I didn't tell her everything, of course. I had learned to keep my mouth shut on certain topics. I told her what my training was like for the Victoria & Co., and that was really it.

Sophia had joined a very prestigious, in her opinion, American company that was known to pick the very best recruits from around America for a chance to become an R.E. Her company was called Belle-Claire. For participants to attempt to become an R.E. for Belle-Claire, the trainee must either have family members in the company or were hand selected by the company's individual hiring committees.

In my opinion, from what I had heard and seen for myself, those selection committees played favoritism to people who fit the company's bogus political agenda. Most of the time, selection of a trainee by big-name trading companies was not always based on skill and qualification. Rather, selection was based on meeting a certain social quota in an effort to appeal to the Terminal and investors.

Once selected, the trainee hopefuls had to go through a strenuous training selection process to be picked by the committee to become a trainee. She said Belle-Claire chose only the best of the best young men and women from the most prestigious colleges, organizations, or references. She claimed the vice president of the United States' own niece tried out to be a trainee for the company, but she was denied.

Sophia claimed she was more than ready for the Trials and had been training this whole year in preparation. She further explained that she sometimes trained in America with other companies' trainees in joint training sessions. That was why she thought it was bizarre she had not seen me before.

I liked her. She was set on the prize and seemed to be a worthy adversary in the Trials. Sophia wanted to show me a few of the other trainees in her circle. I said that I thought it was odd to have friends during this process since in one week we would be trying to kill each other for a coin.

Sophia replied that they were friends on the outside of this process. When it came time for the Trials, she would slit my throat or that of any of her so-called friends without hesitation. I said that was how I was, too.

We followed the promenade to an outside restaurant along the beach. I noticed two women and three men laughing, drinking, and chatting with one another. They were all dressed in fine clothes and drinking red wine. She introduced me to the table.

"Look who Sophia brought," said one of the women scandalously.

"I love fresh bait!" stated one of the young men. His voice sounded strangely familiar. This man turned around to greet me.

"I want all of you to meet my new friend, Christoph Swift," stated Sophia.

My heart stopped for a moment as my eyes locked on this familiar young man.

"That's Tony Torino," said Sophia.

He and I were dead silent. Sophia did not understand there was an issue. The table was perplexed by the encounter.

"Do you know him?" she asked.

"Yes" came the cold reply from Tony Torino, the man from my past.

CHAPTER 21

Dance of the Cauldron

I WAS STANDING there with hesitation. I gazed upon the tormenting figure from my past life in Louisiana. He was my archenemy—the one who disrespected me and disrupted my life, the one whose demeaning words plagued my mind far and wide until I overcame his lies. Now, I was a different man than who I had been when he knew me. Tony Torino may have acted as if he knew me, but like so many people of my past who may have recognized my face, he did not know the creature behind the mask.

I'd grown into a man with a structured mindset and work ethic; I was stronger in the soul and was the commander of my feelings. The past acts done to me by Tony Torino still maintained some weight on my shoulders though it was lighter than a feather.

In Mr. Taft's class, I had stared out that window and dreamed of what the world was like while Tony and Taft chastised me, but I'd had no idea what lay beyond the clouds. I was chained to that desk, held down by oppressive powers, including my own. Once I was free from the chain of that oppressive society, at times heavier than the world of the Terminal, I ascended like a phoenix from the ashes.

On that last day of school, I felt my position of power was weak, but as I stared down Tony Torino with my masked face, I felt my position of power was rather great. And great it was.

Sophia insisted that I sit down next to her at the table. She introduced me to each person. Wayne was a buff, ebony-skinned man, big enough to be a professional football player. He was roughly my age with black hair and a large ego surrounding him. Wayne barely glanced at me. He had a well-kept beard and was dressed in all white with large sunglasses and diamond chains and earrings. In fact, all of them were dressed in white or tan, expensive clothes.

Next to him was Rolando, a large man with a muscular frame. He reminded me of an Italian juicehead who spent hours lifting weights at a gym. He was in his mid-thirties and covered in tattoos; he had tan skin and short, jet-black hair full of gel. He sounded like he was from New York with that Brooklynese accent. Rolando wore a large gold chain and earrings while carrying the same type of confidence as Wayne.

There were two women. The first one was Jessica with pale skin and brown hair. She was slim and appeared to be extremely flexible. She was roughly thirty-two years old. And the last girl was a tall redhead named Killian. She had pale skin and was extremely fit; though not too cute in the face, she looked like she could run for days at a time.

I sat down at the table. Tony could not take his eyes off me. His jaw dropped in astonishment. Silence seized his tongue. I could read him like a children's book. Never could he have imagined someone from his hometown, let alone someone like me, could make it to this prestigious island. Tony would spit on the ground at the mention of my name, but he could not act that way here, especially in front of his new friends.

A gleeful feeling elated my soul as I watched him in astonishment. He looked me up and down with the greatest interest. Fate struck her chord once more with the tune of great justice. Tony may have been the top dog in the past, like in the Golden Age of Greece, but a new empire to the west called Rome was brewing far greater. I was Rome, and his time was up.

"My, my, have you . . . grown! Look at your muscles," Tony commented in complete bewilderment. "How is this possible, Swift?"

"Oh, you know. Been doing a few pushups here and there," I replied coldly.

I withheld all my emotions and grief of my past life, burying it deep in the grave. From then on, he would never know what I thought or felt. I maintained a respectful stature, quiet and quick. After my initial exposure to the past, I returned to the present. I began to connect the strings of Fate.

It should be no surprise that Tony was there, for his father was a Committee chairman. How interesting. Carlos Torino wanted his son to be a Registered Extractor. He had put a great amount of faith in his boy. Sad if something should befall him during the Trials.

No, I told myself. *I must focus on the bigger picture and my path to discovering where my amulet and family fit into this unknown world.* I would not entertain those feelings or ideas of revenge upon Torino. At least I told myself that. No matter what, I could not let the swamp mud of my past hold me down from achieving my true goal.

"A few!" Tony stammered. "And . . . you are here . . . Evisa . . . for the Trials. I never once saw you train at the American academy. Where were you?"

"On the South Pacific islands," I replied.

What I did on the Pacific islands aroused the curious table's attention.

Jessica flipped her hair at me as she took a sip of her spritz. "Oh, I love a good story," she said. "Please, tell us more."

I could tell they did not think much of me and almost felt like they viewed me as far below them. It was a hunch. They carried a superficial air about them. I could tell by how they conversed with one another and the subjects they talked about: clubs, alcohol, exclusive organizations, and their expensive toys at home. I felt they had not yet faced the dirt or any time of swamp mud, though one should never underestimate an opponent. I wanted to leave the moment I sat down.

"Another time, perhaps," I replied with a smile. "After the Trials."

She was put off by my response.

"Yes, after the Trials," smiled Jessica.

Sophia analyzed me closely, watching all my movements and my interactions with the people at the table. She was a smart girl. Everyone at the table continued to converse, but I just listened. Tony could not help but look my way. Painted on his face was a mixture of emotion.

"Are you going to be training tomorrow at the old Roman piazza?" asked Tony.

"Not sure," I replied.

"You should. I hope we see each other again. Maybe you could show me a few things you've learned," said Tony.

"Possibly so," I replied.

My conversation with Tony ended there, for I had little to say to him. After twenty minutes, I gave everyone an adieu and left the table. As I made my way out, Sophia continued to watch me with keen eyes. She was trying to understand something beneath the surface.

I went to my small apartment on the other side of town. The apartment was simple with a nice balcony overlooking the city. No one had come back yet. I took a roughly three-hour nap.

Jeremiah and Marlow woke me up. It looked like they'd been tanning in the sun for a couple hours. They got me up, and we went to a nice café near the apartment. There, I indulged in wonderful chatter about Jeremiah's love life and how good the beach was. Growing tipsier with each shot of limoncello, Jeremiah loved to talk about his past loves from around the world,.

"I tell thee, listen—no, *listen*—the best women in the world are those Germans, beautiful and smart with a tough attitude," Jeremiah said.

"What happened to your German girlfriend? Where is she then?" I inquired.

"Nay, didn't work out. I was too in demand!" replied Jeremiah as he took another shot of limoncello. "Have you seen me? I can't keep the ladies away." He laughed. "Oh, the Italian women, long black hair with hearts as cold as ice! Stay away, lad."

"These women seem to find me," I interjected.

"Is that so?" said Jeremiah, casting his eye at me.

"I take what I can get," shrugged Marlow as he puffed on his cigarette.

"Happened today in the ice cream shop. Beautiful blonde trainee, in fact," I said confidently.

Jeremiah shook his head. "Stay away from other trainees. They are just trying to find your weaknesses. Might be useful in the Trials. Damn snakes!"

"We had a tussle outside the shop," I said.

"See? Searching for your weak points, especially the ones with the look about them," said Jeremiah.

"What's the 'look'?" I asked.

Jeremiah got real close to me, took another shot of limoncello, and pointed his finger at me. "They have a look, a walk, a scent that's different than the others. These trainees are smart. They prey upon those with a different look. They'll follow ye in the Trials without your knowing. Or worse, they let ye handle the hard trials, then at the last second, kill ye for the coin when you least expect it. Alas, beautiful women are notorious for this maneuver. Remember, lad, the Trials are not always about the most brawn. The brain always wins the day."

"Just look at Jeremiah. He's been brawn over brains for this long, and look at him now," Marlow laughed.

"Aye, shut your mouth," replied Jeremiah. "We need rum. Waiter!"

"I'll keep that in mind," I said.

We had a few drinks of rum on ice with lime. Jeremiah could really drink some alcohol. I could barely keep up with the man. Marlow put on sunglasses when he started to drift toward his overly drunk side. We paid our bill, and Jeremiah led us through the winding cobblestone streets of the city. He brought us to a small restaurant with a grand courtyard along a canal.

Wildcat and Fitzroy were seated in quaint courtyard next to a mountain. Wildcat was wearing a white Western-style hat, a white button-down shirt, his favorite blue jeans, and cowboy boots. He was drinking an Italian beer. Fitzroy looked sharp in fine white linen clothes, looking at a menu while drinking a glass of red wine. Jeremiah excitedly sat next to Fitzroy.

"The gang's all here," said Wildcat.

"I ordered us a bottle of wine," Fitzroy said.

"Grape juice, eh?" remarked Jeremiah.

"Beer, partner," Wildcat pointed out.

I took a sip of the wine. It tasted quite nice. Before this, I rarely ever had alcohol, let alone fine alcohol. I was slowly acquiring a taste for fine liquor and wine.

Fitzroy elaborated on why he chose a Spanish wine and what made it special. These men opened my eyes to a new world of taste in fashion, food, drink, women, and fine weaponry—all the things that men loved dearly. I could see Fitzroy's minosblade attached to his belt. His sword was an elegant, curved, and etched with floral designs.

We talked about life, our lost loves, and music that soothed our souls. Fitzroy opened up about the type of music he enjoyed. He loved jazz and Spanish guitar. Jeremiah said classic rock was more his style while Marlow was a hip-hop fan. Wildcat listened to blues and country.

I loved all genres of music but wanted to know more about Fitzroy's taste in things. I liked his style. We laughed, drank, and danced in the courtyard as we listened to the jazz band playing in the background. After we had our delectable Italian cuisine, Jeremiah convinced all our drunken selves to go to an upscale club nearby.

Swaying back and forth, we strolled down the cobblestone walkway for a couple minutes until we came upon a vibrant club called The Octavian. The club was lit by bright orange lights above an old Roman archway. We walked through the tunnel into a mixture of an open-air and enclosed structure built into old Roman ruins, adorned with striped red and orange curtains across the archways.

Jeremiah said this place was extremely high class. We went to the bar and had ourselves some drinks. Fitzroy mentioned he'd been there a few times. Wildcat said he was more of a roadhouse bar kind of guy. Most world leaders and Terminal participants paid a visit to the famous Octavian.

As I was drinking, a received a tap on the shoulder. It was Sophia in a gorgeous blue dress, exposing her curves and features. This was a woman, and I had yet to be with a real woman. Her hair was up in an elegant bun. The rest of my party quickly set their eyes on her.

"You ran off earlier," said Sophia. "I was trying to understand why. Was it me?"

"You?" I smiled. "Never. I just had to be somewhere else."

"I see. A busy gentleman, and yet you are at the Octavian."

"My friends brought me here."

"May I have the honor of meeting them?"

Jeremiah jumped at the chance to meet her. He immediately tried to win her over. He was drunk though and slurred most of his words. Marlow, poor Marlow, was barely standing up at this point. Wildcat introduced himself in a well-mannered way.

"Cowboy, huh?" pointed out Sophia. "Let me hazard a guess. Texas?"

"Did my hat give it away, sweetheart?" Wildcat replied.

"The accent did," smiled Sophia.

"Gets me every time," replied Wildcat.

Sophia enjoyed meeting my outfit. Fitzroy was reserved, keeping to himself. He gave her a brief introduction, and that was all. Sophia and I continued our own chat.

"They are your trainers, am I right?" asked Sophia.

"Possibly. Why do you want to know?" I replied.

She gave a slight laugh under her breath. "Need to know who trained a man with such skill. I'm envious."

"You're the trainee he spoke of," Jeremiah interjected.

"He spoke of me. How thoughtful," smiled Sophia.

"Aye, he did, love, but I told him not to fall for the tricks," Jeremiah replied. "He's smart."

"Tricks? I do nothing of the sort. Rather, I admire your trainee. He's piqued my interest," she replied.

"Pique it elsewhere then. I know what they teach you at Belle-Claire," assured Jeremiah with a smile.

"Oh, you do?" she replied jokingly.

"Indeed, you're beautiful, love, but Christoph," said Jeremiah, "stay as far away as you can from the vipers."

"How rude," she commented.

"I've wrestled with more than a few serpents in my life, both big and small, all the same to ye," Jeremiah exclaimed.

"I can attest to that. I've seen him tango with the worst of 'em," Wildcat said.

"Seems my charm is not welcome here," Sophia said.

"No. No, it's not that," I remarked.

"Oh, it is, and that's fine. I hope to see you soon, Christoph Swift," she smiled and then walked away.

"You gave her your name?" inquired Fitzroy.

"What's wrong with that?" I asked.

"Never give anyone your name here. Do not trust anyone in this place. You understand me?" Fitzroy demanded.

"Yes, of course," I replied.

Fitzroy said he was leaving to prepare for tomorrow and suggested we followed him out. As we were leaving for the exit, we ran into a large group blocking our path.

It was the group I sat with earlier, most especially Tony Torino. Leading them was a tall, pale man with white blond hair cut like a fade. He had sharp features, a pointy nose and chin. He was wearing an all-black suit.

"Lennox," said Jeremiah with a knitted brow.

"Jeremiah," replied Lennox in an English accent.

"Haven't seen ye in a long time," said Jeremiah.

"Been busy, mate," replied Lennox. "Still with old Victoria & Co.?"

"Aye," replied Jeremiah. "Still with the Tughra?"

Lennox laughed to himself. "That's silly. I'm with the best company in the world."

"Hey, it's our friend from earlier," stated Rolando.

"I thought he looked familiar," remarked Wayne.

"Our trainees must've met earlier. How nice," Lennox said.

"What company?" asked Fitzroy. "Obviously, you're not with the King's Company anymore."

"One that pays large dividends." Lennox smirked. "Belle-Claire promised me a ship in the fall per trainee that survives the Trials."

"Watch what you say, funny man," said Wayne.

Lennox laughed, patting Wayne on the back. "See the fire in this one! They grow bigger by the year. My good fellow here played professional American football for a little while, but he wanted more money. I say he chose the right job, eh?"

"At least some of us did," Tony Torino remarked as he gave me a smile wrapped in shallowness.

The groups continued to talk. Tony's remark reminded me of how the social groups, such as the Pack, operated at St. Francis. Conversations were filled with snarky comments that appeared to be nice on the surface but were shallower than a sandbank overpopulated with stinging jellyfish. My wits were too sharp not to notice.

"What'd you say, Torino?" I inquired.

Tony laughed. "Well, not everyone is cut out for this job, just as you weren't cut out for the basketball team at St. Francis."

"Is it a reaction you want?" I replied coldly.

"Come now. Just a jest," said Tony.

"Your mouth is trash filled with dirty daggers. I do not welcome your rotted stench, and I do not jest," I said.

Torino laughed again. "You may feel bigger and better because you're here, but you are still the wormy Swift. I know who you really are a . . . a bottom feeder!"

"Nay, I feel nothing of the sort but regret that I never told you how truly terrible your breath is. Wash it out, would you please? I'm done with this conversation."

Torino was red hot with rage and began to yell all sorts of colorful words in my direction. I maintained my fortified wall of reserve and perfect upright posture. He grabbed the attention of the others in the group.

"Ah, seems our trainees are friends with one another," said Lennox. "That's the Chairman's son, equally as terrifying as the others, and equipped with a frozen heart and deathly black eyes. The crowd will eat him up!"

"Chairman's boy?" Jeremiah inquired.

"Carlos Torino's son," added Lennox.

"It's best we leave," Fitzroy advised.

Tony, followed closely by his other acquaintances, got in my face, still trying to instigate me with demeaning words. Fitzroy broke us up and forced me to leave the bar. I kept my composure to the best of my ability, but Torino's statements still angered me. I tried to overcome those past feelings, but they were like a weight too unbearable to hold up, bringing forth a tidal wave of old emotions and grudges.

I was conflicted as I tried to bury those past feelings, for they were bubbling over. I told myself that I had moved on from the past and that Tony's words wouldn't pierce me like arrows to the heart. My soul was troubled, feeling the angel and devil on each shoulder. And of course, the alcohol did not help. Fitzroy grabbed me, pulling me from my thoughts.

"Whatever happened with Tony in the past is over! Move on. Do not let your emotions skew your judgment," exclaimed Fitzroy. "You must have a clear head and heart, void of feelings and emotions, to make sound decisions. If not, you will perish in the Trials."

"He's right, Christoph," stated Jeremiah with slightly slurred words. "Lennox brought up things of my past. Best not dwell on it."

"I need . . . I need to go on a walk to clear my head," I said with intensity.

"Want Marlow to follow?" asked Jeremiah.

"I'm fine, thank you," I replied.

"Do what you must. But remember, training tomorrow in the morning," said Fitzroy.

"I'll come with you," said Wildcat. "Dangerous to walk alone at night, even here."

"No . . . No, I'll be fine!" I replied.

I could tell my intensity hurt Wildcat's feelings. I was too busy in my head to care about hurting my friends. I gave them a good-bye and decided to walk with no destination in mind, just in the general direction of the apartment.

I was still slightly drunk, which caused me to sway when I walked. Madness consumed my psyche, troubling me on how to feel and think in this chaotic situation. I was being tested, emotionally and physically, at every angle.

Deep in recesses of my dream world, Tony's face sparked in my mind, bringing forth unwanted feelings of sadness and nostalgia pertaining to Axelrod. Tony was the son of the man who tried to kill my only family. Tears flowed from my eyes. My head was a circus of flying acrobats, trying to find a solid place to land. At that moment, all I wanted was the warm embrace of a solid home.

As I was lost in my thoughts, I tripped on a piece of jagged stone along the walkway and fell to the ground. Drunk, I was mentally absent, stuck in swamp mud that kept me from getting up. I yelled out to the crescent moon high up in her celestial throne for relief. I sat on the cobblestone road, lost in my thoughts.

Then, a pale white hand was offered to me in front of my face. I had a strange feeling that I knew who it was.

"Gabriel!" I said. "I had a weird feeling you would be around."

I looked up, and there before me was a shadowed figure in a suit. I could faintly make out his face under the guise of night. The only thing I could see was his flashing magnetic eyes. It was not Gabriel from the church.

"Oh, my bad, sir," I said, pausing slightly. "I thought you were someone else."

"Need a hand?" he asked mysteriously. I was not sure where he was from. His voice was raspy with an accent, from . . . I was not sure. He sounded like a mixture of British English and Middle Eastern.

"Uh, sure," I replied as I took his hand.

"Looked like a tough fall," said the mysterious man.

He did look vaguely familiar as if I had seen him before. This man had a wide smile that showed his teeth.

"I'm . . . I'm all right. Just a bad step in the cobblestone," I said.

"Nothing more? Surely something was bothering you," he replied.

For some odd reason, his voice sounded soothing, as if I wanted to tell him what was wrong, even though he was a stranger.

"Well, trouble from the past seems to have returned," I sighed.

"The past has a way of doing that," the man remarked.

"Fitzroy and Jeremiah were right though. I must move on. I am not my younger self."

"Fitzroy?" inquired the strange man.

"Yes, you know him?"

"We've met before in a past life. My, you look like a strong young lad. Trainee, I presume?"

"Something like that," I replied.

"Don't be so reserved. You're the talk of the town!"

"Oh . . . No, I'm not the talk of the town," I said.

"Indeed, you are. Some say you'll win the Trials by a landslide."

"Really! How did you know I was in the Trials?"

"All of Monte Carlo has heard of this brave, young warrior of the Victoria & Co., the one who's seen the lost chamber of Faustino."

"Wow. How do you know all of this?"

"It's my job to know things, and I was in the courtroom, listening and watching. As for tonight, I just so happened to stumble into you by sheer chance, Christoph Swift."

"You must be a powerful man, someone well-connected with the Committee."

"I have my place," he said with a smile.

"Who are you then?"

"One who roams the earth, going back and forth, watching, listening, and trading."

"A name perhaps?"

"My name is Rime."

"It's a pleasure to meet you, Rime," I said. "What do you trade?"

"All sorts of things."

"I hope to one day trade on the exchange floor at the Terminal."

"Indeed. Great profits come to those that trade on the floor."

"I do it for other reasons," I replied.

"What do you value more than a superfluous amount of equity?" asked Rime. "Women?"

"Answers."

"Ah, I see. Answers to questions that you hold dear."

"Yes," I sighed.

"And no one seems to possess the answer to your questions, or if they hold a piece of the answer, they are unwilling to elaborate on it. Correct?"

"You hit the nail on the head," I replied in a melancholic tone. "At times, I feel my troubles would drift to the wayside if I knew where my place was in the big picture, you know? I tell myself I'm following the path my family set before me, but how do I know for sure? How do I know that this is not all for naught, that it's not pointless and meaningless?"

Rime stared at me, pondering what I said. "Where do you believe these answers would lead you?"

An urge in my soul came forth, unveiling what I desired. "The Labyrinth of Faustino."

"That's what you seek, power and riches," said Rime as he walked around me.

"Yes," I said excitingly.

"With that amount of minosium, you shall be able to defeat your enemies."

"Yes, yes," I repeated.

"Gain the woman of your dreams and reign as king of the world with the greatest minosium deposit at your disposal!"

"Yes, yes, yes!" I said.

"What if I told you I have it in my power to answer the questions you seek?" said Rime.

"I would say, 'Please tell me.' I want to know!"

Rime gave me a wide smile. "Follow me, Christoph Swift, if that is what you seek."

I agreed to follow this mysterious man through a series of alleyways. The moon was high in the sky at this point. The cobblestone road was lit by gas lanterns. The winding roads were empty. He brought me to a rundown building, extremely old and decrepit. There were no signs, only a large wooden door and two glass windows lit by lanterns.

I had uneasy feeling in my stomach. This was clearly in a bad part of the town. I heard someone closing their window above me, then the sound of a cat yowl. It startled me, causing the hairs on the back of my neck to stand up.

"Where are we, Rime?" I asked hesitantly.

"A place with the answers to your questions," insisted Rime as he opened the door.

The large, brown door squeaked open, and he led me down a dark corridor of stairs into a dimly lit bar. The place reeked of tobacco and old beer. There were a good number of people in the bar talking in hushed tones. As we walked through it, I saw a man sitting at a table with a hood over his head staring intently at me, following all of my movements.

It started to freak me out. The hooded man put down his beer and stood up from his seat as I walked away. We went through another door into a dark hallway. I could hear water drip from the stone ceiling above me. This place smelled of death. I passed different rooms with odd occupants. I could hear yelling and banging through the doors.

"I don't like this, Rime," I said. "What answer could possibly be down here? I think I'll go."

"No! You're so close to what you want," he replied.

At the end of the hallway was a vacant room. Rime opened the door, and inside was a large black pot with boiling water. At this point, I was scared out of my wits.

"What is this?" I asked.

"My proposition," said Rime. "I'll give you everything you desire, Christoph—the answers to the mystery of your amulet, the Amulet of Faustino."

"Who told you about that?" I asked.

"Better yet, I'll give you victory in Series Trials and a chance to rid the world of Tony Torino," explained Rime. "You can finally avenge your uncle with me."

My eyes grew wide with fear. This man was blowing my mind.

"You . . . You," I said confused.

"I offer everything you've ever wanted, Christoph," said Rime. His eyes flashed with magnetic pulses, which could only be described in one word—mystery. "I know what happened to your parents, the truth hidden from you."

"Impossible . . ."

"No, all is possible with me," he smiled.

"Tell me. What happened to my parents?"

"That information must be traded," smiled Rime.

"For what in return?" I pleaded.

"Your soul and the souls of the people that shall work for you in the future. All I require is a single drop of your blood in that pot, binding the deal."

My head was rolling with ideas. I was faced with a decision. I could have everything I ever wanted for a single drop of blood, my soul . . . my soul.

My God above, though!

"Are you calling the Most High?" laughed Rime. "He's not here, Christoph. He's in heaven, seated upon his golden throne, while you and I, we underlings, are here now among men, trying to survive. Hear this, I offer you a chance to be greater than Alexander, Caesar, Genghis Khan, Napoleon, and Faustino. Take my knife, and drop your blood into the pot. Seal the deal, and all shall be revealed to you."

Rime's smile grew wide as he took out an elaborate black knife etched with glowing red minosium moving through the knife, like water moving through cracks. The knife had two gargoyles on the hilt. I took the knife from his hand, entranced by his soothing words. I was mesmerized, almost in a hypnotic state. I held my finger up to the boiling pot, but something inside of me would not let me pierce my hand.

"Do it!" screamed Rime.

I couldn't draw the blood. I was fighting the temptation in my head. *I want to know . . . I want to know.*

My eyes grew wide as the blade inched closer to my finger.

Then, the door swung open! The shock of the door's opening pulled me from my hypnotic state. It was the hooded man that was staring at me from the bar above.

"You?!" roared Rime.

Horns, like that of a goat, started to project from Rime's head. Rime's eyes turned to a bright, beastly yellow. The room shook like a dramatic earthquake. I was frozen in place.

The hooded man threw a shard of purple minosium at this horned beast. The sharp shard of minosium pierced Rime's heart, causing electricity colored red, blue, green, yellow, and violet to vibrate around him, like lightning bolts. Rime roared, sounding like a mixture of a man, lion, and bear—horrific and dreadful.

The man grabbed me by the shoulder and tugged me out of the room. The whole hallway was shaking back and forth. We ran to the end of the hallway. I turned around, and in a horrible demonic form, Rime was coming toward us, locked on me with his sinister, yellow eyes.

I was startled, trying to catch my breath. The hooded man grabbed my shoulder once more. We hastily ascended the stairs back into the bar. This time, the bar was completely desolate, filled with cobwebs and dust. It appeared to have been abandoned for many years.

I thought I was going crazy. Just a few minutes ago, the bar was filled with people. The hooded man led me out of the bar and down the street. We put a good distance between us and that decrepit hellhole.

We rested for a moment. I placed my hands above my head, trying to catch my breath and make sense of this strange occurrence. First off, who was this hooded man who saved me?

"Hey," I said. "You saved my life back there!" I ran my hand through my hair, shaking from it the cobwebs of death. "Oh, my . . . What has this world come to?"

The hooded man turned to me and lifted his hood. I couldn't believe it. Here was DuBois, my cabin roommate on the *S.S. Edwards*, the transport ship I took many months ago.

"Nice seezing you herez," said DuBois. "I toldz ya, stay away from the shadow man, and youz not listen!"

DuBois wore a tattered cloak with holes in it. He was tall and skinny like a marathon runner. He had long nails on his fingers. He appeared in his thirties, rough, looking like the type of guy who would sleep in the caboose of a train.

"DuBois!" I cheered as I gave him a strong hug. Relief filled my soul, bringing forth a strangely refreshing air of peace and solidness. "How? . . . Why? . . . Nevermind."

"Feltz like you needed helpz," said DuBois. "Whyz were you following the shadow man?"

"I had no idea that was him. I was desperate, and . . ." I sighed deeply. "I thought he had the answers to my problems."

"Onlyz ye can find the answerz to ye problems. No shortcutz."

"Yes, DuBois. Yes," I said. "This shortcut would've cost me my whole soul. Who exactly is the shadow man, DuBois? He said his name was Rime."

"Biggestz fish in ze fire pond. The Kingfish."

I was perplexed by his answer. "What fire pond?"

He pointed downward toward our feet. "Ze pond where all evil dwellz in fire, and the Kingfish rulez."

"Sounds like hell."

"Kingfish will returnz. Best watch yeez back."

"Sadly, I think you're right. Can I give you anything in return?" I remembered I had a coin in my pocket. I pulled it out. "Here, take this coin. It's the least I can do."

"No, moniez iz no good to me. Saving you was goodz enough."

"Well, if you insist. This must be where your job is, on Evisa like you told me on the ship."

"Here. There. This job bringz me everywherez." He looked around suspiciously. "You shouldz getz going. Never knowz who's watching. Stay quiet about yesz, Christoph."

I tried to talk to DuBois some more, but he wanted none of it. He walked with me for a little while in the direction of my apartment. Then, he went his own way, seamlessly.

It was a strange encounter. Actually, that was an understatement. I needed time to think this over. What in the hell was Rime, Kingfish, and fire pond?

I was pretty shaken up. Should I tell anyone about this? DuBois said to remain quiet.

I made it back to my apartment roughly around 03:00. I quietly made my way inside and lay in bed, staring at the ceiling. At this point, my mind was so far extended with fatigue that darkness was allowed to cover my eyes, and I fell fast asleep.

CHAPTER 22

Waltz of the Roman Ruins

F ITZROY WOKE ME up when the moon was still dressed in her
beautiful nightgown. I stared out over the balcony toward the
fading dark night, reminiscing on the night before. I grabbed
hold of the rail, grounding myself from floating away in pure madness.

I asked myself whether I should I fear Emir, the Tughra, Carlos
Torino, sea serpents, and Trials. Was it even possible to make sense of
this encrypted enigma of my life?

My head was warped from trying to discern fact from fiction,
truth from lie, reality from illusion. I held on to the rail with my physical hands, stretching my mind to its furthest capacity. I grunted with a
cry from the hefty exercise of my mind, and then my attention turned
toward the sun rising upon her celestial throne, adorned in fiery rubies.

Yes, there lay my answer. Staring at the rising sun, I chose to
accept the perpetual, sporadic mystery of life. All I could do was live
in the present—a true gift from God—all the while hanging on for my
dear life for the wild ride to come on the horizon. And wild it would
be.

I went back inside to say my adieu to Wildcat before he left for
Victoria Island that day. Everyone in the apartment gave him a hearty
goodbye and wished him a safe return.

Wildcat pulled me aside before he left. "I'm sorry I won't be
there for the Trials, partner. But you seem happier today for some reason."

"I guess I'm just starting to figure things out," I smiled.

"Ain't we all?" laughed Wildcat. "You'll be in good hands. These men are the best trainers I've ever seen. You'll make it through this, and when you return, you and I will go on one of 'dem big hunts and reminisce on the days I trained with ya. How's that sound?"

"It sounds wonderful. I can't wait 'til we can."

"Aye, 'til we see each other again, Christoph."

We shook hands with great respect for one another.

He then pulled me close. "Give 'em hell, shooter."

I smiled. "You can count on that."

Wildcat went on his way, and my training proceeded.

Fitzroy gave the whole apartment swords to wield. We put them on slings, and Marlow, Jeremiah, Fitzroy, and I went on a run of the ages.

Instead of going to the ground floor, Fitzroy brought us to the top of the roof. Jeremiah stretched his back. Marlow bent over and puked.

"Never mix clear and brown," sighed Marlow.

"Are you good?" I asked.

"Aye, I told him not to mix," said Jeremiah.

"Better than ever," replied Marlow. "Let's do this."

"Good," remarked Fitzroy as he stared over the roof.

"Why are we on the roof?" I asked. "Aren't we going on a run?"

Jeremiah laughed at my question.

"Make sure to keep up," said Fitzroy.

Fitzroy then jumped off the side of the roof. I thought he was mad! I looked over the edge, and to my disbelief, he was running on the roof of the adjacent building. Then, he jumped to the next roof. Jeremiah ran past me, flipped over the roof, and landed on the connecting roof.

"Come on! Jump!" screamed Jeremiah.

I took a deep breath, made the sign of the cross, and ran as fast as I could off the roof. I landed on the adjacent roof.

Jeremiah smiled with delight at me. "Gird ye loins. Can't let Fitzroy drift too far ahead! Jump, Marlow!"

"Go on ahead," said Marlow, trying to pull himself over the roof slowly. "I'll catch up."

Jeremiah shook his head and then started to sprint across the rooftop. I followed closely behind. We jumped from roof top to roof top, running at our top speed over the red tiles. Never in my life would

I have thought I would be doing this. It was exhilarating. Jeremiah and I jumped through open windows, from balcony to balcony, and ascended and descended ladders that hugged the sides of the buildings.

I felt free, unlocking my wings to reach new heights. I felt myself utilizing my balance and strength as I ran on the edge of buildings, pipes, and walls, facing death with each jump. I saw Fitzroy leaving the city and running to the countryside. I jumped to the stone wall fortifying the city. We ran along it until there was an opening in the wall.

Jeremiah and I descended the wall and followed Fitzroy into the open countryside of the island. We continued through the arid land toward a hill in the distance. Fitzroy was waiting for us at the top of it. We ascended the hill with great speed.

We reached the top, and situated in front of us were old Roman ruins, composed of a few Corinthian columns still standing around a marble floor. It used to be a temple to Minerva, the goddess of wisdom.

Fitzroy waited at the center of the marble floor with a drawn sword. Jeremiah drew his sword, as did I. We walked into the ruins. All three of us looked at one another—as opponents, as friends, as teachers and student.

Jeremiah had a sly smile on his face, knowing what was about to happen. We stood a mere eight feet from each other in a triangular formation, staring each other down.

"Every man for himself," stated Fitzroy. "Only the word 'mercy' shall save ye throat."

"Say the word, matey," smiled Jeremiah.

I was ready. A single droplet of sweat fell from my brow. We all drew our swords before one another.

"*En garde!*" Fitzroy yelled.

We sprang into action. Fitzroy swung at me, and I dodged. Jeremiah tried to strike me, but I countered it with my sword. We fought to the teeth, to the death, to new life—withholding nothing. Our swords clashed. Great sounds of colliding steel echoed through the countryside.

Fitzroy cut my arm. I shrieked from the pain. I charged at him, utilizing all my might and skill. We swung up and down, dancing in elegant fashion. I had him on the defense. Jeremiah attempted to strike, but I struck his sword from his hand.

Fitzroy made his last futile attempt to strike me. I dodged and pointed my sword at his throat.

"Mercy," smiled Fitzroy as he held his hands up, yielding to my sword resting upon his throat.

"Ye ready," said Jeremiah excitedly. "The lad's ready, I tell you!" He began to clap with great enthusiasm.

I sheathed my sword. Marlow finally arrived, panting. His sword was drawn. He leaned on one of the pillars.

"I made it!" Marlow exclaimed. Exhausted, he then fell to the ground.

"You've come a long way, Christoph Swift," Fitzroy stated.

"Thanks to you," I smiled gratefully, "and Jeremiah, Marlow, Wildcat, Prince Rock, Zhen, and Kalendar. If it weren't for all of you, I wouldn't be standing here, and for that, I am eternally grateful."

I knelt down before Fitzroy as a sign of deep respect and thankfulness. Not only that, I said a prayer on my knees to the Lord above, thanking him for what I had achieved thus far. A tear trickled from my eye. The feelings of hardship and gain surfaced.

I thought of what Axelrod had gone through to get me here. I thought of the intense training on Victoria Island and the darkness of the jail cell. I saw the sacrifice each of us gave and what it took to prepare for the Trials. I knew I wasn't perfect most of time, but I gave it my all when I could.

Deep in thought and in prayer as I knelt in the Roman ruins, I said to myself, *I will fight in the Series Trials. I will give them everything I have and more, for that is the price to survive, to win. Everything.*

At that moment, I felt at peace. Fitzroy came to me, lifted me up, and looked me in the eye. He spoke through his gaze. He grabbed my shoulder and hugged me. I couldn't hold my feelings back any longer. The tears harbored inside of me poured out of my soul through my eyes like a flowing fountain. A few tears dripped from Jeremiah's eyes. He was a man of passion.

"You got this, Christoph," Fitzroy affirmed. "You will survive the Trials. Hear my words, for I see you adorned in a wreath of victory standing on the victor's podium in the coliseum, and the crowd shall shout your name."

It was a moment in my life that I would never forget: the day I trained at the Roman ruins. After those dear moments, Fitzroy sat at the center of the temple on a ruined marble slab that used to be part of a column. We followed suit, gathering around Fitzroy.

Fitzroy explained, "Many men and women have come to me, asking how I survived the Trials. Most people believe I succeeded by pure chance, a stroke of luck. Alas, do all rich men gain their wealth by pure chance? I think not. They use a process, a methodical approach of judgment, patience, and hard work. This process of evaluation was my secret to success.

"The Trials should be played with wisdom, avoiding traps and hasty decision-making. Judge each situation with a clear head. Do not second-guess yourself; listen to your gut. At times, you will feel lost, pressed for time, confused, and possibly panicked. That is where patience and persistence play their part.

"Take a deep breath, and assess the situation. Even if you feel all hope is lost, I promise you, it is not. Most trainees give up, feeling the weight of hopelessness on their shoulders before they've lost. Be methodical. Be a solid rock. Use the process I have taught you. Persist in analyzing each trial. Analyze the terrain and the trainees.

"Make a sound decision based upon this process of analyzing, deducing, penetrating, and completing each task, for you will not fail or be lost since you have a tangible process of testing the Trials. As I've said, control the game. Test the trials. Do not let them test you. If you must guess, then guess with your first gut instinct. Never the second.

"This is your process, Christoph. This is how I succeeded at the Trials and in life afterward. The Terminal intentionally made trials of complete nonsense, just so the trainee would second-guess himself on the other trials. Do not let your pride overcome you. If you cannot complete a trial or if the trial seems odd, test it. If does not meet your criteria, leave it and move on. Fight only on favorable ground.

"As for the other trainees, be ruthless. Detach from your emotions, and listen closely to your surroundings. Never let your guard down, for there is always another trainee stalking you, waiting to steal your coins. There may be multiple trainees working as a team. Disengage them. Those who join teams never prosper in the Trials unless they are forced by circumstance to partner with other trainees.

"Do not fall for the words other trainees speak. I have seen it time and time again: A trainee joins a team of other trainees in the Trials, only to be killed at the end once his or her purpose was served. If a trainee calls out for help, do not help them. Do not engage.

"Remember, Christoph. These trainees are smart, continually setting traps for you to fall into. Use the process of evaluation. Stick to what is known. Be quick in what you do. Never stop moving, and continue to the next trial. If you have no other choice and must fight a trainee for a coin, then kill him without regret. Listen to what I have said, for this is how I achieved victory in the Series Trials."

I questioned Fitzroy, asking him about which trials to look for and how to avoid the bad ones.

He answered each question precisely, further sharpening my process of evaluation.

I had one more question, which the book vaguely answered: "Why were the Series Trials so important for the Terminal and its members?"

Fitzroy pondered my question and then explained that every year, men and women packed the Trajan Arena, a large modern coliseum located on the island of Aversa, next to Evisa. The Trials took place on Aversa. Some people watched it from Monte Carlo while others from the Trajan Arena.

"As stated earlier, the Series Trials began a week-long celebration called the Festival of the Bazaar, or the Festival of Merchants, in the city of Monte Carlo and on the island of Aversa, honoring the deceased of the Series Trials and those who had died in the contested zones during the last season.

"The celebration marked the beginning of the new extraction season where all the leaders of the companies would come together to honor the Terminal by giving extravagant gifts to the Committee members and donating large sums of money to the Terminal. In return, the Terminal allowed the companies to trade their minosium in large swaths to prospective buyers qualified by the Terminal without imposing their hefty tax on each transaction.

"The Series Trials brought prospective clients from around the world eager to witness the Trials, celebrate, and buy minosium from these companies tax-free. It was the biggest week for trading in the entire world. As for the trainees, we were like ancient gladiators, bringing forth entertainment and equitable opportunities for the companies. The Series Trials brought serious money to the companies and the Terminal.

"In short, this whole week was composed of great trade, partying, and Trials. All members of the company, including privateers, and select individuals determined by the Terminal flocked to Evisa and Aversa for this week of celebration."

Fitzroy asked me a few questions regarding informative facts of the Terminal. I was able to answer all of his questions with ease. Fitzroy had taught me well, showing me how to train and study efficiently, utilizing every hour of the day, and how to approach each task set before me.

We ended that day of training around 16:00. I was exhausted, and so was everyone else. We did this routine for six days straight in preparation of the Trials. There was no horsing around. We all trained together, ate together, and blocked out the world around us.

My friends cared for me and wanted to see me succeed. I could tell that I grew a bond with each of them. I believe that was why they worked so diligently with me, because it was more than a job to them. They were my true friends.

On the last day before the Trials, Fitzroy wanted me to walk with him to the beach near the ruins. I thought we were going to train with Jeremiah and Marlow, but it was only Fitzroy and I.

As we walked along the edge of the city, I could hear the festivities occurring in the distance—sounds of loud talking, laughing, horses galloping, and airships flying into the city. Fitzroy and I walked out of the city and onto a rocky beach near the dock filled with airships coming to and fro. The water looked fresh and vibrant, exuding a brilliant turquoise color brightened from the shining sun above. The waves churned onto the shore.

"What are we doing, Fitzroy?" I asked.

"I am leaving today, Christoph," replied Fitzroy. "I'm boarding an airship on that dock set to leave soon."

"Is this where we part?"

"It is, but I wanted to tell you how much I valued our time spent together. I was unsure of you at first, believing you weren't cut out for this as I've seen too many times before. Alas, you have proven me wrong time and time again."

"I tend to do that," I replied. "You said that you have seen other trainees not cut out for this. Were you referring to your last trainee?"

It took Fitzroy a moment to reply.

"Yes," he said.

"What happened to him?" I asked.

"He was a great kid around your age from America—bright mind, loving heart, and tough as nails. Everyone in the company thought he was going to survive the Trials by his progress. He excelled at everything he did, except one thing: He was weak spiritually, easily broken and swayed."

"A prince's greatest asset is his unbreakable spirit," I said.

"And a desire to learn," replied Fitzroy.

My face lit up. "You read Kalendar's book?"

"Multiple times," said Fitzroy. "Who do you think trained me?"

"You were trained by Kalendar?"

"I was."

"Then, how did your trainee fail with such good guidance?"

"A woman," sighed Fitzroy. "She was a trainee of a different company. They met before the Trials here in Monte Carlo. When the Trials started, they found each other, and she followed him all through the Trials, piggybacking on his success. He even gave her coins from trainees he killed. As you can see, he devalued the coins for an alternative motive—to please her.

"At the very end of the game, on top of the Victor's Volcano when my trainee thought he was safe, she stabbed him in the back and took his coins to pay the gate to enter the last Trial. He failed because of his weak spirit, easily swayed and manipulated by a serpent.

"I trained him for everything—everything, I tell you! Sadly, I never prepared him for a woman's manipulation. May his soul rest in peace." Fitzroy took a moment. "You're different, Christoph. I can feel it in my heart and know you have a great destiny ahead of you, as long as you walk the straight path."

"And follow the process," I replied.

"Aye," smiled Fitzroy. "Stick to it, or you'll be doing burpees 'til ye drop dead on the floor when you return to Victoria Island. I'll make sure of that."

We both laughed and said good-byes. Fitzroy went to the dock, and I went back to the room to rest mentally and physically for tomorrow's Trials.

CHAPTER 23

Entry of the Gladiators

ODAY WAS THE day, the Trials. I awoke with Jeremiah and
Marlow. They accompanied me to the disembarkation point
to the island of Aversa.

As Jeremiah explained to me, airships will transport all the
trainees and their trainers to the Trajan Arena, where each trainee
would be introduced to the crowd. I would then be outfitted with my
uniform. From there, I would be transported via sloop to my starting
point on the island. The Trials would begin, and the clock would start.

A rehash of the rules: I would have twenty-four hours to gather
one coin from the first set of trials, two coins from aerial combat in
phase two, and one final coin at the Victor's Crater on top of the volcano. I would need three coins to pay the gate to enter the final trial at
the Victor's Crater.

We continued through the vibrant city of Monte Carlo, bustling
with activity and entertainment. People were out drinking, laughing,
and dancing to live music. It was still early in the morning, yet people
were gearing up for the beginning of the Series Trials. This was their
pre-game festivity. The city was dressed in red drapes hanging from
the balconies, bridges, and windows.

We eventually reached the disembarkation point on the dock.
A large line of trainees was entering the large airship to transport us
to the Trajan Arena. I could feel the tension growing within myself as
butterflies bounced around in my stomach. I could feel the excitement,
danger, and glory about to be had. I passed by a trainee speaking Arabic, dressed in baggy trousers called *shavlar* that tightened around his

ankles. His trainer was an older man with a long gray beard, dressed in similar Middle Eastern fashion, wearing a *thawb*, a loose garment covering him head to foot. I realized as I passed them that they were praying with each other.

I saw another trainee speaking in what I thought was Hindi, as was his trainer. The trainee wore a turban on his head and loose garments of Indian fashion. He was practicing his swordsmanship with a long, curved sword. His trainer appeared to be a Sikh, wearing similar clothes and a large yellow turban.

I then passed a group of massive Icelandic giants, speaking with one another in their native tongue. They had pale skin, bleached blond hair, blue eyes, and massive muscles. They were stretching with each other.

It was an eclectic group of trainees representing their companies and cultures from around the world.

I could see on the other side of the dock, waiting in line to board the airship, was the Belle-Claire group—Wayne, Rolando, and Tony, accompanied by Lennox. Sophia was not with them.

As we approached the line to board the airship, I gave Marlow an adieu. He wished me luck, and we gave each other a hug. Jeremiah registered our company with the attendant, and we took our spots on the large airship.

The airship was mostly quiet. A trainee next to me was sweating profusely as he recited hymns in a language unknown to me. I heard another trainee throw up in the next aisle. Tensions were high. The airship landed; we disembarked and were individually transported to the arena.

Coming upon the Trajan Arena from our sloop, I noticed it resembled the one in Rome but was much grander in size. It was made of marble, dressed in scarlet drapes, painted in a multiplicity of colors: turquoise, red, gold, green, and violet. The whole coliseum resembled a contemporary version of the old Flavian Colosseum in Rome. It was composed of massive arches that were chiseled with a wide array of floral designs.

A small town similar to Monte Carlo surrounded the arena to service the influx of fans. Many people were moving toward the arena, as was each trainee, ushered by a Terminal cadet. The townspeople surrounded us, clapping and cheering as we passed. I felt like a celebrity. I could tell the people loved a great spectacle of trainees fighting to the death like the old gladiators.

We passed under golden arches and marble walls adorned with painted frescoes of glorified past trainees in combat. An attendee brought us to a small room within the coliseum.

Each trainee had his or her own waiting room. The room had a single window looking out into the small town. A team of attendees came into my room and supplied Jeremiah and me with bountiful food: tuna wrapped in snow crab, steaks, pastas, and other exotic dishes.

They took measurements of my whole body, then went on their way. They were measuring me for my minos-suit, the armor each trainee wore for the Trials.

It was hard for me to eat. My nerves were tense. I felt like my heart could beat out of my chest. I couldn't sit down. Jeremiah insisted we do some deep breathing exercises to stay calm. It helped—barely. Then, I ate what I could.

Jeremiah and I did not speak more than two words to each other. My mind was fixed on the Trials and nothing more. I said a prayer to the Lord above to guide me in the Trials as we waited for our turn to go before the whole arena. Jeremiah was there as my trainer and to represent the Victoria & Co. The light in our room changed to red, signaling our turn.

"Ready?" asked Jeremiah.

"As ready as I'll ever be," I replied.

A cadet led us down the circular hallway to the dressing room. It was filled with different parts of armor and weapons that lined rows of shelves. Workers were welding, drilling, and crafting each piece of armor.

The cadet brought me to a small panel next to other trainees being outfitted. Three workers of the Terminal brought out my suit, but there was no helmet or mask.

"No headgear?" I asked.

"Eh, where's his helmet?" demanded Jeremiah.

The cadet outfitting me said in an odd European accent, "Terminal switching things up this year. Want to see the face."

"Aye, they won't have a face if things get rough," stated Jeremiah.

The cadet then handed me a curved minosblade.

"A minosblade?" I questioned. "This must have replaced the helmet."

Jeremiah cringed. "Aye, a bloody mess to be had."

I could feel the power of the blade in my hand. I put it around my back in a sling. The suit was light, covering my whole body. The suit was all black with the Victoria & Co. orange flag painted on both shoulder pads.

The attendee led Jeremiah and me to another grand arch. I could hear the great roar of the crowd rumbling the arena. Past the grand arches, lit by the bright sun's majesty, was a circular arena composed of sand, and at the center of the arena was a panel with a group of people filming and interviewing each trainee who came forward. I took a deep breath. They called my name, and the crowd roared.

Jeremiah and I walked into the sandy arena to a massive cheering crowd. I looked in all directions in amazement. Jeremiah nudged me forward. I moved to the center of the arena and onto a platform. A group of people with cameras and microphones surrounded me, taking pictures, filming, and recording.

Over the loud intercom, a woman's voice said, "Christoph Swift of the Victoria & Co, represented by Jeremiah Mbombo!" The woman then eloquently gave a brief description of who I was and a few facts about the Victoria & Co.

I could see the screens above me replaying the story of the last Victoria & Co. trainee, the one Fitzroy trained. It showed the woman stabbing him with her sword. It was quite an awful thing to see.

I was then ushered along to another disembarkation station where an attendee waited to bring me to my designated point in the Series Zone. I looked to Jeremiah before I entered the sloop. He was giving me a sincere smile.

"So, is this a farewell?" I asked.

"It's a 'til we meet again," he replied with a smile. "I was never good at goodbyes."

Other sloops around us were taking off, going toward the zone.

Jeremiah grabbed my shoulder and brought me close. "Demand glory, and ye shall have it. Ascend, Christoph Swift. Ascend."

I let go of Jeremiah and boarded the sloop. The attendant flew me to the other side of the island. All I could see below was mountainous jungle. The adrenaline began to kick in.

Here it was, the Trials. It was all or nothing for the next twenty-four hours.

The sloop descended to a small opening the jungle. Nothing was around us except the dense bush. I waited in the sloop for ten minutes, and then a red light came on. The attendant gave me a thumbs up.

Here we go.

I hopped out, and the sloop took off. I checked my wrist, and there was small clock counting down from twenty-four hours . . . and so the Series Trials began.

CHAPTER 24

Dance of the Trials

I HAD FORMULATED a plan in my mind, where I needed to go and what to look for. As with all things in life, nothing went according to plan. This was the fastest twenty-four hours of my life.

I started my trek at a moderate pace, checking my surroundings and keeping a keen eye for traps or potential trials to look for. The jungle was dense but nothing out of the ordinary from what I'd dealt with on Victoria Island. A couple of minutes in, I heard a woman scream. It wasn't far from my position. I was curious to see what happened, but I knew I must keep focused.

I picked up my pace, raising my awareness. I moved through the bush with delicate speed, paying close attention to any irregular movements or sounds. I came upon a marker with a red arrow, signaling me to a trial. I followed in that direction and came upon my first Trial.

I was lucky to find one this early on. Typically, a trainee wandered for hours in search of a trial. It was a large hot spring. I peeked through the bush, waiting to see if anyone was nearby.

Out of the bush came two tan men, working as a team and speaking Portuguese. They looked like Brazilians. They came upon the hot spring with apprehension and blades drawn. I kept myself hidden, just to observe the Trial.

Circling the hot spring were small, elevated, circular platforms, no bigger than twelve inches in diameter, in scattered positions. There was a crystal tablet on a clear podium outside of the circle, marking the Trial. The two Brazilian men moved toward the podium, read the tablet, and then proceeded with the Trial, trying their hand at fortune.

They both jumped on a platform, balancing on it. They began to skip to each one. One of them, while attempting to balance on his right foot, fell off the small platform, landing on the sand around the hot spring.

Instantly, like a geyser at Yosemite, green gas shot up where he landed, burning his whole face and then his body. He continuously coughed up blood as the deadly toxins burned his flesh. I needed a gas mask, or the winds would bring the gas to my lungs. I scanned the panels, and there on a pole in the circle hung a gas mask. That was what I needed.

The other man was scared out of his wits as he tried to maintain his balance. I further analyzed the trial. Each platform was marked with an answer to the question. I knew I couldn't wait, especially since the geyser alerted the other trainees, and gas swirled in the vicinity. I took a deep breath, focused. Gas mask first, then the hot spring.

I sprinted to the crystal podium. The Brazilian, upon seeing me, started to panic and hastily jumped to the next platform. The crystal panel stated the instructions: *Follow the platforms with the correct answers. Then, extract the coin from the tchouplite. Do not fall or jump to the wrong platform.*

The first question: "What can be traded for minosium on the exchange floor?"

Numerous platforms were scattered across the sand, each labeled with a type of product that could be potentially traded for minosium.

I thought to myself, *Only things the Terminal permits to be taxed can be traded for minosium—equity and debt—but can commodities like oil be taxed? Minosium was a commodity though!*

I had to hurry.

The Brazilian trainee was struggling, trying to decide which platform was the answer. We locked eyes. He looked terribly scared and frustrated. I saw the platforms in front of me. The first one said "British pounds."

Equity, yes! I jumped to it. Correct.

The next platform was labeled "Crops." No, they can't be taxed and therefore can't be traded.

"Bonds." Yes! That's debt! Jump. Correct!

The wind started to pick up as it blew through the trees toward me, and I could see the green cloud of gas encroaching, giving my eyes a slight burn. I saw the gas mask a platform away. I jumped to the

"Bonds" platform, grabbed the mask from the pole, and put it on.

The gas mask looked outdated, appearing as if it were from the 1920s. The gas mask was dark green with slight visibility and wrapped tight around my face. The wind picked up. The Brazilian began to cough uncontrollably, then fell off the platform, further releasing more gas into the environment.

I had to focus! I jumped on two more platforms, then approached the last platform that I needed to make it to the hot spring. Two platforms were before me: one labeled "Oil" and the other labeled "Minosium."

This was is it. I had to guess. *Could minosium be traded for other minosium in the terminal? It doesn't make sense. Screw it.*

My gut said oil could not be exchanged for minosium. I had to choose. I jumped to the "Minosium" platform. Nothing came up. Correct!

I jumped to the hot spring. There were minos-drills for me to pick up. The drills were like the ones the Nantucket crew used inside the Faustino chamber. A minos-drill had a body like a spray gun with a long, slender drill etched with purple minosium, which attached to my suit to power it from my internal minosium core.

From the corner of my eye, I noticed two to three other trainees descending upon the Trial. They screamed at each other and then began to duel using their minosblades. I had to stay focused. I picked up the minosdrill and jumped into the hot spring, no more than eight feet across.

I found the yellow rock, the tchouplite. Here it was! I remembered that yellow rock meant the minosium was there. I drilled into the tchouplite, cutting the yellow rock like butter. I hit a crystal box located within the rock, pulled it out, and opened it. A golden coin was in there. I grabbed it and left the hot spring.

On the other side of the circle were two trainees, a tall, pale man with white-blond hair and a smaller, deadly woman with the same complexion. The tall man was cutting the head off another trainee he'd just killed. The woman called out to me in German. Seeing that I did not understand her, she then spoke in English.

"Give us the coin, or you'll end up like our friend!" yelled the German woman.

The tall man threw the head toward me, which landed in the hot spring. I thought for a moment that I couldn't take on both of them

What do I do . . . What do I do?

"You have no choice," screamed the woman, moving closer to me. "Coin or death."

I checked my timer; two hours had passed. I couldn't wait here any longer. More trainees would come. The wind blew once more, carrying the green gas toward them. They began to cough and scream from the pain. The deadly gas was affecting them. Now was my time.

I drew my sword and jumped quickly to each platform, disregarding if I was stepping on the correct one. Large swaths of gas shot up with each wrong step. I barely avoided the steaming gas shooting upward below my feet.

I reached the edge of the circle and jumped onto the sand.

The two Germans, suffocating from the gas, attempted to raise a sword at me, but I quickly cut them both down. It was the first I'd ever killed a man or woman. I kept my mask on, attempting to catch my breath.

Out of the corner of my eyes, I saw one male trainee coming from the bush. He appeared to be Japanese with red war paint on his face, eyeing me down. He was rubbing blood off his blade onto his shoulder pads.

Two ebony-skinned trainees appeared from the bush. Their bodies were painted in black tribal war paint. On the other side of the bush, a fourth trainee came out, a man with a pale turban who briefly displayed his elaborate sword skills. After a brief second, all eyes descended upon me, the one with the coin. I couldn't take on all of them . . . unless I had to.

I darted into the bush, running as fast as I could with my blade drawn. The race was on.

I heard yelling behind me as they chased after me. I was dodging trees and roots, jumping over large boulders. They were tight on my tail. I looked to my right and noticed another trainee running through the jungle toward me.

Above me, I saw a sloop consumed in fire, being chased by another sloop, firing upon the first one. The sloop was descending toward me in a fiery blaze. I entered an open area of the island where the grass was low, void of any trees.

A trainee came at me from my side. It was a woman with her face covered in mud. She swung at me with her minosblade. I blocked it and then swung back, cutting her instantly.

I turned around, and there were at least ten trainees after me. The blazing sloop crashed behind me into the line of trainees, killing at least five of them. It was mayhem.

All I needed to do to enter phase two was cash in my coin to buy a sloop. I just had to find where. Markers indicating where to go should have been around. I re-entered the bush and saw a marker, indicating that the gate to phase two was nearby.

The Japanese trainee caught up with me and started to strike at me. Our swords collided with one another. He was very skilled, working his blade like a samurai cutting through wisps of air. We went back and forth until I gained the upper hand. He charged me. I dodged him and cut right through his stomach. He fell to his knees.

I could see the other trainees gaining on me, so I darted once more. I elegantly moved through the jungle, using its rough terrain to my advantage. I eventually outran the carnivorous group hunting me. I moved behind a large rock face, hidden by the dense jungle. I heard the group of trainees run past me. I held my breath. Moments passed, and they were gone.

I turned my ear to my surroundings and heard sounds of strange machinery operating, sloops flying, guns firing, screaming, and other unidentifiable and horrific sounds that echoed through the jungle.

I opened my hand. There was my golden coin. This was high throttle. I saw why men and women perished in the Trials. It was a chaotic mess.

I looked around, and behind me on the rock face was a painted blue map that outlined the island. The Terminal was tricky where they placed maps and indicators on the island. I analyzed the map and found where the gate to phase two was: north of me in a swampy part of the island.

Trekking toward the swampy part of the island, I used the dense jungle as my cover. I moved diligently. My nerves and jitters faded away. I was aware of the game's mechanics and surroundings. The Trials were brutal, filled with danger at every turn. I had to keep my wits about me.

As I was walking, I noticed a rope tied in a circle on the ground. I almost stepped on it. I followed the line, leading me to look up at a tree. A mangled trainee hung by his ankle, dangling from a tree limb and dripping blood. It was a trap. Ruthless.

I continued on my way and heard movement in the bush next to me. I gripped my blade and moved behind a tree. I saw a male trainee rolling on the ground, laughing and crying.

Watching him enraptured in madness, it occurred to me that he did not fall down the rabbit hole within a few hours, but rather it was the slow process of stress and fatigue built up over time during the training process. The moment the mad trainee stepped foot in the Trials, he cracked under the immense pressure of survival, like a dam with cracks already leaking, allowing the river of madness to finally break his psyche. I could identify with his situation. Mud was his only friend now. I kept my distance and continued on my way.

I finally reached a swampy part of the island. Large oak trees dripping with Spanish moss surrounded me. It strangely resembled where I grew up. How they were able to place a swamp on an island in the Mediterranean was beyond my imagination, but it was here.

The land became mushy with at least a foot of water. I heard movement. I drew my sword and crept along. This could be another trial or trainee. I heard someone struggling. I peeked through the bushes, and there was a woman, trapped waist-deep in swamp mud, unable to move.

I drew closer. It was Sophia, struggling to escape. I looked to her left. Rolando was also stuck in the mud, but he was not moving. He looked blue, most likely dead. *This could be another trap*, I thought, *like a mouse glue trap.*

"Hello! Is someone there? Please, help me!" yelled Sophia. "I know of a trial nearby. If you help me out of here, we can work together. I'll owe you my life. Please!"

I checked my surroundings, which seemed clear. Then, I came out of the bush.

"Christoph!" she pleaded. "How lucky I am! Please. Help me out of here. I don't want to die here. I am too young."

"Why does that matter to me?" I asked.

"Because!" she exclaimed. "I know a secret pertaining to you! I will tell you if you help me."

"I'm sorry," I replied as I continued on my way.

"It's about your uncle!"

I stopped for a moment. How did she know that?

I turned around with apprehension. "Axelrod?"

"Yes!" she insisted.

"You know nothing of him," I replied, slowly inching closer to the thick, inescapable mud.

"I do! I do! I know what happened to him. I know things, things I shouldn't know. I'll tell you all if you get me out of here," she pleaded desperately.

"What do you mean?"

"I know what happened that night you escaped! Help me out, and I'll tell you. No games. Please!"

I thought for a moment. What was she talking about? How could she know this? I had to know the truth.

"Tell me first!" I yelled.

"No, save me, and we can work together."

I couldn't leave her to die. I had to do something. I shook my head in bewilderment, and against my better judgment, I cut off a tree limb, threw it at her, and told her to pull on to the limb.

"Thank you, Christoph. Thank you—Wait, look out!"

Out of nowhere, I was hit on the back of the head and blacked out.

I awoke in a daze, stuck in the swamp mud myself. I couldn't move my arms. Standing before me was Tony Torino and Wayne, going through my bag and taking my coin with delight. Sophia was stuck next to me.

"That bastard," said Sophia.

Tony noticed I was awake.

"Isn't this incredible? See this, Wayne?" smiled Tony. "I knew him in high school. We hated each other, and lo and behold, he fell for our trap! I guess he's not so smart after all!"

"Let's get moving. We don't have all day," Wayne urged as he checked his surroundings. "Let's get to the sloops."

"Pull me out, and fight me like a real man, you coward. Always hiding behind something," I replied.

"No, I like you better in the mud," said Tony. "Keeps you grounded." He laughed. "Don't worry. Soon enough, the gators will be feasting on you. They'll do the dirty work."

"Tony!" yelled Sophia. "Let me out of your trap. You got what you wanted. We were a team. We said we would all work together. I don't want to die here!"

"Yeah, I thought about that," replied Tony. "Wayne and I will do just fine without you. Not enough coins to go around, sweetheart."

"How could you?" Sophia frantically yelled.

"It's easy. He and I will walk away right now," replied Tony as he and Wayne walked into the bush. "Consider your slow deaths as a parting gift from me, for ole time's sake. Bye-bye."

I shook my head. How could I have let this happen? With all my might, I tried to free my arms. My face went blood red from the exertion. I tried once more while letting out a scream. I could not free myself.

"It's no use. We're dead anyway," said Sophia.

"That bastard. That *bastard*!" I grunted. I looked to my right. Rolando's dead body was next to me. It started to smell like a rotted plague.

"He was stabbed by another trainee, bled out a while ago," said Sophia.

"You witch!" I proclaimed.

"Me? No, not at all," pleaded Sophia.

"This was your trap. Pulled a sucker in with your cries only to beat him over the head and throw him in the mud."

"No! I was never part of Tony's trap. I had no idea he was around."

"Speak plainly."

Sophia then elaborated on her story. She said prior to the games, her group planned to stick together and work out each trial safely. At the beginning of the Trials, she found Rolando, and they both linked up with Wayne and Tony on the north side of the island as they had planned. The four of them found a trial, and that was where things went fuzzy.

During the trial, Wayne and Tony went to get the coins while Rolando and Sophia kept watch. A few other trainees tried to bypass Rolando and Sophia, but it didn't go well. Sophia called for Wayne and Tony's help, but they left without a hint of remorse.

Rolando was stabbed in the stomach and began to slowly bleed out. Sophia helped him to his feet, and they stumbled through the bush to escape the other trainees hungry for the coin. While plodding through the swamp, they fell into the mud, trapping themselves. Rolando died shortly after he arrived in the mud pit.

Little did Sophia know that Tony and Wayne had stuck around the mud pit in case a helpless fool tried to save a beautiful damsel in distress. I was that helpless fool with a coin. Now, it was Sophia and I trapped in the swamp mud.

"And what do you know of my uncle?" I asked. "It must've been

Tony who told you something."

"Yes, he did," she replied.

"Explain."

"Tony said he was shocked you were here," said Sophia. "He said you came from a bad family, the black sheep of the Terminal."

"He doesn't know my family. Even I don't." I paused for a moment, wondering how could he know my family. Was he talking of Axelrod . . . or did Carlos talk of my parents? "What did he say about the name Axelrod?"

"He said that he was your uncle, and he hid like a rat from Carlos."

"He never hid from anyone, let alone ever left his shop. Why would he have hidden from Carlos? Did he say?"

"Tony said Carlos wanted something from Axelrod for somebody."

"Like what?!"

"I'm trying to remember."

"Was it an amulet?"

Her eyes lit up. "Yes, it was an amulet! Tony said it belonged to someone important."

"Did he say who?"

"No."

I thought for a moment, internalizing this information. "Did he say anything about what happened to my uncle?"

"I don't recall," she replied. "He never told me. All he said was that your uncle stole from his father, and Carlos went to retrieve the amulet from him. That's all I know. No jest."

I feared the worse for Axelrod. *Oh, I hope Axelrod escaped that night!* I stared at the swamp mud as I slowly sank to the void of hopelessness, realizing my own escape was impossible.

I tried once more to free myself form the mud. With loud cries, I strained every muscle in my body to free myself, but it was futile. Nothing worked.

It seemed the swamp mud had finally gotten me. Rain began to pour down on Sophia and me. Sadness filled me completely, enveloping my thoughts with doubt and madness. All I could do now to escape this exhausting and despairing situation was close my eyes and fall fast asleep.

CHAPTER 25

The Awakening

I AWOKE FROM my brief slumber on account of heavy rainfall. I was further entrenched in the swamp mud, sinking faster than before due to the rainfall. Sophia was asleep. I looked around. Water began to flood around us. I started to worry that the rainwaters wouldn't subside.

I yelled to Sophia, but she would not answer. I screamed for her a second time over the roaring rain. She would not move. I tried with all my might to pull myself out of the mud. I was able to free only my right hand. My heart started to beat rapidly. Panic set in.

Hearing something moving in the bush, I turned my head and through the dark rain saw two yellow eyes locked on me. It was the shadow of a large horned beast slowly moving toward me.

I screamed to Sophia again. She didn't budge. The horned shadow beast moved out of the bush and into the dim light.

It was Rime in human form, wearing his black suit and carrying an umbrella.

I knew this wasn't good. I tried again to pull myself out of the mud with great haste, able to free only my left hand. Lightning struck, illuminating Rime's true face in that brief moment of light. He was a horrible creature with facial features of both a man and a jackal. He had a wide smile, a small snout, sharp teeth, wild yellow eyes, and curled horns upon his head. His face returned to normal when the lightning flash disappeared. I shrieked in great terror, attempting to pull myself out of the mud.

"Tsk, tsk, tsk," said Rime as he walked closer to me. "Stuck perhaps?"

"Back, beast! Stay away!" I yelled.

He walked over the swamp mud without sinking. *Impossible*, I thought. He bent down next to me, then made a hissing sound. His breath reeked of sickness.

"What do you want!" I cried.

"Your soul for your freedom. Nothing can save you now, Christoph Swift. Soon you will join Axelrod, William, and Charlotte," laughed Rime.

Rime had uttered the names of my parents. How would this beast know them?

"Aye," exclaimed Rime. "Your eyes tell all. Yes, your parents and uncle. I know them well."

"Lies!" I cried out.

Rime checked his watch and shook his head.

"Running out of time, my friend, and coins. Let's be honest. You're alone in this world," said Rime. "I'll help you, free you from this mud, and give you your greatest desires."

Appearing from the bush were my parents and Axelrod, gray as death. I hadn't seen my parents since I was a child, no more than three years old. Here they were before me. My mother, Charlotte, shared features similar to mine. I had her smile, high cheekbones, and skinny legs. She was wearing a white dress. My father was tall. I shared his slender frame, upright stature, broad shoulders, and green eyes. He was wearing a suit. Axelrod was in his work attire, looking the same as the night I left him.

"Dad? Mom? Is that you?" I called. "Axelrod!"

They stood motionless next to the swamp mud and appeared lifeless.

"It's me, Christoph! Your boy!" A tear dripped from my eye. "Where have you all been? Don't just stand there. Save me!"

"They can't hear you," smiled Rime. "See the power I possess, Christoph? Give me what I want, and I'll take your pain away, free you from your hopeless, lonely situation. If not, you shall come face-to-face with my two friends here."

Coming from the bush were two large alligators.

"Better decide quickly," Rime said. "They're hungry."

I thought of my lonely days in the past, the anger I had toward my uncle, toward the people in my life, toward my old situation—

stuck in swamp mud. All I ever wanted to do was leave it all behind, start new, and forget about the past—to run away from my past. Alas, here I was, stuck in the same mud, presented with the same past that I thought I'd left behind.

Nay, I thought, *for I am a different person from who I was then.* It may be the same demon of my past coming back to haunt me, stronger than ever before. But I, Christoph Swift, was wiser than ever before, for I had learned that hard work, persistence, and faith could overcome any demon of my past, present, and future—no matter its size, strength, or cunning.

Their tricks would fool me no more. I was not alone in this world, for I had found my true family: those on Victoria Island and those looking out for me from above. They lifted me up from the swamp mud. To them I looked, for them I loved, and with them we would conquer.

I looked up to Rime with zeal in my eyes. "Send them, demon, for you shall not overtake me with your lies, deception, and power. Go back to the place from whence ye came, and take your gators with ye. Begone!"

Rime roared, and at that moment, my eyes were opened. I awoke from my nightmare. Sophia was screaming my name.

"Christoph! Wake up!"

"I'm up," I replied.

"We have a problem."

I turned to my right, and there were two huge alligators feasting on Rolando's body. Another alligator came from the shrubs. I had to act fast. On my right, I noticed a branch split in half due to the downpour. I thought I might be able to grab it. I took a deep breath, made myself as light as possible, and tried to grab the branch. I missed. I tried to grab it once more, but the limb slipped through my fingers.

The alligators were almost done feasting on Rolando's body. I took another deep breath and lunged toward the branch. I got it!

I pulled with everything I had inside of me, letting out a mighty roar. I pulled myself slowly, and then I finally freed myself from the swamp mud. I looked up to the sky and murmured a thank you.

"Christoph!" yelled Sophia, fearing for her life as the alligators moved closer to her.

I grabbed a branch, threw it to her, and quickly pulled her out of the mud before an alligator could snap at her. Without a moment to breathe, we ran away from the mud.

I stopped at tree to catch my breath. Sophia gave me a hug and thanked me endlessly for saving her life. I was still apprehensive of her. I was not interested in receiving a stab in the back while I wasn't looking.

"What now?" she asked.

I checked the timer on my wrist: nine hours left.

"We were in that mud for hours!" I exclaimed.

I had to act fast. I was running out of time. By this point in the game, all the coins from phase one were gone. Hell, some people could be almost done with phase two. I searched my conscience for an answer. The only way to reach the Victor's Crater would be . . . the monster, the ancient beast supposedly on this island protecting a mountain of coins.

The book I read on Victoria Island said those few who are lucky enough to find the cave of the beast would still most likely die from its great jaws. Those that did survive the beast would find a great fortune of coins inside a chamber within the caverns. It was either a child's tale, or it held some truth. I was starting to believe in the latter.

It was a last-ditch effort: Either it was a waste of valuable time or, by some chance, the right move. I pondered the question. Oh Lord, I knew I would be the one to face this thing.

I sighed.

"So?" said Sophia.

"I'm going to find the cave of the beast," I replied.

"Are you mad?" she exclaimed. "How do we know it actually exists? We would do better to search the old trials in hopes of finding a coin."

"Then do that," I replied, then began to walk away.

"Hey, wait!" she exclaimed. "You can't just run off. We need to work together at this point. It's our only chance of surviving this thing."

"I don't do teams," I replied coldly.

"After all we've been through?"

"It's the tale as old as time itself. You'll wait until the end to stab me in the back. What choice do I have?"

"Listen!" yelled Sophia as she moved my way. "I'll make a blood promise to you right here, right now. I won't stab you in the back. I am a woman of honor, and I owe you my life for saving me back there. I know there have been incidents in the past, but that's not me. Understand!"

I pondered the proposition, trying to decide if it was a good idea to trust her. Probably not.

"And like it or not, we need each other!" she exclaimed. "We can win this thing. Together. Besides, the beast is that way."

Sophia pointed in the other direction from where I was walking. Damn, she did have a point. I stared at her intently, then pulled out my sword and gently cut my hand. Blood slowly leaked from the cut. I held out my bleeding hand to her. Sophia smiled, then did the same.

We made a blood pact.

CHAPTER 26

Pas de Deux

W
E MADE OUR way through the swamp into the island's arid but mountainous section, similar to a desert. I was thirsty and hungry with no access to fresh water or food. We came upon an oasis in the middle of the sandy landscape. It was a small paradise in this scorched terrain, containing a few palm trees and shrubs.

I couldn't believe my eyes. Could this really be here? I ran into the oasis, and there before me in the middle of the green shrubs was a pool of fresh, clear water. I bent down in great haste, feeling my survival instinct kick in.

"Wait!" Sophia screamed.

"What?" I objected as my hand dipped into the water.

"Look," pointed Sophia.

On the other edge of the water was a male trainee, who appeared to be from central Asia. He had passed out in the water. Sophia hesitantly approached the man, checked his breath, and then pulled him over. Blood spewed out of his mouth. He was dead.

"The water," said Sophia. "It's poisoned him."

I shook my head. "This is no paradise but a mockery of death."

We continued through the arid desert; it was roughly 05:00. I could see the sun rising in the distance. Seven hours left. We came upon the badlands—an area of rocky, dry terrain with jagged peaks, steep slopes, and a little greenery. The sun began to rise, offering us much-needed light.

"They say the entrance to the cave is in the badlands of the island," I reported.

We entered the winding passages of the badlands. Cliffs surrounded us on every side.

"Do you know where to go?" asked Sophia.

"No," I answered. "But I see something orange in the distance, hanging on to the rock face."

Sophia directed her eyes to where I was pointing.

"Looks like a supply drop from the Terminal," she replied.

"What's a supply drop?" I asked.

"An Easter egg on the island. Might hold food and water."

We continued for two hundred yards through the winding passages and then approached the orange fabric. It was a parachute, tattered with holes, clinging to the rock face. We followed the ropes attached to the parachute. It led to the skeletal remains of a trainee.

"He must've jumped from a sloop," I said.

We approached his dead body. He wore an outdated minos-suit, black in color. Sophia pulled off the dog tag around his neck.

"I think he died on impact," I remarked.

Sophia analyzed the dog tag. "His name was Thomas Sharpe of the American Company, 1972."

I took off his backpack and looked inside. He had a steel box. I opened it. Inside were numerous papers and a few preserved energy bars. I gave the energy bars a sniff, then ate them. I was dying for food. Sophia took the papers from the box and read through them.

"Look!" she declared. "The papers were written by him. He wrote of the entrance to a beast's cave deep in the badlands."

"Sharpe must've been looking for the entrance while on a sloop. Smart man," I said.

"What's a Chamber of Faustino?"

"You must be joking."

"No!" she countered. "Read it for yourself."

She handed me the papers, and I read them. Sophia was right. Sharpe claimed Faustino built the chamber on the island to house his large stash of gold and silver doubloons.

Incredible! It made sense a chamber could be here because the chamber on Victoria Island revealed multiple glowing points on the map. Aye, there could be hundreds of these chambers scattered across the world!

What a strange coincidence, I thought. *What were the odds that the Terminal built the Trials on the same island as a Faustino chamber?* I was starting to see a hidden connection.

Sharpe further stated that a beast lived in the cavern, and only Faustino himself knew how to maneuver past the beast. Sharpe claimed the beast was called the Leviathan, and nothing else was said about it. He included a map that outlined the badlands, charting a red path through its winding mountainside and into the caverns.

I cheered at this discovery. Sophia inquired about a Faustino chamber, of which I related to her what I knew about it from my recent experience on Victoria Island.

We followed the map through the narrow rock formations, eventually arriving at the entrance to a cave. It was just a small opening in the rock that led into complete darkness.

"Think this is it?" Sophia asked. "Doesn't look like much."

"I have a feeling it is," I replied.

We entered the cave and used the suit-powered lights on our wrists to guide us. We climbed over large boulders with jagged edges into the cavern. I reached the floor of the cavern before she did. In an instant, she lost her footing from the rock and fell into my arms. We locked eyes for a moment.

"Um," she said, slightly blushing. "Thanks."

"Yeah . . . No problem," I replied.

Sophia shined her light around the cavern, revealing its massive scale. Her light drifted to a smooth rock wall, revealing a symbol in ancient Egyptian style of a man with a jackal head.

"Christoph!" said Sophia. "Have you seen this before?"

"It's the symbol of Faustino," I remarked as I analyzed the black paint. "Strange."

"What?"

"The symbol I saw on Victoria Island was of the man holding a scepter. In this one, the man is holding an amulet in his hand."

I didn't tell the second part of this revelation to Sophia, but the amulet looked identical to the one I used to wear around my neck. She questioned the significance of the amulet. I downplayed it.

We continued through the dark cavern, using the map to guide our way. After thirty minutes of wandering through this eerily silent and dark passage, Sophia began to complain that we were lost. I pulled out the map, and we both analyzed it.

"The red line outlining the trail stopped back there!" Sophia exclaimed. "What if Sharpe never discovered the way past here?"

"Possibly," I replied. I continued to study the map intently.

"We're running out of time, Christoph," Sophia urged me.

"Hold on." I pulled out his notes and read them. "Ah, he said the only known way through the caverns is by listening to the sounds of an indicator."

"An indicator?" Sophia questioned. "Okay . . . Like bats, light, maybe water?"

I listened intently to the sounds of the cave. I could hear the sound of running water. A smile grew on my face.

"Brilliant, Sophia!" I exclaimed. "The flowing water will guide us."

We followed the sound and came upon a small stream of water flowing in a man-made aqueduct, eight inches across, built into the ground floor and flowing through the cavern in a zigzag pattern.

"Incredible," Sophia remarked.

"This must've been used by Faustino to navigate through the cavern," I said.

We followed the water for a few hundred yards, which led us to a huge open section of the cavern, able to fit a whole mountain inside of it. We looked around in amazement.

As I scanned the cavern with my light, I saw large bones of blue whale carcasses and other sea creatures scattered around the surface. My heart started to beat rapidly. I followed the trail of bones with my light. I started to see bones from not only sea creatures but bones of old trainees still wearing mangled suits.

Then, I came upon an incredible skull of what looked like a serpent, appearing like some sort of dinosaur. It looked similar to the serpents that I saw on Victoria Island.

My light finally fell upon a large pile of bones of all kinds of creatures at least four stories high. Sophia and I were silent as we gazed upon this grand spectacle. At that moment, there was a loud splash on the other side of the cavern. Loud rumbles followed.

"Hide!" I said.

A loud roar echoed through the chamber. We hid behind a rock. I looked at Sophia. Her face was covered in fear. In the distance, the beast came up from a large body of water.

I couldn't see him in the pitch-black cavern. The aqueduct was below our feet. We slowly crept along the water channel. I saw a man-made door in the distance. I pointed to it, and Sophia nodded.

In an instant, large dual lights, like that of flashlight, passed next to us. We quickly ducked down to avoid these strange lights. There were loud sounds of movement in the water. I wanted to see what was going on. I gestured to Sophia to move toward the door while I wanted to capture a view of this beast. I moved to get a better view, but Sophia pulled me down.

I gestured for her not to worry. She shook her head, and then she moved toward the door. I slowly crept closer to the large body of water. From what I could see, we were high above the water on a ledge that circled the cavern. I stood over the cliff and could faintly see this massive beast. Through the pitch blackness, I gazed at a beast larger than anything I could have ever imagined. Sophia made it safely to the door.

"Christoph," Sophia whispered. "Come!"

I turned my eyes to the water. At the center of this lake, high above the water, were two large, glowing eyes. I noticed a large creature struggling to break free from the jaws of this massive beast, like a worm caught in the beak of a bird. The struggling creature looked like a sea serpent with its blue scales and golden underbelly, resembling the ones I encountered on Victoria Island. After a few moments, there was a loud crunching sound, and the serpent went still.

The great beast roared once more, claiming its superiority over all of the seven seas. It was incredible. The more I got a better glimpse of it, the more I fixed my gaze upon its eyes. I needed to see this wonder.

I inched forward. Then, the rocky surface cracked. I fell backward, and the ledge fell into the water.

The beast's eyes locked on me, shining on me like a lighthouse during a stormy night at sea. The beast roared, rumbling the entire cavern. I dashed for the man-made door that was only twenty yards from me. I heard the incredible monster swim toward us.

I reached the door and entered a large, dark hallway in the nick of time. The beast roared on the outside. It couldn't reach us. My heart was beating out of my chest as I tried to catch my breath.

"Great. Now that thing's after us!" Sophia exclaimed as she spoke her mind. "Men are so stubborn."

"It's okay," I replied. "I dealt with large beasts before. Piece of cake."

"Not like that one."

I checked the time: seven hours left. We needed to hurry. I looked around the long corridor we were in. I wondered where the coins would be. My light drifted to the wall, and there before us were the same hieroglyphics from the Faustino chamber on Victoria Island. On the wall, painted in majestic colors, were pictures of the same horned beast from Victoria Island, offering Faustino minosium.

"Hieroglyphics," Sophia commented.

"Yes," I replied. "Do you know how to read it?"

"Roughly. I was taught in school," Sophia said.

"Dang, I should have gone to your school. Which one?"

"Oxford. You?"

"Victoria's school is all I really need."

The beast roared outside of the corridor, reminding us of the danger surrounding us.

Sophia examined the wall with great interest. "My question is . . . why are the hieroglyphics here?"

"Faustino adored the Egyptians."

Sophia moved her hand over the paintings, attempting to decipher their hidden message. "It speaks of a great beast—the Leviathan, placed there by the devil himself—guarding Faustino's labyrinth."

Her hand extended over a picture of a man with angel wings carrying a long sword, standing before the beast.

She read aloud: "A man chosen by God shall vanquish the Leviathan, the feared serpent of the Hebrews. Further, he shall destroy the great minosium deposit deep within the labyrinth so that no man shall be tempted by its power. In doing so, he shall free the world from the curse brought forth by the devil through Faustino. If he shall fail, the world will fall into the hands of the Prince of Darkness."

She moved her hand to the next panel. "Follow the channel through the corridor, which shall lead you to the Amulet Room. There, you shall find the key to Faustino."

I pondered the thought. What was the key?

"We must follow the water channel," Sophia said as she hastily walked down the corridor.

I looked at my feet, and I was standing in the aqueduct. We followed the flowing water with haste. Out of the darkness of the corridor attached to the ceiling were the same majestic blue glowworms from the caves in Victoria Island, lighting the way. Kilbits! The small water channel led out of the corridor back to the open cavern.

"An opening!" Sophia cried.

There was some light breaking into the cavern from the outside world. The small channel moved across the cavern toward another doorframe about seventy yards away. It was lined with bones of all kinds of creatures.

"That must be the chamber," I exclaimed.

The ground rumbled from the large beast moving through the cavern.

"We'll never make it!" she shrieked. "That thing is waiting for us to leave the corridor."

I looked around the cavern, thinking of how to make it to the open cavern. I turned my light to the wall. There was another set of hieroglyphics painted on the smooth rock surface. I started to examine it.

"Sophia, see if there is an answer in this."

Sophia hastily examined the wall. After a few minutes, she said, "Here! I found something."

It was a small picture of a man in rags holding up a blue worm. Next to it was a small inscription in English inscribed on the rock. She read her interpretation aloud: "Job spoke from the Tanakh that the beast has a fear. It's called a kilbit, a worm that attaches to its gills and kills it."

"Unbelievable," I remarked. "The worms! We'll use the worms on the ceiling. Yes, of course."

She continued, "But beware of the luminous eyes of the beast, for it hypnotizes its prey. That explains those bright eyes."

"We'll close our eyes then."

"How will we know where to go?"

I looked to my feet and smiled. "The channel. The water channel will lead us to the door!"

The ground rumbled once more.

"Let's hurry," I remarked.

I propped Sophia up, and she grabbed the long worms from the ceiling, all the while making faces of disgust as she pulled the slimy, wiggly creatures down. They were twelve inches in length and an inch in diameter. We twirled them around our blades.

"Are you ready?" I asked.

She nodded her head.

"Remember, keep your eyes closed," I said.

I could feel the water rushing under my feet. I could tell Sophia was nervous, as her body shook. I clasped her right hand. She looked at me, and the uncertainty in her eyes dissipated as I gripped her hand.

We closed our eyes and followed the channel, holding up our blades wrapped in the glowing worms. The monster roared, emitting loud vibrations that reverberated through my whole body. The ground rumbled from the beast.

Sophia gripped my hand harder. I could hear the bones crunching beneath my feet.

"Keep them closed!" I screamed.

We hastily moved through the channel. The beast moved right above us. I could hear it breathing beside me, smelling like a mixture of the salty sea and rotten fish.

We stayed in the channel. The beast growled loudly once more. Sophia gripped my hand.

Amazingly, the monster did not strike us. I saw only a bright light through my eyelids, but I dared not open them. In an instant, we stumbled into the chamber and crawled further into the room. The ground rumbled, though this time it sounded like the beast was moving away from us. There was a loud splash. The beast must have returned to the watery depths from whence it came. I opened my eyes.

"You can open them. He's gone! He's gone!" I cheered.

Sophia opened her eyes, amazed that we survived. She turned to me with those pretty, passionate eyes of hers while still holding onto my hand, and we fell into a kiss. The feeling of death and fear slowly drifted away with the touch of a lover's lips. We broke from the kiss, and I helped Sophia to her feet.

We were in a dark room. I noticed the same type of black powder from the Faustino chamber on Victoria Island situated on a golden panel along the wall. I lit the black powder, and the whole room was illuminated. It was a large chamber with six pillars adorned with paintings and hieroglyphics. At the center of the room was a mountain of gold coins, the same type of coins the Terminal used in those days.

Past the large pile of coins was a golden throne, and behind that was a painted wall, adorned with scenes depicting the story of creation. This time, the painting style appeared to be like that of the Renaissance in Florence—very vivid, colorful, and fantastical.

The first panel was of God creating the planets, then of Adam and Eve, followed by a serpent tempting them. The paintings continued across the wall, showing the serpent being cast out of the Garden of Eden. The serpent retreated to a fiery pit below the earth.

From there, the serpent bore a larger serpent that spewed from its mouth. The offspring of the serpent grew to be bigger than the world. God restrained this new, larger offspring in this fiery pit beneath the earth.

The paintings then showed the original serpent from the Garden of Eden transform into a horned beast with the head of a jackal. This horned beast decided to leave the fiery pit within the earth's core though he was holding glowing red and purple crystals in his hands.

The paintings then showed the story of Faustino. He appeared to be a sickly man accepting the minosium crystals from the horned beast, or better known as the Devil, drawing the connection from the serpent in the garden to the story of Faustino.

The paintings outlined the whole story of Faustino building a labyrinth around a fiery pit where the Leviathan resided and, supposedly, the place where minosium was first found. The panels continued, demonstrating the workers of Faustino falling into the fiery pit or being eaten alive by this large beast, the Leviathan.

The final panel portrayed the horned beast sitting on a golden throne with souls falling into the fiery pit behind him. The devil was holding a scepter while wearing an amulet around his neck, but the amulet was not there, only an empty circle.

I touched the circle with my hands, feeling the exact dimensions of it. Shivers crept down my spine. My amulet could fit into this circle. My hand then drifted next to the circular hole. Written like graffiti on the wall were three names: William Swift, Reszo Zoltan, and Axelrod Belle-Terre. My eyes grew wide. I slowly stepped back.

That was my father's name, Axelrod's name, and that name . . . Zoltan. My mind rattled with thoughts and ideas.

"Christoph . . . Christoph, what's wrong?" Sophia asked.

"The names," I replied, shaking in complete disbelief.

Sophia looked at the names with curiosity. "That's the name Tony spoke of."

"Yes, Axelrod. I know," I remarked.

"Not just Axelrod."

"What other name then?"

"Zoltan."

"My God . . ."

I had no time to think. We needed to get going. I checked my timer: three hours left.

"Grab enough coins for the both of us. I'm going to look for a way out," I remarked.

I went to the adjacent room, and there, seated on a stone slab with sunlight above, was a first-generation sloop. I couldn't believe it. A sloop? Here? It was full of dust. I brushed my finger along the body, then blew the dust off my finger. Sophia came into the room.

"A sloop!" she exclaimed. "How is this possible?"

"Doesn't matter. We need to go," I urged. "Hop in."

I jumped into the cockpit. I wiped away the dust from the old speedometer. I gripped the wheel. Sophia hopped into the passenger seat behind me.

"Is this thing flyable?" she asked as she snapped her seat belt closed.

"We're about find out," I replied as I adjusted the mirrors.

"This thing is ancient."

I took a deep breath and started the sloop. It clicked on! The whole vehicle lit up, the propellers rotated smoothly, and all the buttons and gears worked well. It seemed this sloop has never been used, or maybe just one time. I pushed the pedal, and the sloop rose into the air. The moment I pulled it up, I heard a ticker start. After a few seconds, a massive explosion occurred in the adjacent room.

"Pull up!" screamed Sophia.

Another explosion occurred in the room with the sloop. I gripped the wheel tightly, aiming us upward, and pushed the pedal; we shot out the roof like a stone out of a slingshot. We soared high into the sky.

Then, the engines cut off. Everything went dead.

We began to free fall back toward the earth's surface. The sloop spiraled out of control. I kept clicking the gauge, and then I pressed the pedal. The vehicle lit up once again, reigniting the engine.

I pulled us out of free fall. I looked below and saw the last explosion occurred over the entrance to the roof where we came from, closing it off from reentering.

"I thought that was the end!" cried Sophia. "Damn traps."

"I'm used to it by now," I replied.

She shook her head. "Keep any eye out for other trainees! Kills by aerial combat are rewarded with a coin, so avoid the other trainees, and get to the Victor's Crater on top of the volcano. We have enough coins to enter the last trial!"

"Got it," I replied as we vaulted across the island.

CHAPTER 27

Final Infernal Waltz and Apotheosis

W E WERE ON the side of the island opposite the volcano. We had to fly over the desert, swamp, and jungle. There was even a section of the island that appeared to be icy. I could see the volcano in the distance. I maintained a level altitude slightly above the treetops. These sloops did better at lower altitudes. I could see in the distance at least fifteen or more sloops dog fighting in the sky.

"Why aren't they moving to phase three?" I asked.

"Still need coins," explained Sophia. "Could be teams helping their comrades out. Bypass them, and get to the crater. We don't need the coins."

We approached a large open area around the giant volcano. The open area circling the volcano was littered with recently destroyed sloops. One sloop in the distance was completely on fire, plummeting from the sky.

The large mass of fighters looked like a swarm of bees around a hive, centered around the tip of the volcano. I deduced that we had to plow through the combat zone to get to the circle. It would be impossible to land under heavy fire.

I knew I would have to think of something. Sophia pulled out a large machine gun attached to the sloop but hidden below the seat. She cocked it and gave me a thumbs up. I checked my missile gauge. Sadly, it was outfitted with none. Thankfully, I had my own machine gun to fire in the front.

"I got your back," said Sophia.

We entered the nest of chaos. Bullets and missiles were flying in all directions, appearing like firebolts cutting through the air. I drifted low, cruising over the treetops.

Two sloops descended toward us, attempting to tail us. Sophia began to fire the machine gun. Aye, she knew how to use that gun. She shot one out of the sky. The other sloop fired a missile at us, but I outmaneuvered it.

I accelerated, pushing for the sky. I noticed that each sloop soaring through the air displayed the flag of its company. I looked in my mirror, and the sloop tailing us collided with another sloop, causing a great explosion. I turned the sloop toward the volcano.

I could see in the crater was a small structure, appearing to descend into the volcano. Sophia pointed at it. That must be the last trial. I attempted to descend to the crater, possibly landing inside of it. Bullets whizzed past our ship. I had to pull up. Sophia unleashed the machine gun.

I thought of a plan: I'd keep circling the crater of the volcano, then curl inside of it in a spiral-like maneuver and land the sloop in the crater. I tried to circle the crater, moving downward. A missile hit near my sloop, causing me to abort the landing.

Lo and behold, I looked to see who it was. The two sloops carried the same flag, a tricolor black, yellow, and green flag: the Belle-Claire Company. It was Wayne and Tony, attempting to bring us down. I pulled up. Both continued to tail us.

I know I had to lose them before I could land. I zipped back into the maelstrom of fighting, dodging incoming sloops and stray bullets.

I was able to escape in the haze. I could see them below us, so I descended upon one of the Belle-Claire sloops, firing my machine gun at them. One sloop caught on fire and plummeted to the ground in a fiery blaze. The poor victim was on fire. He jumped out of the sloop to his death. I couldn't tell if it was Tony or Wayne. The other Belle-Claire sloop still attempted to tail us, like some sort of vendetta.

I went back into the maelstrom of fighting. I knew I could lose him here as he tried to lock onto me. I thought of a plan.

Ascending high in the sky, I knew this Belle-Claire sloop would follow me. Sophia thought I was crazy going this high into the sky. The sloop kept on my tail. I gripped the wheel, pulled up, and looped over him as I had with Rabbit Run. As he passed by me, I fired my machine gun and hit his engine.

I then turned the ship downward toward the crater of the volcano at full speed. I breezed through the maelstrom of combat while holding my breath. Then, with great force, I circled the crater. I brushed up against the crater's rocky surface to slow us down.

It was working. We were sliding on its rocky surface. The propellers were breaking off my sloop. I attempted to control the steering, and then we came to halt. I quickly jumped out. The front of the sloop caught on fire.

I looked to Sophia. She was wounded; a bullet had pierced her arm. I quickly helped her out, and we ran behind a rock. The sloop exploded before us. We didn't have any time to waste. I wrapped up her arm. She grunted from the pain.

Looking skyward, I saw the Belle-Claire sloop, consumed by fire, dive and crash-land into the crater right above our heads. I helped Sophia to her feet, and we hastily descended the stairs into the volcano. It grew more scorching hot the further we descended. The stairs led us to a long, crystal-clear bridge over molten magma. The crystal bridge led to the Victor's Circle on the other side. There was a golden gate before the final trial.

I took Sophia's bag, pulled out the coins, and placed them into the gate. A green light popped on, and we rushed to the other side.

We approached the crystal bridge, no more than six feet in width and sixty yards in length, suspended over fiery, bubbling magma. We were inside the volcano.

A small podium next to the bridge lit up as we approached. A hologram appeared. It was a pre-recorded woman with brown hair and pale skin. "Congratulations on making it to the final phase of the Series Trials. Here lies a special crystal bridge with touch sensitive tiles.

"In this trial, you must choose the correct answer to the question, which will reveal your individual path across the bridge, illuminated by your light. Answer the question correctly, and you will have ten seconds to memorize your pattern on the bridge before it disappears.

"Be warned. Each trainee has a different path and question. If you choose the wrong step, you shall fall to the molten magma below. Complete this trial to enter the Victor's Circle. Good luck!" The holographic woman disappeared.

Sophia and I approached the bridge, and on the first two tiles on the crystal bridge, a question appeared for one trainee.

"We must go together!" she insisted. "At the same time."

She held her right arm. Adrenaline still coursed through her veins, making the true pain of her wound bearable for a short time.

"No, you are hurt. Go first, and memorize the path. I'll meet you on the other side," I replied.

"What if something happens, if I don't make it or . . ."

"Go. I'll be right behind you."

Sophia hugged me as if she were never going to see me again. She ran her hand through my hair as we stared into each other's eyes. She let go, then touched the first tile on the bridge. A question appeared on the clear tile: "Who are the only employees of Trader Companies allowed inside the Traders Terminal?"

"Only Registered Extractors," said Sophia.

She chose the correct answer. Sophia was brilliant and really mastered the art of test-taking. No fancy Ivy League school for me. I had grit and wit alone.

On the crystal bridge, an illuminated green checkerboard pattern appeared for a brief instant, then disappeared. Sophia looked back at me. I gave her a nod, and she started to move in her pattern.

I then received my question: "Who is credited with the discovery of minosium?"

I answered Faustino, and a scattered illuminated blue pattern appeared on the bridge. I memorized it, then started moving from one tile to the next.

A loud yell startled me from behind. It was Tony Torino standing at the gate with his sword drawn. Parts of his face were burnt to a crisp, and his minos-suit seemed to have slightly protected his body from the fire and impact. He deposited his coins, and the gate opened.

"Good job. You killed Wayne," smiled Torino as he moved closer to the bridge. "How funny is this? Once again, it is you and I, Christoph. Destiny always pinned us against one another."

"We can change our destiny, Torino," I replied. "We choose our own path. Who says we must hate each other?"

"I wish it were so, Christoph," smiled Torino. "A strange man in a suit appeared to me in my dreams. He told me that I must kill you, or I shall die if I do not. This was our destiny. It was always going to be you or me."

"Forget about him, Christoph," Sophia called. "Come!"

"Dreams can be misinterpreted," I remarked.

"Look inside yourself. You've always felt that destiny intertwined us together and that only one of us would thrive in the end."

"Yes," I replied.

"Ah, see!" Torino said.

"I used to hate you, Tony, but I've realized there's something much bigger out there than you and me. Move on from the past, for that is our destiny."

Tony laughed. "If only it were that easy, Christoph. The past always comes back to bite ye in the ass. Axelrod learned that the hard way."

"Is it true then? Were your father and his goons there that night?"

"Don't let him in your head. Finish the Trials, Christoph," screamed Sophia from the bridge. "Finish the Trials!"

Tony laughed. "All I can say is that Axelrod begged for you to be free. Poor fool."

"Answer me. Is he dead?" I questioned.

"I don't know," smiled Tony. "Only one way to find out." He pointed to the magma below.

I shook my head. "You are nothing more to me than nuisance. Be gone, demon."

I turned around and continued on the tiles, defeating Tony's comments by moving forward. After a few moments, a yellow color appeared on the bridge. I stopped. I held my breath as I turned around. It was Tony's path intersecting with mine.

"Time to find out, Swift," smiled Tony.

Tony sprinted on his path, attempting to catch up to me. I drew my minosblade in preparation. I moved to my next to tile. Blast! I had trouble remembering my next tile. Tony caught up to me as if he were fueled by otherworldly powers. Our swords collided as we danced over the raging magma below.

I had to place my foot on my own tiles while parrying and dodging Tony's thrusts and strikes. Our blades caught each other's. I pushed him off of me toward the edge of his tile. His foot stepped on a wrong tile, and it disappeared.

He jumped back in place. I was balancing myself with each foot, jumping from each tile—striking, parrying, and using evasive maneuvers. He elbowed me in the face. I fell back on my tile. The tips of my hair touched a wrong tile, causing it to disappear.

Tony used this to his advantage, putting his blade to my neck as my head hung over the side of the clear bridge. I looked over and could see the fiery magma below. I struggled to get free.

"You were always a nobody. A failure. No family, no future, and no hope. Die now, Christoph Swift!"

"Hatred shall be your downfall," I proclaimed.

I pushed my sword with all my power against his blade, slowly pushing him off. His eyes grew wide with fear. He pushed with everything he had, as did I.

Tony yelled into my face, trying to impose his will upon me. I locked my eyes on his, staring the demon in the eyes. I was focused and at peace. I knitted my brow, breathed, and pushed back.

"No!" cried Tony as he tried to push back. "You are not stronger than me."

"I am," I replied.

I gave one final push, causing him to fall backward and roll off the bridge. I stood up and noticed one hand hanging onto the tile.

"Help me, Christoph!" pleaded Tony. "Don't let me die."

"Why was your father at my house that night of Senior Mass on the day the lightning struck with no cloud in the sky?" I stood over him. "Tell me, or face the fiery pits of hell!"

"My father had to!" Tony struggled to hang on. "*He* would have burned down all Fontainebleau searching for the amulet."

"Who? Who would have burned down our home?"

One of Tony's hands slipped. I hastily grabbed onto his right hand, barely holding him up. At that moment, I noticed on his right hand was a tattoo of the Tughra. My eyes were filled with astonishment.

"You . . . the Tughra!" I exclaimed.

Tony's hands slipped through my sweaty palms, and he fell into the magma below. I stood up in disbelief. There was no time to think. My time was running out.

I skipped across the bridge. Sophia was passed out on a rock near the bridge. She was losing too much blood as she was slowly drifting across the River Styx.

"Don't die on me, Sophia!" I cried.

Her eyes slowly opened. I picked her up and helped her through the golden gates that ascended to the Victor's Circle. The moment I passed though those gates, I successfully completed the final trial of the Series Trials.

Epilogue

WHEN I RETURNED to Victoria Island, I was greeted with a wonderful festivity. The whole company came out to celebrate my victory and welcome me into their family. It was a moment I would always cherish. Captain Kalendar placed the wreath of the victory, adorned with colorful hibiscus flowers, upon my head.

Immediately after, I visited with Kalendar alone in his office where he returned my amulet to me. Kalendar questioned me about the Trials and if I saw anything of note. I told him no.

I thought it was best for me to keep what I had witnessed in the Trials to myself. I needed to think about my next steps methodically and piece together this massive puzzle.

At this point, I had learned very well the importance of keeping my mouth shut. I liked Kalendar, but I did not fancy the idea of being thrown back into a jail cell. It would take time for me to build his trust and sort out this mystery of my family, this amulet, and this Zoltan character.

Before I left, Captain Kalendar asked, "Did the prince heed the warning of the wise man to avoid the volcano's destruction?"

"He did," I smiled.

He winked. "Protect the amulet, Christoph. Might come in handy soon."

I nodded and left his office to celebrate at the tiki bar.

Wildcat ordered his beer, and we conversed about kilbits and what I experienced on Aversa. I told him about the second Faustino chamber and the beast. Wildcat said he would look more into these chambers in the coming months.

Zhen wanted to know how the flying went. I told him in-depth about the dog fights on the island. I believed I shot three sloops out of the sky. He said that made me an ace. Zhen further inquired about the Trials, and I told him of all the intricate tests I had to endure. He was happy that it was all over.

One can never forget Jeremiah and Marlow, up to their usual antics. Marlow was smoking a cigarette, checking out the scene, while Jeremiah was trying to sweet-talk Helga at the bar.

Jeremiah eventually brought Helga to our table. She asked for our forgiveness for treating us harshly during the time in the jail cell. I held no hard feelings, as did Wildcat and Marlow. We all took a shot of rum together to a prosperous future.

Jeremiah told me that he noticed my rapport with Sophia during the Trials. My face turned bright rose red at his inquiry; my tongue was tied up with infatuation.

Jeremiah laughed and gave a me a pat on the back. "Aye, she was lovely."

I hadn't seen Sophia since the Trials. I did not have a chance to tell her goodbye. She was quickly taken to the hospital the moment we reached the Victor's Circle as if she were taken up by an angel. I thought about sending her a letter.

Jeremiah, Marlow, and I gleefully toasted with a shot of rum.

They cheered, "To lost love and newfound rum!" It seemed they had toasted with this saying more than a few times before.

Prince Rock was also celebrating with us. He talked with me all about his investment opportunities and future deals for the outfit. Get this: He said jetpacks were the next big thing. Who knew?

Obasa loved to hear about Monte Carlo. I told him about the striking beauty of the city and the people there. Further in my drunken state, I told him about my visit with Rime and DuBois.

Strangely, Obasa grabbed my palm, stared intently at it, and said, "Spirits were drawn to ye, dark and light."

I asked how he knew that.

He told me the bones don't lie. He smiled. "Keep ye eye out. Ye never know who be around."

As we left the tiki bar, Marlow and Jeremiah began to sing old sailor chanteys. The whole bar joined in on the fun. Even Zhen sang along with a smile as he tripped over a chair. Jeremiah picked him up and put his arm around Zhen's shoulder. We all walked out.

I turned around before walking out the door, and there sitting at the bar was DuBois, my roommate on the *S.S. Edwards*, my savior from Rime.

How could he possibly be here? Was I this drunk?

I rubbed my eyes and looked again, but no one was there. I shook my head in astonishment.

I needed to lay off the rum.